RANDOM HOUSE

LARGE PRINT

Alexander McCall Smith

Two Complete Novels

THE FULL CUPBOARD OF LIFE

AND

IN THE COMPANY OF CHEERFUL LADIES

The contents of this book were originally published in two separate volumes under the titles: **In the Company of Cheerful Ladies**, copyright © 2005 Alexander McCall Smith **The Full Cupboard of Life**, copyright © 2004 Alexander McCall Smith

All rights reserved.
This 2008 edition is published in the United States of America by Random House Large Print. Distributed by Random House, Inc., New York.

The Library of Congress has established a Cataloging-in-Publication record for this title.

ISBN: 978-0-7393-2829-3

www.randomhouse.com/largeprint

FIRST LARGE PRINT EDITION

10 9 8 7 6 5 4 3 2 1

This Large Print edition published in accord with the standards of the N.A.V.H.

THE FULL CUPBOARD OF LIFE

Alexander McCall Smith

RANDOM HOUSE
LARGE PRINT

This book is for
Soula Ross
and
Vicky Taylor

THE FULL CUPBOARD OF LIFE

CHAPTER ONE

A GREAT SADNESS AMONG THE CARS OF BOTSWANA

Precious Ramotswe was sitting at her desk at the No. 1 Ladies' Detective Agency in Gaborone. From where she sat she could gaze out of the window, out beyond the acacia trees, over the grass and the scrub bush, to the hills in their blue haze of heat. It was such a noble country, and so wide, stretching for mile upon mile to brown horizons at the very edge of Africa. It was late summer, and there had been good rains that year. This was important, as good rains meant productive fields, and productive fields meant large, ripened pumpkins of the sort that traditionally built ladies like Mma Ramotswe so enjoyed eating. The yellow flesh of a pumpkin or a squash, boiled and then softened with a lump of butter (if one's budget stretched to that), was one of God's greatest gifts to Botswana. And it tasted so good, too, with a slice of fine Botswana beef, dripping in gravy.

Oh yes, God had given a great deal to Botswana, as she had been told all those years ago at Sunday school in Mochudi. "Write a list of Botswana's heavenly blessings," the teacher had said. And the young Mma Ramotswe, chewing on the end of her indelible pencil, and feeling the sun bearing down on the tin roof of the Sunday school, heat so insistent that the tin creaked in protest against its restraining bolts, had written: **(1) the land; (2) the people who live on the land; (3) the animals, and specially the fat cattle.** She had stopped at that, but, after a pause, had added: **(4) the railway line from Lobatse to Francistown.** This list, once submitted for approval, had come back with a large blue tick after each item, and the comment written in: **Well done, Precious! You are a sensible girl. You have correctly shown why Botswana is a fortunate country.**

And this was quite true. Mma Ramotswe was indeed a sensible person and Botswana was a fortunate country. When Botswana had become independent all those years ago, on that heart-stilling night when the fireworks failed to be lit on time, and when the dusty wind had seemed to augur only ill, there had been so little. There were only three secondary schools for the whole country, a few clinics, and a measly eight miles of tarred road. That was all. But was it? Surely there was a great deal more than that. There was a country so large that the land seemed to have no limits; there was a sky so wide and so free that the spirit could rise and soar and not feel in the least constrained; and there were the people, the quiet, patient people, who had survived in this land, and who loved it. Their tenacity was rewarded, because underneath the land there were the diamonds, and the cattle prospered, and brick by brick the people built a country of which anybody could be proud. That was what Botswana had, and that is why it was a fortunate country.

Mma Ramotswe had founded the No. 1 Ladies' Detective Agency by selling the cattle left her by her father, Obed Ramotswe, a good man whom everybody respected. And for this reason she made sure that his picture was on the office wall, alongside, but slightly lower than, the picture of the late President of Botswana,

Sir Seretse Khama, paramount chief of the Bangwato, founding president of Botswana, and gentleman. The last of these attributes was perhaps the most important in Mma Ramotswe's eyes. A man could be a hereditary ruler, or an elected president, but not be a gentleman, and that would show in his every deed. But if you had a leader who was a gentleman, with all that this meant, then you were lucky indeed. And Botswana had been very lucky in that respect, because all three of her presidents had been good men, gentlemen, who were modest in their bearing, as a gentleman should be. One day, perhaps, a woman might become president, and Mma Ramotswe thought that this would be even better, provided, of course, that the lady in question had the right qualities of modesty and caution. Not all ladies had those qualities, Mma Ramotswe reflected; some of them being quite conspicuously lacking in that respect.

Take that woman who was always on the radio—a political woman who was always telling people what to do. She had an irritating voice, like that of a jackal, and a habit of flirting with men in a shameless way, provided that the men in question could do something to advance her career. If they could not, then they were ignored. Mma Ramotswe had seen this happening; she had seen her ignoring the Bishop at a public function, in order to talk to an important government minister who might put in a good word for her in the right place. It had been transparent. Bishop Theophilus had opened his mouth to say something about the rain and she had said, "Yes, Bishop, yes. Rain is very important." But even as she spoke, she was looking in the direction of the minister, and smiling at him. After a few minutes, she had slipped away, leaving the Bishop behind, and sidled up to the minister to whisper something to him. Mma Ramotswe, who had watched the whole thing, was in no doubt about what that something had been, for she knew women of this sort and there were many of them. So they would have to be careful before choosing a woman as president. It would have to be the right sort of woman; a woman who knew what hard work was and what it was like to bear half the world upon your shoulders.

On that day, sitting at her desk, Mma Ramotswe allowed her thoughts to wander. There was nothing in particular to do. There were no outstanding matters to investigate, as

she had just completed a major enquiry on behalf of a large store that suspected, but could
not prove, that one of its senior staff was em-
bezzling money. Its accountants had looked at
the books and had found discrepancies, but
had been unable to find how and where the
money had disappeared. In his frustration at
the continuing losses, the managing director
had called in Mma Ramotswe, who had com-
piled a list of all the senior staff and had decided to look into their circumstances. If
money was disappearing, then there was every
likelihood that somebody at the other end
would be spending it. And this elementary
conclusion—so obvious really—had led her
straight to the culprit. It was not that he
had advertised his ill-gotten wealth; Mma
Ramotswe had been obliged to elicit this information by placing temptation before each suspect. At length, one had succumbed to the
prospect of an expensive bargain and had been
able to offer payment in cash—a sum beyond
the means of a person in such a position. It was
not the sort of investigation which she enjoyed,
because it involved recrimination and shame,
and Mma Ramotswe preferred to forgive, if at
all possible. "I am a forgiving lady," she said,

which was true. She did forgive, even to the extent of bearing no grudge against Note Mokoti, her cruel former husband, who had caused her such suffering during their brief, ill-starred marriage. She had forgiven Note, even though she did not see him any more, and she would tell him that he was forgiven if he came to her now. Why, she asked herself, why keep a wound open when forgiveness can close it?

Her unhappiness with Note had convinced her that she would never marry again. But then, on that extraordinary evening some time ago, when Mr J.L.B. Matekoni had proposed to her after he had spent all afternoon fixing the dispirited engine of her tiny white van, she had accepted him. And that was the right decision, for Mr J.L.B. Matekoni was not only the best mechanic in Botswana, but he was one of the kindest and most gracious of men. Mr J.L.B. Matekoni would do anything for one who needed help, and, in a world of increasing dishonesty, he still practised the old Botswana morality. He was a good man, which, when all is said and done, is the finest thing that you can say about any man. He was a good man.

It was strange at first to be an engaged lady; a status somewhere between spinsterhood and marriage; committed to another, but not yet another's spouse. Mma Ramotswe had imagined that they would marry within six months of the engagement, but that time had passed, and more, and still Mr J.L.B. Matekoni had said nothing about a wedding. Certainly he had bought her a ring and had spoken freely, and proudly, of her as his fiancée, but nothing had been said about the date of the wedding. She still kept her house in Zebra Drive, and he lived in his house in the Village, near the old Botswana Defence Force Club and the clinic, and not far from the old graveyard. Some people, of course, did not like to live too close to a graveyard, but modern people, like Mma Ramotswe, said that this was nonsense. Indeed, there were many differences of opinion here. The people who lived around Tlokweng, the Batlokwa, had a custom of burying their ancestors in a small, mud-walled round house, a rondavel, in the yard. This meant that those members of the family who died were always there with you, which was a good practice, thought Mma Ramotswe. If a mother died, then she might be buried under the hut of the children, so that her spirit could watch over them. That must have been comforting for children, thought Mma Ramotswe, to have the mother under the stamped cattle-dung floor.

There were many good things about the old ways, and it made Mma Ramotswe sad to think that some of these ways were dying out. Botswana had been a special country, and still was, but it had been more special in the days when everybody—or almost everybody—observed the old Botswana ways. The modern world was selfish, and full of cold and rude people. Botswana had never been like that, and Mma Ramotswe was determined that her small corner of Botswana, which was the house on Zebra Drive, and the office that the No. 1 Ladies' Detective Agency and Tlokweng Road Speedy Motors shared, would always remain part of the old Botswana, where people greeted one another politely and listened to what others had to say, and did not shout or think just of themselves. That would never happen in that little part of Botswana, ever.

That morning, sitting at her desk, a steaming mug of bush tea before her, Mma Ramotswe was alone with her thoughts. It was nine o'clock, which was well into the working morning (which started at seven-thirty), but Mma Makutsi, her assistant, had been instructed to go to the post office on her way to work and would not arrive for a little while yet. Mma Makutsi had been hired as a secretary, but had quickly proved her value and had been promoted to assistant detective. In addition to this, she was Assistant Manager of Tlokweng Road Speedy Motors, a role which she had taken on with conspicuous success when Mr J.L.B. Matekoni had been ill. Mma Ramotswe was lucky to have such an assistant; there were many lazy secretaries in Gaborone, who sat in the security of their jobs tapping at a keyboard from time to time or occasionally picking up the telephone. Most of these lazy secretaries answered the telephone in the same tone of voice, as if the cares of being a secretary were overwhelming and there was nothing that they could possibly do for the caller. Mma Makutsi was quite unlike these; indeed she answered the telephone rather too enthusiastically, and had sometimes scared callers away altogether. But this was a minor fault in one who brought with her the distinction of being the most accomplished graduate of her year from the Botswana Secretarial College, where she had scored ninety-seven per cent in the final examinations.

As Mma Ramotswe sat at her desk, she heard

sounds of activity from the garage on the other side of the building. Mr J.L.B. Matekoni was at work with his two apprentices, young men who seemed entirely obsessed with girls and who were always leaving grease marks about the building. Around each light switch, in spite of many exhortations and warnings, there was an area of black discolouration, where the apprentices had placed their dirty fingers. And Mma Ramotswe had even found greasy fingerprints on her telephone receiver and, more irritatingly still, on the door of the stationery cupboard.

"Mr J.L.B. Matekoni provides towels and all that lint for wiping off grease," she had said to the older apprentice. "They are always there in the washroom. When you have finished working on a car, wash your hands before you touch other things. What is so hard about that?"

"I always do that," said the apprentice. "It is not fair to talk to me like that, Mma. I am a very clean mechanic."

"Then is it you?" asked Mma Ramotswe, turning to the younger apprentice.

"I am very clean too, Mma," he said. "I am always washing my hands. Always. Always."

"Then it must be me," said Mma Ramotswe.

"I must be the one with greasy hands. It must be me or Mma Makutsi. Maybe we get greasy from opening letters."

The older apprentice appeared to think about this for a moment. "Maybe," he said.

"There's very little point in trying to talk to them," Mr J.L.B. Matekoni had observed when Mma Ramotswe subsequently told him of this conversation. "There is something missing in their brains. Sometimes I think it is a large part, as big as a carburettor maybe."

Now Mma Ramotswe heard the sound of voices coming from the garage. Mr J.L.B. Matekoni was saying something to the apprentices, and then there came a mumbling sound as one of the young men answered. Another voice; this time raised; it was Mr J.L.B. Matekoni.

Mma Ramotswe listened. They had done something again, and he was reprimanding them, which was unusual. Mr J.L.B. Matekoni was a mild man, who did not like conflict, and always spoke politely. If he felt it necessary to raise his voice, then it must have been something very annoying indeed.

"Diesel fuel in an ordinary engine," he said, as he entered her office, wiping his hands on a large piece of lint. "Would you believe it, Mma Ramotswe? That . . . that silly boy, the younger one, put diesel fuel into the tank of a non-diesel vehicle. Now we have to drain everything out and try to clean the thing up."

"I'm sorry," said Mma Ramotswe. "But I am not surprised." She paused for a moment. "What will happen to them? What will happen when they are working somewhere else—somewhere where there is no longer a kind person like you to watch over them?"

Mr J.L.B. Matekoni shrugged. "They will ruin cars left, right, and centre," he said. "That is what will happen to them. There will be great sadness among the cars of Botswana."

Mma Ramotswe shook her head. Then, on a sudden impulse, and without thinking at all why she should say this, she asked, "And what will happen to us, Mr J.L.B. Matekoni?"

The words were out, and Mma Ramotswe looked down at her hands on the desk, and at the diamond ring, which looked back up at her. She had said it, and Mr J.L.B. Matekoni had heard what she had said.

Mr J.L.B. Matekoni looked surprised. "Why do you ask, Mma? What do you mean when you ask what will happen to us?"

Mma Ramotswe raised her eyes. She thought that she might as well continue, now that she had begun. "I was wondering what would happen to us. I was wondering whether we would ever get married, or whether we would continue to be engaged people for the rest of our lives. I was just wondering, that was all."

Mr J.L.B. Matekoni stood quite still. "But we are engaged to be married," he said. "That means that we will get married. Everybody knows that."

Mma Ramotswe sighed. "Yes, but now they are saying: when will those two get married? That is what they are all saying. And maybe I should say that too."

For a few moments Mr J.L.B. Matekoni said nothing. He continued to wipe his hands on the lint, as if concentrating on a delicate task, and then he spoke. "We will get married next year. That is the best thing to do. By then we will have made all the arrangements and saved enough money for a big wedding. Weddings cost a lot, you know. Maybe it will be next year, or the year after that, but we shall certainly get married. There is no doubt about that."

"But I have got money in the Standard

Chartered Bank," said Mma Ramotswe. "I could use that or I could sell some cattle. I still have some cattle that my father left me. They have multiplied. I have almost two hundred now."

"You must not sell cattle," said Mr J.L.B. Matekoni. "It is good to keep cattle. We must wait."

He stared at her, almost reproachfully, and Mma Ramotswe looked away. The subject was too awkward, too raw, to be discussed openly, and so she did not pursue the matter. It seemed as if he was frightened of marriage, which must be the reason why he was proving so slow to commit himself. Well, there were men like that; nice men who were fond enough of women but who were wary of getting married. If that was the case, then she would be realistic about it and continue to be an engaged lady. It was not a bad situation to be in, after all; indeed, there were some arguments for preferring an engagement to a marriage. You often heard of difficult husbands, but how often did you hear of difficult fiancés? The answer to that, thought Mma Ramotswe, was never.

Mr J.L.B. Matekoni left the room, and Mma Ramotswe picked up her mug of bush tea. If she was going to remain an engaged lady, then she would make the most of it, and one of the ways to do this would be to enjoy her free time. She would read a bit more and spend more time on her shopping. And she might also join a club of some sort, if she could find one, or perhaps even form one herself, perhaps something like a Cheerful Ladies' Club, a club for ladies in whose lives there was some sort of gap—in her case a gap of waiting—but who were determined to make the most of their time. It was a sentiment of which her father, the late Obed Ramotswe, would have approved; her father, that good man who had always used his time to good effect and who was always in her thoughts, as constantly and supportively as if he were buried under the floor directly beneath her.

CHAPTER TWO

HOW TO RUN
AN ORPHAN FARM

MMA SILVIA POTOKWANE, the matron of the orphan farm, was sorting out bits of carpeting for a jumble sale. The pieces of carpet were scattered about the ground under a large syringa tree, and she and several of the housemothers were busy placing them in order of desirability. The carpets were not old at all, but were off-cuts which had been donated by a flooring firm in Gaborone. At the end of every job, no matter how careful the carpet layers were, there would always be odd pieces which simply did not fit. Sometimes these were quite large, if the end of a roll had been used, or the room had been a particularly awkward shape. But none of them was square or rectangular, and this meant that their usefulness was limited.

"Nobody has a room this shape," said one of the housemothers, drawing Mma Potokwane's attention to a triangular piece of flecked red carpet. "I do not know what we can do with this."

Mma Potokwane bent down to examine the carpet. It was not easy for her to bend, as she was an unusually traditional shape. She enjoyed her food, certainly, but she was also very active, and one might have thought that all that walking about the orphan farm, peering into every corner just to keep everybody on their toes, would have shed the pounds, but it had not. All the women in her family had been that build, and it had brought them good fortune and success; there was no point, she felt, being a thin and unhappy person when the attractions of being a comfortable person were so evident. And men liked women like that too. It was a terrible thing that the outside world had done to Africa, bringing in the idea that slender ladies, some as thin as a sebokoldi, a millipede, should be considered desirable. That was not what men really wanted. Men wanted women whose shape reminded them of good things on the table.

"It is a very strange shape," agreed Mma Potokwane. "But if you put together two triangles, then do you not get a square, or something quite close to a square? Do you not think that is true, Mma?"

The housemother looked blank for a moment, but then the wisdom of Mma Potokwane's suggestion dawned upon her and she smiled broadly. There were other triangular pieces, and she now reached for one of these, and held it in position alongside the awkward red piece. The result was an almost perfect square, even if the two pieces of carpet were a different colour.

Mma Potokwane was pleased with the result. Once they had sorted out the carpets, they would put up a notice in the Tlokweng Community Centre and invite people to a carpet sale. They would have no difficulty in selling everything, she thought, and the money would go into the fund that they were building up for book prizes for the children. At the end of each term, those who had done well would receive a prize for their efforts; an atlas, perhaps, or a

Setswana Bible, or some other book which would be useful at school. Although she was not a great reader, Mma Potokwane was a firm believer in the power of the book. The more books that Botswana had, in her view, the better. It would be on books that the future would be based; books and the people who knew how to use them.

It would be wonderful, she thought, to write a book which would help other people. In her case, she would never have the time to do it, and even if she had the time, then she very much doubted whether she would have the necessary ability. But if she were to write a book, then the title would undoubtedly be **How to Run an Orphan Farm.** That would be a useful book for whomever took over from her when she retired, or indeed for the many other ladies who ran orphan farms elsewhere. Mma Potokwane had spent some time thinking about the contents of such a work. There would be a great deal about the ordinary day-to-day business of an orphan farm: the arranging of meals, the sorting out of duties and so on. But there would also be a chapter on the psychology which went into running an orphan farm. Mma Potokwane knew a great deal about that. She could tell you, for example, of the importance of keeping brothers and sisters together, if at all possible, and of how to deal with behavioural problems. These were almost always due to insecurity and had one cure and one cure alone: love. That, at least, had been her experience, and even if the message was a simple one, it was, in her view, utterly true.

Another chapter—a very important one—would be on fund raising. Every orphan farm needed to raise money, and this was a task which was always there in the background. Even when you had successfully performed every other task, the problem of money always remained, a persistent, nagging worry at the back of one's mind. Mma Potokwane prided herself on her competence in this. If something was needed—a new set of pots for one of the houses, or a pair of shoes for a child whose shoes were wearing thin—she would find a donor who could be persuaded to come up with the money. Few people could resist Mma Potokwane, and there had been an occasion when the Vice-President of Botswana himself, a generous man who prided himself on his open door policy, had thought ruefully of those countries where it was inconceivable that any citizen could claim the right to see the second most important person in the country. Mma Potokwane had made him promise to find somebody to sell her building materials, and he had agreed before he had thought much about it. The building materials had been purchased from a firm which was prepared to sell them cheaply, but it had taken up a great deal of time.

At the very head of Mma Potokwane's list of supporters was Mr J.L.B. Matekoni. She had relied on him for years to take care of various bits of machinery on the orphan farm, including the water pump, which he had now insisted on being replaced, and the minivan in which the orphans were driven into town. This was an old vehicle, exhausted by years of bumping along on the dusty road to the orphanage, and had it not been for Mr J.L.B. Matekoni's expert hand, it would have long since come to the end of its life. But it was a van which he understood, and it was blessed with a Bedford engine that had been built to last and last, like a strong old mule that pulls a cart. The orphan farm could probably afford a new van, but Mma Potokwane saw no reason to spend money on something new when you had something old which was still working.

That Saturday morning, as they sorted out the carpet pieces for the sale, Mma Potokwane suddenly looked at her watch and saw that it was almost time for Mr J.L.B. Matekoni to arrive. She had asked him whether he could come out to look at a ladder which was broken and needed welding. A new ladder would not have cost a great deal, and would probably have been safer, but why buy a new ladder, Mma Potokwane had asked herself. A new ladder might be shiny, but would hardly have the strength of their old metal ladder, which had belonged to the railways and had been given to them almost ten years ago.

She left the housemothers discussing a round piece of green carpet and returned to her office. She had baked a cake for Mr J.L.B. Matekoni, as she usually did, but this time she had taken particular care to make it sweet and rich. She knew that Mr J.L.B. Matekoni liked fruit cake, and particularly liked raisins, and she had thrown several extra handfuls of these into the mixture, just for him. The broken ladder might have been the ostensible reason for his invitation, but she had other business in mind and there was nothing better than a cake to facilitate agreement.

When Mr J.L.B. Matekoni eventually did arrive, she was ready for him, sitting directly in front of the fan in her office, feeling the benefit of the blast of air from the revolving blades, looking out of the window at the lushness of the trees outside. Although Botswana was a dry country, at the end of the rainy season it was always green, and there were pockets of shade at every turn. It was only at the beginning of the summer, before the rains arrived, that everything was desiccated and brown. That was when the cattle became thin, sometimes painfully so, and it broke the heart of a cattle-owning people to see the herds nibbling at the few dry shreds of grass that remained, their heads lowered in lassitude and in weakness. And it would be like that until the purple clouds stacked up to the east and the wind brought the smell of rain—rain which would fall in silver sheets over the land.

That, of course, was if the rain came. Sometimes there were droughts, and a whole season would go by with very little rainfall, and the dryness would become an ache, always there, like dust in the throat. Botswana was lucky of course; she could import grain, but there were countries which could not, for they had no money, and in those places there was nothing to stand between the people and starvation. That was Africa's burden, and by and large it was borne with dignity; but it still caused pain to Mma Potokwane to know that her fellow Africans faced such suffering.

Now, though, the trees were covered with green leaves, and it was easy for Mr J.L.B. Matekoni to find a shady place for his car outside the orphan farm offices. As he emerged from the car, a small boy came up to him and took his hand. The child looked up at him with grave eyes, and Mr J.L.B. Matekoni smiled down on him. Reaching into his pocket, he withdrew a handful of wrapped peppermints, and slipped these into the palm of the child's hand.

"I saw you there, Mr J.L.B. Matekoni," said Mma Potokwane, as her visitor entered her room. "I saw you give sweets to that child. That child is cunning. He knows you are a kind man."

"I am not a kind man," said Mr J.L.B. Matekoni. "I am an ordinary mechanic."

Mma Potokwane laughed. "You are not an ordinary mechanic. You are the best mechanic in Botswana! Everybody knows that."

"No," said Mr J.L.B. Matekoni. "Only you think that."

Mma Potokwane shook her head vigorously. "Then why does the British High Commissioner take his car to you? There are many big garages in Botswana who would like to service a car like that. But he still goes to you. Always."

"I cannot say why," said Mr J.L.B. Matekoni. "But I think that he is a good man and likes to go to a small garage." He was too modest to accept her praise, and yet he was aware of his reputation. Of course, if people knew about his apprentices, and how bad they were, they might think differently of Tlokweng Road Speedy Motors, but the apprentices were not going to be there forever. In fact, they were due to complete their training in a couple of months and that would be the end of them. How peaceful it would be once they had moved on! How comfortable it would be not to have to think of the damage that they were doing to the cars entrusted to him. It would be a new freedom for him; a release from a worry which hung about his shoulders each day. He had done his best to train them properly, and they had picked up something over the years, but they were impatient, and that was a fatal flaw in the personality of any mechanic. Donkeys and cars required patience.

One of the older girls had made tea, and now she brought this in, together with the rich fruit cake on a plate. Mr J.L.B. Matekoni saw the cake, and for a moment he frowned. He knew Mma Potokwane, and the presence of a large cake, specially made for the occasion, was an unambiguous signal that she had a request to make of him. A cake of this size, and emitting such a strong smell of raisins, would mean a major mechanical problem. The minivan? He had replaced the brake pads recently, but he was concerned about the engine seals. At that age, engine seals could go and the block could heat up and . . .

"I've made you a cake," said Mma Potokwane brightly.

"You are a very generous person, Mma," said Mr J.L.B. Matekoni flatly. "You always remember that I like raisins."

"I have many more packets of raisins," said Mma Potokwane, making a generous gesture, as might one with an unlimited supply of raisins. She reached over to the plate and cut a large portion of cake for her guest. Mr J.L.B. Matekoni watched her, and he thought: once I eat this cake I will have to say yes. But then he went on to think: I always say yes anyway, cake or no cake. What difference is there?

"I should think that Mma Ramotswe makes you many cakes these days," said Mma Potokwane as she slid a generous portion of cake onto her own plate. "She is a good cook, I think."

Mr J.L.B. Matekoni nodded. "She is best at cooking pumpkin and things like that," he said. "But she can also make cakes. You ladies are very clever."

"Yes," agreed Mma Potokwane, pouring the tea. "We are much cleverer than you men, but unfortunately you do not know that."

Mr J.L.B. Matekoni looked at his shoes. It was probably true, he thought. It was difficult being a man sometimes, particularly when women reminded one of the fact that one was a man. But there were clever men about, he thought, and these men would give ladies like Mma Potokwane a good run for their money. The problem was that he was not one of these clever men.

Mr J.L.B. Matekoni looked out of the window. He thought that perhaps he should say something, but nothing came into his mind. Outside the window, the branch of the flamboyant tree, on which a few red flowers still grew, moved almost imperceptibly. New seed pods were growing, while last year's pods, long blackened strips, clung to branches here and there. They were good trees, flamboyants, he thought, with their shade and their red flowers, and their delicate fronds of tiny leaves, like feathers, swaying gently in the wind . . . He stopped. The thin green branch just outside the open window seemed to be unwinding itself and extending tentatively, as if some exaggerated process of growth were occurring.

He rose to his feet, putting down his half-finished piece of cake.

"You've seen something?" asked Mma Potokwane. "Are the children up to something out there?"

Mr J.L.B. Matekoni took a step closer to the window and then stopped. "There is a snake on that branch out there, Mma. A green snake."

Mma Potokwane gasped and stood up to peer out of her window. She narrowed her eyes briefly, peering into the foliage, and

then reached suddenly for Mr J.L.B. Matekoni's arm.

"You are right, Rra! There is a snake! Ow!
Look at it!"

"Yes," said Mr J.L.B. Matekoni. "It's a long
snake too. Look, its tail goes all the way down
there."

"You must kill it, Rra," said Mma Potokwane. "I will fetch you a stick."

Mr J.L.B. Matekoni nodded. He knew that
people were always telling you not to kill
snakes on sight, but you could not allow snakes
to come so close to all the orphans. It might be
different in the bush, where there was a place
for snakes, and they had their own roads and
paths, going this way and that, but here it was
different. This was the orphan farm front yard,
and at any moment the snake could drop down
on an orphan as he or she walked under that
tree. Mma Potokwane was right; he would have
to kill the snake.

Armed with the broomstick which Mma
Potokwane had fetched from a cupboard, Mr
J.L.B. Matekoni, followed at a discreet distance
by the matron, walked round the corner of the
office building. The syringa tree seemed higher
when viewed from outside, and he wondered

whether he would be able to reach the branch on which the snake had been sitting. If he could not, then there was nothing that he could do. They would simply have to warn the orphans to stay away from that tree for the time being.

"Just climb up there and hit it," whispered Mma Potokwane. "Look! There it is. It is not moving now."

"I cannot go up there," protested Mr J.L.B. Matekoni. "If I get too close, it could bite me." He shuddered as he spoke. These green tree snakes, boomslangs they called them, were amongst the most poisonous snakes, worse even than the mambas, some people said, because they had no serum in Botswana to deal with their bite. They had to telephone through to South Africa to get supplies of it if somebody was bitten.

"But you must climb up," urged Mma Potokwane. "Otherwise, it will get away."

Mr J.L.B. Matekoni looked at her, as if to confirm the order. He looked for some sign that she did not really mean this, but there was none. He could not climb up the tree, into the snake's domain; he simply could not.

"I cannot," he said. "I cannot climb up

there. I shall try to reach him with my stick from here. I shall poke at the branch."

Mma Potokwane looked doubtful, standing back as he took a tentative step forward. She raised a hand to watch as the broom handle moved up into the foliage of the tree. For his part Mr J.L.B. Matekoni held his breath; he was not a cowardly man, and indeed was braver than most. He never shirked his duty and knew that he had to deal with this snake, but the way to deal with snakes was to keep an advantage over them, and while it was in the tree this snake was in its element.

What happened next was the subject of much discussion amongst the staff of the orphan farm and amongst the small knot of orphans which was by now watching from the security of the office verandah. Mr J.L.B. Matekoni might have touched the snake with the broom handle or he might not. It is possible that the snake saw the stick approaching and decided on evasive action, for these are shy snakes, in spite of their powerful venom, and do not seek confrontation. It moved, and moved quickly, slipping through the leaves and branches with a fluid, undulating motion.

Within a few seconds it was sliding down the trunk of the tree, impossibly attached, and then was upon the ground and darting, arrow-like, across the baked earth. Mma Potokwane let out a shriek, as the snake seemed to be heading for her, but then it swerved and shot away towards a large hibiscus bush that grew on a patch of grass behind the office. Mr J.L.B. Matekoni gave a shout, and pursued it with his broom, thumping the end of the stick upon the earth. The snake moved faster, and reached the grass, which seemed to help it in its flight. Mr J.L.B. Matekoni stopped; he did not wish to kill this long green stripe of life, which would surely not linger here any longer and was no danger to anyone. He turned to Mma Potokwane, who had raised her hand to her mouth and had uttered a brief ululation, as was traditional, and quite proper, at moments of celebration.

"You brave man!" she shouted. "You chased that snake away!"

"Not really," said Mr J.L.B. Matekoni. "I think it had decided to go anyway."

Mma Potokwane would have none of this. Turning to the group of orphans, who were chattering excitedly amongst themselves, she said, "You see this uncle? You see how he has saved us all from this snake?"

"Ow!" called out one of the orphans. "You are very brave, uncle."

Mr J.L.B. Matekoni looked away in embarrassment. Handing back the broom to Mma Potokwane, he turned to go back into the office, where the rest of his cake was awaiting him. He noticed that his hands were shaking.

"Now," SAID Mma Potokwane as she placed another, particularly generous, slice of cake on Mr J.L.B. Matekoni's plate. "Now we can talk. Now I know you are a brave man, which I always suspected anyway."

"You must stop calling me that," he said. "I am no braver than any other man."

Mma Potokwane seemed not to hear. "A brave man," she went on. "And I have been looking for a brave man now for over a week. At last I have found him."

Mr J.L.B. Matekoni frowned. "You have had snakes for that long? What about the men around here? What about the husbands of all those housemothers? Where are they?"

"Oh, not snakes," said Mma Potokwane. "We have seen no other snakes. This is about something else. I have a plan which needs a brave man. And you are the obvious person. We need a brave man who is also well-known."

"I am not well-known," said Mr J.L.B. Matekoni quickly.

"But you are! Everybody knows your garage. Everybody has seen you standing outside it, wiping your hands on a cloth. Everybody who drives past says, 'There's Mr J.L.B. Matekoni in front of his garage. That is him.'"

Mr J.L.B. Matekoni looked down at his plate. He felt a strong sense of foreboding, but he would eat the cake nonetheless while Mma Potokwane revealed whatever it was that she had in store for him. He would be strong this time, he thought. He had stood up to her not all that long ago on the question of the pump, and the need to replace it; now he would stand up to her again. He picked up the piece of cake and bit off a large piece. The raisins tasted even better now, in the presence of danger.

"I want you to help me raise money," said Mma Potokwane, "We have a boy who can sing very well. He is sixteen now, one of the older boys, and Mr Slater at the Maitisong Festival wants to send him to Cape Town to take part in a competition. But this costs money, and this boy has none, because he is just an orphan. He can only go if we raise the money for him. It will be a big thing for Botswana if he goes, and a big thing for that boy too."

Mr J.L.B. Matekoni put down the rest of the cake. He need not have worried, he thought: this sounded like a completely reasonable request. He would sell raffle tickets at the garage if she wanted, or donate a free car service as a prize. Why that should require courage, he could not understand.

And then it became clear. Mma Potokwane picked up her tea cup, took a sip of tea, and then announced her plan.

"I'd like you to do a sponsored parachute jump, Mr J.L.B. Matekoni," she said.

CHAPTER THREE

MMA RAMOTSWE VISITS
HER COUSIN IN MOCHUDI,
AND THINKS

Mma Ramotswe did not see Mr J.L.B. Matekoni that Saturday, as she had driven up to Mochudi in her tiny white van. She planned to stay there until Sunday, leaving the children to be looked after by Mr J.L.B. Matekoni. These were the foster children from the orphan farm, whom Mr J.L.B. Matekoni had agreed to take into his home, without consulting Mma Ramotswe. But she had been unable to hold this against him, even if many women would have felt that they should have been consulted about the introduction of children into their lives; it was typical of his generosity that he should do something like this. After a few days, the children had come to stay with her, which was better than their living in his house, with its engine parts that littered the floor and with its empty store cupboards (Mr J.L.B. Matekoni did not bother to buy much food). And so they had moved to the house in Zebra Drive, the girl and her brother; the girl in a wheel-chair, for illness had left her unable to walk, and the brother, much younger than she, and still needing special attention after all that had happened to him.

Mma Ramotswe had no particular reason to go up to Mochudi, but it was the village in which she had grown up and one never really needed an excuse to visit the place in which one had spent one's childhood. That was the mar-vellous thing about going back to one's roots; there was no need for explanation. In Mochudi everybody knew who she was: the daughter of Obed Ramotswe, who had gone off to Gab-orone, where she had made a bad marriage to a trumpet player she had met on a bus. That was all common knowledge, part of the web of memories which made up the village life of Botswana. In that world, nobody needed to be a stranger; everybody could be linked in some way with others, even a visitor; for visitors came for a reason, did they not? They would be associated, then, with the people whom they were visiting. There was a place for everybody.

Mma Ramotswe had been thinking a great deal recently about how people might be fitted in. The world was a large place, and one might have thought that there was enough room for everybody. But it seemed that this was not so. There were many people who were unhappy, and wanted to move. Often they wished to come to the more fortunate countries—such as Botswana—in order to make more of their lives. That was understandable, and yet there were those who did not want them. This is our place, they said; you are not welcome.

It was so easy to think like that. People wanted to protect themselves from those they did not know. Others were different; they talked different languages and wore different clothes. Many people did not want them living close to them, just because of these differences. And yet, they were people, were they not? They thought the same way, and had the same hopes as anybody else did. They were our brothers and sisters, whichever way you looked at it, and you could not turn a brother or sister away.

Mochudi was busy. There was to be a wedding at the Dutch Reformed Church that afternoon, and the relatives of the bride were arriving from Serowe and Mahalapye. There was also something happening at one of the schools—a sports day, it seemed—and as she passed the field (or patch of dust, she noted ruefully) a teacher in a green floppy hat was shouting at a group of children in running shorts. Ahead of her on the road a couple of donkeys ambled aimlessly, flicking at the flies with their moth-eaten tails. It was, in short, a typical Mochudi Saturday.

Mma Ramotswe went to her cousin's house and sat on a stool in the lelapa, the small, carefully swept yard which forms the immediate curtilage of the traditional Botswana house. Mma Ramotswe was always pleased to see her cousin, as these visits gave her the opportunity to catch up on village news. This was information one would never see in any newspaper, yet it was every bit as interesting—more so, in many respects—than the great events of the world which the newspapers reported. So she sat on a traditional stool, the seat of which was woven from thin strips of rough-cured leather, and listened to her cousin tell her what had taken place. Much had happened since Mma Ramotswe's last visit. A minor headman, known for his tendency to drink too much beer, had fallen into a well, but had been saved because a young boy passing by had happened to mention that he had seen somebody jump into the well.

"They almost didn't believe that boy," said the cousin. "He was a boy who was always telling lies. But happily somebody decided to check."

"That boy will grow up to be a politician," said Mma Ramotswe. "That will be the best job for him."

The cousin had shrieked with laughter. "Yes, they are very good at lying. They are always promising us water for every house, but they never bring it. They say that there are not enough pipes. Maybe next year."

Mma Ramotswe shook her head. Water was the source of many problems in a dry country and the politicians did not make it any easier by promising water when they had none to deliver.

"If the opposition would only stop arguing amongst themselves," the cousin went on, "they would win the election and get rid of the government. That would be a good thing, do you not think?"

"No," said Mma Ramotswe.

The cousin stared at her. "But it would be very different if we had a new government," she said.

"Would it?" asked Mma Ramotswe. She was not a cynical woman, but she wondered whether one set of people who looked remarkably like another set of people would run things any differently. But she did not wish to provoke a political argument with her cousin, and so she changed the subject by asking after the doings of a local woman who had killed a neighbour's goat because she thought that the neighbour was flirting with her husband. It was a long-running saga and was providing a great deal of amusement for everyone.

"She crept out at night and cut the goat's throat," said the cousin. "The goat must have thought she was a tokolosh, or something like that. She is a very wicked woman."

"There are many like that," said Mma Ramotswe. "Men think that women can't be wicked, but we are quite capable of being wicked too."

"Even more wicked than men," said the cousin. "Women are much more wicked, don't you agree?"

"No," said Mma Ramotswe. She thought that the levels of male and female wickedness were about the same; it just took slightly different forms.

The cousin looked peevishly at Mma Ramotswe. "Women have not had much of a chance to be wicked in a big way," she muttered. "Men have taken all the best jobs, where you can be truly wicked. If women here were allowed to be generals and presidents and the like, then they would be very wicked, same as all those wicked men. Just give them the chance. Look at how those lady generals have behaved."

Mma Ramotswe picked up a piece of straw and examined it closely. "Name one," she said.

The cousin thought, but no names came to her, at least no names of generals. "There was an Indian lady called Mrs Gandhi."

"And did she shoot people?" asked Mma Ramotswe.

"No," said the cousin. "Somebody shot her. But . . ."

"There you are," said Mma Ramotswe. "I assume that it was a man who shot her, or was it some lady, do you think?"

The cousin said nothing. A small boy was

peering over the wall of the lelapa, staring at the two women. His eyes were large and round, and his arms, which protruded from a scruffy red shirt, were thin. The cousin pointed at him.

"He cannot speak, that little boy," she said. "His tongue does not work properly. So he just watches the other children play."

Mma Ramotswe smiled at him, and called out to him gently in Setswana. But the little boy might not have heard, for he turned away without replying and walked slowly away on his skinny legs. Mma Ramotswe was silent for a moment, imagining what it would be like to be a little boy like that, thin and voiceless. I am fortunate, she thought, and turned to say to her cousin, "We are lucky, aren't we? Here we are, traditionally built ladies, and there's that poor little boy with his thin arms and legs. And we can talk and he can make no sound at all."

The cousin nodded. "We are very lucky to be who we are," she said. "We are fortunate ladies, sitting here in the sun with so much to talk about."

So much to talk about—and so little to do. Here in Mochudi, away from the bustle of Gaborone, Mma Ramotswe could feel herself lapsing again into the rhythms of country life, a life much slower and more reflective than life in town. There was still time and space to think in Gaborone, but it was so much easier here, where one might look out up to the hill and watch the thin wisps of cloud, no more than that, float slowly across the sky; or listen to the cattle bells and the chorus of the cicadas. This was what it meant to live in Botswana; when the rest of the world might work itself into a frenzy of activity, one might still sit, in the space before a house with ochre walls, a mug of bush tea in one's hand, and talk about very small things: headmen in wells, goats and jealousy.

CHAPTER FOUR

A WOMAN WHO KNOWS ABOUT HAIR

THAT MONDAY, Mma Ramotswe had an appointment. Most of her clients did not bother to arrange a time to see her, preferring to drop in unannounced and—in some cases—without disclosing their identity. Mma Ramotswe understood why people should wish to do this. It was not easy to consult a detective agency, especially if one had a problem of a particularly private nature, and many people had to pluck up considerable courage before they knocked on her door. She understood that doctors sometimes encountered similar behaviour; that patients would talk about everything except the real problem and then, at the last moment, mention what was really troubling them. She had read somewhere—in one of the old

magazines that Mma Makutsi liked to page
through—of a doctor who had been consulted
by a man wearing a paper bag over his head.
Poor man, thought Mma Ramotswe. It must
be terrible to feel so embarrassed about something that one would have to wear a paper
bag over one's head! What was wrong with
that man? she wondered. Things did go wrong
with men sometimes that they were ashamed
to talk about, but there was really no need to
feel that way.

Mma Ramotswe had never encountered
embarrassment of such a degree, but she had
certainly had to draw stories out of people.
This happened most commonly with women
who had been let down by their husbands, or
who suspected that their husbands were having
an affair. Such women could feel anger and a
sense of betrayal, both of which were entirely
understandable, but they could also feel shame
that such a thing had happened to them. It was
as if it was their fault that their husband had
taken up with another woman. This could be
so, of course; there were women who drove
their husbands away, but in most cases it was
because the husband had become bored with
his marriage and wanted to see a younger

woman. They were always younger, Mma Ramotswe reflected; only rich ladies were able to take up with younger men.

The thought of rich ladies reminded her: the woman who was coming to see her that day was undoubtedly a rich lady. Mma Holonga was well-known in Gaborone as the founder of a chain of hairdressing salons. The salons were successful, but what had proved even more profitable was her invention, and marketing, of Special Girl Hair Braiding Preparation. This was one of those mixtures which women put on their hair before they braided it; its efficacy was doubtful, but the hair products market was not one which required a great deal of scientific evidence. What mattered was that there was a sufficient number of people who believed that their favourite preparation worked.

Mma Ramotswe had never met Mma Holonga. She had seen her picture in **Mmegi** and the **Botswana Guardian** from time to time, and in the photographs she had noticed a pleasant, rather round face. She knew, too, that Mma Holonga lived in a house in the Village, not far from Mr J.L.B. Matekoni. She was intrigued to meet her, because from what she had seen in the newspapers she had formed the impression that Mma Holonga was an unusual rich lady. Many such women were spoilt and demanding, and frequently had an exaggerated idea of their own importance. Mma Holonga did not seem like that.

And when she arrived for her appointment, at exactly the right time (which was another point in her favour), Mma Holonga confirmed Mma Ramotswe's advance impressions.

"You are very kind to see me," she said as she sat down on the chair in front of Mma Ramotswe's desk. "I can imagine how busy you must be."

"Sometimes I am busy," said Mma Ramotswe. "And then sometimes I am not. I am not busy today. I am just sitting here."

"That is very good," said Mma Holonga. "It is good just to sit sometimes. I like to do that, if I get the chance. I just sit."

"There is a lot to be said for that," agreed Mma Ramotswe. "Although we would not want people to do it all the time, would we?"

"Oh no," said Mma Holonga hurriedly. "I would never recommend that."

For a few moments there was silence. Mma Ramotswe looked at the woman in front of her. As the newspaper photographs had suggested, she was traditionally built about the face, but also everywhere else, and her dress was straining at the sides. She should move up a size or two, thought Mma Ramotswe, and then those panels on the side would not look as if they were about to rip. There really was no point in fighting these things: it is far better to admit one's size and indeed there is even a case for buying a slightly larger size. That gives room for manoeuvre.

Mma Holonga was also taking the opportunity to sum up Mma Ramotswe. Comfortable, she thought; not one of these undernourished modern ladies. That is good. But her dress is a bit tight, and she should think of getting a slightly larger size. But she has a friendly face— a good, old-fashioned Botswana face that one can trust, unlike these modern faces which one saw so much of these days.

"I am glad that I came to see you," said Mma Holonga. "I had heard that you were a good person for this sort of thing. That's what people tell me."

Mma Ramotswe smiled. She was a modest person, but a compliment was never unwelcome. And she knew, of course, how important it was to compliment others; not in any insin-

cere way, but to encourage people in their work
or to make them feel that their efforts had been
worthwhile. She had even complimented the
apprentices on one occasion, when they had
gone out of their way to help a customer, and
for a short time it seemed as if this had inspired
them to take a pride in their work. But after a
few days she assumed that her words had been
forgotten, as they forgot everything else, since
they returned to their usual, sloppy habits.

"Oh yes," Mma Holonga continued. "You
may not know it, Mma, but your reputation in
this town is very high. People say that you are
one of the cleverest women in Botswana."

"Oh that cannot be true," said Mma Ramotswe, laughing. "There are many much cleverer ladies in Botswana, ladies with BAs and
BScs. There are even lady doctors at the hospital. They must be much cleverer than I am.
I have just got my Cambridge Certificate, that
is all."

"And I haven't even got that," said Mma
Holonga. "But I don't think that I am any less
intelligent than those apprentices out there in
the garage. I assume they have their Cambridge
Certificate too."

"They are a special case," said Mma

Ramotswe. "They have passed their Cambridge Certificate, but they are not a very good advertisement for education. Their heads are quite empty. They have nothing in them except thoughts of girls."

Mma Holonga glanced through the doorway to where one of the apprentices could be seen sitting on an upturned oil-drum. She appeared to study him for a moment before she turned back to Mma Ramotswe. Mma Ramotswe noticed; it was only a momentary stare, she thought, but it told her something: Mma Holonga was interested in men. And why should she not be? The days when women had to pretend not to be interested in men were surely over, and now they could talk about it. Mma Ramotswe was not sure whether it was a good idea to talk too openly about men—she had heard some quite shocking things being said by some women, and she would never condone such shamelessness—but it was, on the whole, better for women to be able to express themselves.

"I have come to see you about men," said Mma Holonga suddenly. "That is why I am here."

Mma Ramotswe was taken aback. She had

wondered why Mma Holonga had come and had assumed that it was something to do with one of her businesses. But now it seemed it was going to be something rather more personal than that.

"There are many women who come to see me about men," she said quietly. "Men are a major problem for many women."

Mma Holonga smiled at this. "That is no exaggeration, Mma. But many women have problems just with one man. I have problems with four men."

Mma Ramotswe gave a start. This was unexpected: four men! It was conceivable that somebody might have two boyfriends, and hope that neither found out about the other, but to have four! That was an invitation for trouble.

"It's not what you may think," said Mma Holonga hurriedly. "I do not have four boyfriends. At the moment I have no boyfriend, except for these four . . ."

Mma Ramotswe raised her hand. "You should start at the beginning," she said. "I am getting confused already." She paused. "And to help you talk, I shall make some bush tea. Would you like that?"

Mma Holonga nodded. "I will talk while

you are making the tea. Then you will hear all my troubles while the water is boiling."

"I AM a very ordinary lady," Mma Holonga began. "I did not do very well at school, as I have told you. When other girls were looking at their books, I was always looking at magazines. I liked the fashion magazines with all their pictures of bright clothes and smart models. And I specially liked looking at pictures of people's hair and of how hair could be braided and made beautiful with all those beads and henna and things like that.

"I thought it very unfair that God had given African ladies short hair and all the long hair had been taken by everybody else. But then I realised that there was no reason why African hair should not be very beautiful too, although it is not easy to do things with it. I used to braid my friends' hair, and soon I had quite a reputation amongst the other girls at school. They came to see me on Friday afternoons to have their hair braided for the week-end, and I would do it outside our kitchen. The friends would sit on a chair and I would stand behind them, talking and braiding hair in the afternoon sun. I was very happy doing that.

"You'll know all about hair braiding, Mma. You'll know that it can sometimes take a long time. Most of the time I would only spend an hour or two on somebody's hair, but there were times when I spent over two days on a design. I was very proud of all the circles and lines, Mma. I was very proud.

"By the time I was ready to leave school, there was no doubt in my mind what I wanted to do for a living. I had been promised a job in a hair salon that a lady had opened in the African Mall. She had seen my work and knew that I would bring a lot of business because I was so well-known as a hair braider. She was right. All my friends came to this salon although now they had to pay for me to do their hair.

"After a while I started my own business. I found a small tuck shop that was closing down and I started off in there. It was very cramped, and I had to bring the water I needed in a bucket, but all my customers moved with me and said that they did not mind if the new place was very small. They said that the important thing was to have somebody who really knew about hair, and they said I was such a person. One of them said that a person who knew as much about hair only comes along once or twice in a century. I was very pleased to hear this and asked that person to write out what they had said. I then had a sign-writer paint it on a board and passers-by would stop and read that remark and look at me with respect as I stood there with my scissors ready to cut their hair. I was very happy, Mma. I was very happy.

"I built up my business and eventually I bought a proper salon. Then I bought another one and another after that up in Francistown. Everything went very well and all this time the money was piling up in the bank. I had so much money that I could not really spend it all myself, and so I gave some to my brother and asked him to use it to buy some other businesses for me. He bought me a shop and a place where they make dresses. So I had a factory now, and this made me even richer. I was very happy with all that money, and I went into the bank every Thursday to check how much I had. They were very polite to me now, as I had all that money and banks like people with lots of money.

"But you know what I didn't have, Mma? I didn't have a husband. I had been so busy cutting hair and making money that I had forgotten to get married. Three months ago, when I had my fortieth birthday, I suddenly thought: where is your husband? Where are all your children? And the answer was that there were none of these. So I decided that I would find a husband. It may be too late to have children now, but at least I would find a husband.

"And do you think that was easy, Mma? What do you think?"

Mma Ramotswe had by now made the bush tea and was pouring it into her client's cup. "I think it would be easy for a lady like you," she said. "I would not think you would find it hard."

"Oh?" said Mma Holonga. "And why would I not find it hard?"

Mma Ramotswe hesitated. She had answered without thinking very much about it, and now she wondered how she would explain herself. She had probably thought that it would be easy for Mma Holonga to find a husband because she was rich. It was easy for rich people to do anything, even to find a husband. But could she say that? Would it not seem insulting to Mma Holonga that the only reason why Mma Ramotswe should think she could find a husband was because she was rich, and not because she was beautiful or desirable.

"There are many men . . ." began Mma Ramotswe, and then stopped. "There are many men looking for wives."

"But many women say that it is not all that easy," said Mma Holonga. "Why should they find it hard while I should find it easy? Can you explain that?"

Mma Ramotswe sighed. It was best to be honest, she thought, and so she said, quite simply, "Money, Mma. That is the reason. You are a lady with a large chain of hair salons. You are a rich lady. There are many men who like rich ladies."

Mma Holonga sat back in her chair and smiled. "Exactly, Mma. I was waiting to see if you would say that. Now I know that you really do understand things."

"But they would also like you because you are an attractive lady," added Mma Ramotswe hurriedly. "Traditional Botswana men like ladies who are more traditionally shaped. You and I, Mma. We remind men of how things used to be in Botswana before these modern-shaped ladies started to get men all confused."

Mma Holonga nodded, but in a rather distracted fashion. "Yes, Mma. That may be quite true, but I think that my problem remains. I must tell you what happened when I let it be known that I was looking for a suitable husband. A very interesting thing happened." She paused. "But would you pour me more of that tea, Mma? It is very fine tea and I am thirsty again."

"It is bush tea," said Mma Ramotswe as she reached for the tea-pot. "Mma Makutsi—my assistant—and I drink bush tea because it helps us to think."

Mma Holonga raised her refilled cup to her lips and drained it noisily.

"I shall buy bush tea instead of ordinary tea," she said. "I shall put honey in it and drink it every day."

"That would be a very good thing to do," said Mma Ramotswe. "But what about this husband business? What happened?"

Mma Holonga frowned. "It is very difficult for me," she said. "When word got round, then I received many telephone calls. Ten, twenty calls. And they were all from men."

Mma Ramotswe raised an eyebrow. "That is a large number of men," she said.

Mma Holonga nodded. "Of course, I realised that some of them were no good right there and then. One even telephoned from the prison and the telephone was snatched away from him. And one was only a boy, about thirteen or fourteen, I think. But I agreed to see the others, and from these I ended up with a list of four."

"That is a good number to choose from," said Mma Ramotswe. "Not too large a list of men, but not too small."

Mma Holonga seemed pleased by this. She looked at Mma Ramotswe uncertainly. "You do not think it strange to have a list, Mma? Some of my friends . . ."

Mma Ramotswe raised a hand to interrupt her. Many of her clients referred to advice from friends, and in her experience this advice was often wrong. Friends tried to be helpful, but tended to misadvise, largely because they had unrealistic ideas of what the friend whom they were advising was really like. Mma Ramotswe believed that it was usually better to seek the advice of a stranger—not just any stranger, of course, as one could hardly go out onto the street and confide in the first person one encountered, but a stranger whom you knew to be wise. We do not talk about wise men or wise ladies any more, she reflected; their place had been taken, it seemed, by all sorts of shallow people—actors and the like—who were only too ready to pronounce on all sorts of subjects. It was worse, she thought, in other countries, but it was beginning to happen in Botswana and she did not like it. She, for one, would never pay any attention to the views of such people; she would far rather listen to a person who had done something real in life; these people knew what they were talking about.

"I'm not sure if you should worry too much about what your friends think, Mma," she said. "I think that it is a good idea to have a list. What is the difference between a list of things to buy at a shop, or a list of things to do, and a list of men? I do not see the difference."

"I am glad that you think that," said Mma Holonga. "In fact, I have been glad to hear everything that you have said."

Mma Ramotswe was always embarrassed by compliments, and rapidly went on.

"You must tell me about this list," she said. "And you must tell me about what you want me to do."

"I want you to find out about these men," said Mma Holonga. "I want you to see which men are interested in my money and which are interested in me."

Mma Ramotswe clapped her hands in delight. "Oh, this is the sort of work I like," she said. "Judging men! Men are always looking at women and judging them. Now we have the chance to do some judging back. Oh, this is a very good case to take on."

"I can pay you very well," said Mma Holonga, reaching for the large black handbag she had placed by the side of her chair. "If you tell me how much it will cost, I shall pay it."

"I shall send you a bill," said Mma Ramotswe. "That is what we do. Then you can pay me for my time." She paused. "But first, you must tell me about these men, Mma. I shall need some information on them. Then I shall set to work."

Mma Holonga sat back in her seat. "I am happy to talk about men, Mma. And now I shall begin with the first of these men."

Mma Ramotswe looked into her tea cup. It

was still half-full of bush tea. That would be enough to see her through one man, perhaps, but not four. So she reached forward, picked up the tea-pot, and offered to fill Mma Holonga's cup before attending to her own. That was the old Botswana way of doing things, and that is how Mma Ramotswe behaved. Modern people could say what they liked, but nobody had ever come up with a better way of doing things and in Mma Ramotswe's view nobody ever would.

CHAPTER FIVE

MR J.L.B. MATEKONI HAS CAUSE TO REFLECT

IT WAS some time before it dawned on Mr
J.L.B. Matekoni that Mma Potokwane may
have thought that he was agreeing to her
proposition. His own recollection of what had
happened was very clear. He had said, "I shall
think about it, Mma," which is very different—as anybody could see—from saying that
one would definitely do something. It might
have been better had he refused her there and
then, but Mr J.L.B. Matekoni was a kind man
and like all kind men he did not enjoy saying
no. There were many who had no such com-
punction, of course; they would refuse things
outright, even if it meant hurting another's
feelings.

Mr J.L.B. Matekoni thought very carefully.

After the initial bombshell, when Mma Potokwane had revealed what she had in mind,
he had remained silent for a moment. At first,
he thought that he had misheard her, and that
she had said that she wanted him to **fix** a parachute, just as she was always asking him to fix
some piece of equipment. But of course she
had not asked him that, as there would have
been plenty of people around the orphan farm
who would be much better placed to fix a
parachute than he. Fixing a parachute was a
sewing job, he assumed, and most of the
housemothers were adept at that; they were always sewing the orphans' clothes, repairing
rents in the seats of boys' trousers or undoing
the hems of skirts that were now a little bit too
short. These ladies could easily have stitched
up a torn parachute, even if the parachute
would end up with a patch made out of a boy's
trousers. No, that was not what Mma Potokwane could have had in mind.

Her next remark made this clear. "It's a very
good way of raising money," she had said.
"The hardship project did it last year. That
man from the radio—the well-known one
with the funny voice—he agreed to jump.
And then that girl who almost became Miss

Botswana said she would jump too. They raised a lot of money. A lot."

"But I cannot jump," Mr J.L.B. Matekoni had protested. "I have never even been in an aeroplane. I would not like to jump from one."

It was as if Mma Potokwane had not heard him. "It is a very easy thing to do. I have spoken to somebody in the Flying Club and they say that they can teach you how to do it. They have a book, too, which shows you how to put your feet when you land. It is very simple. Even I could do it."

"Then why don't you?" he had said, but not loudly enough to be heard, for Mma Potokwane had continued as if he had not spoken.

"There is no reason to be afraid," she said. "I think that it will be very comfortable riding down in the air like that. They might drop you over one of our fields and I will get one of the housemothers to have a cake ready for you when you land. And we have a stretcher too. We can have that close by, just in case."

"I do not want to do it," Mr J.L.B. Matekoni had intended to say, but for some reason the words came out as, "I'll think about it."

THE FULL CUPBOARD OF LIFE

And that, he realised, was where he had made his mistake. Of course it would be easy enough to undo. All that he would have to do would be to telephone Mma Potokwane and tell her, as unambiguously and as finally as he could, that he had now thought about it and he had decided that he would not do it. He would be happy to give some money to whomsoever she managed to persuade to do it for her, but that person, he was sorry to say, would not be him. This was the only way with Mma Potokwane. One had to be firm with her, just as he had been firm with her on the issue of the pump. One had to stand up to a woman like that.

The difficulty, of course, with standing up to women was that it appeared to make little difference. At the end of the day, a man was no match for a woman, especially if that woman was somebody like Mma Potokwane. The only thing to do was to try to avoid situations where women might corner you. And that was difficult, because women had a way of ensuring that you were neatly boxed in, which was exactly what had happened to him. He should have been more careful. He should have been on his guard when she offered him cake. That was her technique, he now understood; just as Eve had used an apple to trap Adam, so Mma Potokwane used fruit cake. Fruit cake, apples; it made no difference really. Oh foolish, weak men!

Mr J.L.B. Matekoni looked at his watch. It was nine o'clock in the morning, and he should have been at the garage by eight, at the latest. The apprentices had plenty to do—simple servicing tasks that morning—and he could probably leave them to get on with it, but he did not like to leave the business in their hands for too long. He looked out of the window. It was a comfortable sort of day, not too hot for the time of year, and it would be good to drive out into the lands somewhere and just walk along a path. But he could not do that, as he had his clients to think of. The best thing to do was to stop thinking about it, and to get on with the ordinary business of the day. There were exhaust pipes to be looked at, tyres to be changed, brake linings to be renewed; these were the things that really mattered, not some ridiculous parachute drop which Mma Potokwane had dreamed up and which he was not proposing to do anyway. That could be disposed of—with a little resolve. All he had to do was to lift up the telephone and say no to Mma Potokwane. He imagined the conversation.

"No, Mma. That's all: no."

"No what?"

"No. I'm not doing it."

"What do you mean no?"

"By no, I mean no. That's what I mean. No."

"No? Oh."

That, at least, was the theory. When it came actually to speaking, it might be considerably more difficult than that. But at least he had an idea of what he might say and the tone he would adopt.

MR J.L.B. MATEKONI, trying—and largely succeeding—not to think of parachutes or aeroplanes, or even the sky, started the short journey from his house to Tlokweng Road Speedy Motors. It was a journey that he had made so often that he knew every bump in the road, every gateway past which he drove, and, extraordinarily, the people whom he would often see standing at much the same place as they always stood. People like their places, Mr J.L.B. Matekoni reflected. There was that rather ragged man who used to walk about the end of Maratadiba Road, looking as if he had lost something. He was the father, he believed, of the maid who worked in one of the houses there and she had given him the spare room in her quarters. That was the right thing for a daughter to do, of course, but if Mr J.L.B. Matekoni were that man, or the daughter for that matter, he would think that the best place for a father who was slightly confused would be back in the village, or even out at the lands or at a cattle post. In the village he would be able to stand in one spot and watch everything happen without his moving about. He could watch cattle, which was very important for older people, and a good hobby for older men. There was a great deal to be learned just by watching cattle and noting their different colours. That would have kept that man busy.

And then, just round the corner, on Boteli Road, on Fridays and Saturdays one might see a very interesting car parked under the shade of a thorn tree. The car belonged to the brother of a man who lived in one of the houses on Boteli Road. He was a butcher from

Lobatse, who came up to Gaborone for the weekends, which started, for him, on Friday morning. Mr J.L.B. Matekoni had seen his butchery store down in Lobatse. It was large and modern, with a picture of a cow painted on the side. In addition, this man owned a plastering business, and so Mr J.L.B. Matekoni imagined that he was a fairly wealthy man, at least by the standards of Lobatse, if not the standards of Gaborone. But it was not his prosperity which singled him out in the eyes of Mr J.L.B. Matekoni; it was the fact that he had such a fine car and had clearly taken such good care of it.

This car was a Rover 90, made in 1955, and therefore very old. It was painted blue, and on the front there was a silver badge showing a boat with a high prow. The first time he had driven past it, Mr J.L.B. Matekoni had stopped to examine it and had noted the fine red leather seats and the gleaming silver of the gear lever. These external matters had not impressed him; it was the knowledge of what lay within: the knowledge of the 2.6-litre engine with its manual transmission **and its famous free wheel option**. That was something one would not see these days, and indeed Mr J.L.B. Matekoni had once brought his apprentices to look at the car, from the outside, so that they could get some sense of fine engineering. He knew of course that there was very little chance of that, but he tried anyway. The apprentices had whistled, and the older one, Charlie, had said, "That is a very fine car, Rra! Ow!" But no sooner had Mr J.L.B. Matekoni turned his back for a moment than that very same apprentice had leant forward to admire himself in the car's wing mirror.

Mr J.L.B. Matekoni had realised then that it was hopeless. Between these young men and himself there was a gulf that simply could not be crossed. The apprentice had recognised that it was a fine car, but had he really understood what it was that made it fine? He doubted that. They were impressed with the spoilers and flashy aluminium wheels that car manufacturers added these days; things which meant nothing, just nothing, to a real mechanic like Mr J.L.B. Matekoni. These were the externals, the outside trim designed, as often as not, to impress those who had no knowledge of cars. For the real mechanic, mechanical beauty lay in the accuracy and intricacy of the thousand moving pieces within the breast of the car: the rods, the cogs, the pistons. These were the things that mattered, not the inanimate parts that did nothing but reflect the sun.

Mr J.L.B. Matekoni slowed down and gazed at the fine car under the thorn tree. As he did so, he noticed, to his alarm, that there was something under the car—something that a casual observer might not notice but which he would never miss. Drawing up at the side of the road, he switched off the engine of his truck and got out of the cab. Then, walking over to the blue Rover, he went down on his hands and knees and peered at the dark underbelly of the car. Yes, it was as he thought; and now he went down on his stomach and crawled under the car to get a better view. It took him only a moment to realise what was wrong, of course, but the sight made him draw in his breath sharply. A pool of oil had leaked out onto the ground below the car and had stained the sand black.

"What are you doing, Rra?"

The sound surprised Mr J.L.B. Matekoni,

but he knew better than to lift his head up sharply; that was the sort of thing that the apprentices kept doing. They often bumped their heads on the bottom of cars when the telephone rang or when something else disturbed them. It was a normal human reaction to look up when disturbed, but a mechanic learned quickly to control it. Or a mechanic should learn that quickly; the apprentices had not done so, and he suspected that they never would. Mma Makutsi knew this, of course, and she had once rather mischievously called out Charlie's name when he was underneath a car. "Charlie," she had cried, and there had followed a dull thump as the unfortunate young man had sat up and hit his head on the sump of the car. Mr J.L.B. Matekoni had not really approved of this little joke, but he had found it difficult not to smile when he caught her eye. "I was just checking up that you were all right," shouted Mma Makutsi. "Be careful of your head down there. That brain needs to be looked after, you know."

Mr J.L.B. Matekoni wriggled his way out from under the car and stood up, dusting his trousers as he did so. As he had thought, it was the butcher himself, a corpulent man with a thick neck, like the neck of a bull. It was obvious to anyone, from the very first glance, that this was a wealthy man, even if they did not know about the butchery and the plastering business, nor indeed about this wonderful car with its silver badge.

"I was looking at your car, Rra," he said. "I was underneath it."

"So I see," said the butcher. "I saw your legs sticking out. When I saw that, I knew that there was somebody under my car."

Mr J.L.B. Matekoni smiled. "You must be wondering what I was doing, Rra."

The butcher nodded. "You are right. That is what I was wondering."

"You see, I am a mechanic," said Mr J.L.B. Matekoni. "I have always thought very highly of this car. It is a very good car."

The butcher seemed to relax. "Oh, I see, Rra. You are one who understands old cars like this. I am happy for you to go back under and look."

Mr J.L.B. Matekoni acknowledged the generosity of the offer. He would go back under the car, but it would be more than out of mere curiosity. If he went back, it would be on a mission of repair. He would have to tell the butcher of what he had seen.

"There is oil, Rra," he began. "Your car is leaking oil."

The butcher lifted up a hand in a gesture of tiredness. There was always oil. It was a risk with old cars. Oil; the smell of burning rubber; mysterious rattles: old cars were like the bush at night—there were always strange sounds and smells. He kept taking the car back to the garage and getting them to fix this problem and that problem, and yet these problems always recurred. And now here was another mechanic—one he did not even know—who was talking about oil leaks.

"I have had trouble with oil," he said. "There are always oil leaks and I always have to put more oil in the front. Every time I make the journey up from Lobatse, I have to put in more oil."

Mr J.L.B. Matekoni grimaced. "That is bad, Rra. But you should not have to do it. If the person who serviced this car made sure that the rubber seal on the rod that holds the oil cylinder was in its proper place, then this sort of thing would not happen." He paused. "I could fix this for you. I could do it in ten minutes."

The butcher looked at him. "I cannot bring the car in to your garage now," he said. "I have to talk to my brother about our sister's boy. He is a difficult boy, that one, and we have to work something out. And anyway, I cannot be paying all sorts of mechanics to look at this car. I have already paid a lot of money to the garage."

Mr J.L.B. Matekoni looked down at his shoes. "I would not have charged you, Rra. That is not why I offered."

For a few moments there was silence. The butcher looked at Mr J.L.B. Matekoni and knew, immediately, what sort of man he was dealing with. And he knew, too, that his assumption that Mr J.L.B. Matekoni would want payment was a gross misreading of the situation; for there were people in Botswana who still believed in the old Botswana ways and who were prepared to do things for others just to help them and not in prospect of some reward. This man, whom he had found lying underneath his car, was such a man. And yet he had paid such a great deal of money to those mechanics and they had assured him that all was in order. And the car, after all, worked reasonably well, even if there was a small problem with oil.

The butcher frowned, slipping a hand inside his collar and tugging at it, as if to loosen the material. "I do not think there can be anything wrong with my car," he said. "I think that you must be wrong, Rra."

Mr J.L.B. Matekoni shook his head. Without saying anything, he pointed to the edge of the dark oil stain, just discernible beneath the body of the car. The butcher's gaze followed his hand, and he shook his head vigorously. "It is impossible," he said. "I take this car to a good garage. I pay a great deal of money to have it looked after. They are always tinkering with the engine."

Mr J.L.B. Matekoni raised an eyebrow. "Always tinkering? Who are these people?" he asked.

The butcher gave the name of the garage, and Mr J.L.B. Matekoni knew immediately. He had spent years trying to improve the image of the motor trade, but whatever he, and others like him, did they would always be thwarted by the activities of people like the butcher's mechanics; if indeed they were mechanics at all—Mr J.L.B. Matekoni had strong doubts about the qualifications of some of them.

Mr J.L.B. Matekoni took his handkerchief out of his pocket and wiped his brow.

"If you would let me look at the engine, Rra," he said. "I could very quickly check your oil level. Then we would know whether it was safe for you to drive off to have more oil put in."

The butcher hesitated for a moment. There was something humiliating about being called to account in this way, and yet it would be churlish to reject an offer of help. This man was obviously sincere, and seemed to know what he was talking about; so he reached into his pocket for the car keys, opened the driver's door, and set about pulling the silver-topped lever that would release the catch on the engine cover.

Mr J.L.B. Matekoni stood back respectfully. The revealing of an engine of this nature— an engine which was older than the Republic of Botswana itself—was a special moment, and he did not want to show unseemly curiosity as the beautiful piece of engineering was exposed to view. So he stood where he was and only leaned forward slightly once he could see the engine; and quickly drew in his breath, and was silent—not in admiration, as he had expected, but in shock. For this was not the engine of a 1955 Rover 90, lovingly preserved; he saw, instead, an engine which had been cobbled together with all manner of parts. A flimsy carburettor, of recent vintage and crude construction; a modern oil filter, adapted and tacked onto the only original part that he could make out—the great, solid engine block that had been put into the car at its birth all those years ago. That at least was intact, but what mechanical company it had been obliged to keep!

The butcher looked at him expectantly. "Well, Rra?"

Mr J.L.B. Matekoni found it hard to reply. There were times when, as a mechanic, one had to give bad news. It was never easy, and one often wished that there were some way round the brute truth. But there were occasions when just nothing could be done, and he feared that this was one of them. "I'm sorry, Rra," he began. "This is very sad. A terrible thing has been done to this car. The engine parts . . ." He could not go on. What had been done was an act of such mechanical vandalism that Mr J.L.B. Matekoni could not find the words to express the feelings within him. So he turned away and shook his head, as might one who had seen some great work of art destroyed before his eyes, cast low by the basest Philistines.

CHAPTER SIX

MR MOPEDI BOBOLOGO

MMA HOLONGA sat back in her chair and closed her eyes. From the other side of the desk, Mma Ramotswe watched her client. She had observed that some people found it easier to tell a story if they shut their eyes, or if they looked down, or focused on something in the distance—something that was there but not there. It did not matter to her; the important thing was that clients should feel comfortable and that they should be able to talk without embarrassment. It might not be easy for Mma Holonga to talk about this, as these were intimate matters of the heart, and if closing her eyes would help, then Mma Ramotswe thought that a good idea. One of her clients, ashamed of what he had to say, had talked from behind cupped hands; that had been difficult, as what he had said had been far from clear. At least Mma Holonga, addressing her from her private darkness, could be understood perfectly well.

"I'll start with the man I like best," she said. "Or at least I think he is the one I like the best."

Then why not marry him? thought Mma Ramotswe. If you liked a man, then surely you could trust your judgment? But no, there were men who were likeable—charming in fact—but who were dangerous to women: Note Makoti, thought Mma Ramotswe. Her own first husband, Note Makoti, was immensely attractive to women, and only later would they discover what sort of man he really was. So Mma Holonga was right: the man you liked might not be the right man.

"Tell me about this man," said Mma Ramotswe. "What does he do?"

Mma Holonga smiled. "He is a teacher."

Mma Ramotswe noted this information on a piece of paper. **First man**, she wrote. **Teacher**. It was important information, because everybody in Botswana had their place, and one simple word could describe a world. Teachers were respected in Botswana, even if so many attitudes were changing. In the past, of course, it had been an even more important thing to be a schoolteacher, and the moral authority of the teacher was recognised by all. Today, more people had studied for diplomas and certificates and these people considered themselves to be every bit as good as teachers. But often they were not, because teachers had wisdom, while many of these people with paper qualifications had not. The wisest man Mma Ramotswe had ever known—her own father, Obed Ramotswe, had no Cambridge Certificate, not even his Standard Six, but that had made no difference. He had wisdom, and that counted for very much more.

She looked out of the window while Mma Holonga began to explain who the teacher was. She tried to concentrate, but the thought of her father had taken her back to Mochudi, and to the memories that the village had for her; of afternoons in the hot season when nothing happened but the heat and when it seemed that nothing could ever have happened; when there was time to sit in front of one's house in the evening and watch the birds flying back to the trees and the sky to the West fill with swathes of red as the sun went down over the Kalahari; when it seemed that you would be fifteen years old for ever and would always be here in Mochudi. And you were not to know then what the world would bring; that the life you imagined for yourself elsewhere might not be as good as the life you already had. Not that this was the case with Mma Ramotswe's life, which had on the whole been a happy one; but for many it was true—those quiet days in their village would prove to be the best time for them.

Mma Ramotswe's thoughts were interrupted by Mma Holonga. "A teacher, Mma," the other woman said. "I said that he was a teacher."

"I'm sorry," said Mma Ramotswe. "I was dreaming there for a moment. A teacher. Yes, Mma, that is a good job to have, in spite of the cheekiness of young people these days. It is still a good thing to be a teacher."

Mma Holonga nodded, acknowledging the truth of this observation. "His name is Bobologo," she went on. "Mopedi Bobologo. He is a teacher at the school over there near the University gate. You know that one."

"I have driven past it many times," said Mma Ramotswe. "And Mr J.L.B. Matekoni, who is the man who runs this garage behind us;

he has a house nearby and he says that he can hear the children singing sometimes if the wind is coming from that school."

Mma Holonga listened to this, but was not interested. She did not know Mr J.L.B. Matekoni, and could not picture him, as Mma Ramotswe now did, standing on his verandah, listening to the singing of the children.

"This man is called Mr Mopedi Bobologo, although he is not like the famous Bobologo. This one is tall and thin, because he comes from the North, and they are often tall up there. Like the trees. They are just like the trees up in the North.

"He is a very clever man, this Bobologo. He knows everything about everything. He has read many books, and can tell you what is in all of them. This books says that. This book says this. He knows the contents of many books."

"Oh," said Mma Ramotswe. "There are many, many books. And all the time, more books are coming. It is difficult to read them all."

"It is impossible to read them all," said Mma Holonga. "Even those very clever people at the University of Botswana—people like Professor Tlou—they have not read everything."

"It must be sad for them," observed Mma Ramotswe reflectively. "If it is your job to read books and you can never get to the end of them. You think that you have read all the books and suddenly you see that there are some new ones that have arrived. Then what do you do? You have to start over again."

Mma Holonga shrugged. "I don't know what you do. It is the same with every job, I suppose. Look at hairdressing. You braid one head of hair and then another head of un-braided hair comes along. And so it goes on. You cannot finish your work." She paused. "Even you, Mma. Look at you. You deal with one case and then somebody knocks at the door and there is another case. Your work is never finished."

They were both silent for a moment, think-ing of the endless nature of work. It was true, thought Mma Ramotswe, but it was not some-thing to worry too much about. If it were not true, one might have real cause to be con-cerned.

"Tell me more about this Mr Bobologo," said Mma Ramotswe. "Is he a kind man?"

Mma Holonga thought for a moment. "He

is kind, I think. I have seen him smiling at the schoolchildren and he has never spoken roughly to me. I think he is kind."

"Then why has he not been married?" asked Mma Ramotswe. "Or is his wife late?"

"There was a wife," said Mma Holonga. "But she died. He did not have time to get married again, as he was so busy reading. Now he thinks that it is time."

Mma Ramotswe looked out of the window. There was something wrong with this Mr Bobologo; she could sense it. So she wrote on her piece of paper: **No wife. Reads books. Tall and thin.** She looked up. It would not take long to deal with Mr Bobologo, she thought; then they could move on to the second, third, and fourth man. There would be something to worry about with each of them, she thought pessimistically, but then she corrected herself, reminding herself that it was no use giving up on a case before one even started. Clovis Andersen, author of **The Principles of Private Detection**, would never have countenanced that. **Be confident**, he wrote—and Mma Ramotswe remembered the very passage— **Everything can be found out in time. There are very few circumstances in which the true**

facts are waiting to be tripped over. And never, ever reach a decision before you start.

That was very wise advice, and Mma Ramotswe was determined to follow it. So while Mma Holonga continued to talk about Mr Bobologo, she deliberately thought of the positive aspects of this man who was being described to her. And there were many. He was very neat, she heard, and he did not drink too much. On one occasion, when they had a meal together, he had made sure that she had the bigger piece of meat and he had taken the smaller. That was a very good sign, was it not? A man who did that must have very fine qualities. And of course he was educated, which would mean that he could teach Mma Holonga things, and improve her outlook on life. All of this was positive, and yet there was still something wrong, and she could not drive the suspicion from her mind. Mr Bobologo would have an ulterior motive. Money? That was the obvious one, but was there something more to it than that?

MMA HOLONGA had just finished talking that morning when Mr J.L.B. Matekoni arrived at the garage. He was preoccupied with his encounter with the butcher and he was eager to tell Mma Ramotswe about it. He had heard a great deal about that other garage, and from time to time he had seen the results of their fumbling when one of their disgruntled clients had switched to Tlokweng Road Speedy Motors. But those cases were but as nothing compared with the deliberate fraud—and there really was no other word for it—which his glance at the engine of the Rover 90 had revealed. This was dishonesty of a calculated and prolonged variety, all perpetrated against a man who had trusted them, and, what was perhaps even more shocking, against an important car that had been placed in their hands. That was a particular and aggravated wrong: a mechanic had a duty towards machinery, and these ones had demonstrably failed to discharge that duty. If you were a conscientious mechanic you would never deliberately subject an engine to stress. Engines had their dignity—yes, that was the word—and Mr J.L.B. Matekoni, as one of Botswana's finest mechanics, was not ashamed to use such terms. It was a question of morality. That was what it was.

As he parked his truck in its accustomed

place—under the acacia tree at the side of the garage—Mr J.L.B. Matekoni reflected on the sheer effrontery of those people. He imagined the butcher going into the garage and describing some problem, and being reassured, when he collected the car, that it had been attended to. Perhaps they even lied about the difficulties of obtaining parts; he was sure that they would have charged him for the genuine spare parts, which they would have had to order from a special dealer in South Africa, or even England, all that way away. He thought of the factory in England where they made Rover cars; under a grey sky, with rain, which they had in such abundance and of which Botswana had so little; and he thought too of those Englishmen, his brother mechanics, standing over the metal lathes and drills that would produce those beautiful pieces of machinery. What would they have felt, he wondered, if they were to know that far away in Botswana there were unscrupulous mechanics prepared to put all sorts of unsuitable parts into the engine which they had so lovingly created? What would they think of Botswana if they knew that? It made him burn with indignation just to contemplate. And he was sure that Mma Ramotswe would share his outrage when he told her. He had noticed her reaction to wrongdoing when she heard about it. She would go quiet, and shake her head, and then she would utter some remark which always expressed exactly what he was feeling, but in a way which he could never achieve. He was a man of machinery, of nuts and bolts and engine blocks, not a man of words. But he appreciated the right words when he heard them, and particularly when they came from Mma Ramotswe, who, in his mind, spoke for Botswana.

Rather than enter the garage through the workshop, Mr J.L.B. Matekoni went round to the side, to the door of the No. 1 Ladies' Detective Agency. Normally this was kept open, which meant that chickens sometimes wandered in and annoyed Mma Makutsi by pecking at the floor around her toes, but today it was closed, which suggested that Mma Ramotswe and Mma Makutsi were out, or that there was a client inside. Mr J.L.B. Matekoni leaned forward to listen at the keyhole, to see if he could hear voices within, and at that moment, as he bent forward, the door was suddenly opened from inside.

Mma Holonga stared in astonishment at the

sight of Mr J.L.B. Matekoni, bent almost double. She half turned to Mma Ramotswe. "There is a man here," she said. "There is a man here listening."

Mma Ramotswe shot Mr J.L.B. Matekoni a warning glance. "He has hurt his back, I think, Mma. That is why he is standing like that. And anyway, it's only Mr J.L.B. Matekoni, who owns the garage. He is entitled to be standing there. He is quite harmless."

Mma Holonga looked again at Mr J.L.B. Matekoni, who, feeling that he had to authenticate Mma Ramotswe's explanation, put a hand to his back and tried to look uncomfortable.

"I thought that he was trying to listen to us," said Mma Holonga. "That's what I thought, Mma."

"No, he would not do that," said Mma Ramotswe. "Sometimes men just stand around. I think that is what he was doing."

"I see," said Mma Holonga, making her way past Mr J.L.B. Matekoni with a sideways glance. "I shall go now, Mma. But I shall wait to hear from you."

"Well, well!" said Mma Ramotswe as they watched Mma Holonga get into her car. "That was very awkward. What were you doing listening in at the keyhole?"

Mr J.L.B. Matekoni laughed. "I was not listening. Or I was not listening, but just trying to hear . . ." He trailed off. He was not explaining it well.

"You wanted to see if I was busy," prompted Mma Ramotswe. "Is that it?"

Mr J.L.B. Matekoni nodded. "That was all I was doing."

Mma Ramotswe smiled. "You could always knock and say Ko, Ko. That is how we normally do things, is it not?"

Mr J.L.B. Matekoni took the reproach in silence. He did not wish to argue with Mma Ramotswe over this; he was keen to tell her about the butcher's car and he looked eagerly at the tea-pot. They could sit over a cup of bush tea and he would tell her about the awful thing that he had discovered quite by chance and she would tell him what to do. So he made a remark about being thirsty, as it was such a hot day, and Mma Ramotswe immediately suggested a cup of tea. She could sense that there was something on his mind and it was surely the function of a wife to listen to her husband when there was something troubling him. Not that I'm actually a wife, she told herself; I'm only a fiancée. But even then, fiancées should listen too, and could give exactly the same sort of advice as wives gave. So she put on the kettle and they had bush tea together, sitting in the shade of the acacia tree, beside Mr J.L.B. Matekoni's parked truck. And in the tree above them, an African grey dove watched them from its branch, silently, before it flew off in search of the mate which it had lost.

MMA RAMOTSWE'S reaction to Mr J.L.B. Matekoni's story was exactly as he had thought it would be. She was angry; not angry in the loud way in which some people were angry, but quietly, with only pursed lips and a particular look in her eye to show what she was feeling. She had never been able to tolerate dishonesty, which she thought threatened the very heart of relationships between people. If you could not count on other people to mean what they said, or to do what they said they would do, then life could become utterly unpredictable. The fact that we could trust one another made it possible to undertake the simple tasks of life. Everything was based on trust, even day-to-day things like crossing the road—which required trust that the drivers of cars would be paying attention—to buying the food from a roadside vendor, whom you trusted not to poison you. It was a lesson that we learned as children, when our parents threw us up into the sky and thrilled us by letting us drop into their waiting arms. We trusted those arms to be there, and they were.

Mma Ramotswe was silent for a while after Mr J.L.B. Matekoni finished speaking. "I know that garage," she said. "A long time ago, when I first had my white van, I used to go there. That was before I started coming to Tlokweng Road Speedy Motors of course."

Mr J.L.B. Matekoni listened intently. This explained the state of the tiny white van when he had first seen it. He had assumed that the worn brake pads and the loose clutch were the results of neglect by Mma Ramotswe herself, rather than a consequence of the van having been looked after—if one could call it that—by First Class Motors, as it had the temerity to call itself. The thought made his heart skip a beat; it would have been so very easy for Mma Ramotswe to have had an accident as a result of her faulty brakes, and if that had happened he might never have met her and he would never have been what he was today—the fiancé of one of the finest women in Botswana. But he recognised that there was no point in entertaining such thoughts. History was littered with events that had changed everything and might easily not have done so. Imagine if the British had given in to South African pressure and had agreed to make what was then the Bechuanaland Protectorate into part of the Cape Province. They might easily have done that, and then there would be no Botswana today, and that would have been a loss for everybody. And his people would have suffered so much too if that had happened; all those years of suffering which others had borne but which they had been spared; and all that had stood between them and that was the decision of some politician somewhere who may never even have visited the Protectorate, or cared very much. And then, of course, there was Mr Churchill, whom Mr J.L.B. Matekoni admired greatly, although he had been no more than a small boy when Mr Churchill had died. Mr J.L.B. Matekoni had read in one of Mma Makutsi's magazines that Mr Churchill had almost been run over by a car when he was visiting America as a young man. If he had been standing six inches further into the road when the car hit him he would not have survived, and that would have made history very different, or so the article suggested. And then there was President Kennedy, who might have leaned forward just at the moment when that trigger was pulled, and might have lived to change history even more than he had already done. But Mr Churchill had survived, as had Mma Ramotswe, and that was the important thing. Now the tiny white van was scrupulously maintained, with its tight clutch and its responsive brakes. And Mr J.L.B. Matekoni had fitted a new, extra-large seat belt in the front, so that Mma Ramotswe could strap herself in without feeling uncomfortable. She was safe, which was what he wanted above all else; it would be unthinkable for anything to happen to Mma Ramotswe.

"You will have to do something about this," said Mma Ramotswe suddenly. "You cannot leave it be."

"Of course not," said Mr J.L.B. Matekoni. "I have told the butcher to bring the car round here next week, and I shall start to fix it for him. I shall have to order special parts, but I think I know where I can find them. There is a man in Mafikeng who knows all about these old cars and the parts they need. I shall ask him."

Mma Ramotswe nodded. "That will be a kind thing to do," she said. "But I was really thinking that you would have to do something about First Class Motors. They are the ones who have been cheating him. And they will be cheating others."

Mr J.L.B. Matekoni looked thoughtful. "But I don't know what I can do about them," he said. "You can't make good mechanics out of bad ones. You cannot teach a hyena to dance."

"Hyenas have nothing to do with it," said Mma Ramotswe firmly. "But jackals do. Those men in that garage are jackals. You will have to stop them."

Mr J.L.B. Matekoni felt alarmed. Mma Ramotswe was right about those mechanics, but he really did not see what he could do to stop them. There was no Chamber of Mechanics to which he could complain (Mr J.L.B. Matekoni had often thought that a Chamber of Mechanics would have been a good idea), and he had no proof that they had committed a crime. He would never be able to convince the police that fraud had been perpetrated because there would be no proof of what they had said to the butcher. They could argue that they had told him all along that they would have to put in substitute parts, and there would be many other mechanics who could go into court and testify that this was a reasonable thing for any mechanic to do in the circumstances. And if there were no help from the police, then Mr J.L.B. Matekoni would have to speak to the manager of First Class Motors, and he did not relish the prospect of that. This man had an unpleasant look on his face and was known to be something of a bully. He would not stand for allegations being made by somebody like Mr J.L.B. Matekoni, and the situation could rapidly turn threatening. It was all very well, then, for Mma Ramotswe to tell him to go and deal with the dishonest garage, but she did not understand that one could not police the motor trade single-handed.

Mr J.L.B. Matekoni said nothing. He felt that the whole day had taken an unsatisfactory turn—right from the beginning. He had encountered a shocking case of dishonesty, he had been suspected of listening in at doors (when all he had been doing was listening in), and now there was this uncomfortable expectation on the part of Mma Ramotswe that he would confront the unpleasant mechanics at First Class Motors. This was all very unsettling to a man who in general only wanted a quiet life; who liked nothing more than to be bent over the engine of a car, coaxing machinery back into working order. Everything, it seemed to him, was becoming more complicated than it need be, and—here he shuddered as the thought occurred to him—there was also hanging over him the awful threat of an involuntary parachute descent. This was far worse than anything else; a summons to a seat of judgment, an undischarged debt that sooner or later he would have to pay.

He turned to Mma Ramotswe. He should tell her now, as it would be so much easier if there was somebody to share his anxiety. She might accompany him to see Mma Potokwane to make it clear to her that there would be no parachute jump, at least not one made by him. She could handle Mma Potokwane, as women were always much better at dealing with other dominant women than were men. But when he opened his mouth to tell her, he found that the words were not there.

"Yes?" said Mma Ramotswe. "What is it, Mr J.L.B. Matekoni?"

He looked at her appealingly, willing her to help him in his torment, but Mma Ramotswe, seeing only a man staring at her with a vague longing, smiled at him and touched him gently on the cheek.

"You are a good man," she said. "And I am a very lucky woman to have such a fiancé."

Mr J.L.B. Matekoni sighed. There were cars to fix. This hill of problems could wait for its resolution until that evening when he went to Mma Ramotswe's house for dinner. That would be the time to talk, as they sat in quiet companionship on the verandah, listening to the sounds of the evening—the screeching of insects, the occasional snatch of music drifting across the waste ground behind her house, the barking of a dog somewhere in the darkness. That was when he would say, "Look, Mma Ramotswe, I am not very happy." And she would understand, because she always understood, and he had never once seen her make light of another's troubles.

But that evening, as they sat on the verandah, the children were with them, Motholeli and Puso, the two orphans whom Mr J.L.B.

Matekoni had so precipitately fostered, and the moment did not seem to right to discuss these matters. So nothing was said then, nor at the kitchen table, where, as they ate the meal which Mma Ramotswe had prepared for them, the talk was all about a new dress which Motholeli had been promised and about which it seemed there was great deal to say.

CHAPTER SEVEN

EARLY MORNING AT TLOKWENG ROAD SPEEDY MOTORS

Mma Makutsi woke early that day, in spite of having been to bed late and having slept very little. She had arisen at five, just before the first signs of dawn in the sky, and had gone outside to wash at the tap which she shared with two other houses. It was not ideal this sharing, and she looked forward to the day when she would have her own tap—and perhaps even a shower. This day was coming, which was one of the reasons why she had found it difficult to sleep. The previous afternoon she had found a couple of rooms to rent in another, rather better, part of town, which made up almost half—and the best half, too—of a low-cost house, and which had rudimentary plumbing all of their own. She had been told that it would not be expensive to install a simple shower, and was assured that this could be arranged within a week or two of her moving in. The information had prompted her into paying a deposit straightaway, which meant that she could make the move in little more than a week.

The rent of the new rooms was almost three times the rent which she was currently paying, but, rather to her surprise, she found that she could easily afford it. Her financial position had improved out of all recognition since she had started her part-time typing school, the Kalahari Typing School for Men. This school met several evenings a week in a church hall and offered supportive and discreet typing instruction for men. There had been many takers—she had been obliged to keep a waiting list—and the money which she had made had been carefully husbanded. Now there was enough for the deposit and more: if she chose to empty her account, she would be able to pay at least eight months' rent and still send a substantial sum back to her family in Bobonong. She had already doubled the amount that she sent to them, and had received an appreciative letter from an aunt. "We are eating well now," her aunt had written. "You are a kind girl, and we think of you every time we eat the good food which you make it possible for us to buy. Not all girls are like you. Many are interested only in themselves (and I have a long list of such girls), but you are interested in aunties and cousins. That is a very good sign."

Mma Makutsi had smiled as she had read this letter. This aunt was a favourite of hers and one day she would pay for her to come on a visit to Gaborone. The aunt had never been out of Bobonong and it would be a great treat for her to come all the way down to Gaborone. But would it be an altogether good idea, she wondered? If you had never been anywhere in your life it could be disturbing suddenly to discover a new place. The aunt was content in Bobonong, but if she were to see how much bigger and more exciting was Gaborone, then she might find it hard to return to Bobonong, to all those rocks, and baked land, and hot sun. So perhaps the aunt would stay where she was, but Mma Makutsi could perhaps send her a picture of Gaborone, so that she would have some idea of what it was like to be in a city.

Mma Makutsi made her way out of her room and walked towards the tap at the side of the neighbouring house. She and the other people who used this tap paid the neighbour twenty pula a month for the privilege, and even then they were discouraged from using too much water. If the tap was left running while one doused one's face under it, then the owner was apt to appear and make a comment about the shortage of water in Botswana.

"We are a dry country," she had once said while Mma Makutsi was trying to wash her hair in the running water.

"Yes," said Mma Makutsi from under the stream of deliciously cool water. "That is why we have taps."

The owner had stormed off. "It is people like you," she had remarked over her shoulder, "it is people like you who are causing droughts and making all the dams empty. You be careful or the whole country will dry up and we shall have to go somewhere else. You just be careful."

This had irritated Mma Makutsi, as she was a careful user of water. But one had to turn the tap on sometimes; there was no point just standing there and looking at it, even if that is what the tap's owner would really have wanted.

This morning there was no sign of the

owner, and Mma Makutsi got down on her hands and knees and allowed the water to run over her head and shoulders. After a while, she changed her position and put her feet under the water, in this way experiencing a satisfactory tingling sensation that went all the way up her calves to her knees. Then, washed and refreshed, she returned to her room. She would make breakfast now, and give her brother Richard a bowl of freshly boiled porridge . . . She stopped. For a few moments she had forgotten that Richard was no longer there, and that the corner of her room which she had curtained off for his sickbed was now empty.

Mma Makutsi stood in her doorway, looking down at the place where his bed had been. Only four months ago he had been there, struggling with the illness which was causing his life to ebb away. She had nursed him, doing her best to make him comfortable in the morning before she went off for work, and bringing him whatever small delicacies she could afford from her meagre salary. They had told her to make sure that he ate, even if his appetite was tiny. And she had done so, bringing him sticks of biltong, ruinously expensive though they were, and watermelons, which cooled his mouth and gave him the sugar that he needed.

But none of this—none of the special food, the nursing, or the love which she so generously provided—could alter the dreadful truth that the disease which was making his life so hard could never be beaten. It could be slowed down, or held in check, but it would always assert itself in the long run.

She had known, on that awful day, that he might not be there when she came back from work, because he had looked so tired, and his voice had been so reedy, like the voice of a thin bird. She had toyed with the idea of staying at home, but Mma Ramotswe was away from the office during the morning and there had to be somebody there. So she had said goodbye to him in a fairly matter-of-fact way, although she knew that this might be the last time she spoke to him, and indeed her intuition had been right. Shortly after lunchtime she had been summoned by a neighbour who looked in on him several times a morning, and she had been told to come home. Mma Ramotswe had offered to drive her back in the tiny white van, and she had accepted. As they made their way past the Botswana Technical College, she had suddenly felt that it was too late, and she had sat back in her seat, her head sunk in her hands, knowing what she would find when she arrived at her room.

Sister Banjule was there. She was the nurse from the Anglican Hospice and the neighbour had known to call her too. She was sitting by his bedside, and when Mma Makutsi came in she rose to her feet and put her arm around her, as did Mma Ramotswe.

"He said your name," she whispered to Mma Makutsi. "That is what he said before the Lord took him. I am telling you the truth. That is what he said."

They stood together for several minutes, the three women; Sister Banjule in the white uniform of her calling, Mma Ramotswe in her red dress, that she would now change for black, and Mma Makutsi in the new blue dress that she had treated herself to with some of the proceeds of the typing school classes. And then the neighbour, who had been standing near the door, led Mma Makutsi away so that Sister Banjule could ensure in private the last dignities for a man whose life had not amounted to much, but who now received, as of right, the unconditional love of one who knew how to give just that. **Receive the soul of our brother, Richard**, said Sister Banjule as she gently took from the body its stained and threadbare shirt and replaced it with a garment of white, that a poor man might leave this world in cleanliness and light.

SHE WISHED that he could have seen her new place, as he would have appreciated the space and the privacy. He would have loved the tap too, and she would have probably ended up being as bad as the woman who watched the water, telling him off for using too much. But that was not to be, and she accepted that, because she knew now that his suffering was at an end.

The new place, when she moved into it, would be much closer to work. It was not far from the African Mall, in an area which everybody called Extension Two. The streets there were nothing like Zebra Drive, which was leafy and quiet, but at least they were recognisably streets, with names of their own, rather than being the rutted tracks which dodged this way and that round Naledi. And the houses there were neatly set in the middle of small plots of land, with paw-paw trees or flowering bushes dotted about the yards. These houses, although small, were suitable for clerks, or the managers of small stores, or even teachers. It was not at all inappropriate that somebody of her status—a graduate of the Botswana Secretarial College and an assistant detective—should live in a place like that, and she felt proud when she thought of her impending move. There would be less smell, too, which would be good, as there were proper drains and not so much litter. Not that Botswana smelled; anything but, though there were small corners of it—one of these near Mma Makutsi's room—where one was reminded of humanity and heat.

The fact that Mma Makutsi had two rooms in a house of four rooms meant, in her mind, that she could say that she would now be living in a house. **My house**—she tried the words out, and at first they seemed strange, almost meretricious. But it was true; she would shortly be responsible for half a roof and half a yard, and that justified the expression **my house**. It was a comforting thought—anther milestone on the road that had led her from that constrained life in Bobonong, with its non-existent possibilities and its utter isolation, via the Botswana Secretarial College, with its crowning moment of the award of ninety-seven per cent in the final examinations, to the anticipated elevation to the status of householder, with a yard, and paw-paw trees of her own, and a place where the washing could be hung out to dry in the wind.

The furnishing and decoration of the new house was a matter of the utmost importance, and had been the subject of lengthy discussion with Mma Ramotswe. There were long hours at the office when nothing very much happened, and these might be spent in conversation, or crocheting perhaps, or in simply looking up at the ceiling, with its little fly tracks, like miniature paths through the bush. Mma Ramotswe had strong views on the subject of decoration, and had put these into effect in the house on Zebra Drive, where the living room was unquestionably the most comfortable room Mma Makutsi had ever seen. When she had first visited Mma Ramotswe at home, Mma Makutsi had stood for a moment in the living room doorway, marvelling at the matching suite of sofa and chairs, with their thick cushions, so inviting for a tired or discouraged person, and at the treasures on the shelves—the commemorative plate of Sir Seretse Khama and the Queen Elizabeth II tea cup, with the Queen smiling out in such a reassuring way; and the framed picture of Nelson Mandela with the late King Moshoeshoe II of Lesotho; and the illuminated motto which called for peace and understanding in the house. She had stood there and realised that there had been little beauty in her life; that she had never had a room which in any way expressed her striving for something better, but that perhaps one day she would. And now it was happening.

Mma Ramotswe had been generous. When she first heard of the move, she had taken Mma Makutsi to the house on Zebra Drive and she had gone through the whole place, room by room, identifying household effects which she could pass on to her assistant. There was a chair which nobody used any more, but which had a bright red seat. She could have that. And then there were the yellow curtains, which had been replaced by a new set; Mma Makutsi had scarcely dared to ask for those, but they had been offered, and she had accepted with alacrity.

Now, sitting at her desk in the morning, it seemed to her that her life could hardly get any better. There was her new home to look forward to, furnished in part with Mma Ramotswe's generous gifts; there was the prospect of having a little spare money in her pocket, rather than having to count every thebe; and there was the knowledge that she had a good job, with good people, and that her work made things better, at least for some. Since she had started at the No. 1 Ladies' Detective Agency, she had managed to help quite a number of clients. They had gone away feeling the better for what she had done for them, and that, more than any fee, made her work worthwhile. So those glamorous girls who had gone to work in those companies with new offices; those girls who had never achieved much more than fifty per cent in the examinations at the Botswana Secretarial College; those girls may have highly paid jobs, **but did they enjoy their work**? Mma Makutsi was sure that they did not. They sat at their desks, pretending to type, watching the hands of the clock approach five. And then, exactly on the hour, they disappeared, eager to get as far away as possible from their offices. Well, it was not like that for Mma Makutsi. Sometimes she would be there in the office well after six, or even seven. Occasionally she found that she was so absorbed in what she was doing that she would not even notice that it had become dark, and when she walked home it would be through the night, with all its sounds and the smells of wood-smoke from cooking fires, and with the sky up above like a great black blanket.

Mma Makutsi rose from her chair and went to look out of the window. Charlie, the older apprentice, was getting out of a minibus which had drawn off the main road. He waved to somebody who remained inside, and then began to walk towards the garage, his hands stuck in his pockets, his lips moving as he whistled one of those irritating tunes which he picked up. Just as he reached the garage, he began a few steps of a dance, and Mma Makutsi grimaced. He was thinking of girls, of course, as he always did. That explained the dance.

She drew back from the window, shaking her head. She knew that the apprentices were popular with girls, but she could not imagine what anybody saw in them. It was not that they had much to talk about—cars and girls seemed to be their only interest—and yet there were plenty of girls who were prepared to giggle and flirt with them. Perhaps those girls were in their own way as bad as the apprentices themselves, being interested only in boys and make-up. There were plenty of girls like that, Mma Makutsi thought, and maybe they would make very good wives for these apprentices when they were ready to marry.

The door, which was ajar, was now opened and the apprentice stuck his head round.

"Dumela, Mma," he said. "You have slept well?"

"Dumela, Rra," Mma Makutsi replied. "Yes, I have. Thank you. I was here very early and I have been thinking."

The apprentice smiled. "You must not think too much, Mma," he said. "It is not good for women to think too much."

Mma Makutsi decided to ignore this remark, but after a moment she had to reply. She could not let this sort of thing go unanswered; he would never have said something like that if

Mma Ramotswe had been present, and if he thought that he could get away with it then she would have to disabuse him of that idea.

"It is not good for men if women think too much," she retorted. "Oh yes, you are right there. If women start thinking about how useless some men are, then it is bad for men in general. Oh yes, that is true."

"That is not what I meant," said the apprentice.

"Hah!" said Mma Makutsi. "So now you are changing your mind. You did not know what you were saying because your tongue is out of control. It is always walking away on its own and leaving your head behind. Perhaps there is some medicine for that. Maybe there is an operation that can fix it for you!"

The apprentice looked cross. He knew that there was no point in trying to better Mma Makutsi in an argument, but anyway he had not come into the office to argue; he had come in to impart some very important news.

"I have read something in the paper," he said. "I have read something very interesting."

Mma Makutsi glanced at the paper which

he had extracted from his pocket. Already it had been smudged with greasy fingerprints, and she wrinkled her nose in distaste.

"There is something about Mr J.L.B. Matekoni in here," said the apprentice. "It is on the front page."

Mma Makutsi drew in her breath. Had something happened to Mr J.L.B. Matekoni? Newspapers were full of bad news about people, and she wondered whether something unpleasant had happened to Mr J.L.B. Matekoni. Or perhaps Mr J.L.B. Matekoni had been arrested for something or other; no, that was impossible. Nobody would ever arrest Mr J.L.B. Matekoni. He was the last person who would ever do anything that would send him to jail. They would have to arrest the whole population of Botswana before they got to Mr J.L.B. Matekoni.

The apprentice, relishing the interest which his comment had aroused, unfolded the newspaper and handed it to Mma Makutsi. "There," he said. "The Boss is going to do something really brave. Ow! I'm glad that it's him and not me!"

Mma Makutsi took the newspaper and

began to read. "Mr J.L.B. Matekoni, pro-prietor of Tlokweng Road Speedy Motors, and a well-known figure in the Gaborone motor trade," began the report, "has agreed to per-form a parachute jump to raise money for the Tlokweng orphan farm. Mma Silvia Potok-wane, the matron of the orphan farm, said that Mr J.L.B. Matekoni made the surprise offer only a few days ago. She expects him to be able to raise at least five thousand pula in spon-sorship. Sponsorship forms have already been distributed and many sponsors are coming for-ward."

She read the report aloud, the apprentice standing before her and smiling.

"You see," said the apprentice. "None of us would have imagined that the Boss would be so brave, and there he is planning to jump out of an aeroplane. And all to help the orphan farm! Isn't that good of him?"

"Yes," said Mma Makutsi. It was very kind, but she had immediately wondered what Mma Ramotswe would think of her fiancé making a parachute jump. If she had a fiancé herself, then she was not sure whether she would ap-prove of that; indeed the more she thought about it the more she realised that she would not approve. Parachute jumps went wrong; everybody knew that.

"They go wrong, these parachute jumps," said the apprentice, as if he had picked up the direction of her thoughts. "There was a man in the Botswana Defence Force whose parachute didn't open. That man is late now."

"That is very sad," said Mma Makutsi. "I am sorry for that man."

"The other men were watching from the ground," the apprentice continued. "They looked up and shouted to him to open his emergency parachute—they always carry two, you see—but he did not hear them."

Mma Makutsi looked at the apprentice. What did he mean: **he didn't hear them?** Of course he wouldn't hear them. This was typical of the curious, ill-informed way in which the apprentices, and so many young men like them, viewed the world. It was astonishing to think that they had been to school, and yet there they were, with a good Cambridge Certificate. As Mma Ramotswe pointed out, it must be very difficult being the Minister of Education and having to deal with raw material like this.

"But he would never be able to hear them,"

said Mma Makutsi. "They were wasting their breath."

"Yes," said the apprentice. "It is possible that he had fallen asleep."

Mma Makutsi sighed. "You would not fall asleep while you were jumping from an aeroplane. That doesn't happen."

"Oh yes?" challenged the apprentice. "And what about falling asleep at the wheel—while you're driving? I saw a car go off the Francistown Road once, just because of that. The driver had gone to sleep and the next thing he knew he had hit a tree and the car rolled over. You can go to sleep anywhere."

"Driving is different," said Mma Makutsi. "You do that for a long time. You become hot and drowsy. But when you jump out of an aeroplane, you are not likely to feel hot and drowsy. You will not go to sleep."

"How do you know?" said the apprentice. "Have you jumped out of an aeroplane, Mma? Hah! You would have to watch your skirt! All the boys would be standing down below and whistling because your skirt would be over your head. Hah!"

Mma Makutsi shook her head. "It is no good talking to somebody like you," she said.

"And anyway, here's Mr J.L.B. Matekoni's truck. We can ask him about this parachute business. We can find out if what the paper says is true."

Mr J.L.B. Matekoni parked his truck in the shade under the acacia tree beside the garage, making sure to leave enough room for Mma Ramotswe to park her tiny white van when she arrived. She would not arrive until nine o'clock, she had told him, because she was taking Motholeli to the doctor. Dr Moffat had telephoned to say that a specialist was visiting the hospital and that he had agreed to see Motholeli. "I do not think that he will be able to say much more than we have said," Dr Moffat had warned. "But there's no harm in his seeing her." And Dr Moffat had been right; nothing new could be said.

Mr J.L.B. Matekoni was pleased that he was getting to know the children better. He had always been slightly puzzled by children, and felt that he did not really understand them. There were children all round Botswana, of course, and nobody could be unaware of them, but he had been surprised at how these orphans thought about things. The boy, Puso, was a case in point. He was behaving very much better than he had in the past—and Mr J.L.B. Matekoni was thankful for that—but he was still inclined to be on the moody side. Sometimes, when he was driving with Mr J.L.B. Matekoni in his truck, he would sit there, staring out of the window, and saying nothing at all.

"What are you thinking of?" Mr J.L.B. Matekoni would ask, and Puso would shake his head and reply, "Nothing."

That could not be true. Nobody thought of nothing, but it was difficult to imagine what thoughts a boy of that age would have. What did boys do? Mr J.L.B. Matekoni tried to remember what he had done as a boy, but there was a curious gap, as if he had done nothing at all. This was strange, he thought. Mma Ramotswe remembered everything about her childhood and was always describing the details of events which had happened all those years ago. But when he tried to do that, Mr J.L.B. Matekoni could not even remember the names of the other boys in his class, apart from one or two very close friends with whom he had kept in touch. And it was the same with the initiation school, when all the boys were sent off to be inducted into the traditions of men. That was a great moment in your life, and you were meant to remember it, but he had only the vaguest memories.

Engines were different, of course. Although his memory for people's names and for people themselves was not terribly good, Mr J.L.B. Matekoni remembered virtually every engine that he had ever handled, from the large and loyal diesels which he had learned to deal with during his apprenticeship to the clinically efficient, and characterless, motors of modern cars. And not only did he remember the distinguished engines—such as that which powered the British High Commissioner's car—but he also remembered their more modest brothers, such as that which drove the only NSU Prinz which he had ever seen on the roads of Botswana; a humble car, indeed, which looked the same from the front or the back and which had an engine very like the motor on Mma Ramotswe's sewing machine. All of these engines were like old friends to Mr J.L.B. Matekoni—old friends with all the individual quirks which old friends inevitably had, but which were so comfortable and reassuring.

Mr J.L.B. Matekoni got out of his truck and stretched his limbs. He had a busy day ahead of him, with four cars booked in for a routine service, and another which would require the replacement of the servo system on its brakes. This was a tricky procedure, because it was difficult to get at in the first place, and then, when one got there, it was very easy to replace incorrectly. The problem, as Mr J.L.B. Matekoni had explained to the apprentices on numerous occasions, was that the ends of the brake pipes were flared and one had to put a small nut into these flared ends. This nut allowed you to connect the servo mechanism to the pipes, but, and this was the real danger, if you cross-threaded the nuts you would get a leak. And if you avoided this danger, but if you were too rough, then you could twist a brake pipe. That was a terrible thing to do, as it meant that you had to replace the entire brake pipe, and these pipes, as everybody knew, ran through the body of the car like arteries. The apprentices had caused both of these disasters in the past, and he had been obliged to spend almost a whole day sorting things out. Now he no longer trusted them to do it. They could

watch if they wished, but they would not be allowed to touch. This was the main problem
with the apprentices; they had the necessary
theoretical knowledge, or some of it, but so
often they were slipshod in the way they finished a job—as if they had become bored with
it—and Mr J.L.B. Matekoni knew that you
could never be slipshod when it came to brake
pipes.

He went into the garage and, hearing voices
from the detective agency, he knocked on the
door and looked in to see Mma Makutsi handing Charlie a folded-up newspaper. They
turned and stared at him.

"Here's the Boss," said the apprentice.
"Here's the brave man himself."

"The hero," echoed Mma Makutsi, smiling.

Mr J.L.B. Matekoni frowned. "What is
this?" he asked. "Why are you calling me a
brave man?"

"Not just us," said the apprentice, handing
him the newspaper. "The whole town will be
calling you brave now."

Mr J.L.B. Matekoni took the newspaper. It
can only be one thing, he thought, and as his
eye fell upon the article his fears were con-

firmed. He stood there, his hands shaking slightly as he held the offending newspaper, the dismay mounting within him. This was Mma Potokwane's doing. Nobody else could have told the newspaper about the parachute jump, as he had spoken to nobody about it. She had no right to do this, he thought. She had no right at all.

"Is it true?" asked Mma Makutsi. "Did you really say that you would jump out of an aeroplane?"

"Of course he did," exclaimed the apprentice. "The Boss is a brave man."

"Well," began Mr J.L.B. Matekoni, "Mma Potokwane said to me that I should and then . . ."

"Oh!" said Mma Makutsi, clapping her hands with delight. "So it is true then! This is very exciting. I will sponsor you, Rra. Yes, I will sponsor you up to thirty pula!"

"Why do you say 'up to'?" asked the apprentice.

"Because that's what these sponsorship forms normally say," said Mma Makutsi. "You put down a maximum amount."

"But that's only because when a person is

doing something like a sponsored walk they may not reach the end," said the apprentice. "In the case of a parachute jump, the person you have sponsored usually reaches the end—one way or the other." He laughed at his observation, but Mr J.L.B. Matekoni merely stared at him.

Mma Makutsi was annoyed with the apprentice. It was not right to make remarks like that in the presence of one who would be taking such a great personal risk for a good cause. "You must not talk like that," she said severely. "This is not a joke for you to laugh at. This is a brave thing that Mr J.L.B. Matekoni is doing."

"Oh it's brave all right," said the apprentice. "It is surely a brave thing, Mma. Look what happened to that poor Botswana Defence Force man . . ."

"What happened to him?" asked Mr J.L.B. Matekoni.

Mma Makutsi glowered at the apprentice. "Oh that has nothing to do with you, Mr J.L.B. Matekoni," she said quickly. "That is another thing. We do not need to talk about that thing."

Mr J.L.B. Matekoni looked doubtful. "But

he said that something happened to a Botswana Defence Force man. What is that thing?"

"It is not an important thing," said Mma Makutsi. "Sometimes the Botswana Defence Force makes silly mistakes. It is only human after all."

"How do you know it was the Defence Force's mistake?" interjected the apprentice. "How do you know that it wasn't that man's fault?"

"What man?" asked Mr. J.L.B. Matekoni.

"I do not know his name," said Mma Makutsi. "And anyway, I am tired of talking about these things. I want to get some work done before Mma Ramotswe comes in. There is a letter here which we shall have to reply to. There is a lot to do."

The apprentice smiled. "All right," he said. "I am also busy, Mma. You are not the only one." He gave a small jump, which could have been the beginnings of one of his dances, but which also could have been just a small jump. Then he left the office.

Mma Makutsi returned to her desk in a businesslike fashion. "I have drawn up the accounts for last month," she said. "It was a much better month."

"Good," said Mr J.L.B. Matekoni. "Now about this Defence Force man . . ."

He did not finish, as Mma Makutsi interrupted him with a screech. "Oh," she cried, "I have forgotten something. Oh, I am very stupid. Sorry, Mr J.L.B. Matekoni, I have forgotten to enter those receipts over there. I am going to have to check everything."

Mr J.L.B. Matekoni shrugged. There was something which she did not want him to be told, but he thought that he knew exactly what it was. It was about a parachute that had not opened.

CHAPTER EIGHT

TEA IS ALWAYS THE SOLUTION

Mma Ramotswe swept up to the premises of Tlokweng Road Speedy Motors, bringing her tiny white van to a halt under the acacia tree. She had been thinking as she drove in, not of work, but of the children, who were proving such surprising people to live with. Children were never simple—she knew that—but she had always assumed that brothers and sisters had at least something in common in their tastes and behaviour. Yet here were these two orphans, who were children of the same mother and same father (or so Mma Potokwane had told her) and yet who were so thoroughly different. Motholeli was interested in cars and trucks, and liked nothing better than to watch Mr J.L.B. Matekoni with his spanners and wrenches and all the other mysterious tools of his calling. She was adamant that she would be a mechanic, in spite of her wheelchair and in spite of the fact that her arms were not as strong as the arms of other girls of her age. The illness which had deprived her of the use of her legs had touched at other parts of her body too, weakening the muscles and sometimes constricting her chest and lungs. She never complained, of course, as it was not in her nature to do so, but Mma Ramotswe could tell when a momentary shadow of discomfort passed over her face, and her heart went out to the brave, uncomplaining girl whom Mr J.L.B. Matekoni, almost by accident, had brought into her life. Puso, the boy, whom Motholeli had rescued from burial with their mother, scraping the hot sand from his face and breathing air into his struggling lungs, shared none of his sister's interest in machinery. He was indifferent to cars, except as a means of getting around, and he was happiest in his own company, playing in the patch of scrub bush behind Mma Ramotswe's house in Zebra Drive, throwing stones at lizards or tricking those minute creatures known as ant lions into showing themselves. These insects, small as ticks but quicker and more energetic, created little conical wells in the sand, snares for any ants that might wander that way. Once on the edge of the trap, the ant would inevitably trigger a miniature landslide, tumbling down the sides of it. The ant lion, hidden under grains of sand at the bottom, would burrow out and seize its prey, dragging it back underground to provide a tasty meal. If you were a boy, and so minded, you could tickle the edge of the trap with a blade of grass and create a false alarm to bring the ant lion out of its lair. Then you could flip it out with a twig and witness its confusion. That was an entertaining pastime for a boy, and Puso liked to do this for hours on end.

Mma Ramotswe had imagined that he would play with other boys, but he seemed to be quite happy on his own. She had invited a friend to send her sons over, and these boys had arrived, but Puso had simply stared at them and said nothing.

"You should talk to these boys," Mma Ramotswe admonished him. "They are your guests, and you should talk to them."

He had mumbled something, and they had gone off into the garden together, but when she had looked out of the window a few minutes later, Mma Ramotswe had seen the two visiting boys entertaining themselves by climbing a tree while Puso busied himself with a nest of white ants which he had found underneath a mopipi tree.

"Leave him to do what he wants to do," Mr J.L.B. Matekoni had advised her. "Remember where he comes from. Remember his people."

Mma Ramotswe knew exactly what he meant. These children, although not pure-bred Masarwa, had at least some of that blood in their veins. It was easy to forget that, because they did not look like bushmen, and yet here was the boy taking this strange, almost brooding interest in the bush and in creatures that most other people would not ever notice. That, she imagined, was because he had been given the eyes to see these things; as we are given the eyes of those who have gone before us, and can see the world in the way in which they saw it. In her case, she knew that she had her father's eye for cattle, and could tell their quality in an instant, at first glance. That was something she just knew—she just knew it. Perhaps Mr J.L.B. Matekoni could do the same with cars; one glance, and he would know.

She got out of the tiny white van and walked

round the side of the building to the door that led directly into the No. 1 Ladies' Detective Agency. She could tell that they were busy in the garage, and she did not want to disturb them. In an hour or so it would be time for tea-break, and she could chat to Mr J.L.B. Matekoni then. In the meantime there was a letter to sign—Mma Makutsi had started to type it yesterday—and there might be new mail to go through. And sooner or later she would have to begin the investigation of Mma Holonga's list of suitors. She had no idea how she was going to tackle that, but Mma Makutsi might be able to come up with a suggestion. Mma Makutsi had a good mind—as her ninety-seven per cent at the Botswana Secretarial College had demonstrated to the world— but she was inclined to unrealistic schemes. Sometimes these worked, but on other occasions Mma Ramotswe had been obliged to pour cold water on over-ambitious ideas.

She entered the office to find Mma Makutsi polishing her large spectacles, staring up at the ceiling as she did so. This was always a sign that she was thinking, and Mma Ramotswe wondered what she was thinking about. Perhaps the morning post, which Mma Makutsi now picked up from the post office on her way into work, had contained an interesting letter, possibly from a new client. Or perhaps it had brought one of those anonymous letters which people inexplicably sent them; letters of denunciation which the senders thought that they would be interested to receive, but which were no business of theirs. Such letters were usually mundane, revealing nothing but human pettiness and jealousy. But sometimes they contained a snippet of information which was genuinely interesting, or gave an insight into the strange corners of people's lives. Mma Makutsi could be thinking about one of these, thought Mma Ramotswe, or she could just be staring at the ceiling because there was nothing else to do. Sometimes, when people stared, there was nothing else in their minds, and all they were doing was thinking of the ceiling, or of the trees, or of the sky, or of any of the things that it was so satisfying just to stare at.

"You're thinking of something, Mma," said Mma Ramotswe. "Whenever I see you polishing your glasses like that, I know that you are thinking of something."

Mma Makutsi looked round sharply, disturbed by the sudden sound of her employer's voice. "You surprised me, Mma," she said. "I was sitting here and I suddenly heard your voice. It made me jump."

Mma Ramotswe smiled. "Mr J.L.B. Matekoni says that I creep up on him too. But I do not mean to do that." She paused. "So what were you thinking about, Mma?"

Mma Makutsi replaced her glasses and adjusted their position on the bridge of her nose. She had been thinking about Mr J.L.B. Matekoni and his parachute drop and about how Mma Ramotswe would react to the news, that is assuming that she had not heard it already.

"Have you seen the paper today?" she asked.

Mma Ramotswe shook her head as she walked over to her desk. "I have not seen it," she said. "I have been busy taking the children here and there. I have had no time to sit down." She threw Mma Makutsi a quizzical glance. "Is there something special in it?"

So she does not know, thought Mma Makutsi. Well, she would have to tell her, and it would probably be a shock for her.

"Mr J.L.B. Matekoni is going to jump," she said. "It is in the paper this morning."

Mma Ramotswe stared at Mma Makutsi. What was she talking about? What was this nonsense about Mr J.L.B. Matekoni jumping?

"Out of a plane," went on Mma Makutsi quickly. "Mr J.L.B. Matekoni is going to do a parachute jump."

Mma Ramotswe laughed. "What nonsense!" she said. "Mr J.L.B. Matekoni would never do something like that. Who has put such nonsense in the newspapers?"

"It's true," said Mma Makutsi. "It's one of these charity jumps. Mma Potokwane . . ."

She had to say no more. At the mention of Mma Potokwane's name, Mma Ramotswe's expression changed. "Mma Potokwane?" she said sharply. "She has been forcing Mr J.L.B. Matekoni to do things again? A parachute jump?"

Mma Makutsi nodded. "It is in the paper," she said. "And I have spoken to Mr J.L.B. Matekoni myself. He has confirmed that it is true."

Mma Ramotswe sat quite still. For a moment she said nothing, as the implications of Mma Makutsi's revelations sank in. Then she thought, I shall be a widow. I shall be a widow before I am even married.

Mma Makutsi could see the effect the news was having on Mma Ramotswe and she searched for words that might help.

"I don't think he wants to do it," she said quietly. "But now he is trapped. Mma Potokwane has told the newspapers."

Mma Ramotswe said nothing, while Mma Makutsi continued. "You must go into the garage right now," she said. "You must put a stop to it. You must forbid him. It is too dangerous."

Mma Ramotswe nodded. "I do not think that it is a good idea. But I'm not sure that I can forbid him. He is not a child."

"But you are his wife," said Mma Makutsi. "Or you are almost his wife. You have the right to stop him doing something dangerous."

Mma Ramotswe frowned. "No, I do not have that right. I can talk to him about it, but if you try to stop people from doing things they can resent it. I do not want Mr J.L.B. Matekoni to think that I am telling him what to do all the time. That is not a good start for a marriage."

"But it hasn't started yet," protested Mma Makutsi. "You are just an engaged lady. And you've been an engaged lady for a long time now. There is no sign of a wedding." She stopped, realising that perhaps she had gone too far. What she said was quite true, but it did not help to draw attention to their long engagement and to the conspicuous absence of any wedding plans.

Mma Ramotswe was not offended. "You are right," she said. "I am a very engaged lady. I have been waiting for a long time. But you cannot push men around. They do not like it. They like to feel that they are making their own decisions."

"Even when they are not?" interjected Mma Makutsi.

"Yes," said Mma Ramotswe. "We all know that it is women who take the decisions, but we have to let men think that the decisions are theirs. It is an act of kindness on the part of women."

Mma Makutsi took off her glasses and polished them on her lace handkerchief, now threadbare but so loved. This was the handkerchief that she had bought when she was at the Botswana Secretarial College, at a time when she had virtually nothing else, and it meant a great deal to her.

"So we should say nothing at the moment?" she said. "And then . . ."

"And then we find a chance to say something very small," said Mma Ramotswe. "We shall find some way to get Mr J.L.B. Matekoni out of this. But it will be done carefully, and he will think that he has changed his mind."

Mma Makutsi smiled. "You are very clever with men, Mma. You know how their minds work."

Mma Ramotswe shrugged. "When I was a girl I used to watch little boys playing and I saw what they did. Now that I am a lady, I know that there is not much difference. Boys and men are the same people, in different clothes. Boys wear short trousers and men wear long trousers. But they are just the same if you take their trousers off."

Mma Makutsi stared at Mma Ramotswe, who, suddenly flustered, added quickly, "That is not what I meant to say. What I meant to say is that trousers mean nothing. Men think like boys, and if you understand boys, then you understand men. That is what I meant to say."

"I thought so," said Mma Makutsi. "I did not think that you meant anything else."

"Good," said Mma Ramotswe briskly. "Then let us have a cup of tea and think about how we are going to deal with this problem which Mma Holonga brought us the other day. We cannot sit here all day talking about men. We must get down to work. There is much to do."

Mma Makutsi made the bush tea and they sipped on the dark red liquid as they discussed the best approach to the issue of Mma Holonga's suitors. Tea, of course, made the problem seem smaller, as it always does, and by the time they reached the bottom of their cups, and Mma Makutsi had reached for the slightly chipped tea-pot to pour a refill, it had become clear what they would have to do.

CHAPTER NINE

HOW TO HANDLE YOUNG MEN THROUGH THE APPLICATION OF PSYCHOLOGY

A<small>T THE</small> end of that day's work Mma Ramotswe so engineered matters that she was standing at the door of her tiny white van at precisely the time—one minute to five—that the two apprentices came out of the garage entrance, wiping their greasy hands on a handful of the loose white lint provided by Mr J.L.B. Matekoni. Mr J.L.B. Matekoni knew all about oil-dermatitis, the condition which stalked mechanics and which had struck several of his brother mechanics over the years, and he made every effort to drum the lesson into the heads of his apprentices. Not that this worked, of course; they were still inclined to limit themselves to a quick plunge of the hands into a bucket of luke-warm water, but at least on occasion they resorted to lint and made some effort to do it properly. There was an old barrel for the used lint, and for other detritus of their calling, but they tended to ignore this and now Mma Ramotswe saw the lint tossed casually to the ground. As they did so, the older apprentice looked up and saw her watching them. He muttered something to his friend, and they dutifully picked up the lint and walked off to deposit it in the barrel.

"You are very tidy," called out Mma Ramotswe when they re-emerged. "Mr J.L.B. Matekoni will be pleased."

"We were going to put it there anyway," said the younger apprentice reproachfully. "You don't have to tell us to do it, Mma."

"Yes," said Mma Ramotswe. "I knew that. I thought perhaps you had just dropped it by mistake. That sometimes happens, doesn't it? I have often seen you drop things by mistake. Sweet papers. Chip bags. Newspapers."

The apprentices, who had now drawn level with the tiny white van, looked at their shoes sheepishly. They were no match for Mma Ramotswe, and they knew it.

"But I don't want to talk about litter," said Mma Ramotswe kindly. "I can see that you have been working very hard today, and I thought I would drive you both home. It will save you waiting for a minibus."

"You are very kind, Mma," said the older apprentice.

Mma Ramotswe gestured to the passenger seat. "You sit in there, Charlie. You are the older one. And you," she looked at the younger apprentice and pointed to the back of the van, "you can go there. Next time you can ride in front."

She had a rough idea where the two young men lived. The younger one stayed with his uncle in a house beyond the Francistown Road brewery and the older one lodged with an aunt and uncle near the orphan farm at Tlokweng. It would take over half an hour to deliver them both, and the children would be waiting for her at home, but this was important and she would do it cheerfully.

She would deliver the younger one first, skirting the edge of the town, driving past the university and the Sun Hotel and the road to Maru-a-Pula. Then Nyerere Drive bore left, past the end of Elephant Road, and ran down to Nelson Mandela Drive, which she still thought of as the old Francistown Road. They crossed the dry course of the Segoditshane River and then the older apprentice directed her to a side road lined by a row of small, well-kept houses.

"That is his uncle's place over there," he said, pointing to one of the houses. "He lives in that shack on the side. That is where he sleeps, but he eats inside with the family."

They stopped outside the gate and the younger apprentice jumped out of the van and clapped his hands in gratitude. Mma Ramotswe smiled and said through the open window, "I am glad that I saved you a walk." Then she waved and they drove off.

"He is a good boy," said Mma Ramotswe. "He will make a good husband for some girl one day."

"Hah!" said the older apprentice. "That girl will have to catch him first. He is a quick runner, that boy. It will not be easy for the girls!"

Mma Ramotswe pretended to look interested. "But what if a very beautiful girl with lots of money saw him? What then? Surely he would like to marry a girl like that and have a large car? Perhaps even one of those German cars that you think are so smart. What then?"

The apprentice laughed. "Oh, I would

marry a girl like that double-quick. But girls like that won't look at boys like us. We are just apprentice mechanics. Girls like that want boys from rich families or with very good jobs. Accountants. People like that. We just get ordinary girls."

Mma Ramotswe clucked her tongue. "Oh! That is very sad. It is a pity that you don't know how to attract more glamorous girls. It is a great pity." She paused before saying, almost as an aside, "I could tell you, of course."

The apprentice looked at her incredulously. "You, Mma? You could tell me how to attract that sort of girl?"

"Of course I could," said Mma Ramotswe. "I am a woman, remember? I used to be a girl. I know how girls think. Just because I am a bit older now and I do not run round looking at boys doesn't mean that I have forgotten how girls think."

The apprentice raised an eyebrow. "You tell me then," he said. "You tell me this secret."

Mma Ramotswe was silent. This, she thought, was the difficult part. She had to make sure that the apprentice would take what she had to say seriously, and that meant that she should not be too quick to impart the information.

"I don't know whether I should tell you," she said. "I cannot just tell anybody. I would only want to tell a man who would be kind to these glamorous girls. Just because they are glamorous doesn't mean that they do not have their feelings. Maybe I should wait a few years before I tell you."

The apprentice, who had been smiling, now frowned. "I would treat such a girl very well, Mma. You can count on me."

Mma Ramotswe concentrated on her driving. There was an elderly man on a bicycle ahead of them, a battered hat perched on his head, and a red hen tied to the carrier on the back of his cycle. She slowed down, giving him a wide berth.

"That hen is making its last journey," she said. "He will be taking it to somebody who will eat it."

The apprentice glanced behind him. "That is what happens to all hens. That is what they are for."

"They may not think that," said Mma Ramotswe.

The apprentice laughed. "They cannot think. They have very small heads. There are no brains in a chicken."

"What is in their heads, then?" asked Mma Ramotswe.

"There is just blood and some bits of meat," said the apprentice. "I have seen it. There is no brain."

Mma Ramotswe nodded. "Oh," she said. There was no point in arguing with these boys about matters of this sort; they were usually quite adamant that they were right, even if there was no basis for what they said.

"But what is this thing about girls?" the apprentice persisted. "You can tell me, Mma. I may talk about girls a lot, but I am very kind to them. You ask Mr J.L.B. Matekoni. He has seen how well I treat girls."

They were now nearing the Tlokweng Road, and Mma Ramotswe thought that the time was ripe. She had aroused the apprentice's attention and now he was listening to her.

"Well then," she began, "I will tell you a very certain way to attract the attention of one of these glamorous girls. You must become well-known. If you are well-known—if your name is in the papers—then these girls cannot resist you. You look about you and see what sort of man has that sort of lady. It is always the ones who are in the papers. They get those girls every time."

The apprentice looked immediately defeated. "That is not good news for me," he said. "I shall never be well-known. I shall never get into the papers."

"Why not?" asked Mma Ramotswe. "Why give up before you have started?"

"Because nobody is ever going to write about me," said the apprentice. "I am just an unknown person. I am not going to be famous."

"But look at Mr J.L.B. Matekoni," said Mma Ramotswe. "Look at him. He was in the papers today. Now he is well-known."

"That is different," the apprentice retorted. "He is in the papers because he is going to do a parachute jump."

"But you could do that," said Mma Ramotswe, as if the idea had just occurred. "If you were to jump out of an aeroplane you would be all over the papers and the glamorous girls would notice all right. They would be all over you. I know how these girls think."

"But . . ." began the apprentice.

He did not finish. "Oh yes they would," Mma Ramotswe went on. "There is nothing— nothing—that they like more than bravery. If you jumped out of the plane—maybe instead of Mr J.L.B. Matekoni, who is possibly too old to do that these days—then you would be the one who would get all the attention. I guarantee it. Those girls would be waiting for you. You could take your pick. You could choose the one with the biggest car."

"If she had the biggest car then she would also have the biggest bottom," said the apprentice, smiling. "She would need a big car to fit her bottom in. Such a girl would be very nice."

Mma Ramotswe would normally not have let such a remark pass without a sharp retort, but this was not the occasion, and she simply smiled. "It seems simple to me," she said. "You do the jump. You get the girl. It's perfectly safe."

The apprentice thought for a moment. "But what about that Botswana Defence Force man? The one whose parachute didn't open. What about him?"

Mma Ramotswe shook her head. "You are wrong there, Charlie. His parachute would have opened **if he had pulled the cord**. You yourself said to Mma Makutsi that that man had probably gone to sleep. There was nothing wrong with his parachute, you see. You are much cleverer than that man. You will not forget to pull the cord."

The apprentice thought for a moment. "And you think that the papers will write about me?"

"Of course they will," said Mma Ramotswe. "I shall get Mma Potokwane to talk to them again. She is always giving them stories about the orphan farm. She will tell them to put a big photograph of you on the front page. That will certainly be read by the sort of girl we are talking about."

Mma Ramotswe slowed down. A small herd of donkeys had wandered onto the road ahead of them and had stopped in the middle, looking at the tiny white van as if they had never before encountered a vehicle. She brought the van to a halt, glancing quickly at the apprentice as she did so. Psychology, she thought; that is what they called it these days, but in her view it was something much older than that. It was woman's knowledge, that was what it was; knowledge of how men behaved and how they could be persuaded to do something if one approached the matter in the right way. She had told the apprentice no lies; there were girls who would be impressed by a young man who did a parachute jump and who had his photograph in the papers. If men were prepared to use psychology, which they usually were not, then they too could get women to do what they wanted them to do. Perhaps it was fortunate, then, that men were so bad at psychology. Men got women to do what they wanted through making them feel sorry for them, or making them feel guilty. Men did not do this deliberately, of course, but that was the effect.

The apprentice leaned out of his window and shouted at the donkeys, who looked at him balefully before they began to move slowly out of the way. Then, sitting back in his seat, he turned to Mma Ramotswe. "I think I will do it, Mma. I think that maybe it is a good idea to help the orphan farm. We should all do that we can."

WHEN MMA RAMOTSWE returned to Zebra Drive it was already beginning to get dark. Mr J.L.B. Matekoni's truck was parked at the side of the house, in the special spot that she had set aside for him, and she tucked the tiny white van into its own place near the kitchen door. Lights were on in the house, and she heard the sound of voices. They would be wondering, she thought, where she was, and they would be hungry.

She went into the kitchen, kicking off her shoes as she entered. Motholeli was in her wheelchair, behind the kitchen table, chopping carrots, and Puso was stirring something on the stove. Mr J.L.B. Matekoni, standing just behind the boy, was dropping a pinch of salt into the mixture in the pot.

"We are cooking your dinner tonight," said Mr J.L.B. Matekoni. "You can go and sit down, with your feet on a stool. We will call you when everything is ready."

Mma Ramotswe gave a cry of delight. "That is a very big treat for me," she said. "I am very tired for some reason."

She went through to the sitting room and dropped into her favourite chair. Although the children helped in the kitchen, it was unusual for them to cook a full meal. It must have been Mr J.L.B. Matekoni's idea, she reflected, and the thought filled her with gratitude that she had such a man who would think to cook a meal. Most husbands would never do that—

would regard it as beneath their dignity to work in the house—but Mr J.L.B. Matekoni was different. It was as if he knew what it was like to be a woman, to have all that cooking to do, for the rest of one's life, a whole procession of pots and pans stretching out into the distance, seemingly endless. Women knew all about that, and dreamed about cooking and pots and the like, but here was a man who seemed to understand.

When they sat down to table half an hour later, Mma Ramotswe watched proudly as Mr J.L.B. Matekoni and Puso brought in the plates of good rich food and set them at each place. Then she said grace, as she always did, her eyes lowered to the tablecloth, as was proper.

"May the Lord look down kindly on Botswana," said Mma Ramotswe. "And now we thank Him for the food on our plates which has been cooked so well." She paused. There was more to be said about that, but for the time being she felt that what she had said was enough and since everybody was very hungry they should all begin.

"This is very good," she said after the first mouthful. "I am very happy that I have such good cooks right here in my own house."

"It was Mr J.L.B. Matekoni's idea," said Motholeli. "Maybe he could start a Tlokweng Road Speedy Restaurant."

Mr J.L.B. Matekoni laughed. "I could not do that. I am only good at fixing cars. That is all I can do."

"But you can jump by parachute," said Motholeli. "You can do that too. They were talking about it at school."

There was a sudden silence, and it seemed as if a cloud had passed over the gathering. Mr J.L.B. Matekoni's fork paused where it was, half way to his mouth, and Mma Ramotswe's knife stopped cutting into a large piece of pumpkin. She looked up at Mr J.L.B. Matekoni, who held her glance only for a moment before he looked away.

"Oh that," said Mma Ramotswe. "That is all a mistake. Mr J.L.B. Matekoni was going to do a parachute jump, but now Charlie, the apprentice at the garage, has offered to do it instead. I have already spoken to Mma Poto-kwane about it and she is very pleased with the new arrangements. She said that she was sure that Mr J.L.B. Matekoni would want to give that young man a chance, and I said I would ask him what he thought."

They all looked at Mr J.L.B. Matekoni, whose eyes had opened wide as Mma Ramotswe spoke.

"Well?" said Mma Ramotswe, returning to her task of cutting the pumpkin. "What would you like to do, Mr J.L.B. Matekoni? Would you like to give that boy a chance?"

Mr J.L.B. Matekoni looked up at the ceiling. "I could do, I suppose," he said.

"Good," said Mma Ramotswe. "You are a very generous man. Charlie will be very pleased."

Mr J.L.B. Matekoni smiled. "It is nothing," he said. "Nothing."

They continued with the meal. Mma Ramotswe noticed that Mr J.L.B. Matekoni appeared to be in a very good mood and made several amusing remarks about the day's events, including a joke about a gearbox, which they all laughed at but which none of them understood. Then, when the plates were cleared away and the children were out of the room, Mr J.L.B. Matekoni left his chair and, standing over Mma Ramotswe's chair, he took her hand and said, "You are a kind woman, Mma Ramotswe, and I am very lucky to have found a lady like you. My life is a very happy one now."

"And I am happy too," said Mma Ramotswe. She was not going to be a widow after all, and she had managed to make it seem as if it had been his decision. That was what men liked—she was sure of it—and why should men not be allowed to think that they were getting what they liked, occasionally at least? She saw no reason why not.

CHAPTER TEN

MR J.L.B. MATEKONI'S DREAM

Mr J.L.B. Matekoni was, of course, immensely relieved that Mma Ramotswe had presented him with the opportunity to withdraw from the parachute jump. She had done it so graciously, and so cleverly, that he had been saved all embarrassment. Throughout that day he had been plagued by anxiety as he reflected on the position in which Mma Potokwane had placed him. He was not a cowardly man, but he had felt nothing but fear, sheer naked fear, when he thought about the parachute jump. Eventually, by mid-afternoon, he had reached the conclusion that this was going to be the way in which he would die, and he had spent almost an hour thinking about the terms of a will which he would draw up the following day.

Mma Ramotswe would get the garage, naturally, and she could run it with Mma Makutsi, who could become Manager again. His house would be sold—it would get a very good price—and the money could then be distributed amongst his cousins, who were not well-off and who would be able to use it to buy cattle. Mma Ramotswe should keep some of it, perhaps as much as half, as this would help to keep the children, who were his responsibility after all. And then there was his truck, which could go to the orphan farm, where a good use would be found for it.

At this point he stopped. Leaving the truck to the orphan farm was tantamount to leaving it to Mma Potokwane, and he was not at all sure whether this was what he wanted. It was Mma Potokwane, after all, who had caused this crisis in the first place and he saw no reason why she should profit from it. In one view of the matter, Mma Potokwane would be responsible for his death, and perhaps she should even be put on trial. That would teach her to push people around as she did. That would be a lesson to all powerful matrons, and he suspected that there were many such women. Men would simply have to fight back, and this could be done, on their behalf, by the Attorney-General of Botswana himself, who could start a show trial of Mma Potokwane—for homicide—for the sake of all men. That would at least be a start.

Such unworthy thoughts were now no longer necessary, and after that glorious release pronounced by Mma Ramotswe at the dinner table, Mr J.L.B. Matekoni felt no need to plan his will. That night, after he had returned to his house near the old Botswana Defence Force Club, he contemplated his familiar possessions, not with the eye of one who was planning their testamentary disposal, but with the relief of one who knew that he was not soon to be separated from them. He looked at his sofa, with its stained arms and cushions, and thought about the long Saturday afternoons that he had spent just sitting there, listening to the radio and thinking about nothing in particular. Then he looked at the velvet picture of a mountain that hung on the wall opposite the sofa. That was a fine picture which must have taken the artist a great deal of time to make. Mr J.L.B. Matekoni knew every detail of it. All of this would go over to Mma Ramotswe's house one of these days, but for the time being it was reassuring to see things so firmly and predictably in their proper place.

It was almost midnight by the time Mr J.L.B. Matekoni went to bed. He read the paper for a few minutes before he put out the light, drowsily dropping the paper by his bedside, and then, enveloped in darkness, he drifted into the sleep that had always come so easily to him after a day of hard work. Sleep was welcome; the nightmare that he had experienced had been a diurnal one, and now it was resolved. There was to be no drop, no plummet to the ground, no humiliation as his fear made itself manifest to all . . .

That was in the waking world; the sleeping world of Mr J.L.B. Matekoni had not caught up with the events of that evening, with the release from his torment, and at some point that night, he found himself standing on the edge of the tarmac at the airport, with a small white plane of the sort used by the Kalahari Flying Club taxiing towards him. A door of the plane was opened, and he was beckoned within by the pilot, who, as it happened, was Mma Potokwane herself.

"Get in, Mr J.L.B. Matekoni," shouted Mma Potokwane above the noise of the engine.

She seemed vaguely annoyed that he was holding things up in some way, and Mr J.L.B. Matekoni obeyed, as he always did.

Mma Potokwane seemed quite confident, leaning forward to flick switches and adjust instruments. Mr J.L.B. Matekoni reached to touch a switch that appeared to need attention, as an orange light was flashing behind it, but his hand was brushed away by Mma Potokwane.

"Don't touch!" she shouted, as if addressing an orphan. "Dangerous!"

He sat back, and the little plane shot forward down the runway. The trees were so close, he thought, the grass so soft that he could jump out now, roll over, and escape; but there was no getting away from Mma Potokwane, who looked at him crossly and shook a finger in admonition. And then they were airborne, and he looked out of the window of the plane at the land below him, which was growing smaller and smaller, a miniaturised Botswana of cattle like ants and roads like thin strips of twisting brown thread. Oh, it was so beautiful to look down on his land and see the clouds and the blue and all the air. One might so easily step out onto such clouds and drift away, off to the

West, over the great brown, and alight some-where where the lions walked and where there were springs of water and tall trees and little sign of man.

Mma Potokwane pulled on the controls of the plane and they circled, hugging the edge of the town so far below. He looked down and he saw Zebra Drive; it was so easy to spot it, and was that not Mma Ramotswe waving to him from her yard, and Mma Makutsi, in her new green shoes? They were waving, smiling up at him, pointing to a place on the ground where he might land. He turned to Mma Potokwane, who smiled at him now and pointed to the handle of the door.

He reached out and no more than touched the door before it flew open. He felt the wind on his face, and the panic rose in him, and he tried to stop himself falling, holding onto one of the levers in the plane, a little thing that gave him no purchase. Mma Potokwane was shout-ing at him, taking her hands off the controls of the plane to shove him out, and now kicked him firmly in the back with those flat brown shoes which she wore to walk about the orphan farm. "Out!" she cried, and Mr J.L.B. Matekoni, mute with fear, slipped out into the empty air and tumbled, head over heels, now looking at the sky, now at the ground, down to the earth that was still so far away beneath him.

There was no parachute, of course, just pyjamas, and they were billowing about him, hardly slowing him up at all. **This is how it ends**, thought Mr J.L.B. Matekoni, and he began to think of how good life had been, and how precious; but he could not think of these things for long, for his fall was over in seconds and he landed on his feet, perfectly, as if he might have hopped off an old orange box at the garage; and there he was, out in the bush, beside a termite mound. He looked about him; it was an unfamiliar landscape, perhaps Tlokweng, perhaps not, and he was studying it when he heard his father's voice behind him. He turned round, but there was no sign of his father, who was there but not quite there, in the way in which the dead can come to us in our dreams. There was much that he wanted to ask his father, there was much that he wanted to tell him about the garage, but his father spoke first, in a voice which was strange and reedy—for a dead man has no breath to make a voice—and asked a question which woke up Mr J.L.B. Matekoni, wrenching him from his dream with its satisfactory soft landing by the termite mound.

"When are you going to marry Mma Ramotswe?" asked his father. "Isn't it about time?"

CHAPTER ELEVEN

MEETING MR BOBOLOGO

Mma Ramotswe had not been ignoring Mma Holonga's case. It was true that she had as yet done nothing, but that did not mean that she had not been thinking about how she would approach this delicate issue. It would not do for any of the men to discover that they were being investigated, as this would give offence and could easily drive away any genuine suitor. This meant that she would have to make enquiries with discretion, talking to people who knew these men and, if at all possible, engineering a meeting with them herself. That would require a pretext, but she was confident that one could be found.

The first thing she would have to do, she thought, was to talk to somebody who worked at Mr Bobologo's school. This was not difficult, as Mma Ramotswe's maid, Rose, had a cousin who had for many years been in charge of the school kitchen. She had stopped working now, and was living in Old Naledi, where she looked after the children of one of her sons. Mma Ramotswe had never met her, but Rose had mentioned her from time to time and assured her employer that a visit would be welcome.

"She is one of these people who is always talking," said Rose. "She talks all day, even if nobody listens to her. She will be very happy to talk to you."

"Such people are very helpful in our work," said Mma Ramotswe. "They tell us things we need to know."

"This is such a lady," said Rose. "She will tell you everything she knows. It makes her very happy to do that. You will need a long, long time."

There were many people like that in Botswana, Mma Ramotswe reflected, and she was glad that this was so. It would be strange to live in a country where people were silent, passing one another in the street wordlessly, as if frightened of what the other might think or say. This was not the African way, where people would call out and converse with one another from opposite sides of a road, or across a wide expanse of bush, careless of who heard. Such conversations could be carried on by people walking in different directions, until voices grew too faint and too distant to be properly heard and words were swallowed by the sky. That was a good way of parting from a friend, so less abrupt than words of farewell followed by silence. Mma Ramotswe herself often shouted out to the children after they had left the house for school, reminding Puso to be careful of how he crossed the road or telling him to make sure that his shoelaces were tied properly, not that boys ever bothered about that sort of thing. Nor did boys ensure that their shirts were tucked into their trousers properly, but that was another issue which she could think about later, when the demands of clients were less pressing.

Rose's cousin, Mma Seeonyana, was at home when Mma Ramotswe called on her. Her house was not a large one—no more than two small rooms, Mma Ramotswe saw—but her yard was scrupulously clean, with circles traced in the sand by her wide-headed broom. This was a good sign; an untidy yard was a sign of a woman who no longer bothered with the traditional Botswana virtues, and such people, Mma Ramotswe found, were almost always unreliable or rude. They had no idea of **botho**, which meant respect or good manners. **Botho** set Botswana apart from other places; it was what made it a special place. There were people who mocked it, of course, but what precisely did they want instead? Did they want people to be selfish? Did they want them to treat others unkindly? Because if you forgot about **botho**, then that was surely what would happen; Mma Ramotswe was sure of that.

She saw Mma Seeonyana standing outside her front door, a brown paper bag in her hand. As she parked the tiny white van at the edge of the road, she noticed the older woman watching her. This was another good sign. It was a traditional Botswana pursuit to watch other people and wonder what they were up to; this modern habit of indifference to others was very hard to understand. If you watched people, then it was a sign that you cared about them, that you were not treating them as complete strangers. Again, it was all a question of manners.

Mma Ramotswe stood at the gate and called

out to Mma Seeonyana. The other woman responded immediately, and warmly, inviting Mma Ramotswe to come in and sit with her at the back of the house, where it was shadier. She did not ask her visitor what she wanted, but welcomed her, as if she were a friend or neighbour who had called in for a chat.

"You are the woman who lives over that way, on Zebra Drive," said Mma Seeonyana. "You are the woman who employs Rose. She has told me about you."

Mma Ramotswe was surprised that she had been recognised, but further explanation was quickly provided. "Your van is very well-known," said Mma Seeonyana. "Rose told me about it, and I have seen you driving through town. I have often thought: I would like to get to know that lady, but I never thought I would have the chance. I am very happy to see you here, Mma."

"I have heard of you too," said Mma Ramotswe. "Rose has spoken very well of you. She was very proud that you were in charge of those school kitchens."

Mma Seeonyana laughed. "When I was in that place I was feeding four hundred children every day," she said. "Now I am feeding two little boys. It is much easier."

"That is what we women must do all the time," said Mma Ramotswe. "I am feeding three people now. I have a fiancé and I have two children who are adopted and who come from the orphan farm. I have to make many meals. It seems that women have been put in the world to cook and keep the yard tidy. Sometimes I think that is very unfair and must be changed."

Mma Seeonyana agreed with this view of the world, but frowned when she thought of the implications. "The trouble is that men would never be able to do what we do," she said. "Most men will just not cook. They are too lazy. They would rather go hungry than cook. That is a big problem for us women. If we started to do other things, then the men would fade away and die of hunger. That is the problem."

"We could train them," said Mma Ramotswe. "There is much to be said for training men."

"But you have to find a man to train," said Mma Seeonyana. "And they just run away if you try to tell them what to do. I have had three men run away from me. They said that I talked too much and that they had no peace. But that is not true."

Mma Ramotswe clicked her tongue in sympathy. "No, Mma, it cannot be true. But sometimes men seem not to like us to talk to them. They think they have already heard what we have to say."

Mma Seeonyana sighed. "They are very foolish."

"Yes," said Mma Ramotswe. Some men were foolish, she thought, but by no means all. And there were some very foolish women too, if one thought about it.

"Even teachers," said Mma Seeonyana. "Even teachers can be foolish sometimes."

Mma Ramotswe looked up sharply. "You must have known many teachers, Mma," she said. "When you were working in that place you must have known all the teachers."

"Oh I did," said Mma Seeonyana. "I knew many teachers. I saw them come as junior teachers and I saw them get promotion and become senior teachers. I saw all that happening. And I saw some very bad teachers too."

Mma Ramotswe affected surprise. "Bad teachers, Mma? Surely not."

"Oh yes," said Mma Seeonyana. "I was astonished over what I found out. But I suppose teachers are the same as anybody else and they can be bad sometimes."

Mma Ramotswe looked down at the ground. "Who were these bad teachers?" she asked. "And why were they bad?"

Mma Seeonyana shook her head. "They came and went," she said. "I do not remember all their names. But I do remember a man who came to the school for six months and then the police took him away. They said he had done a very bad thing, but they never told us what it was."

Mma Ramotswe shook her head. "That must have been very bad." She paused, and then, "The good teachers must have been ashamed. Teachers like Mr Bobologo, for example. He's a good teacher, isn't he?"

She had not expected the reply, which was a peal of laughter. "Oh that one! Yes, Mma. He's very good all right."

Mma Ramotswe waited for something more to be said, but Mma Seeonyana merely smiled, as if she were recalling some private, amusing memory. She would have to winkle this out without giving the impression of being too interested. "Oh," she said. "So he's a ladies' man, is he? I might have suspected it. There are so many ladies' men these days. I am surprised that there are any ordinary husbands left at all."

This brought forth another burst of laughter from Mma Seeonyana, who wiped at her eyes with the cuff of her blouse. "A ladies' man, Mma? Yes, I suppose you could say that! A ladies' man! Yes. Mr Bobologo would be very pleased to hear that, Mma."

Mma Ramotswe felt a momentary irritation with Mma Seeonyana. It was discourteous, in her view, to make vague allusions in one's conversation with another—allusions which the other could not understand. There was nothing more frustrating than trying to work out what another person was saying in the face of coyness or even deliberate obfuscation. If there was something which Mma Seeonyana wanted to say about Mr Bobologo, then she should say it directly rather than hinting at some private knowledge.

"Well, Mma," said Mma Ramotswe in a firm tone. "Is Mr Bobologo a ladies' man, or is he not?"

Mma Seeonyana stared at her. She was still smiling, but she had picked up the note of irritation in her visitor's voice and the smile was fading. "I'm sorry, Mma," she said. "I didn't mean to laugh like that. It's just that . . . well, it's just that you touched upon a very funny thing with that man. He is a ladies' man, but only in a very special sense. That was what was so funny."

Mma Ramotswe nodded encouragingly. "In what sense is he a ladies' man then?"

Mma Seeonyana chuckled. "He is one of those men who is worried about street ladies. These bad girls who hang about in bars. That sort of woman. He disapproves of them very strongly and he and some friends of his have been trying for years to save these girls from their bad ways. It is his hobby. He goes to the bus station and hands leaflets to young girls coming in from the villages. He warns them about what can happen in Gaborone."

Mma Ramotswe narrowed her eyes. This was very interesting information, but it was difficult to see what exactly it told her. Everybody was aware of the problem of bar girls, who were the scourge of Africa. It was sad to see them, dressed in their shoddy finery, flirting with older men who should know better, but who almost inevitably did not. Nobody liked this, but most people did nothing about it. At least Mr Bobologo and his friends were trying.

"It's a hopeless task," Mma Seeonyana continued. "They have set up some sort of place where these girls can go and live while they try to get honest jobs. It is over there by the African Mall." She stopped and looked at Mma Ramotswe. "But I'm sure that you didn't come here to talk about Mr Bobologo, Mma. There are better things to talk about."

Mma Ramotswe smiled. "I have been very happy to talk about him," she replied. "But if there are other things you would like to talk about, I am happy with that."

Mma Seeonyana sighed. "There are so many things to talk about, Mma. I don't really know where to start."

This, thought Mma Ramotswe, was a good cue, and she took it. She remembered Rose's warning, and she could see the afternoon, her precious Sunday afternoon, disappearing before her. "Well, I could always come back to visit you, Mma . . ."

"No," said Mma Seeonyana quickly. "You must stay, Mma. I will make you some tea and then I can tell you about something that has been happening around here that is very strange."

"You are very kind, Mma."

Mma Ramotswe sat down on the battered chair which Mma Seeonyana had pulled out of the doorway. This was duty, she supposed, and there were more uncomfortable ways of earning a living than listening to ladies like Mma Seeonyana gossiping about neighbourhood affairs. And one never knew what one might learn from such conversations. It was her duty to keep herself informed, as one could not tell when some snippet of information gathered in such a way would prove useful; just as the information about Mr Bobologo and the bar girls might prove useful, or might not. It was difficult to tell.

MMA MAKUTSI was also busy that Sunday, not on the affairs of the No. 1 Ladies' Detective Agency, but on the move to her new house. The simplest way of doing this would have been to ask Mma Ramotswe to bring her tiny white van to carry over her possessions, but she was unwilling to impose in this way. Mma Ramotswe was generous with her time, and would have readily agreed to help her, but Mma Makutsi was independent and decided to hire a truck and a driver for the hour or so it would take to move her effects to their new home. There was not much to move, after all: her bed, with its thin coir mattress which she would soon replace, her single chair, her black tin trunk with her clothes folded within it, and a box containing her shoes, her pot, pan, and small primus stove. These were the worldly goods of Mma Makutsi which were quickly piled up in the back of the truck by the muscular young man who drove up the bumpy track that morning.

"You have packed this well," he said, making conversation as they drove the short distance to her new house. "I move things for people all the time. But they often have many boxes and plastic bags full of things. Sometimes they also have a grandmother to be moved, and I have to put the old lady in the back of the truck with all the other things."

"That is no way to treat a grandmother," said Mma Makutsi. "The grandmother should ride in the front."

"I agree, Mma," said the young man. "Those people who put their grandmother in the back of the truck, they will feel sorry when the grandmother is late. They will remember that they put her in the back of the truck, and it will be too late to do anything about it."

Mma Makutsi replied to this observation civilly, and the rest of the journey was completed in silence. She had the key of the house in the pocket of her blouse and she felt for it from time to time just to reassure herself that it was really there. She was thinking, too, of how she would arrange the furniture—such as it was—and how she might see about a rug for her new bedroom. That was a previously undreamed-of luxury; she had woken every day of her life to a packed earth floor or to plain concrete. Now she might afford a rug which would feel so soft underfoot, like a covering of new grass. She closed her eyes and thought of what lay ahead—the luxury of having her own shower—with hot water!—and the pleasure, the sheer pleasure, of having an extra room in which she could entertain people if she wished. She could invite friends to have a meal with her, and nobody would have to sit on a bed or look at her tin trunk. She could buy a radio and they could listen to music together, Mma Makutsi and her friends, and they would talk about important things, and all the humiliations of the shared stand-pipe would be a thing of the past.

She kept her eyes closed until they were almost there and then opened them and saw the house, which seemed smaller now than she had remembered it, but which was still so beautiful in her eyes, with its sloping roof and its paw-paw trees.

"This is your place, Mma?" asked the driver.

"It's my house," said Mma Makutsi, savouring the words.

"You're lucky," said the young man. "This is a good place to live. How many pula is the rent? What do you pay?"

Mma Makutsi told him and he whistled. "That is a lot! I could not afford a place like this. I have to live in half a room over that way, half way to Molepolole."

"That cannot be easy," said Mma Makutsi.

They drew up in front of the gate, and Mma Makutsi walked down the short path that led to the front door. She had that door, and the part of the house which was lived in by the other tenants was reached by the door at the back. She felt proud that the front door was hers, even if it looked as if it was in need of a coat of paint. That could be dealt with later;

what counted now was that she had the key to this door in her hand, paid for by the first month's rent, and hers by right.

It took the young man very little time to move her possessions into the front room. She thanked him, and gave him a ten-pula tip—overly generous, perhaps, but she was a proper householder now and these things would be expected of her. As she handed over the money, which he took from her with a wide smile, she reflected on the fact that she had never done this before. She had never before been in a position where she had given largesse, and the thought struck her forcibly. It was an unfamiliar, slightly uncomfortable feeling; I am just Mma Makutsi, from Bobonong, and I am giving this young man a ten-pula note. I have more money than he has. I have a better house. I am where he would like to be, but isn't.

By herself now, in the house, Mma Makutsi moved about her two rooms. She touched the walls; they were solid. She loosened a window latch, letting in a warm breeze for a moment, and then closed the window again. She switched on a light, and a bulb glowed above her; she turned on a tap, and water, fresh, cold water came out and splashed into a stainless steel sink, so polished and shiny that she could see her face reflected at her, the face of a person who was looking at the world with the cautious wonder of ownership, or at least of something close to it, of tenancy.

There was a side door to the house, and she opened this and peered out onto the yard. The paw-paw trees had incipient fruit upon them, which would be ready in a month or so. There were one or two other plants, shrubs that had wilted in the heat but which had the dogged determination of indigenous Botswana vegetation. These would survive even if never watered; they would cling on in the dry ground, making the most of what little moisture they could draw from the soil, tenacious because they lived here in this dry country, and had always lived here. Mma Ramotswe had once described the traditional plants of Botswana as loyal and yes, that was right, thought Mma Makutsi, that is what they are—our old friends, our fellow survivors in this brown land that I love and love so much. Not that she thought about that love very often, but it was there, as it was in the hearts of all Batswana. And that was surely what most people wanted, at the end of the day; to live on the land that they love, and nowhere else; to be where their people had been before them, as long as anybody could remember.

She drew back from the door, and looked about her house again. She did not see the grubby finger marks on the wall, nor the place where the floor had buckled. What she saw was a room with bright curtains and with friends about a table, and herself at the head; what she heard was a pot of water boiling on a stove, to the soft hissing of a flame.

CHAPTER TWELVE

MR BOBOLOGO TALKS ON THE SUBJECT OF LOOSE WOMEN

THE FACT that the schools were on holiday was convenient. Had Mr Bobologo been teaching, then Mma Ramotswe would have been obliged to wait until half past three, when she could have accosted him on his way to the house that he occupied in the neat row of teachers' houses at the back of the school. As it was, that Monday she was able to arrive at his house at ten o'clock and find him, as Mma Seeonyana said she would, sitting on a chair in the sun outside his back door, a Bible on his lap. She approached him carefully, as one always should when coming across somebody reading the Bible, and greeted him in the approved, traditional fashion. Had he slept well?

Was he well? Would he mind if she talked to him?

Mr Bobologo looked up at her, squinting against the sunlight, and Mma Ramotswe saw a tall man of slim build, carefully dressed in khaki trousers and an open-necked white shirt, and wearing a pair of round, pebble-lensed glasses. Everything about him, from the carefully polished brown shoes to the powerful glasses, said **teacher**, and she had to make an effort to prevent herself from smiling. People were so predictable, she thought, so true to type. Bank managers dressed exactly as bank managers were expected to dress—and behaved accordingly; you could always tell a lawyer from that careful, rather watchful way they listened to what you had to say, as if they were ready to pounce on the slightest slip; and, since she had come to know Mr J.L.B. Matekoni, there was no mistaking mechanics, who looked at things as if they were ready to take them apart and make them work better. Not that this applied to all mechanics, of course; the apprentices would be mechanics before too long and yet they looked at things as if they were about to break them. So per-

haps it took years before a calling began to tell
on a person.

Did she look like a detective, she wondered?
This was an intriguing question. If somebody
saw her in the street, they would probably not
look twice at her. She was just an ordinary
Motswana lady, in the traditional mould, going
about her daily business as so many other
women did. Surely nobody would suspect her
of **watching**, which is what she had to do in
her job. Perhaps it was different with Mma
Makutsi, with those large glasses of hers. People noticed those glasses and clearly thought
about them. They might wonder, might they
not, why somebody would need such large
glasses and they might conclude that this was
because she was interested in looking closely at
things, at magnifying them. That, of course,
was an absurd vision of what she and Mma
Makutsi did; they very rarely had to examine
any physical objects—human behaviour was
what interested them, and all that this required
was observation and understanding.

Her observation of Mr Bobologo lasted only
a few seconds. Now he stood up, closing the
Bible with some regret, as one might close a

riveting novel in which one had become immersed. Of course Mr Bobologo would know the end of the story—which was not a happy ending, if one thought about it carefully—but one might still be absorbed even in the completely familiar.

"I am sorry to disturb you," said Mma Ramotswe. "The school holidays must be a good time for you teachers to catch up on your reading. You will not like people coming along and disturbing you."

Mr Bobologo responded well to this courteous beginning. "I am happy to see you, Mma. There will be plenty of time for reading later on. You may sit on this chair and I will fetch another."

Mma Ramotswe sat on the teacher's chair and waited for him to return. It was a good spot that he had chosen to sit, hidden from passersby on the road, but with a view of the children's playground where even now in the holidays the children of the school staff were engaged in some complicated game with a ball. It would be good to sit here, she thought, knowing that the Government was still paying one's salary every month, and that reading, and becoming wiser and wiser, was exactly what one was expected to do.

Mr Bobologo returned with another chair and seated himself opposite Mma Ramotswe. He looked at her through the thick lenses of his spectacles, and then dabbed gently at the side of his mouth with a white handkerchief, which he then folded neatly and placed in the pocket of his shirt.

Mma Ramotswe looked back at him and smiled. Her initial impression of Mr Bobologo had been favourable, but she found herself wondering why it was that a successful, rather elegant person such as Mma Holonga should take up with this teacher, who, whatever his merits might be, was hardly a romantic figure. But such speculation was inevitably fruitless. The choices that people made in such circumstances were often inexplicable, and perhaps it was no more than sheer chance. If you were in the mood for falling in love, or marrying, then perhaps it did not matter very much whom you would see when you turned the corner. You were looking for somebody, and there was somebody, and you would convince yourself that this random person was what you were really looking for in the first place. **We find**

what we are looking for in life, her father had once said to her; which was true—if you look for happiness, you will see it; if you look for distrust and envy and hatred—all those things—you will find those too.

"So, Mma," said Mr Bobologo. "Here I am. You have come to see me about your child, I assume. I hope I can say that this boy or this girl is doing well at school. I am sure I can. But first you must tell me what your name is, so I know which child it is that I am talking about. That is important."

For a few moments Mma Ramotswe was taken aback, but then she laughed. "Oh no, Rra. Do not worry. I am not some troublesome mother who has come to talk about her difficult child. I have come because I have heard of your other work."

Mr Bobologo took out his handkerchief and dabbed again at the side of his mouth.

"I see," he said. "You have heard of this work that I do." There was a note of suspicion in his voice, Mma Ramotswe noticed, and she wondered why this should be. Perhaps he was laughed at by others, or labelled a prude, and the thought irritated her. There was nothing to be ashamed of in the work that he did, even if it seemed strange for a man to have such strong views on such a matter. At least he was trying to help address a social problem, which was more than most people did.

"I have heard of it," said Mma Ramotswe. "And I thought that I would like to hear more about it. It is a good thing that you are doing, Rra."

Mr Bobologo's expression remained impassive. Mma Ramotswe thought that he was still unconvinced by what she had said, and so she continued, "The problem of these street girls is a very big one, Rra. Every time I see them going into bars, I think: **That girl is somebody's daughter**, and that makes me sad. That is what I think, Rra."

These words had a marked effect on Mr Bobologo. While she was still speaking, he sat up in his chair, sharply, and stared intensely at Mma Ramotswe.

"You are right, Mma," he said. "They are all the daughters of some poor person. They are all children who have been loved by their parents, and by God himself, and now where are they? In bars! That is where. Or in the arms of some man. That is also where." He paused, looking down at the ground. "I am sorry to use such strong language, Mma. I am not a man who uses strong language, but when it comes to this matter, then I am like a dog who has been kicked in the ribs."

Mma Ramotswe nodded. "It is something that should make us all angry."

"Yes," said Mr Bobologo. "It should. It should. But what does the Government do about this? Do you see the Government going down to these bars and chasing these bad girls back to their villages? Do you see that, Mma?"

Mma Ramotswe mused for a moment. There were many things, she thought, that one could reasonably expect the Government to do, but it had never occurred to her that chasing bar girls back to their villages was one of them. For a moment she imagined the Minister of Roads, for example, a portly man who inevitably wore a wide-brimmed hat to shade him from the sun, chasing bar girls down the road to Lobatse, followed, perhaps, by his Under-Secretary and several clerks from the Ministry. It was an intriguing picture, and one which would normally have made her smile, but there was no question of smiling now, in front of the righteous indignation of Mr Bobologo.

"So I decided—together with some friends," continued Mr Bobologo, "that we should do something ourselves. And that is how we started the House of Hope."

Mma Ramotswe listened politely as Mr Bobologo listed the difficulties he had encountered in finding a suitable building for the House of Hope and how eventually they had obtained a ruinously expensive lease on a house near the African Mall. It had three bedrooms and a living room which was not enough, he explained, for the fourteen girls who lived there. "Sometimes we have even had as many as twenty bad girls in that place," he said. "Twenty girls, Mma! All under one roof. When it is that full, then there is not enough room for anybody to do anything. They must sleep on the floor and doubled-up in bunks. That is not a good thing, because when things get that crowded they run away and we have to look for them again and persuade them to come back. It is very trying."

Mma Ramotswe was intrigued. If the girls ran away, then it implied that they were kept there against their will, which surely could not be the case. You could keep children in one place against their will, but you could not do that to bar girls, if they were over eighteen. There were obviously details of the House of Hope which would require further investigation.

"Would you show me this place, Rra?" she asked. "I can drive you down there in my van if you would show me. Then I will be able to understand the work that you are doing."

Mr Bobologo seemed to weigh this request for a moment, but then he rose to his feet, taking his glasses off and stowing them in his top pocket. "I am happy to do that, Mma. I am happy for people to see what we are doing so that they may tell other people about it. Perhaps they will even tell the Government and persuade them to give us money so that we can run the House of Hope on a proper basis. There is never ever enough money, and we have to rely on what we can get from churches and some generous people. The Government should pay for this, but do they help us? The answer to that, Mma, is no. The Government is not concerned about the welfare of ladies in this country. They think only of new roads and new buildings. That is what they think of."

"It is very unfair," agreed Mma Ramotswe. "I also have a list of things that I think the Government should do."

"Oh yes?" said Mr Bobologo. "And what is on your list, Mma?"

This question caught Mma Ramotswe by surprise. She had spoken of her list idly, as a conversational ploy; there was no list, really.

"So?" pressed Mr Bobologo. "So what is on this list of yours, Mma?"

Mma Ramotswe thought wildly. "I would like to see boys taught how to sew at school," she said. "That is on my list."

Mr Bobologo stared at her. "But that is not possible, Mma," he said dismissively. "That is not something that boys wish to learn. I am not surprised that the Government is not trying to teach boys this thing. You cannot teach boys to be girls. That is not good for boys."

"But boys wear clothes, do they not, Rra?" countered Mma Ramotswe. "And if these clothes are torn, then who is there to sew them up?"

"There are girls to do that," said Mr Bobologo. "There are girls and ladies. There are plenty of people in Botswana to do all the necessary sewing. That is a fact. I am a very experienced teacher and I know about these matters. Do you have anything else on your list, Mma?"

There would have been a time when Mma Ramotswe would not have allowed this to pass, but she was on duty now, and there was no need to antagonise Mr Bobologo. She owed it to her client to find out more about him, and that was a more immediate duty than her duty to the women of Botswana. So she merely looked up at the sky, as if looking for inspiration.

"I would like the Government to do many things," she said. "But I do not want to make them too tired. So I shall have to think about my list and make it a bit smaller."

Mr Bobologo looked at her approvingly. "I think that is very wise, Mma. If one asks for too many things at the same time, then one does not usually get them. If you ask for one thing, then you may get that one thing. That is what I have found in life."

"Ow!" exclaimed Mma Ramotswe. "You are a clever man, Rra!"

Mr Bobologo acknowledged the compliment with a brief nod of the head, and then indicated that he was now ready to follow Mma Ramotswe to the van. She stood aside and invited him to precede her, as was proper when dealing with a teacher. Whatever Mr Bobologo might prove to be like, he was first and foremost a teacher, and Mma Ramotswe believed very strongly that teachers should be treated with respect, as they always had been before the old Botswana morality had started to unravel. Now people treated teachers like anybody else, which was a grave mistake; no wonder children were so cheeky and ill-behaved. A society that undermined its teachers and their authority only dug away at its own sure foundations. Mma Ramotswe thought this was obvious; the astonishing thing was that many people simply did not understand that this was the case. But there was a great deal that people did not understand and would only learn through bitter experience. In her view, one of these things was the truth of the old African saying that it takes an entire village to raise a child. Of course it does; of course it does. Everybody in a village had a role to play in bringing up a child—and cherishing it—and in return that child would in due course feel responsible for everybody in that village. That is what makes life in society possible. We must love one another and help one another in our daily lives. That was the traditional African way and there was no substitute for it. None.

IT WAS only a few minutes' drive from the teachers' quarters to the House of Hope, a drive during which Mr Bobologo held on firmly to the side of the passenger seat, as if fearing that any moment Mma Ramotswe would steer the tiny white van off the road. Mma Ramotswe noticed this, but said nothing; there were some men who would never be happy with women drivers, even although the statistics were plain for them to see. Women had fewer accidents because they drove more sedately and were not trying to prove anything to anybody. It was men who were the reckless drivers—particularly young men (such as the apprentices) who felt that girls would be more impressed by speed than by safety. And it was young men in red cars who were the most dangerous of all. Such people were best given a wide berth, both in and out of the car.

"That is the House of Hope," said Mr Bobologo. "You can park under the tree here.

Carefully, Mma. You do not wish to hit the tree. Careful!"

"I have never hit a tree in my life," retorted Mma Ramotswe. "But I have known many men who have hit trees, Rra. Some of those men are late now."

"It may not have been their fault," muttered Mr Bobologo.

"Yes," said Mma Ramotswe evenly. "It could have been the fault of the trees. That is always possible."

She was incensed by his remark and struggled to contain her anger. Unfortunately, her battle with her righteous indignation overcame her judgment, and she hit the tree; not hard, but with enough of a jolt to make Mr Bobologo grab onto his seat once again.

"There," he said, turning to her in triumph. "You have hit the tree, Mma."

Mma Ramotswe turned off the engine and closed her eyes. Clovis Andersen, author of her professional vade mecum, **The Principles of Private Detection,** had advice which was appropriate to this occasion, and Mma Ramotswe now called it to mind. **Never allow your personal feelings to cloud the issue**, he had written. **You may be seething with anger over something, but do not—and I repeat not—do not allow it to overcome your professional judgment. Keep your calm. That is the most important thing. And if you find it difficult, close your eyes and count to ten**.

By the time she reached ten, Mr Bobologo had opened his door and was waiting for her outside. So Mma Ramotswe swallowed hard and joined him, following him up the short garden path that led to the doorway of an unexceptional white-washed house, of much the same sort as could be seen on any nearby street, and which from the road would never have been identified—without special knowledge—as a house of hope, or indeed of despair, or of anything else for that matter. It was just a house, and yet here it was, filled to the brim with bad girls.

"Here we are, Mma," said Mr Bobologo as he approached the front door. "Take up hope all you who enter here. That is what we say, and one day we shall have it written above the door."

Mma Ramotswe looked at the unprepos-

sessing door. Her reservations about Mr
Bobologo were growing, but she was not quite
sure why this should be so. He was irritating,
of course, but so were many people, and being
irritating was not enough for him to be written
off. No, there was something more than that.
Was it smugness, or singularity of purpose?
Perhaps that was it. It was always disconcerting
to meet those who had become so obsessed
with a single topic that they could not see their
concerns in context. Such people were uncomfortable company purely because they lacked
normal human balance, and this, she thought,
might be the case with Mr Bobologo. And yet
she had not been asked to find out whether Mr
Bobologo was an interesting man, or even a
nice man. She had been asked to find out
whether he was after Mma Holonga's money.
That was a very specific question, and her feelings for Mr Bobologo had nothing to do with
the answer to that question. So she would give
him the benefit of the doubt, and keep her personal opinions to herself. She herself would
never marry Mr Bobologo—or any man like
him—but it would be wrong of her to interfere until she had very concrete proof of the
exact issue at stake. And that had not yet ap-

peared, and might never appear. So for the time being, the only thing to do was to concentrate on inspecting the House of Hope and wait until Mr Bobologo put a foot wrong and gave himself away. And she had a feeling now—a fairly strong feeling—that he might never do that.

CHAPTER THIRTEEN

MR J.L.B. MATEKONI RECEIVES THE BUTCHER'S CAR; THE APPRENTICES RECEIVE AN ANONYMOUS LETTER

WHILE MMA RAMOTSWE was visiting Mr Bobologo and his House of Hope, Mr J.L.B. Matekoni was completing a tricky repair at Tlokweng Road Speedy Motors. He was relieved, of course, about the cancellation of the parachute jump, but at the same time he was concerned about the fact that one of the apprentices was going to do it in his stead. He knew that these boys were feckless, and he knew that they would do anything to impress girls, but he was their apprentice-master, after all, and he considered that he had a moral responsibility for them until they had served out their apprenticeship. Many people would say that this did not extend to cover what they did in their own time, but Mr J.L.B. Matekoni was not one to take a narrow view of these matters and he could not avoid feeling at least slightly paternal towards these young men, irritating though they undoubtedly were. He was not sure, though, how he could deal with this issue. If he persuaded the young man not to jump, then Mma Potokwane might insist that he do the jump after all. If she did so, then that would lead to a row between her and Mma Ramotswe, and that could become complicated. There might be no more fruit cake, for example, and he would miss his trips out to see the orphans, even if he was inevitably given some task to perform the moment he arrived at the orphan farm.

The repair took less time than he had anticipated, and well before it was time for the morning break Mr J.L.B. Matekoni found himself wiping the steering wheel and the driver's seat to make the car ready for collection by its owner. He was always very careful to ensure that cars were returned to the customer in a clean state—something he had attempted to drill into the apprentices, but without success.

"How would you feel if your car came back

to you with greasy fingerprints all over it?" he said to them. "Would you like it?"

"I would not see them," said one of the young men. "I am not worried about fingerprints. As long as a car goes fast, that is the only thing."

Mr J.L.B. Matekoni could barely credit what he had heard. "Do you mean to say that the only thing that advantages is speed? Is that what you really think?"

The apprentice had looked at him blankly before he gave his reply. "Of course. If a car goes fast, then it is a good car. It has a strong engine. Everybody knows that, Boss."

Mr J.L.B. Matekoni shook his head in despair. How many times had he explained about solid engineering and the merits of a reliable gearbox? How many times had he spelled out to these young men the merits of an economical engine, particularly a good diesel engine that would give years and years of service with very little trouble? Diesel-powered cars did not usually go very fast, but that was not the point; they were good cars anyway. None of these lessons, it appeared, had sunk in. He sighed. "I have been wasting my time," he muttered. "Wasting my time."

The apprentice smiled. "Wasting your time, Boss? What have you been doing? Dancing? You and Mma Ramotswe going dancing at one of those clubs? Hah!"

Mr J.L.B. Matekoni wanted to say, "Trying to teach a hyena to dance," but did not. Where had he heard that expression before? It seemed familiar, and then he remembered he had said it himself only a few days ago when he had been discussing First Class Motors with Mma Ramotswe. The memory made him start, and put the apprentices quite out of his mind. There was something hanging over him; he had forgotten what it was, but now it came back: he still had to deal with the issue of the butcher's car, which was due to be brought into the garage that morning. The thought appalled him: he would be able to effect a temporary repair, until such time as he tracked down the right parts, but there was more to it than that. He had agreed that he would confront the Manager of First Class Motors and tell him that his wrongdoing had been discovered. He did not relish this, in view of the other man's reputation. Indeed, it might have been moderately more attractive to do a parachute jump, perhaps, rather than meet the Manager of First Class Motors.

"You look worried," said the apprentice. "Is there something troubling you, Boss?"

Mr J.L.B. Matekoni sighed. "I have an unpleasant duty to do," he said. "I have to go and speak to some bad mechanics about their work. That is what is troubling me."

"Who are these bad mechanics?" asked the apprentice.

"Those people at First Class Motors," said Mr J.L.B. Matekoni. "The man who owns it and the men who work for him. They are all bad, every one of them."

The apprentice whistled. "Yes, they are bad all right. I have seen those people. They know nothing about cars. They are not like you, Mr J.L.B. Matekoni, who knows everything about all sorts of cars."

The compliment from the apprentice was unexpected, and Mr J.L.B. Matekoni, in spite of his modesty, was touched by the young man's tribute.

"I am not a great mechanic," he said softly. "I am just careful, that is all, and that is what I have always wanted you to be. I would want you to be careful mechanics. It would make me very happy if you would be that."

"We will be," said the apprentice. "We will try to be like you. We hope that people will always look at our work and think: they learned that from Mr J.L.B. Matekoni."

Mr J.L.B. Matekoni smiled. "**Some** of your work, maybe . . ." he began, but the apprentice interrupted him.

"You see," he said, "my father is late. He became late when I was a small boy—just that high—very small. And I did not have uncles who were any good, and so I think of you as my father, Rra. That is what I think. You are my father."

Mr J.L.B. Matekoni was silent. He had always had difficulty in expressing his emotions—as mechanics often do, he thought—and it was hard for him now. He wanted to say to this young man: What you have said makes me very proud, and very sad, all at the same time—but he could not find these words. He could, however, place a hand on the young man's shoulder and leave it there for a moment, to show that he understood what had been said.

"I have never said thank you, Rra," went on the apprentice. "And I would not want you to die without being thanked by me."

Mr J.L.B. Matekoni gave a start. "Am I going to die?" he asked. "I am not all that old surely. I am still here."

The apprentice smiled. "I did not mean that you were going to die soon, Rra. But you will die one of these days, like everybody else. And I wanted to say thank you before that day came."

"Well," said Mr J.L.B. Matekoni, "what you say is probably true, but we have spent too much time standing here talking about these things. There is work to be done in the garage. We have to get rid of that dirty oil over there. You can take it over to the special dump for burning. You can take the spare truck."

"I will do that now," said the apprentice.

"And don't pick up any girls in the truck," warned Mr J.L.B. Matekoni. "You remember what I told you about the insurance."

The apprentice, who had been already walking away, suddenly stopped in his tracks, guiltily, and Mr J.L.B. Matekoni knew immediately that this was precisely what he had been planning to do. The young man had made a moving statement, and Mr J.L.B. Matekoni had been touched by what he had said, but some things obviously never changed.

A FEW HOURS later, as the sun climbed up the sky and made shadows short and even the birds were lethargic, when the screeching of the cicadas from the bush behind Tlokweng Road Speedy Motors had reached a high insistent pitch, the butcher drew up in his handsome old Rover. He had had the time to reflect on what Mr J.L.B. Matekoni had told him, and he now spoke angrily of First Class Motors, with whom he intended to have no further dealings. Only shame, the shame of being a victim, prevented him from returning there to ask for his money back.

"I shall do that for you, Rra," said Mr J.L.B. Matekoni. "I feel responsible for what my brother mechanics have done to you."

The butcher took Mr J.L.B. Matekoni's hand and shook it firmly. "You have been very good to me, Rra. I am glad that there are still some honest men left in Botswana."

"There are many honest men in Botswana," said Mr J.L.B. Matekoni. "I am no better than anybody else."

"Oh yes you are," said the butcher. "I see many men in my work and I can tell . . ."

Mr J.L.B. Matekoni cut him short. This was clearly a day for excessive compliments, and he was beginning to feel embarrassed. "You are very kind, Rra, but I must get on with my work. The flies will be settling on the cars if I don't look out."

He had spoken the words without thinking that a butcher might take such a remark as a slight, as a suggestion that his own meat was much beset by flies. But the butcher did not appear to mind, and he smiled at the metaphor. "There are flies everywhere," he said. "We butchers know all about that. I would like to find a country without flies. Is there such a place, do you think, Rra?"

"I have not heard of such a country," said Mr J.L.B. Matekoni. "I think that in very cold places there are no flies. Or in some very big towns, where there are no cattle to bring the flies. Perhaps in such places. Places like New York."

"Are there no cattle in New York?" asked the butcher.

"I do not think so," said Mr J.L.B. Matekoni.

The butcher thought for a moment. "But there is a big green part of the town. I have seen a photograph. This part, this bit of bush, is in the middle. Perhaps they keep the cattle there. Do you think that is the place for cattle, Rra?"

"Perhaps," said Mr J.L.B. Matekoni, glancing at his watch. It was time for him to go home for his lunch, which he always ate at noon. Then, after lunch, fortified by a plate of meat and beans, he would drive round to First Class Motors and speak to the Manager.

MMA MAKUTSI ate her own lunch in the office. Now that she had a bit more money from the Kalahari Typing School for Men, she was able to treat herself to a doughnut at lunchtime, and this she ate with relish, a magazine open on the desk before her, a cup of bush tea at her side. It was best, of course, if Mma Ramotswe was there too, as they could exchange news and opinions, but it was still enjoyable to be by oneself, turning the pages of the magazine with one hand and licking the sugar off the fingers of the other.

The magazine was a glossy one, published in Johannesburg, and sold in great numbers at the

Botswana Book Centre. It contained articles about musicians and actors and the like, and about the parties which these people liked to attend in places like Cape Town and Durban. Mma Ramotswe had once said that she would not care to go to that sort of party, even if she were to be invited to one—which she never had been, as Mma Makutsi helpfully pointed out—but she was still sufficiently interested to peer over Mma Makutsi's shoulder and comment on the people in the pictures.

"That woman in the red dress," Mma Ramotswe had said. "Look at her. She is a lady who is only good for going to parties. That is very clear."

"She is a very famous lady, that one," Mma Makutsi had replied. "I have seen her picture many times. She knows where there are cameras and she stands in front of them, like a pig trying to get to the food. She is a very fashionable lady over in Johannesburg."

"And what is she famous for?"

"The magazine has never explained that," Mma Makutsi had said. "Maybe they do not know either."

This had made Mma Ramotswe laugh. "And then that woman there, that one in the middle, standing next to . . ." She had stopped, suddenly, as she recognised the face in the photograph. Mma Makutsi, engrossed in the contemplation of another photograph, had not noticed anything untoward. So she did not see the expression on Mma Ramotswe's face as she recognised, in the middle of the group of smiling friends, the face of Note Mokoti, trumpet player, and, for a brief and unhappy time, husband of Precious Ramotswe and father—not that it had meant anything to him—of her tiny child, the one who had left her after only those few, cherished hours.

Now, though, Mma Makutsi paged through the magazine on her own, while from within the garage there came the sound of a car's wheels being taken off. The sounds of wheel-nuts being thrown into an upturned hub-cap was one she recognised well, and was reassuring, in a strange way, just as the sound of the cicadas in the bush was a comforting one. The sounds that were alarming were those that came from nowhere, strange sounds that occurred at night, which might be anything.

She abandoned her magazine and reached for her tea cup, and it was at that point that she saw the envelope at the end of her desk. She had not noticed it when she came in that day, and it was not there last night, which meant that it must have been put there first thing in the morning. Mr J.L.B. Matekoni had opened the garage and the office, and he must have found it slipped under a door. Sometimes customers left notes that way, when they passed by and the garage was closed. Bills were even settled like this, with the money tucked into an envelope and pushed into the office through a crack in the door. That worried Mma Makutsi, who imagined that it would be very easy for money to go missing, but Mr J.L.B. Matekoni seemed unconcerned about it, and said that his customers had always paid in all sorts of ways and money had never been lost.

"One man used to pay his bills with bags of coins," he said. "Sometimes he would drive past, throw out one of those old white Standard Bank bags, wave, and drive off. That is how he settled his bills."

"That's all very well," Mma Makutsi had said. "But that would never have been recommended to us at the Botswana Secretarial College. They taught us there that the best way to pay bills was by cheque, and to ask for a receipt."

That was undoubtedly true, and Mr J.L.B. Matekoni had not cared to argue with one who had achieved the since then unequalled score of ninety-seven per cent in her final examinations at the Botswana Secretarial College. This letter, though, was plainly not a bill. As Mma Makutsi stretched across her desk to pick it up, she saw, written across the front of the envelope: **To Mr Handsome, Tlokweng Road Speedy Motors**.

She smiled. There was no means of telling who this Mr Handsome was—there were, after all, three men who worked at the garage and it could be addressed to any one of them—and this meant that she would be quite within her rights to open it.

There was a single sheet of paper inside the envelope, and Mma Makutsi unfolded this and began to read. **Dear Mr Handsome**, the letter began. **You do not know who I am, but I have been watching out for you! You are very handsome. You have a handsome face and handsome legs. Even your neck is handsome. I hope that you will talk to me one day. I am waiting for you. There is a lot we could talk about. Your admirer**.

Mma Makutsi finished reading and then

folded the letter up and put it back in the envelope. People did send such notes to one another, she knew, but the senders usually made sure that the letters were picked up by those for whom they were intended. It was strange that this person, this admirer, whoever she was, should have put the letter under the door without giving any further clue as to which Mr Handsome she had in mind. Now it was up to her to decide who should get this letter. Mr J.L.B. Matekoni? No. He was not a handsome man; he was pleasant-looking in a comfortable sort of way, but he was not handsome, in that sense. And anyway, whoever it was who had left the letter had no business in sending a letter like that to an engaged man and she, Mma Makutsi, would most certainly never pass on a letter of this nature to Mr J.L.B. Matekoni, even if it had been intended for him.

It was much more likely, then, that the letter was intended for the apprentices. But which one? Charlie, the older apprentice, was certainly good-looking, in a cheap sort of way she thought, but the same could probably be said of the younger one, perhaps even more so, when one considered the amount of hair gel that he seemed to rub on his head. If one were a young woman, somebody aged perhaps seventeen or eighteen, it is easy to see how one would be taken in by the looks of these young men and how one might even write a letter of this sort. So there was really no way of telling which of the young men was the intended recipient. It might be simpler, then, to throw the letter in the bin, and Mma Makutsi had almost decided to do this when the older apprentice walked into the room. He saw the envelope on the desk before her and, with a typical lack of respect for what is right, peered at the writing on the envelope.

"To Mr Handsome," he exclaimed. "That letter must be for me!"

Mma Makutsi snorted. "You are not the only man around here. There are two others, you know. Mr J.L.B. Matekoni and that friend of yours, that one with the oil on his hair. It could be for either of them."

The apprentice stared at her uncomprehendingly. "But Mr J.L.B. Matekoni is at least forty," he said. "How can a man of forty be called Mr Handsome?"

"Forty is not the end," said Mma Makutsi. "People who are forty can look very good."

"To other people who are forty maybe," said the apprentice, "but not to the general public."

Mma Makutsi drew in her breath, and held it. If only Mma Ramotswe had been here to listen to this; what would she have done? She certainly would not have let any of this pass. The effrontery of this young man! The sheer effrontery! Well, she would teach him a lesson, she would tell him what she thought of his vanity; she would spell it out . . . She stopped. A better idea had materialised; a wonderful trick that would amuse Mma Ramotswe when she told her about it.

"Call the young one in," she said. "Tell him I want to tell him about this letter you have received. He will be impressed, I think."

Charlie left and soon returned with the younger apprentice.

"Charlie here has received a letter," said Mma Makutsi. "It was addressed to Mr Handsome and I shall read it out to you."

The younger apprentice glanced at Charlie, and then looked back at Mma Makutsi. "But that could be for me," he said petulantly. "Why should he think that such a letter is addressed to him? What about me?"

"Or Mr J.L.B. Matekoni?" asked Mma Makutsi, smiling. "What about him?"

The younger apprentice shook his head. "He is an old man," he said. "Nobody would call him Mr Handsome. It is too late."

"I see," said Mma Makutsi. "Well, at least you are agreed on that. Well, let me read out the letter, and then we can decide."

She opened the envelope again, extracted the piece of paper, and read out the contents. Then, putting the letter down on the table, she smiled at the two young men. "Now who is being described in that letter? You tell me."

"Me," they both said together, and then looked at one another.

"It could be either," said Mma Makutsi. "Of course, I now remember who must have put that letter there. I have remembered something."

"You must tell me," said the older apprentice. "Then I can look out for this girl and talk to her."

"I see," said Mma Makutsi. She hesitated; this was a delicious moment. Oh, silly young men! "Yes," she continued, "I saw a man outside the garage this morning, first thing. Yes, there was a man."

There was complete silence. "A man?" said the younger apprentice eventually. "Not a girl?"

"It was for him, I think," said the older apprentice, gesturing at the younger one. And the younger one, his mouth open, was for a few moments unable to talk.

"It was not for me," he said at last. "I do not think so."

"Then I think that we should throw the letter into the bin, where it belongs," said Mma Makutsi. "Anonymous letters should always be ignored. The best place for them is the bin."

Nothing more was said. The apprentices returned to their work and Mma Makutsi sat at her desk and smiled. It was a wicked thing to have done, but she could not resist it. After all, one could not be good all the time, and occasional fun at the expense of another was harmless. She had told no lies, strictly speaking; she had seen a man walking away from the garage, but she had recognised him as one who did occasionally take a shortcut that way. The real sender of the letter was obviously some young girl who had been dared to write it by her friends. It was a piece of adolescent nonsense which everybody would soon forget about. And perhaps the boys had been taught some sort of lesson, about vanity certainly, but also, in an indirect way, about tolerance of the feelings of others, who might be a bit different from oneself. She doubted if they had learned the latter lesson, but it was there, she thought, visible if one bothered to think hard enough about it.

CHAPTER FOURTEEN

INSIDE THE HOUSE OF HOPE

Mma Ramotswe surveyed the House of Hope. It was a rather grand name for a modest bungalow which had been built in the early seventies, at a time when Gaborone was a small town, inching out from the cluster of buildings around Government Headquarters and the small square of shops nearby. These houses had been built for government employees or for expatriates who came to the country on short-term contracts. They were comfortable, and were large by the standards of most people's houses, but it seemed ambitious to use them for institutions, such as the House of Hope. But there was no choice, she imagined: larger buildings simply were not available, least of all to charities, which would have to scrimp and save to meet their costs.

There was a large garden, though, and this had been well-tended. In addition to a stand of healthy-looking paw-paw trees at the back, there were several clusters of bougainvillea and a mopipi tree. A vegetable garden, rather like the vegetable garden which Mr J.L.B. Matekoni had established in Mma Ramotswe's own yard, appeared to be growing beans and carrots with some success, although Mma Ramotswe reflected that in the case of carrots one could never really tell until one pulled them out of the ground. There were all sorts of insects which competed with us for carrots, and often what appeared from above to be a healthy plant would reveal itself as riddled with holes once pulled out of the soil.

There was a verandah to the side of the house, and somebody had thoughtfully placed shade netting over the side of this. That would be a good place to sit, thought Mma Ramotswe, and one might even drink tea there, on a hot afternoon, and feel the sun on one's face, but filtered by the shade netting. And then the thought occurred to her that all of

Gaborone, the whole town, might be covered with shade netting, held aloft on great poles, and that this would keep the town cool and hold in the water which people put on their plants. It would be comfortable under this shade netting in summer, and then when winter came, and the air was cooler, they could roll back the shade netting to let in the winter sun, which would warm them, like the smile of an old friend. It was such a good idea, and it would surely not be too expensive for a country that had all those diamonds, but she knew that nobody would ever take it seriously. So they would continue to complain about the hot weather when it was hot and about the cold weather when it was cold.

The front door of the House of Hope opened immediately into the living room. This was a large room for that style of house, but the immediate and overwhelming impression it gave Mma Ramotswe was one of clutter. There were three or four chairs in the centre of the room—tightly arranged in a circle—and around them there were tables, storage boxes, and, here and there, a suitcase. On the wall, fixed with drawing pins, were pictures ripped from magazines; pictures of families and of mothers and children; of Mother Teresa with her characteristic headscarf; of Nelson Mandela waving to a crowd; and of a line of African nuns, all clad in white, walking down a path through thick undergrowth, their hands joined in prayer. Mma Ramotswe's eye dwelt on the picture of the nuns. Where was the photograph taken, and where were these ladies going? They looked so peaceful, she thought, that perhaps it did not matter whether they were going anywhere, or nowhere in particular. People sometimes walked simply because walking was an enjoyable thing to do, and better than standing still, perhaps, if that was all you otherwise had to do. Sometimes she herself walked around her garden for no reason, and found it very relaxing, as perhaps it was for those nuns.

"You are interested in the pictures," said Mr Bobologo, behind her. "We think that it is important that these bar girls should be reminded of a better life. They can sit here and look at the pictures."

Mma Ramotswe nodded. She was not convinced that it would be much fun for a bar girl, or for anybody else for that matter, to be sitting on one of those chairs in that crowded room, looking at these pictures from the magazines. But then it would be better than listening to Mr Bobologo, she thought.

Mr Bobologo now came to Mma Ramotswe's side and pointed in the direction of the corridor that led off the living room. "I will be happy to show you the dormitories," he said. "We may find some of the bad girls in their rooms."

Mma Ramotswe raised an eyebrow. It was not very tactful of him to call them bad girls, even if they were. People rose to the descriptions of themselves, and it might have been better, she thought, to call them young ladies, in the hope that they might behave as young ladies behaved. But then, to be realistic, they probably would not behave that way, as it took a great deal to change somebody's ways.

The corridor was tidy enough, with only a small bookcase along one wall and the floor well-polished with that fresh-smelling polish that Mma Ramotswe's maid, Rose, so liked to use. They stopped outside a half-open bedroom door and Mr Bobologo knocked upon this before he pushed it open.

Mma Ramotswe looked inside. There were two bunk-beds in the room, both of them triple-deckers. The top bed was just below the ceiling, barely allowing enough space for anybody to fit in. Mma Ramotswe reflected that she herself would never fit in that space, but then these girls were younger, and some of them might be quite small.

There were three girls in the room, two lying fully clothed on the lower bunks and one wearing a dressing gown, and sitting on a middle bunk, her legs hanging down over the edge. As Mr Bobologo and Mma Ramotswe entered the room, they stared at them, not with any great interest, but with a rather vacant look.

"This lady is a visitor," Mr Bobologo announced, somewhat obviously, thought Mma Ramotswe.

One of the girls muttered something, which may have been a greeting but which was difficult to make out. The other one on the lower bunk nodded her head, while the girl sitting on the middle bunk managed a weak smile.

"You have a nice house here," said Mma Ramotswe. "Are you happy?"

The girls exchanged glances.

"Yes," said Mr Bobologo. "They are very happy."

Mma Ramotswe watched the girls, who

did not appear inclined to contradict Mr Bobologo.

"And do you get good food here, ladies?" she asked.

"Very good food," said Mr Bobologo. "These good-time bar girls do not eat properly. They just drink dangerous liquor. When they are here they are given good, Botswana cooking. The food is very healthy."

"It is good to hear you telling me all this," Mma Ramotswe said, pointedly addressing her remark to the girls.

"That is all right," said Mr Bobologo. "We are happy to talk to visitors." He touched Mma Ramotswe's elbow and pointed out into the corridor. "I must show you the kitchen," he said. "And we must allow these girls to get on with their work."

It was not very apparent to Mma Ramotswe what this work was, and she had to suppress a smile as they walked back down the corridor towards the kitchen. He really was a most irritating man, this Mr Bobologo, with his tendency to speak for others and his one-track mind. Mma Holonga had struck Mma Ramotswe as being a reasonable woman, and yet she was seriously entertaining Mr Bobologo as a suitor, which seemed very strange. Surely Mma Holonga, with her wealth and position, could find somebody better than this curious teacher with his ponderous, didactic style.

They now stood at the door of the kitchen, in which two young women, barefoot and wearing light pink housecoats, were chopping vegetables on a large wooden chopping board. A pot of stew was boiling on the stove—boiling too vigorously, thought Mma Ramotswe—and a large cup of tea was cooling on the table. It would be good to be offered tea, she thought longingly, and that very cup looked just right.

"These girls are chopping vegetables," said Mr Bobologo solemnly. "And there is stew for our meal tonight."

"So I see," said Mma Ramotswe. "And I see, too, that they have just made tea."

"It is better for them to drink tea than strong liquor," intoned Mr Bobologo, looking disapprovingly at one of the girls, who cast her eyes downwards, in shame.

"Those are my views too," said Mma Ramotswe. "Tea refreshes. It clears the mind. Tea is good at any time of the day, but especially at mid-day, when it is so hot." She paused, and then added, "As it is today."

"You are right, Mma," said Mr Bobologo. "I am a great drinker of tea. I cannot understand why anybody would want to drink anything else when there is tea to be had. I have never been able to understand that."

Mma Ramotswe now used an expression which is common in Setswana and which indicates understanding, and firm endorsement of what another has said. "Eee, Rra," she said, with great depth of feeling, drawing out the vowels. If anything could convey to this man that she needed a cup of tea, this would. But it did not.

"This habit of drinking coffee is a very bad thing," went on Mr Bobologo. "Tea is better for the heart than coffee is. People who drink coffee strain their hearts. Tea has a calming effect on the heart. It makes the heart go more slowly. Thump, thump. That is what the heart should sound like. I have always said that."

"Yes," agreed Mma Ramotswe, weakly. "That is very true."

"That is why I am in favour of tea," pronounced Mr Bobologo with an air of finality, as might a speaker at a kgotla meeting make his concluding statement.

They stood there in silence. Mr Bobologo

looked at the girls, who were still chopping vegetables with an air of studied concentration. Mma Ramotswe looked at the cup of tea. And the girls looked at the vegetables.

AFTER THEY had finished inspecting the kitchen—which was very clean, Mma Ramotswe noticed—they went out and sat on the verandah. There was still no tea, and when Mma Ramotswe, in a last desperate bid, mentioned that she was thirsty, a glass of water was called for. She sipped on this in a resigned way, imagining that it was bush tea, which helped slightly, but not a great deal.

"Now that you have seen the House of Hope," said Mr Bobologo, "you can ask me anything you like about it. Or you can tell me what you think. I don't mind. We have nothing to hide in the House of Hope."

Mma Ramotswe lifted her glass to her lips, noticing the greasy fingerprints around its rim, the fingerprints of those girls in the kitchen, she imagined. But this did not concern her. We all have fingerprints, after all.

"I think that this is a very good place," she began. "You are doing very good work."

"Yes, I am," said Mr Bobologo.

Mma Ramotswe looked out at the garden, at the rows of beans. A large black dung beetle was optimistically rolling a tiny trophy, a fragment of manure from the vegetable beds, back towards its home somewhere—a small bit of nature struggling with another small bit of nature, but as important as anything else in the world.

She turned to Mr Bobologo. "I was wondering, Rra," she began. "I was wondering why the girls come here. And why do they stay, if they want to be bar girls in the first place?"

Mr Bobologo nodded. This was clearly the obvious question to ask. "Some of them are very young and are sent here by the social work department or the police when they see them going into bars. Those girls have to stay, or the police will take them back to their village.

"Then there are the other bad girls, the ones our people meet down at the bus station or outside the bars. They may have nowhere to stay. They may be hungry. They may have been beaten up by some man. They are ready to come here then."

Mma Ramotswe listened carefully. The

House of Hope might be a rather dispiriting place, but it was better than the alternative.

"This is very interesting. Most of us are doing nothing about these things. You are doing something. That is very good." She paused. "But how did you come to do this work, Rra? Why do you give up all your time to this thing? You are a busy teacher, and you have much to do at the school. Instead, you very kindly come and give up all your time to this House of Hope."

Mr Bobologo thought for a moment. Mma Ramotswe noticed that his hands were clasped together; her question had unsettled him.

"I will tell you something, Mma," he said after a few moments. "I would not like you to speak about it, please. Will you give me your word that you will not speak about it?"

Instinctively Mma Ramotswe nodded, immediately realising that this would put her in difficulty if he said something that she needed to report to her client. But she had agreed to keep his secret, and she would honour that.

Mr Bobologo spoke quietly. "Something happened to me, Mma. Something happened some years ago, and I have not forgotten this thing. I had a daughter, you see, by my wife who is late. She was our first born, and our only child. I was very proud of her, as only a father can be proud. She was clever and did well at Gaborone Secondary School.

"Then one day she came back from school, and she was a different girl. Just like that. She paid no attention to me and she started to go out at night. I tried to keep her in and she would scream at me and stamp her feet. I did not know what to do. I could not raise a hand to her, as there was no mother, and a father does not strike a motherless child. I tried to reason with her, and she just said that I was an old man and I did not understand the things that she now understood.

"And then she left. She was just sixteen when this happened. She left, and I looked everywhere and asked everybody about her. Until one day I heard that she had been seen over the border, down in Mafikeng, and that this place where she had been seen, this place . . ." He faltered, and Mma Ramotswe reached out to him, in a gesture of sympathy and reassurance.

"You can carry on when you are ready, Rra," she said. But she already knew what he was going to say and he need not have continued.

"This place was a bar down there. I went there and my heart was hammering within me. I could not believe that my daughter would be in such a place. But she was, and she did not want to talk to me. I cried out to her and a man with a broken nose, a young man in a smart suit, a tsotsi type, came and threatened me. He said, **Go home, uncle. Your daughter is not your property. Go home, or pay for one of these girls, like everybody else**. Those were his words, Mma."

Mma Ramotswe was silent. Her hand was on his shoulder, and it remained there.

Mr Bobologo raised his head and looked up into the sky, high above the shade netting. "And so I said to myself that I would work to help these girls, because there are other fathers, just like me, who have this awful thing happen to them. These men are my brothers, Mma. I hope that you understand that."

Mma Ramotswe swallowed. "I understand very well," she said. "I understand. Your heart is broken, Rra. I understand that."

"It is broken inside me," echoed Mr Bobologo. "You are right about that, Mma."

There was not much else to be said, and they made their way down the path to Mma Ramotswe's tiny white van, parked under a tree. But as they walked, Mma Ramotswe decided to ask another question, more by way of making conversation than to elicit information.

"What are your plans for the House of Hope, Rra?"

Mr Bobologo turned and looked back at the house. "We are going to build an extension there at the side," he said. "We shall have new showers and a room where the girls can learn sewing. That is what we are going to do."

"That will be expensive," said Mma Ramotswe. "Extensions always seem to cost more than the house itself. These builders are greedy men."

Mr Bobologo laughed. "But I will shortly be in a position to pay," he said. "I think that I may be a rich man before too long."

Had Mma Ramotswe been less experienced than she was, had she not been the founder of the No. 1 Ladies' Detective Agency, this remark would have caused her to falter, to miss her step. But she was an experienced woman, whose job had shown her all of human life, and so she appeared quite unperturbed by what he had said. But these last few words that Mr Bobologo uttered—every one of them—fell into the pond of memory with a resounding splash.

CHAPTER FIFTEEN

BAD MEN ARE JUST
LITTLE BOYS, UNDERNEATH

THE FOLLOWING morning at Tlokweng Road Speedy Motors, when the morning rush had abated, Mma Ramotswe decided to stretch her legs. She had been sitting at her desk, dictating a letter to a client, while Mma Makutsi's pencil moved over the page of her notepad with a satisfactory squeak. Shorthand had been one of her strongest subjects at the Botswana Secretarial College, and she enjoyed taking dictation.

"Many secretaries these days don't have shorthand," Mma Makutsi had remarked to Mma Ramotswe. "Can you believe it, Mma? They call themselves secretaries, and they don't have shorthand. What would Mr Pitman think?"

"Who is this Mr Pitman?" asked Mma Ramotswe. "What is he thinking about?"

"He is a very famous man," said Mma Makutsi. "He invented shorthand. He wrote books about it. He is one of the great heroes of the secretarial movement."

"I see," said Mma Ramotswe. "Perhaps they should put up a statue to him at the Botswana Secretarial College. In that way he would be re-membered."

"That is a very good idea," said Mma Makutsi. "But I do not think they will do it. They would have to raise the money from the graduates, and I do not think that some of those girls—the ones who do not know any-thing about shorthand, and who only managed to get something like fifty per cent in the exams—I do not think they would pay."

Mma Ramotswe nodded vaguely. She was not particularly interested in the affairs of the Botswana Secretarial College, although she al-ways listened politely when Mma Makutsi sounded off about such matters. Most people had something in their lives that was particularly im-portant to them, and she supposed that the Botswana Secretarial College was as good a cause as any. What was it in her own case, she wondered? Tea? Surely she had something more important than that; but what? She looked at Mma Makutsi, as if for inspiration, but none came, and she decided to return to the subject later, in an idle moment, when one had time for this sort of unsettling philosophical speculation.

Now, the morning's dictation finished and the letters duly signed, Mma Ramotswe arose from her desk, leaving Mma Makutsi to address the envelopes and find the right postage stamps in the mail drawer. Mma Ramotswe glanced out of the window; it was precisely the sort of morning she appreciated—not too hot, and yet with an empty, open sky, flooded with sunlight. This was the sort of morning that birds liked, she thought; when they could stretch their wings and sing out; the sort of morning when you could fill your lungs with air and inhale nothing but the fragrance of acacia and the grass and the sweet, sweet smell of cattle.

She left the office by the back door and stood outside, her eyes closed, the sun on her face. It would be good to be back in Mochudi, she thought, to be sitting in front of somebody's house peeling vegetables, or crocheting something perhaps. That's what she had done when she was a girl, and had sat with her cousin, who was adept at crocheting and made place mat after place mat in fine white thread; so many place mats that every table in Botswana could have been covered twice over, but which somebody, somewhere, bought and sold on. These days she had no time for crocheting, and she wondered whether she would even remember how to do it. Of course, crocheting was like riding a bicycle, which people said that you never forgot how to do once you had learned it. But was that true? Surely there were things that one might forget how to do, if enough time elapsed between the occasions on which one had to do whatever it was that one had forgotten. Mma Ramotswe had once come across somebody who had forgotten his Setswana, and she had been astonished, and shocked. This person had gone to live in Mozambique as a young man and had spoken Tsonga there, and had learned Portuguese too. When he came back to Botswana, thirty years later, it seemed as if he were a foreigner, and she had seen him look puzzled when people used quite simple, everyday Setswana words. To lose your own language was like forgetting your mother, and as sad, in a way. We must not lose Setswana, she thought, even if we speak a great deal of English these days, because that would be like losing part of one's soul.

Mma Makutsi, of course, had another language tucked away in her background. Her mother had been a speaker of Ikalanga, because she had come from Marapong, where they spoke a dialect of Ikalanga called Lilima. That made life very complicated, thought Mma Ramotswe, because that meant that she spoke a minor version of a minor language. Mma Makutsi had been brought up speaking both Setswana, her father's language, and this strange version of Ikalanga, and then had learned English at school, because that was how one got on in life. You could never even get to the Botswana Secretarial College if you spoke no English, and you would certainly never get anywhere near ninety-seven per cent unless your English was almost faultless, like the English that schoolteachers **used** to speak.

Mma Ramotswe had more or less forgotten that Mma Makutsi spoke Ikalanga until one day she had used an Ikalanga word in the middle of a sentence, and it had stuck out.

"I have hurt my gumbo," Mma Makutsi had said.

Mma Ramotswe had looked at her in surprise. "Your gumbo?"

"Yes," said Mma Makutsi. "When I was walking to work today, I stepped into a pothole and hurt my gumbo." She paused, noticing the look of puzzlement on Mma Ramotswe's face. Then she realised. "I'm sorry," she said. "**Gumbo** is foot in Ikalanga. If you speak Ikalanga, your foot is your gumbo."

"I see," said Mma Ramotswe. "That is a very strange word. Gumbo."

"It is not strange," said Mma Makutsi, slightly defensively. "There are many different words for foot. It is **foot** in English. In Setswana it is **lonao**, and in Ikalanga it is **gumbo**, which is what it really is."

Mma Ramotswe laughed. "There is no **real** word for foot. You cannot say it is really gumbo, because that is true only for Ikalanga-speaking feet. Each foot has its own name, depending on the language which the foot's mother spoke. That is the way it works, Mma Makutsi."

That had ended the conversation, and no more was said of gumbos.

These, and other, thoughts went through Mma Ramotswe's head as she stood outside the office that morning, stretching, and allowing her mind to wander this way and that. After a few minutes, though, she decided that it was time to get back into the office. Mma Makutsi would have finished addressing the letters by now, and she wanted to tell her about yesterday's visit to the House of Hope. There was a lot to be said about that, and she thought it would be useful to discuss it with her assistant. Mma Makutsi often came up with very shrewd observations, although in the case of Mr Bobologo no particular shrewdness was required to work out what his motives were. And yet, and yet . . . One could not say that he was an insincere man. He was patently sincere when it came to bar girls, but marriage, perhaps, was another matter. Mma Makutsi might have valuable insights into this, and this would help clarify the situation in Mma Ramotswe's mind.

Mma Ramotswe opened her eyes and started to make her way back into the office. She was intercepted in the doorway, though, by Mma Makutsi, who looked anxious.

"There is something wrong," Mma Makutsi whispered to her. "There is something wrong with Mr J.L.B. Matekoni. Back there." She gestured towards the garage. "There is something wrong with him."

"Has he hurt himself?" Mma Ramotswe always dreaded the possibility of an accident, particularly with those careless apprentices being allowed to raise cars on ramps and do other dangerous things. Mechanics hurt themselves, it was well-known, just as butchers often had parts of fingers missing, a sight which always made Mma Ramotswe's blood run cold, although the enthusiasm of the butchers for their great chopping knives—the guilty blades, no doubt—seemed undiminished.

Mma Makutsi set her mind at rest. "No, there has not been an accident. But I saw him sitting in the garage with his head in his hands. He looked very miserable, and he hardly greeted me when I walked past him. I think something has happened."

This was not good news. Even if there had been no accident, Mr J.L.B. Matekoni's recovery from his depressive illness was recent enough to make any apparent drop in mood a cause for concern. Dr Moffat, who had treated Mr J.L.B. Matekoni during his illness—with the assistance of Mma Potokwane, it must be recalled, who had taken Mr J.L.B. Matekoni in hand and made him take his pills—had warned that these illnesses could recur. Mma Ramotswe remembered his very words: "You must be watchful, Mma Ramotswe," the doctor had said, in that kind voice he used when he spoke to everybody, even to his rather ill-tempered brown spaniel. "You must be watchful because this illness is like a dark cloud in the sky. It is often there, just over the horizon, but it can blow up very quickly. Watch, and tell me if anything happens."

So far, the recovery had seemed complete, and Mr J.L.B. Matekoni had been as equable and as constant as he always had been. There had been no sign of the lassitude that had come with the illness; no sign of the dark, introspective brooding which had so reduced him. But perhaps this was it coming back. Perhaps the cloud had blown over and had covered his sky.

Mma Ramotswe thanked Mma Makutsi and made her way into the garage. The two apprentices were bent over the engine of a car, spanners in hand, and Mr J.L.B. Matekoni was sitting on his old canvas chair near the compressor, his head sunk in his hands, just as Mma Makutsi had seen him.

"Now then, Mr J.L.B. Matekoni," said Mma Ramotswe breezily. "You seem to be thinking very hard about something. Can I make you a cup of tea to help you think?"

Mr J.L.B. Matekoni looked up, and as he did so Mma Ramotswe realised, with relief, that the illness had not returned. He looked worried, certainly, but it was a very different look from the haunted look he had developed during the illness. This was a real worry, she thought; not a worry about shadows and imaginary wrongs and dying; all those things which had so tormented him when he was ill.

"Yes, I am thinking," he said. "I am thinking that I have dug myself into a mess. I am like a potato in . . ." He stopped, unable to complete the metaphor.

"Like a potato?" asked Mma Ramotswe.

"Like a potato in a . . ." He stopped again. "I don't know. But I have done a very foolish thing in involving myself in this business."

Mma Ramotswe was perplexed, and asked him what business he meant.

"This whole business with that butcher's car," he said. "I went round to First Class Motors yesterday afternoon."

"Ah!" said Mma Ramotswe, and thought:

this is my fault. I urged him to go and now this has happened. So, rather than say Ah! again, she said, "Oh!"

"Yes," went on Mr J.L.B. Matekoni miserably. "I went up there yesterday afternoon. The man who runs the place was at a funeral in Molepolole, and so I spoke to one of his assistants. And this man said that he had seen the butcher's car round at my garage and he had mentioned it to his boss, who was very cross. He said that I was taking his clients, and that he was going to come round and see me about it this morning, when he arrived back from Molepolole. He said that his boss was going to 'sort me out.' That's what he said, Mma Ramotswe. Those were his words. I didn't even have the chance to complain, as I had intended to. I didn't even have the chance."

Mma Ramotswe folded her arms. "Who is this man?" she snapped angrily. "What is his name, and who does he think he is? Where is he from?"

Mr J.L.B. Matekoni sighed. "He is called Molefi. He is a horrible man from Tlokweng. People are scared of him. He gives mechanics a bad name."

Mma Ramotswe said nothing for a moment. She felt sorry for Mr J.L.B. Matekoni, who was a very peaceful man and who did not like conflict. He was not one to start an argument, and yet she rather wished that he would stand up to this Molefi man a bit more. Such people were bullies and the only thing to do was to stand up to them. If only Mr J.L.B. Matekoni were a bit braver . . . Did she really want him to fight, though? It was quite out of character, and that was just as well. She could not abide men who threw their weight around, and that was one of the reasons why she so admired Mr J.L.B. Matekoni. Although he was physically strong from all that lifting of engines, he was gentle. And she loved him for that, as did so many others.

She unfolded her arms and walked over to stand beside Mr J.L.B. Matekoni. "When is this man coming?" she asked.

"Any time now. They said this morning. That is all they said."

"I see." She turned away, intending to go over to the apprentices and have a word with them. They would have to rally round to deal with this Molefi person. They were young men . . . She stopped. Tlokweng. Mr J.L.B. Matekoni had said that Molefi was from Tlokweng, and Tlokweng was where the orphan farm was, and the orphan farm made her think of Mma Potokwane.

She turned back again, ignoring the apprentices, and walked briskly back into her office. Mma Makutsi looked up at her expectantly as she came in.

"Is he all right? I was worried."

"He is fine," she said. "He is worried about something. That man at First Class Motors has been threatening him. That's what's going on."

Mma Makutsi whistled softly, as she sometimes did in moments of crisis. "That is very bad, Mma. That is very bad."

Mma Ramotswe nodded. "Mma Makutsi," she said. "I am going out to Tlokweng right now. This very minute. Please telephone Mma Potokwane and tell her that I am coming to fetch her in my van and that we need her help. Please do that right now. I am going."

WHEN MMA RAMOTSWE arrived at the orphan farm, Mma Potokwane was not in her office. The door was open, but the large, rather shabby chair in which Mma Potokwane was often to be found—when she was not bustling round the kitchens or the houses—was empty. Mma Ramotswe rushed outside again and looked about anxiously. It had not occurred to her that Mma Potokwane might not be found; she was always on duty, it seemed. And yet she could be in town, doing some shopping, or she could even be far away, down in Lobatse, perhaps, picking up some new orphan.

"Mma Ramotswe?"

She gave a start, looking about her. It was Mma Potokwane's voice, but where was she?

"Here!" came the voice. "Under this tree! Here I am, Mma Ramotswe."

The matron of the orphan farm was in the shade of a large mango tree, merging with the shadows. Mma Ramotswe had looked right past her, but now Mma Potokwane stepped out from under the drooping branches of the tree.

"I have been watching a special mango," she said. "It is almost ready and I have told the children that they are not to pick it. I am keeping it for my husband, who likes to eat a good mango." She dusted her hands on her skirts as she walked towards Mma Ramotswe. "Would you like to see this mango, Mma Ramotswe?" she asked. "It is very fine. Very yellow now."

"You are very kind, Mma," called out Mma

Ramotswe. "I will come and see it some other time, I think. Right now there is something urgent to talk to you about. Something very urgent."

Mma Potokwane joined her friend outside the office, and Mma Ramotswe quickly explained that she needed her to come to the garage, "to help with Mr J.L.B. Matekoni." Mma Potokwane listened gravely and nodded her agreement. They could go straight away, she said. No, she would not need to fetch anything from her office. "All I need is my voice," she said, pointing to her chest. "And it is all there. Ready to be used."

They travelled back to the garage in the tiny white van, now heavily laden and riding low on its shock absorbers. Mma Ramotswe drove more quickly than she normally did, sounding the horn impatiently at indolent donkeys and children on wobbling cycles. There was only one hold-up—a small herd of rickety cattle, badly looked after by all appearances, which blocked the road until Mma Potokwane opened her window and shouted at them in a stentorian voice. The cattle looked surprised, and indignant, but they moved, and the tiny white van continued its journey.

They drew up at Tlokweng Road Speedy Motors a few minutes after the arrival of Molefi. A large red truck was parked outside the garage, blocking the entrance, and on this was written FIRST CLASS MOTORS in ostentatious lettering. Mma Potokwane, to whom the situation had been explained by Mma Ramotswe on the way back, saw this and snorted.

"Big letters," she murmured. "Big nothing."

Mma Ramotswe smiled. She was sure that the summoning of Mma Potokwane was the right thing to do and this remark made her even more certain. Now, as they negotiated their way round the aggressively parked truck and she saw Molefi standing in front of Mr J.L.B. Matekoni, who was looking down at the ground as his visitor remonstrated with him, she realised that they had not arrived a minute too early.

Mma Potokwane bustled forward. "So," she said. "Who do we find here in Mr J.L.B. Matekoni's garage? Molefi? It's you, isn't it? You've come to discuss some difficult mechanical problem with Mr J.L.B. Matekoni, have you? Come for his advice?"

Molefi looked round and glowered. "I am

here on business, Mma. It's business between me and Mr J.L.B. Matekoni." His tone was rude and he compounded the offence by turning his back on Mma Potokwane and facing Mr J.L.B. Matekoni again. Mma Potokwane glanced at Mma Ramotswe, who shook her head in disapproval of Molefi's rudeness.

"Excuse me, Rra," said Mma Potokwane, stepping forward. "I think that perhaps you might have forgotten who I am, but I certainly know exactly who you are."

Molefi turned around in irritation. "Listen, Mma . . ."

"No, you listen to me, Rra," Mma Potokwane said, her voice rising sharply. "I know you, Herbert Molefi. I know your mother. She is my friend. And I have often felt sorry for her, with a son like you."

Molefi opened his mouth to speak, but no sound came.

"Oh yes," went on Mma Potokwane, shaking a finger at him. "You were a bad little boy, and now you are a bad man. You are just a bully, that's what you are. And I have heard this thing about the butcher's car. Oh, yes, I have heard it. And I wonder whether your mother knows it, or your uncles? Do they know it?"

Molefi's collapse was sudden and complete. Mma Ramotswe watched the effect of these words and saw the burly figure shrink visibly in the face of Mma Potokwane's tongue-lashing.

"No? They have not heard about it?" she pressed on. "Well, I think I might just let them know. And you, you, Herbert Molefi, who thinks that he can go round bullying people like Mr J.L.B. Matekoni here, had better think again. Your mother can still tell you a thing or two, can't she? And your uncles. They will not be pleased and they might just give their cattle to somebody else when they die, might they not? I think so, Rra. I think so."

"Now, Mma," said Molefi. "I am just talking to Mr J.L.B. Matekoni, that is all I am doing."

"Pah!" retorted Mma Potokwane. "Don't you try to tell me your lies. You just shut that useless mouth of yours for a little while and let Mr J.L.B. Matekoni tell you what to do about that poor man you've cheated. And I'll just stand here and listen, just in case. Then we'll think about whether your people out at Tlokweng need to be told about this."

Molefi was silent, and he remained silent while Mr J.L.B. Matekoni quietly and reasonably told him that he would have to make a refund to the butcher and that he should be careful in the future, as other garages in the town would be watching what he did. "You let us all down, you see," said Mr J.L.B. Matekoni. "If one mechanic cheats, then all mechanics are blamed. That is what happens, and that is why you should change your ways."

"Yes," said Mma Ramotswe, making her first contribution. "You just be careful in future, or Mma Potokwane will hear of it. Do you understand?"

Molefi nodded silently.

"Has a goat eaten your tongue?" asked Mma Ramotswe.

"No," said Molefi quietly. "I understand what you have said, Mma."

"Good," said Mma Potokwane. "Now the best thing you can do is to move that truck of yours and get back to your garage. I think that you will have an envelope in your office. That will do for the letter you are going to write to that man in Lobatse." She paused before adding, "And send me a copy, if you don't mind."

There was not much more to be said after that. Molefi reversed his truck and drove angrily

away. Mr J.L.B. Matekoni thanked Mma Potokwane, rather sheepishly, thought Mma
Ramotswe, and the two women went into the
office of the No. 1 Ladies' Detective Agency,
where Mma Makutsi had boiled the kettle for
tea. Mma Makutsi had listened to the encounter from the doorway. She was somewhat
in awe of Mma Potokwane, but now she asked
her a question.

"Is his mother that fierce?"

"I have no idea," said Mma Potokwane.
"I've only seen his mother; I've never met her,
and I took a bit of a risk with that. But usually
bullies have severe mothers and bad fathers,
and they are usually frightened of them. That is
why they are bullies, I think. There is something wrong at home. I have found that with
children in general and this applies to men as
well. I think that I shall have to write about
that if I ever write a book about how to run an
orphan farm."

"You must write that book, Mma," urged
Mma Ramotswe. "I would read it, even if I was
not planning to run an orphan farm."

"Thank you," said Mma Potokwane.
"Maybe I shall do that one day. But at the moment I am so busy looking after all those or-

phans and making tea and baking fruit cake and all those things. There seems very little time for writing books."

"That is a pity," said Mma Makutsi. It had just occurred to her that she might write a book herself, if Mma Potokwane, of all people, was considering doing so. **The Principles of Typing**, perhaps, although that was not perhaps the most exciting title one might imagine. **How to Get Ninety-Seven Per Cent**. Now that was much, much better, and would be bought by all those people, those many, many people who would love to get ninety-seven per cent in whatever it was that they were doing and who knew that perhaps they never would. At least they could hope, which was an important thing. We must be able to hope. We simply must.

CHAPTER SIXTEEN

MMA POTOKWANE AND MMA RAMOTSWE DISCUSS MARRIAGE

THESE MATTERS were distractions, of course, but at least the matter of the butcher's car was now sorted out and Mr J.L.B. Matekoni, only so recently worried on two fronts—the parachute jump and First Class Motors—could now look forward to the immediate future with greater equanimity. Mma Potokwane had been magnificent, as she always was, and had dispatched the bullying Herbert Molefi with the same ease as she dealt with ten-year-old bullies. She had been happy to do this, as she owed Mr J.L.B. Matekoni a great deal, with his constant and unquestioning availability to fix bits and pieces of machinery on the orphan farm. And Mma Potokwane, like everybody else who came into

contact with him, recognised in Mr J.L.B.
Matekoni those qualities which endeared him
to so many and which meant that most people
would do anything for him: his courtesy, his
reliability, his sheer decency. If only all men,
or even more men, were like that, thought
Mma Potokwane, indeed thought all the
women of Botswana. If only you could trust
men in the same way in which you could trust
a close woman friend; instead of which, men
tended to let women down, not always deliberately, but just because they were selfish or
they became bored, or their heads were turned
in some way. It was very easy to turn a man's
head; a glamorous woman could do it just by
looking at a man and lowering her eyelids
once or twice. That could make an apparently
steadfast man quite unpredictable, particularly if that man were of an age where he was
starting to feel unsure of himself as a man.

Mma Ramotswe was lucky to be engaged
to Mr J.L.B. Matekoni, thought Mma Potokwane. He was exactly the right choice for her,
as she was a fine woman and she deserved a
good man like Mr J.L.B. Matekoni with
whom to share her life. It was hard being a

woman by oneself, particularly when one was in a job such as Mma Ramotswe's, and it was important to have a man on whom one could call for assistance and support. So Mma Ramotswe had made a wise choice, even if all those years ago she had shown a distinct lack of judgment in marrying Note Mokoti, the trumpet player. Mokoti, Matekoni: similar names, reflected Mma Potokwane, but how different the men who bore the names.

Of course there was the question of the length of the engagement and the slowness with which preparations were being made for the wedding, indeed if any preparations were being made at all. This was a puzzle to Mma Potokwane, and while Mma Makutsi made tea that day, after the disposal of Herbert Molefi, Mma Potokwane decided to raise the matter with Mma Ramotswe. She was direct rather than allusive; rather too direct, thought Mma Makutsi, who listened but did not say anything. She tended to feel inhibited in the presence of Mma Potokwane, largely because she felt the other woman was so much more confident and experienced than she was. There was also an element of disapproval in

Mma Makutsi's attitude—not that she would ever have expressed it. She thought that Mma Potokwane was too ready to take advantage of Mr J.L.B. Matekoni's good nature. The kindness of men like that could be exploited by forceful women, and there was no doubt but that Mma Potokwane was in the vanguard of the forceful women of Botswana, their very standard bearer, their champion.

So Mma Makutsi said nothing, but listened very carefully as Mma Potokwane raised the subject of marriage and weddings, virtually under the nose of Mr J.L.B. Matekoni, who had resumed work on a car next door. And what if he had walked in the door and heard her speaking in these terms; what then? Mma Makutsi was astonished at the matron's tactlessness.

"Such a very good man," came the opening gambit. "He has been very helpful to us at the orphan farm. All the children love him and call him their special uncle. So there he is an uncle, but not yet a husband!"

Mma Ramotswe smiled. "Yes, he is a fine man. And he will make a good husband one day. That is why I agreed to his proposal."

Mma Potokwane looked at her fingernails, as if absorbed by some cuticular matter. "One day?" she said. "Which day? When is this day you are talking about? Next week, do you think? Or next year?"

"Not next week," said Mma Ramotswe evenly. "Maybe next year. Who knows?"

Mma Potokwane was quick to press home on this question. "But does he know? That's the important thing. Does Mr J.L.B. Matekoni know?"

Mma Ramotswe made a gesture which indicated that she did not know the answer and that indeed the matter was not important as far as she was concerned. "Mr J.L.B. Matekoni is not a man who makes hasty decisions. He likes to think about things for a long time."

Mma Potokwane shook her head. "That is a weakness, Mma Ramotswe," she said. "I'm sorry to have to say this, but there are some men who need to be organised by women. Every woman knows this. It is only now, in these modern days, with men getting ideas about running their lives without any help from women—those dangerous, bad ideas—it is only now that we see how much these poor men need our assistance. It is a very sad thing."

"I don't know about that," countered Mma Ramotswe. "I know that ladies have to help men in many things. Sometimes it is necessary to push men a little bit. But one should not take it too far."

"Well it's not going too far to push men to the altar," retorted Mma Potokwane. "Women have always done that, and that is how marriages take place. If you left it up to men, they would never get there. Nobody would be married. You have to remind men to get married."

Mma Ramotswe looked at her guest thoughtfully. Should she allow Mma Potokwane to help her to get Mr J.L.B. Matekoni a little bit further along the road to matrimony? It was awkward for her; she did not want him to form the impression that she was interfering too much in his life; men did not like that, and many men would simply leave if they felt this was happening. At the same time, if Mr J.L.B. Matekoni did need slight prompting, it would be easier for this to come from Mma Potokwane, who had a long history of pushing Mr J.L.B. Matekoni about, most of it with considerable success. One only had to remember the matter of that old pump at the orphan farm which she had cajoled him into maintaining well beyond the point where he had formed the professional opinion that it should be scrapped. And one only had to recall the recent instance of the parachute jump, which was another example of Mr J.L.B. Matekoni being made to agree to something to which he did not wish to agree. Perhaps there was a case for assistance in this matter too . . .

No, no, no! thought Mma Makutsi, willing her employer not to yield to the imprecations of the manipulative Mma Potokwane. She could see that Mma Ramotswe was tempted, and if only Mma Potokwane had not been there she would have urged Mma Ramotswe in the most vocal terms not to do anything which could have serious consequences for the engagement or, even more importantly, for Mr J.L.B. Matekoni's state of health. Dr Moffat had told them all that Mr J.L.B. Matekoni was not to be put under any stress, and what could be more stressful than to be the object of a determined campaign by Mma Potokwane? Look at that Herbert Molefi man, crushed by her tongue and unable to do anything to defend himself. If only the Botswana Defence Force could have seen it, thought Mma Makutsi, they would have signed her up immediately and made her a sergeant-major or a general or whatever they called those soldiers who ordered all the other soldiers about. Or even better, Mma Potokwane could have been used as a weapon to intimidate the enemy, whoever they were. They would see Mma Potokwane coming towards them and they would be incapable of doing anything, reduced by the sight to mute and helpless boys.

None of these thoughts reached Mma Ramotswe, although she did briefly glance across the room to where Mma Makutsi was busying herself with the tea. But Mma Makutsi was turned away at the time and Mma Ramotswe did not see her expression, so she had no idea of the other woman's feelings.

"Well," began Mma Ramotswe cautiously, "how would we help Mr J.L.B. Matekoni to make a decision? How would we do it?"

"We don't have to help him make any decision," replied Mma Potokwane firmly. "He has already made the decision to marry you, has he not? What is an engagement? It is an agreement to marry. That decision is made, Mma. No, all we have to do is to arrange for him to carry it out. We need to get a date, and then we need to make sure that he gets to the right place on the date. And in my view that means that we should make all the plans and then pick him up on the day and take him there. That's right, we'll **take** him there."

At this, Mma Makutsi spun round and stared at Mma Ramotswe open-mouthed. Surely Mma Ramotswe would see the danger in this? If you took a man to the church, he would simply run away. No man would be forced in this way, and certainly not a mature and intelligent man like Mr J.L.B. Matekoni. This was the stuff of disaster, and Mma Ramotswe should put a stop to these ridiculous fantasies at once. But instead—and here Mma Makutsi drew in her breath in astonishment—instead she was nodding her head in agreement!

"Good," said Mma Potokwane enthusiastically. "I can see that you agree with me. So now all we have to do is to plan the wedding and get everything ready—in secret of course—and then on the day get him into a suit somehow . . ."

"And how would you do that?" interrupted Mma Ramotswe. "You know the sort of clothes that Mr J.L.B. Matekoni normally wears. Those overalls. That old hat with grease round the rim. Those suede veldschoens. How will we get him out of those and into suitable clothes for church?"

"Leave that side of it to me," said Mma Potokwane confidently. "In fact, simply leave the whole thing to me. We can have the wedding out at the orphan farm. I will get my house-mothers to cook all the food. I will make all the arrangements and all you will have to do is to get there at the time I will tell you. Then you will be married. I promise you."

Mma Ramotswe looked doubtful and was about to open her mouth to say something when Mma Potokwane continued. "You needn't worry, Mma Ramotswe. I am a very tactful person. I know how to do these things. You know that."

Mma Makutsi's eyes widened, but she knew that there was no stopping Mma Potokwane now, and that events would run their course whatever she tried to do. And what was there for her to do? She could attempt to persuade Mma Ramotswe to forbid Mma Potokwane from proceeding with her plan, but that would be unlikely to happen once Mma Ramotswe had agreed to it. She could warn Mr J.L.B. Matekoni that he was in danger of being pushed into his own wedding, but then that would seem appallingly disloyal to Mma Ramotswe, and if she did that she might be responsible for his doing something really foolish, such as calling off the engagement altogether. No, there was only one thing for Mma Makutsi to do, and that was to keep out of the whole affair, although she would allow herself one remark, perhaps, just as an aside, to register her disapproval of the whole scheme.

Mma Potokwane did not stay long, but every minute of the visit seemed to drag terribly. An icy atmosphere had developed, with Mma Makutsi sitting in almost complete silence, responding to Mma Potokwane's remarks only in the briefest and most unhelpful of terms.

"You must be very busy," the matron said to her, pointing to the papers on her desk. "I have heard that you are a very efficient secretary. Perhaps you will come out to the orphan farm one day and sort out my office! That would be a good thing to do. You could have a big bonfire of all the spare papers. The children would like that."

"I am too busy," said Mma Makutsi. "Perhaps you should employ a secretary. There is a very fine secretarial college, you know, the Botswana Secretarial College. They will provide you with a name. They will also tell you what the right salary will be."

Mma Potokwane took a sip of her tea and looked at Mma Makutsi over the rim of the cup.

"Thank you, Mma," she said. "That is a good suggestion. But of course we are an orphan farm and we do not have very much money for secretaries and the like. That is why kind people—people like Mr J.L.B. Matekoni—offer their services free."

"He is a kind man," agreed Mma Makutsi. "That is why people take advantage of him."

Mma Potokwane put down her cup and turned to Mma Ramotswe. "You are very lucky to have an assistant who can give you good advice," she said politely. "That must make your life easier."

Mma Ramotswe, who had been quite aware of the developing tension, did her best to smooth over the situation.

"Most tasks in this life are better done by two people," she said. "I am sure that you get a lot of support from the housemothers. I am sure that they have good advice to give too."

Mma Potokwane rose to her feet to leave. "Yes, Mma," she said, glancing at Mma Makutsi. "We must all help one another. That is very true."

One of the apprentices was detailed to drive Mma Potokwane back to the orphan farm, leaving Mma Ramotswe and Mma Makutsi alone in the office once again. Mma Makutsi, sitting at her desk, looked down at her shoes, as she often did in moments of crisis; her shoes, always her allies, but now so unhelpfully mute, as if to convey: **don't look at us, we said nothing. You were the one, Boss.** (In her mind, her shoes always addressed her as Boss, as the apprentices addressed Mr J.L.B. Matekoni. This was right for shoes, which should know their place.)

"I'm sorry, Mma," Mma Makutsi suddenly burst out. "I had to stand there making tea while that woman gave you that terrible, terrible advice. And I couldn't say anything because I always feel too small to say anything when she's around. She makes me feel as if I'm still six years old."

Mma Ramotswe looked at her assistant with concern. "She is just trying to help. She's bossy, of course, but that is because she is a matron. Every matron is bossy; if they weren't then nothing would get done. Mma Potokwane's job is to be bossy. But she is just trying to help."

"But it won't help," wailed Mma Makutsi. "It won't help at all. You can't force Mr J.L.B. Matekoni to get married."

"Nobody's forcing him," said Mma Ramotswe. "He asked me to marry him. I said yes. He has never once, not once, said that he does not want to get married. Have you ever heard him say that? No, well there you are."

"But he will agree to a wedding one day," said Mma Makutsi. "You can wait."

"Can I, Mma?" said Mma Ramotswe quickly. "Can I wait forever? And why should I wait all this time and put up with all this uncertainty? My life is going past. Tick, tick. Like a clock that is running too fast. And all the time I remain an engaged lady. People are talking, believe me. They say: there's that lady who's engaged forever to Mr J.L.B. Matekoni. That's what they are saying."

Mma Makutsi was silent, and Mma Ramotswe continued, "I don't want to force Mr J.L.B. Matekoni to do anything he doesn't want to do. But in this case I think that there is some sort of block—there is some sort of reason why he cannot make up his mind. I think it is in his nature. Dr Moffat said that when people had that illness—that depression thing—then they might not be able to make decisions. Even when they seem quite well. Maybe there is a little corner of that in Mr J.L.B. Matekoni. So all we are trying to do is help him."

Mma Makutsi shook her head. "I don't know, Mma. You may be right, but I am very worried. I do not think that you should let Mma Potokwane stick her nose into this business."

"I understand what you are saying to me," said Mma Ramotswe. "But I have reached the end of waiting. I have waited, waited,

waited. No date has been mentioned. Nothing has been said. No cattle have been bought for the feast. No chairs have been fixed up. No aunties have been written to. Nothing has been done. Nothing. No lady can accept that, Mma."

Mma Makutsi again looked down at her shoes. This time the shoes were vocal: **you just be quiet now**, they said rather rudely.

CHAPTER SEVENTEEN

MR SPOKES SPOKESI, THE AIRWAVE RIDER

IF MMA Ramotswe was still on the shelf, then the following day she was on the wall. She was sitting on the wall in question, the waist-high wall that surrounded the car park of Radio Gabs, enjoying the effervescent company of two seventeen-year-old girls. They were attractive girls, dressed in jeans and bright-coloured blouses that must have cost them a great deal, thought Mma Ramotswe; too much, in fact, because the most expensive parts of their outfit, the labels, were prominently displayed. Mma Ramotswe had never been able to understand why people wanted to have their labels on the outside. In her day, labels had been tucked in, which is where they belonged in her view. One did not walk around the town with one's birth certificate stuck on one's back; why then should clothes have their labels on the outside? It was a very vulgar display, she felt, but it did not really matter with these nice girls, who were talking so quickly and in such an amusing way about all the things which interested them, which was not very much, at the end of the day; in fact which was only one subject when one came to think of it, or two, possibly, if one included fashion.

"Some people say that there are no good-looking men in Gaborone," said Constance, the girl sitting to Mma Ramotswe's right. "But I think that is nonsense. There are many good-looking men in Gaborone. I have seen hundreds, just in one day. Hundreds."

Her friend, Kokotso, looked dubious. "Oh?" she said. "Where can I go to see all these good-looking men? Is there a club for good-looking men maybe? Can I go and stand outside the door and watch?"

"There is no such club," laughed Constance. "And if there were, then the men would not be able to get near it, for all the girls standing at the door. It would not work."

Mma Ramotswe decided to join in. It

was many years since she had participated in such a conversation, and she was beginning to enjoy it. "It all depends on what you mean by good-looking," she said. "Some men are good-looking in one department and not so good-looking in another. Some men have nice wide shoulders, but very thin legs. Very thin legs are not so good. I know one girl who left a good boyfriend because his legs were too thin."

"Ow!" exclaimed Kokotso. "That girl made a very bad move. If he was a good boyfriend in other ways, then why leave him because of his thin legs?"

"Perhaps she felt that she wanted to laugh whenever she saw his legs," suggested Constance. "That would not have made him happy. Men do not like to be laughed at. Men do not think they are funny."

This made Mma Ramotswe smile. "That is very amusing! Men do not think they are funny! That is very true, Mma. Very true. You must not laugh at a man, or he will go and hide away like a village dog."

"But there is a serious point," said Kokotso. "Can you call a man good-looking if he has a handsome face but very short legs? I have known men like that. They are good-looking when they are sitting down, but when they stand up and you see how short their legs are you think Oh my God, these are short, short legs!"

"And sometimes, have you noticed," Constance interjected, "have you noticed how men's legs go out at the knees and make a circle? Have you seen that? That is very funny. I always want to laugh when I see men like that."

Kokotso now lowered herself off the wall and began to walk in a circle, her arms hanging loose, her chin stuck out. "This is how men walk," she said. "Have you seen it? They walk like this, almost like monkeys."

It was difficult not to laugh, and if she had thought that these girls seriously entertained this low opinion of men she would have frowned instead, but she knew that these were girls who liked men, a great deal, and so joined Constance in shrieking with laughter at Kokotso's imitation of . . . of the apprentices! How accurate she was, and she did not even know them. To imitate one young man of that sort, then, was to imitate them all.

Kokotso resumed her seat on the wall and

for a moment there was silence. Mma
Ramotswe was rather surprised at herself, sitting there on a wall with two young women
less than half her age, talking about good-
looking men. She had seen them when she
had driven past the Radio Gabs station at
lunch-time, not intending to call in until later
that afternoon, but realising that this was exactly the opportunity she was looking for. So
she had parked the tiny white van round the
corner and had walked back, casually, as one
who was spending the lunch hour in a quiet
ramble. She had stopped at the entrance to
the car park and had gone up to the girls
to ask them if they knew the correct time.
From there it had been easy. The question
about the time had been followed by a remark
on how tiring it was to have to walk all the
way into town and would they mind if she sat
on the wall with them for a few minutes while
she summoned up her energy?

Of course she had suspected that these girls
were not sitting on the wall just because it was
any wall. This was the Radio Gabs wall, and
these young ladies were watching the entrance
to the radio station. And if one were to ask
oneself why girls like this would be watching

the entrance to the radio station, it was surely not to see who went in, but who came out. And amongst those who were likely to come out, in terms of good looks and general interest to fashion-conscious girls of seventeen or so, who could it be but Mr Spokes Spokesi, the well-known disc-jockey and radio personality? Spokes Spokesi's show, which stretched from nine in the morning until one-thirty in the afternoon, **Cool Time with Spokes**, was a favourite of younger people in Gaborone. The apprentices listened to it while they were working—although Mr J.L.B. Matekoni, when he could bear it no longer, would switch off their radio in a gesture of defiance. He at least had good taste and a limited tolerance for the inane patter which such radio stations pumped out with great enthusiasm. Mma Ramotswe would have had a similar lack of interest in Spokes except for one thing: he was the second name on the list of Mma Holonga's suitors, unlikely though that was, and this meant that she would have to speak to him at some stage.

"Do you listen to this station?" she asked casually.

Constance clapped her hands. "All the time! All the time! It's the best station there is. The latest music, the latest everything, and . . ."

"And Spokes, of course," supplied Kokotso. "Spokes!"

Mma Ramotswe pretended to look blank. "Spokes? Who is this Spokes? Is he a band?"

Kokotso laughed. "Oh, Mma, you're out of touch. Spokes does a show—the best show you can listen to. Can he talk! Oh my! You hear him talking about music and you can just see him sitting there in front of the mike. Oh!"

"And is he good-looking too?" asked Mma Ramotswe.

"He's fabulous," said Constance. "The best-looking man in Gaborone."

"In all Botswana," suggested Kokotso.

"My!" said Mma Ramotswe. "And will we see him if we sit here long enough? Will we see him coming out?"

"Yes," said Constance. "We come here once a week usually just to see Spokes. He talks to us sometimes; sometimes he just waves. He thinks that we work in that building over there and are just sitting here to pass the lunch hour. He doesn't know that we come to see him."

Mma Ramotswe tried to look intrigued. "How old is this Spokes?" she asked.

"Just the right age," said Constance. "He's twenty-eight. And his birthday is . . ."

"The twenty-fourth of July," said Kokotso. "We shall come here on that day with a present for him. He will like that."

"You are very kind," said Mma Ramotswe. She studied the girls for a moment, trying to imagine what it must be like to worship somebody who was, after all, almost a stranger to them. Why did people behave this way with entertainers? What was so special about them? And then she stopped, for she had remembered Note Mokoti and her own feelings for him all those years ago when she was hardly older than these girls. And the memory made her humble; for we should not forget what it is to be young and to have ideas and attitudes that may later seem so fanciful.

"Will he be out soon?" she asked. "Will we have to wait long?"

"It depends," said Constance. "Sometimes he sits inside and talks to the station manager for hours. But on other days he comes out the moment his show goes off the air and he gets into his car. That is his car over there, that red one with the yellow curtains in the back. It is a very smart car."

Mma Ramotswe glanced at the car. First Class Motors, she thought dismissively, but then Kokotso grabbed her arm and Constance whispered in her ear: Spokes!

He came out of the front door, dressed in his hip-hugging jeans, his shirt open to the third button down, a gold chain round his neck; Spokes Spokesi himself, Gaborone icon, silver-tongued rider of the airwaves, good-looking, confident, ice-cool, flashing white teeth.

"Spokes!" murmured Kokotso, and as if he had heard her barely articulated prayer, he turned in their direction, waved, and began to make his way over the car park to where they sat.

"Hiya, girls! Dumela and all the rest of it, etcetera, etcetera, etcetera!"

Kokotso dug Mma Ramotswe in the ribs. "He's coming to speak to us," she whispered. "He's seen us!"

"Hallo there, Spokes," called out Constance. "Your show today was great. Fantastic. That band you played at ten o'clock. To die for!"

"Yes," said Spokes, who was now standing before them, smiling his devastating smile. "Good sound. A good sound."

"This lady hasn't listened to you yet, Spokes," said Kokotso, gesturing towards Mma Ramotswe. "Now she knows. She'll be listening tomorrow morning, won't you, Mma."

Mma Ramotswe smiled. She did not like to lie and would not lie now. "No," she said. "I won't be listening."

Spokes looked at her quizzically. "Why not, Mma? My music's wrong for you? Is that it? Maybe I can play some more oldies."

"That would be nice," said Mma Ramotswe politely. "But please don't worry about me. You play what your listeners want to hear. I'll be all right."

"I like to please everybody," said Spokes agreeably. "Radio Gabs is for everyone."

"And everyone listens, Spokes," said Kokotso. "You know we listen."

"What are you doing today, Spokes?" asked Constance.

Spokes winked at her. "You know I'd like to

take you to the movies, but I have to go and look after the cattle. Sorry about that."

They all laughed at this witticism, Mma Ramotswe included. Then Mma Ramotswe spoke.

"Haven't I seen you before, Rra?" she said, looking at him closely, as if inspecting him. "I'm sure that I've seen you."

Spokes drew back slightly, but seemed bemused. "You see me here and there. Gaborone is not a big place. You might have seen my picture in the papers."

Mma Ramotswe looked doubtful. "No, it wasn't in the papers. No . . ." She paused, as if trying to drag something out of her memory, and then continued, "Yes! That's it. I remember now. I've seen you with that lady who owns the hair-braiding salons. You know the one. I've seen you with her somewhere or other. A party maybe. You were with her. Is she your girlfriend, Rra?"

Her remark made, she watched its effect on him. The easy smile disappeared, and in its place there was a look of anxiety. He glanced at the young girls, who were looking at him eagerly. "Oh that lady! She is my aunty! She is not my girlfriend!"

The girls giggled, and Spokes leaned forward to touch Kokotso lightly on the shoulder. "Meet you later?" he asked. "Metro Club?"

Kokotso squirmed with pleasure. "We'll be there."

"Good," said Spokes, and then, to Mma Ramotswe, "Nice meeting you, aunty. Go carefully."

MMA MAKUTSI listened intently to what Mma Ramotswe had to say when she returned that afternoon from her meeting with Constance, Kokotso, and Spokes.

"I have spent two days on this matter so far," said Mma Ramotswe. "I have met and interviewed two of the suitors on Mma Holonga's list, and neither of them is in the slightest bit suitable. Both can only be interested in her money. One by his own admission—he said it himself, Mma—and the other by the way he behaved."

"Poor Mma Holonga," said Mma Makutsi. "I have read that it is not easy being rich. I have read that you can never tell who is really interested in you or who is interested only in your money."

Mma Ramotswe agreed. "I am going to have to speak to her soon and tell her what progress I have made. I am going to have to say that the first two are definitely unsuitable."

"That is very sad," said Mma Makutsi, thinking how sad it was, too, that there was Mma Holonga with four suitors and there was she with none.

CHAPTER EIGHTEEN

THE PARACHUTE JUMP, AND A UNIVERSAL TRUTH ABOUT THE GIVING AND TAKING OF ADVICE

MMA RAMOTSWE was hoping that Mma Potokwane would forget all about the parachute jump which Charlie, the older apprentice, had agreed to take over from Mr J.L.B. Matekoni. Unfortunately, neither Mma Potokwane nor Charlie himself forgot, and indeed Charlie had actively been seeking sponsorship. People were generous; a parachute jump was a considerably more exciting project than a sponsored walk or run—anybody could do those. A parachute jump required courage and there was always the possibility that it could go badly wrong. This made it difficult to refuse a donation.

The jump was planned for a Saturday. The plane would take off from the airport, out near the ostrich abattoir, would circle the town and would then fly out towards Tlokweng and the orphan farm. At the appropriate moment the apprentice would be given the signal to jump and would land, it was hoped, in a large field at the edge of the orphan farm. All the children would be there, waiting to see the parachute come down, and the ranks of the children would be swelled by several press photographers, an official from the Mayor's office—the Mayor himself would be away at the time—a colonel from the Botswana Defence Force (invited by Mr J.L.B. Matekoni) and the Principal of the Botswana Secretarial College (invited by Mma Makutsi). Mma Ramotswe had invited Dr Moffat, and had asked him whether he could possibly bring his medical bag with him—just in case anything went wrong, which she was certain it would not. She had also invited Mma Holonga, not only because she was something of a public figure who might be expected to attend a charity event as a matter of course, but also because she wanted to speak to her. Apart from these people, the public at large could attend, if it wished. The event had been given wide publicity in the papers, and even Spokes Spokesi had mentioned it on his show on Radio Gabs. He claimed to have done a parachute jump himself, and that it was nothing, "as long as you were brave enough." But things could go wrong, he warned, although he did not propose to say anything more on that subject just then.

Charlie himself seemed very calm. On the day before the jump, Mma Ramotswe had a private word with him at the garage, telling him that there would be no dishonour in his withdrawing, even at this late stage.

"Nobody will think the less of you if you phone Mma Potokwane right now and tell her that you have changed your mind. Nobody will think that you are a coward."

"Yes, they will," said Charlie. "And anyway, I want to do it. I have been practising and I know everything there is to know about parachutes now. You count ten—or is it fifty?—and then you pull the cord. So. Like that. Then you keep your feet together and you roll over on the ground once you land. That is all there is to it."

Mma Ramotswe wanted to say that it was not so simple, but she kept her own counsel.

"You could come with me, Mma Ramotswe," said Charlie, jokingly. "They could make an extra big parachute for you."

Mma Ramotswe ignored this. He could be right, of course; perhaps you needed an especially large parachute if you were of traditional build, or perhaps you just came down faster. But then parachutists of traditional build would land more softly and comfortably, being better padded, and those of particularly traditional build might just roll over when they landed, as barrels do when you drop them.

"Well," she said, after a while, "in your case you must be hoping to land on your bottom, which is much bigger than normal. That will be the best place for you to land. Put your feet up when you get close to the ground and sit down."

The apprentice looked annoyed, but he did not say anything. Instead, he looked in a small mirror which he had hung on a pin near the door that led from the garage into the office. He could often be found standing before this mirror, preening himself, or doing a small, shuffling dance while he looked at his reflection.

ON THE day in question, they all met at Tlokweng Road Speedy Motors: Mma Ramotswe;

the two children, Motholeli and Puso; Mr
J.L.B. Matekoni; Mma Makutsi; and the
younger apprentice. Charlie himself had been
collected from his home several hours earlier
and driven to the airfield by the pilot of the
light aircraft from which he was to jump.

They drove out to the orphan farm in Mma
Ramotswe's tiny white van and in Mr J.L.B.
Matekoni's truck, Mma Makutsi travelling in
the van with Mma Ramotswe and the children
sitting in the back. Motholeli's wheelchair was
secured in the back of the van by a system of
ropes which Mr J.L.B. Matekoni had devised,
and this gave her a very good view of the passing countryside. People waved to her, and she
waved back, "like the Queen," she said. Mma
Ramotswe had told her all about the Queen
Elizabeth and about how she had been a friend
of Sir Seretse Khama himself. She loved
Botswana, explained Mma Ramotswe, and she
did her duty all the time, all the time, visiting
people and shaking their hands and being
given flowers by children. She had been on
duty for fifty years, Mma Ramotswe said, just
like Mr Mandela, who had given his whole life
for justice and had never once thought of himself. How unlike these people were modern

politicians, who thought only of power and tricks.

By the time they drew up at the orphan farm, the trees outside the office already had cars under them, and they were obliged to leave the tiny white van out on the road. People had obviously already begun to arrive, and some of the children were on duty at the gate, standing smartly and greeting the guests, telling them where they should go for tea and cake before the jump took place. Some of the younger children were wearing cardboard aeroplane badges which they had cut out and coloured themselves, and some of these were on sale for two pula at a small table under a tree.

Mma Potokwane saw them from her office, and she rushed out to meet them just as Mr J.L.B. Matekoni and the younger apprentice arrived in the truck. Then Dr Moffat arrived, with his wife, in his pick-up truck, and Mma Potokwane immediately seized him and led him off to look at one of the children who had developed a high fever and was being watched over by her housemother. Mrs Moffat stayed with Mma Ramotswe and Mma Makutsi and together they made their way to the spot under a wide jacaranda tree where two of the housemothers were dispensing heavily-sugared tea from a very large brown tea-pot. There was cake too, but it was not free. Mma Ramotswe bought a slice for all of them and they sat down on stools and drank the tea and ate the cake while further spectators arrived. Then, after half an hour or so, they heard the distant drone of an aircraft engine and the children began to squeal with excitement, pointing at the sky to the west. Mma Ramotswe looked up, straining her eyes; the sound was clear enough now, and yes, there it was, a small plane, white against the great empty sky, much higher than she had imagined it would be. How small we must all look from up there, she thought; and poor Charlie, for all his faults, now just a tiny dot in the sky, a tiny dot that would come tumbling down to the hard earth below.

"I shouldn't have asked him to do this," she said to Mma Makutsi. "What if he's killed?"

Mma Makutsi put a reassuring hand on Mma Ramotswe's forearm. "He won't be," she said. "These things are very safe these days. They check everything two or three times."

"But it still might not open. And what if he

freezes with shock and doesn't pull the cord? What then?"

"His instructor will be jumping with him," soothed Mma Makutsi. "He would dive down and pull the cord for him. I saw a picture in the **National Geographic** of that being done. It is very easy for these people."

They became silent as the plane passed overhead. Now they could see the markings underneath the wings and the undercarriage, and then the opening door and a figure and a blur of shapes. Suddenly there were two little packages, but packages with arms and legs flailing about in the rushing wind, and some of the children shrieked and pointed upwards. Mr J.L.B. Matekoni looked up too, and gulped, imagining that it could have been him up there, and remembering that disturbing dream. Mma Ramotswe closed her eyes, and then opened them again, and still the figures were falling against the empty sky, and she thought: his parachute is not going to open, and she clutched at Mma Makutsi who had muttered something under her breath, a prayer perhaps.

But the parachutes did open, and Mma Ramotswe let out her breath and felt weak at the knees. Mrs Moffat smiled at her and said, "I was worried then. It seemed such a time," and Mma Ramotswe was too overcome to say anything in response, but vowed to herself that she would make it up to this boy in the future; she would be kind to him and not be so impatient at the irritating things he said and did.

As they drifted down, floating beneath the great white canopies, the two figures separated. One of them waved to the other, and seemed to be gesturing, but the other did nothing and continued to float away. The gesturing one was now getting fairly close to the ground, and within seconds he had landed in the field, scarcely a few hundred yards from the spectators. There was a cheer, and the children ran forward, in spite of the calls from the housemothers to stay where they were until the second parachutist had landed safely.

They need not have worried. The other parachutist, now revealed to be Charlie, had so drifted off course that he did not land in the field at all, but disappeared behind the tree tops of the scrub bush on the other side. The spectators watched silently as this happened, and then people turned to one another in uncertainty.

"He will be dead," cried out one of the smaller children. "We must fetch a box."

IT WAS Mr J.L.B. Matekoni, Mma Potokwane's husband, and the instructor (not freed of his equipment) who discovered Charlie. He was hanging a few feet above the ground, his parachute covering the upper branches of a large acacia tree, snagged and snared by the thorny limbs of the tree. He shouted out to them as they approached, and the instructor soon had him out of the harness and down on the ground.

"That was a soft landing," said the instructor. "Well done. You were just a bit off target, that's all. I think you were pulling on the wrong side of the canopy. That's why you sailed off here."

The apprentice nodded. He had a curious expression on his face, half way between sheer relief and pain.

"I think that I am injured," he said.

"You can't be," said the instructor, dusting down the green parachute suit. "The tree completely broke your fall."

The apprentice shook his head. "There is

something hurting me. It is very sore. It is there. Please see what it is."

Mr J.L.B. Matekoni looked at the seat of Charlie's trousers. There was a large rip in the fabric and a very nasty-looking acacia thorn, several inches long, embedded in the flesh. Deftly he took this between his fingers and extracted it with one swift movement. The apprentice gave a yelp.

"That was all," said Mr J.L.B. Matekoni. "A big thorn . . ."

"Please do not tell them," said the apprentice. "Please do not tell them where it was."

"Of course I will not," said Mr J.L.B. Matekoni. "You are a brave, brave young man."

The apprentice smiled. He was recovering from his shock now. "Are the newspaper people there?" he asked. "Did they come?"

"They are there," said Mma Potokwane's husband. "And many girls too."

Back under the trees he received a hero's welcome. The children ran round him, tugging at his sleeves, the housemothers fussed over him with mugs of tea and large slices of cake, and the girls looked on admiringly. Charlie basked in the glory of it all, smiling at the photographers when they approached with their cameras, and patting children on the head, just as an experienced hero might do. Mma Ramotswe watched with amusement, and considerable relief, and then went off to talk to Mma Holonga, whom she had spotted arriving rather late, when the jump had already taken place. She took her client a mug of tea and led her to a private place under a tree, where they could both sit in privacy and talk.

"I have started making enquiries for you," she began. "I have spoken to two of the men on your list and I can give you a report on what I have found out so far."

Mma Holonga nodded. "Well, yes. I must say that there have been developments since I saw you. But tell me anyway. Then I shall tell you what I have decided to do."

Mma Ramotswe could not conceal her surprise. What was the point of consulting her if Mma Holonga was going to make a decision before receiving even a preliminary report?

"You've decided something?" she asked.

"Yes," said Mma Holonga, in a matter-of-fact voice. "But you go ahead and tell me what you found out. I'm very interested."

Mma Ramotswe began her account. "A few days ago I met your Mr Spokesi," she said. "I had a conversation with him and in the course of this conversation I realised that he was not being honest with you. He is a man who likes younger ladies and I do not think that he is serious about marrying you. I think that he would like to have a good time using your money, and then he would go back to the other ladies. I'm sorry about that, Mma, but there it is."

"Of course," said Mma Holonga, tossing back her head. "That man is very vain and is interested only in himself. I think I knew that all along. You have confirmed my views, Mma."

Mma Ramotswe was slightly taken aback by this. She had expected a measure of disappointment on Mma Holonga's part, an expression of regret, instead of which Mr Spokes Spokesi, who must have been a lively suitor, was being consigned to oblivion quite insouciantly.

"Then there is the teacher," Mma Ramotswe went on. "Mr Bobologo. He is a much more serious man than that Spokesi person. He is a clever man, I think; very well-read."

Mma Holonga smiled. "Yes," she said. "He is a good man."

"But a very dull one too," said Mma

Ramotswe. "And he is interested only in getting hold of your money to use for his House of Hope. That is all that interests him. I think that . . ."

Mma Ramotswe tailed off. Her words were having a strange effect on Mma Holonga, she thought. Her client was now sitting bolt upright, her lips pursed in disapproval of what Mma Ramotswe was telling her.

"That is not true!" Mma Holonga expostulated. "He would never do a thing like that."

Mma Ramotswe sighed. "I am sorry, Mma. In my job I often have to tell people things that they do not want to hear. I think that you might not want to hear what I have to say, but I must say it nonetheless. That is my duty. That man is after your money."

Mma Holonga stared at Mma Ramotswe. She rose to her feet, dusting at her skirts as she did so. "You have been very good, Mma," she said coldly. "I am very grateful to you for finding out about Spokesi. Oh yes, you have done well there. But when it comes to my fiancé, Mr Bobologo, you must stop talking about him in this way. I have decided to marry him, and that is it."

Mma Ramotswe did not know what to say

and for a few moments she struggled with herself. Clovis Andersen, as far as she could remember, had never written about what to do in this precise situation and she was thrown back on first principles. There was her duty to her client, which was to carry out the enquiries which she had been asked to conduct. But then there was her duty to warn—a simple human duty which involved warning somebody of danger which they were courting. That duty existed, of course, but at the same time one should not be paternalistic and interfere in matters in which another person wished to choose for themselves. It was not for Mma Ramotswe to make Mma Holonga's decisions for her.

She decided to be cautious. "Are you sure about this, Mma?" she asked. "I hope that you do not think I am being rude in asking, but are you sure that you wish to marry this man? It is a very major decision."

Mma Holonga seemed to be pacified by Mma Ramotswe's tone, and she smiled as she replied. "Well, Mma, you are right about its being a very major decision. I am well aware of that. But I have decided that my destiny lies with that man."

"And you know all about his . . . his interests?"

"You mean his good works? His work for others?"

"The House of Hope. The bar girls . . ."

Mma Holonga looked out over the orphan farm field, as if searching for bar girls. "I know all about that. In fact, I am very much involved in that good work. Since I came to see you, he has shown me the House of Hope and I have been doing work there. I have started hair-braiding classes for those bad girls and then they can come and work in my salons."

"That is a very good idea," said Mma Ramotswe. "And then there is the possible extension . . ."

"That too," interrupted Mma Holonga. "I shall be paying for that. I have already talked to a builder I know. Then, after that is done, I am going to build a House of Hope out at Mole-polole, for bad girls from that region. That was all my idea, not Bobologo's."

Mma Ramotswe listened to all this and realised that she was in the presence of a woman who had found her vocation. So there was nothing more for her to say, other than to congratulate her on her forthcoming marriage and to reflect on the truth that when people ask for advice they very rarely want your advice and will go ahead and do what they want to do anyway, no matter what you say. That applied in every sort of case; it was a human truth of universal application, but one which most people knew little or nothing about.

CHAPTER NINETEEN

A VERY RICH CAKE IS SERVED

AFTER SHE had finished her surprising discussion with Mma Holonga, Mma Ramotswe moved over to join Mr J.L.B. Matekoni and Mma Makutsi, who were sitting at a table under a tree near the children's dining room. More tea had been produced and was being served by the housemothers, and Mma Ramotswe noticed that there were many people in the crowd whom she knew. Indeed, some of them were relatives of hers; her cousin and husband, for example, and some of Mr J.L.B. Matekoni's people. Mma Potokwane had obviously been very active in gathering people for the parachute drop.

She walked over to join her cousin, who said that she would not be prepared to do a parachute drop, even if asked by the President himself. "I would have to say, I'm sorry Rra, but there are some things one cannot do, even for Botswana. I cannot jump from an aeroplane. I would die straightaway."

The cousin's husband agreed. He would be prepared to give all his money, and all his cattle, to charity rather than jump.

"You should not let Mma Potokwane hear that," said Mma Ramotswe. "It might give her ideas."

Then there was a conversation with the Reverend Trevor Mwamba from the Anglican Cathedral. He, too, confessed that he would not like to do a parachute jump, and he felt that the same could be said for the Bishop. For a moment Mma Ramotswe entertained a mental picture of the Bishop jumping from an aeroplane, dressed in his episcopal robes and clutching his mitre as he fell.

"It is nothing, you know," said Charlie, who had come up to join them, a glass of beer in his hand, and clearly enjoying his fame. "I wasn't at all frightened. I just jumped and then bump! the chute opened above me and I came down. That's all there is to it. I will do it again tomorrow if Mma Potokwane asks me. In fact, I think I might offer to join the Botswana Defence Force. I could look after their aeroplane engines and then do some jumping in my spare time."

Mma Ramotswe saw that this made Mr J.L.B. Matekoni look anxious, but the conversation moved on to another topic and no more was said of the looking-after of aeroplane engines.

The event had now turned into something of a party. Some of the older children, who had been helping with the tea cups and with arranging chairs under the trees, now formed up as a choir and sang several songs while one of them, a talented marimba player, provided an accompaniment. Then, after the singing, Mma Potokwane came over to Mma Ramotswe's side and invited her to join her for a moment in the office. The same invitation was extended to Mr J.L.B. Matekoni, and it was explained that a very special cake had been prepared for him but that it could not be produced in public as there was not enough for everybody.

They went into the office. The Reverend Trevor Mwamba was already there, a plate of cake before him. He stood up and smiled at Mr J.L.B. Matekoni.

"Now," said Mma Potokwane, putting a large slice of the special cake on Mr J.L.B. Matekoni's plate. "Here is the special cake I have made."

"You are very kind to us, Mma," said Mr J.L.B. Matekoni. "This looks like a very rich cake. Very rich." He paused, the cake half way to his mouth. He looked at Mma Potokwane. Then he looked at the Reverend Trevor Mwamba. Finally he looked at Mma Ramotswe. Nobody spoke.

Mma Potokwane broke the silence. "Mr J.L.B. Matekoni," she said. "We all know how proud you are of Mma Ramotswe. We all know how proud you are to be her fiancé and how you wish to be her husband. I am right, am I not, in saying that you wish to be her husband?"

Mr J.L.B. Matekoni nodded. "I do. Of course I do."

"Well, do you not think that the moment has come?" she went on. "Do you not think that this would be the right time to marry Mma Ramotswe? Right now. Not next month or next year or whenever, but right now. Because if you do not do something about this, you may never do it. Life is perilous. At any

time it could be too late. When you love another person, you must tell her, but you must
also show her. You must do that thing that says
to the world that you love that person. And this
must never be put off, never."

She paused, watching the effect of her words
on Mr J.L.B. Matekoni. He was staring at her,
his eyes slightly moist, as if he was about to
burst into tears.

"You do wish to marry Mma Ramotswe, do
you not?" Mma Potokwane urged.

Now there was a further silence. The Reverend Trevor Mwamba slipped a small piece of
cake into his mouth and chewed on it. Mma
Ramotswe herself looked down at the ground,
at the edge of Mma Potokwane's carpet. And
then Mr J.L.B. Matekoni spoke.

"I will marry Mma Ramotswe right now,"
he said. "If that is what Mma Ramotswe
wishes, then I shall do that. I shall be proud
to do that. There is no other lady I would
ever wish to marry. Just Mma Ramotswe.
That is all."

It was a long speech for Mr J.L.B. Matekoni,
but every word was filled with passion and a
new determination.

"In that case," said the Reverend Trevor

Mwamba, wiping the crumbs from the edge of his lips. "In that case I have the prayer books in my car and I have the Bishop's authority to perform the ceremony right here."

"We can do it under the big tree," said Mma Potokwane. "I will tell the children's choir to get ready. And I will also tell the guests to prepare themselves. They will be surprised."

THEY ASSEMBLED under the boughs of the great jacaranda tree. A table had been covered with a clean white sheet and served as an altar, and before this altar stood Mr J.L.B. Matekoni, waiting for Mma Ramotswe to be led up to him by Mma Potokwane's husband, who had offered to give the bride away on behalf of her late father, Obed Ramotswe. Mma Potokwane had produced a suitable dress for Mma Ramotswe, in just the right size as it happened, and Mr J.L.B. Matekoni had been put into a suit by Mma Potokwane's husband. The Reverend Trevor Mwamba had fetched his robes from his car.

When Mma Ramotswe came out of the office and walked with Mma Potokwane's husband up to the group of people and the waiting groom, there were enthusiastic ululations from the crowd. This was how people showed their delight and pleasure and the sound was strong that day.

"Dearly beloved," began the Reverend Trevor Mwamba, "we are gathered here together in the sight of God and in the presence of this congregation to join this man and this woman in holy matrimony, which is an honourable estate . . ."

The words which Mma Ramotswe had heard so many times for others, those echoing words, she now heard for herself, and she made the responses clearly, as did Mr J.L.B. Matekoni. Then, taking their hands and placing them together, in accordance with the authority vested in him, the Reverend Trevor Mwamba pronounced them man and wife, and the ladies present, led by Mma Potokwane, ululated with pleasure.

The choir had been waiting, and now they sang, while Mma Ramotswe and Mr J.L.B. Matekoni sat down on chairs which had been placed before the altar, and signed the register which the Reverend Trevor Mwamba had also happened to have in the back of his car. The choir sang, the sweet voices of the children rising through the branches of the tree above them, and filling the still, clear air with sound. There was an old Botswana hymn, one which everybody knew, and then, because it was a favourite of Mma Ramotswe's father, they sang that song which distils all the suffering and the hope of Africa; that song which had inspired and comforted so many, "Nkosi Sikeleli Afrika," God Bless Africa, give her life, watch over her children.

Mma Ramotswe turned to face her friends, and smiled, and they smiled back. Then she and Mr J.L.B. Matekoni stood up and walked down through the crowd to the place where the children had taken more tables and where, quite miraculously, as at Cana of Galilee, the housemothers had set out large plates of food, ready for the wedding feast.

IN THE COMPANY OF
CHEERFUL LADIES

Alexander McCall Smith

RANDOM HOUSE
LARGE PRINT

This book is for
Helena Kennedy

IN THE COMPANY OF
CHEERFUL LADIES

CHAPTER ONE

HONESTY, TEA, AND THINGS
IN THE KITCHEN

Mma Ramotswe was sitting alone in her favourite café, on the edge of the shopping centre at the Gaborone end of the Tlokweng Road. It was a Saturday, the day that she preferred above all others, a day on which one might do as much or as little as one liked, a day to have lunch with a friend at the President Hotel, or, as on that day, to sit by oneself and think about the events of the week and the state of the world. This café was a good place to be, for several reasons. Firstly, there was the view, that of a stand of eucalyptus trees with foliage of a comforting dark green which made a sound like the sea when the wind blew through the leaves. Or that, at least, was the sound which Mma Ramotswe imagined the sea to make. She had never seen the ocean, which was far away from land-locked Botswana; far away across the deserts of Namibia, across the red sands and the dry mountains. But she could imagine it when she listened to the eucalyptus trees in the wind and closed her eyes. Perhaps one day she would see it, and would stand on the shore and let the waves wash over her feet. Perhaps.

The other advantage which this café had was the fact that the tables were out on an open verandah, and there was always something to watch. That morning, for instance, she had seen a minor dispute between a teenage girl and her boyfriend—an exchange of words which she did not catch but which was clear enough in its meaning—and she had witnessed a woman scrape the side of a neighbouring car while she tried to park. The woman had stopped, quickly inspected the damage, and had then driven off. Mma Ramotswe had watched this incredulously, and had half-risen to her feet to protest, but was too late: the woman's car had by then turned the corner and disappeared and she did not even have time to see its number-plate.

She had sat down again and poured herself

another cup of tea. It was not true that such a thing could not have happened in the old Botswana—it could—but it was undoubtedly true that this was much more likely to happen today. There were many selfish people about these days, people who seemed not to care if they scraped the cars of others or bumped into people while walking on the street. Mma Ramotswe knew that this was what happened when towns became bigger and people became strangers to one another; she knew too that this was a consequence of increasing prosperity, which, curiously enough, just seemed to bring out greed and selfishness. But even if she knew why all this happened, it did not make it any easier to bear. The rest of the world might become as rude as it wished, but this was not the way of things in Botswana and she would always defend the old Botswana way of doing things.

Life was far better, thought Mma Ramotswe, if we knew who we were. In the days when she was a schoolgirl in Mochudi, the village in which she had been born, everybody had known exactly who you were, and they often knew exactly who your parents, and your parents' parents, had been. Today when she went back to Mochudi, people would greet her as if she had barely been away; her presence needed no explanation. And even here in Gaborone, where things had grown so much, people still knew precisely who she was. They would know that she was Precious Ramotswe, founder of the No. 1 Ladies' Detective Agency, daughter of the late Obed Ramotswe, and now the wife (after a rather protracted engagement) of that most gracious of mechanics, Mr J.L.B. Matekoni, proprietor of Tlokweng Road Speedy Motors. And some of them at least would also know that she lived in Zebra Drive, that she had a tiny white van, and that she employed one Grace Makutsi as her assistant. And so the ramifications of relationships and ties would spread further outwards, and the number of things that might be known would grow. Some might know that Mma Makutsi had a brother, Richard, who was now late; that she had achieved the previously unheard-of result of ninety-seven per cent in the final examinations of the Botswana Secretarial College; and that following upon the success of the Kalahari Typing School for Men, she had recently moved to a rather better house in Extension Two. Knowledge of this sort—everyday, hu-

man knowledge—helped to keep society together and made it difficult to scrape the car of
another without feeling guilty about it and
without doing something to let the owner
know. Not that this appeared to make any difference to that selfish woman in the car, who
had left the scrape unreported, who clearly did
not care.

But there was no point in throwing up one's
hands in despair. People had always done
that—the throwing up of hands, the shrug—
but one got nowhere in doing so. The world
might have changed for the worse in some respects, but in others it was a much better place,
and it was important to remember this. Lights
went off in some places, but went on in others.
Look at Africa—there had been so much to
shake one's head over—corruption, civil wars,
and the rest—but there was also so much
which was now much better. There had been
slavery in the past, and all the suffering which
that had brought, and there had been all the
cruelties of apartheid just those few miles away
over the border, but all that was now over.
There had been ignorance, but now more and
more people were learning to write, and were
graduating from universities. Women had been

held in such servitude, and now they could vote and express themselves and claim lives for themselves, even if there were still many men who did not want such things to be. These were the good things that happened and one had to remember them.

Mma Ramotswe raised her tea cup to her lips and looked out over the brim. At the edge of the car park, immediately in front of the café, a small market had been set up, with traders' stalls and trays of colourful goods. She watched as a man attempted to persuade a customer to buy a pair of sunglasses. The woman tried on several pairs, but was not satisfied, and moved on to the next stall. There she pointed to a small piece of silver jewellery, a bangle, and the trader, a short man wearing a wide-brimmed felt hat, passed it across to her to try on. Mma Ramotswe watched as the woman held out her wrist to be admired by the trader, who nodded encouragement. But the woman seemed not to agree with his verdict, and handed the bangle back, pointing to another item at the back of the stall. And at that moment, while the trader turned round to stretch for whatever it was that she had singled out, the woman quickly slipped another bangle into the pocket of the jacket she was wearing.

Mma Ramotswe gasped. This time, she could not sit back and allow a crime to be committed before her very eyes. If people did nothing, then no wonder that things were getting worse. So she stood up, and began to walk firmly towards the stall where the woman had now engaged the trader in earnest discussion about the merits of the merchandise which he was showing her.

"Excuse me, Mma."

The voice came from behind her, and Mma Ramotswe turned round to see who had addressed her. It was the waitress, a young woman whom Mma Ramotswe had not seen at the café before.

"Yes, Mma, what is it?"

The waitress pointed an accusing finger at her. "You cannot run away like that," she said. "I saw you. You're trying to go away without paying the bill. I saw you."

For a moment Mma Ramotswe was unable to speak. The accusation was a terrible one, and so unwarranted. Of course she had not been trying to get away without paying the bill—she would never do such a thing; all she was doing was trying to stop a crime being committed before her eyes.

She recovered herself sufficiently to reply. "I am not trying to go away, Mma," she said. "I am just trying to stop that person over there from stealing from that man. Then I would have come back to pay."

The waitress smiled knowingly. "They all find some excuse," she said. "Every day there are people like you. They come and eat our food and then they run away and hide. You people are all the same."

Mma Ramotswe looked over towards the stall. The woman had begun to walk away, presumably with the bangle still firmly in her pocket. It would now be too late to do anything about it, and all because of this silly young woman who had misunderstood what she was doing.

She went back to her table and sat down. "Bring me the bill," she said. "I will pay it straightaway."

The waitress stared at her. "I will bring you the bill," she said. "But I shall have to add something for myself. I will have to add this if you do not want me to call the police and tell them about how you tried to run away."

As the waitress went off to fetch the bill, Mma Ramotswe glanced around her to see if people at the neighbouring tables had witnessed the scene. At the table next to hers, a woman sat with her two young children, who were sipping with evident pleasure at large milkshakes. The woman smiled at Mma Ramotswe, and then turned her attention back to the children. She had not seen anything, thought Mma Ramotswe, but then the woman leaned across the table and addressed a remark to her.

"Bad luck, Mma," she said. "They are too quick in this place. It is easier to run away at the hotels."

FOR A FEW minutes Mma Ramotswe sat in complete silence, reflecting on what she had seen. It was remarkable. Within a very short space of time she had seen an instance of barefaced theft, had encountered a waitress who thought nothing of extorting money, and then, to bring the whole matter to a shameful conclusion, the woman at the next table had disclosed a thoroughly dishonest view of the world. Mma Ramotswe was frankly astonished. She thought of what her father, the late Obed Ramotswe, a fine judge of cattle but also a man of the utmost propriety, would have thought of this. He had brought her up to be scrupulously honest, and he would have been mortified to see this sort of behaviour. Mma Ramotswe remembered how she had been walking with him in Mochudi when she was a young girl and they had come across a coin on the edge of the road. She had fallen upon it with delight and was polishing it with her handkerchief before he noticed what had happened and had intervened.

"That is not ours," he said. "That money belongs to somebody else."

She had yielded the coin reluctantly, and it had been handed in to a surprised police sergeant at the Mochudi Police Post, but the lesson had been a vivid one. It was difficult for Mma Ramotswe to imagine how anybody could steal from another, or do any of the things which one read about in the **Botswana Daily News** court reports. The only explanation was that people who did that sort of thing had no understanding of what others felt; they simply did not understand. If you knew what it was like to be another person, then how could you possibly do something which would cause pain?

The problem, though, was that there seemed to be people in whom that imaginative part was just missing. It could be that they were born that way—with something missing from their brains—or it could be that they became like that because they were never taught by their parents to sympathise with others. That was the most likely explanation, thought Mma Ramotswe. A whole generation of people, not only in Africa, but everywhere else, had not been taught to feel for others because the parents simply had not bothered to teach them this.

She continued to think of this as she drove in her tiny white van, back through that part of town known as the Village, back past the University, with its growing sprawl of buildings, and finally along Zebra Drive itself, where she lived. She had been so disturbed by what she had seen that she had quite forgotten to do the shopping that she had intended to do, with the result that it was only when she pulled into her driveway and came to a halt beside the kitchen wall that she remembered that she had none of the items she needed to make that night's dinner. There were no beans, for example, which meant that their stew would be accompanied by no greens; and there would be no custard for the pudding which she had planned to make for the children. She sat at the wheel of the van and contemplated retracing her tracks to the shops, but she just did not have the energy. It was a hot day, and the house looked cool and inviting. She could go inside, make herself a pot of bush tea, and retire to her bedroom for a sleep. Mr J.L.B. Matekoni and the children had gone out to Mojadite, a small village off the Lobatse Road, to visit his aunt, and would not be back before six or seven. She would have the house to herself for several hours yet, and this would be a good time for a rest. There was plenty of food in the house— even if it was the wrong sort for the dinner that she had planned. They could have pumpkin with the stew, rather than beans, and the children would be perfectly happy with a tin of peaches in syrup rather than the custard and semolina pudding that she had thought of making. So there was no reason to go out again.

Mma Ramotswe stepped out of the tiny white van and walked round to the kitchen door, unlocking it to let herself in. She could remember the days when nobody locked their doors in Botswana, and indeed when there were many doors that had no locks to lock anyway. But they had to lock their doors now and there were even people who locked their gates too. She thought of what she had seen only a short time before. That woman who had stolen from the trader with the wide-brimmed felt hat; she lived in a room somewhere which she no doubt kept locked, and yet she was prepared to steal from that poor man. Mma Ramotswe sighed. There was much in this world over which one might shake one's head. Indeed, it would be possible to go through life today with one's head in constant motion, like a puppet in the hands of a shaky puppeteer.

The kitchen was cool, and Mma Ramotswe slipped out of her shoes, which had been pinching her recently (could one's feet put on weight?). The polished concrete floor was comfortable underfoot as she moved over to the sink to pour herself a glass of water. Rose, her maid, was away for the weekend, but had tidied the kitchen before she left on Friday evening. Rose was conscientious and kept all the surfaces scrupulously clean. She lived in a small house on the far edge of Tlokweng, which she maintained with the same rigour as she devoted to her work for Mma Ramotswe. She was one of those women, thought Mma Ramotswe, in whom there seemed to be an unending capacity for hard work. She had raised a family—and raised them well—with little help from the fathers of the children. She had provided for these children on the small wages that she had earned as a maid and by the payment, scant though it was, that she received for the sewing work that she undertook. Africa was full of such women, it seemed, and if there was to be any hope for Africa it would surely come from women such as these.

Mma Ramotswe filled the kettle from the kitchen tap and put it on the cooker. She did this automatically, as one performs familiar tasks, and it was only after she had done this that she noticed that the kettle had not been in its accustomed place. Rose always left it on the small wooden chopping block beside the sink, and the children, Motholeli and Puso, knew to leave it there too. That was the kettle's place, and it would not have occurred to anybody to leave it on the low wooden dresser on the other side of the kitchen. Certainly Mr J.L.B. Matekoni would not have done that—and indeed she had never seen Mr J.L.B. Matekoni touch the kettle in all the six months since their marriage and his arrival in the house on Zebra Drive. Mr J.L.B. Matekoni liked tea, of course—it would have been very difficult to marry a man who did not like tea—but he very rarely seemed to make any tea for himself. She had not thought about this before now, but it was rather interesting, was it not, that somebody might believe that tea just happened along? Mr J.L.B. Matekoni was not a lazy man, but it was remarkable to reflect how most men imagined that things like tea and food would simply appear if they waited long enough. There would always be a woman in the background—a mother, a girlfriend, a wife—who would ensure that these needs would be met. This should change, of course, and men should learn how to look after themselves, but very few men seemed to be doing this yet. And there was not much hope for the younger generation, looking at the two apprentices and how they behaved. They still expected women to look after them and, unfortunately, there seemed to be enough young women who were prepared to do this.

It was while she was thinking this that Mma Ramotswe noticed that one of the drawers in the kitchen dresser was not as she had left it. It was not fully open, but had definitely been pulled out and then not closed properly. She frowned. This was very strange. Again, Rose always shut everything after she used it and the only other person who had been in the kitchen since Rose left had been Mma Ramotswe herself. She had been in there early that morning, when she had got out of bed to make breakfast for Mr J.L.B. Matekoni and the children before they went off to Mojadite. Then she had seen them off on their early start and had gone back into the kitchen to tidy up. She had not needed anything from that drawer, which contained string, scissors, and other items that she would only use from time to time. Somebody else must have opened it.

She moved over to that side of the kitchen and opened the drawer further to inspect it. Everything seemed to be there, except . . . and now she noticed the ball of string which was sitting on the top of the dresser. She picked this up and examined it. This was her ball of string, indeed, and it had been taken out of the drawer and left out by the person who had opened the drawer and, she imagined, who had also moved the kettle from its accustomed place.

Mma Ramotswe stood quite still. It now occurred to her that there had been an intruder, and that whoever it was who had come into the house had been disturbed by her return. That person might have run out of the front of the house when she came into the kitchen, but then the front door, which provided the only means of leaving on that side of the house, would have been left firmly locked. This meant that the intruder might still be inside.

For a few moments she wondered what to do. She could telephone the police and tell them that she suspected that somebody was in the house, but what if they came out to investigate and there was nobody? They would hardly be pleased to be called out for no reason at all and they would probably mutter comments about nervous women who should know better than to waste police time while there were real crimes to be looked into. So perhaps it was premature to call the police and she should, instead, go through the house herself, moving from room to room to see if there was anybody there. Of course that was risky. Even in peaceful Botswana there were cases of people being attacked by intruders when they came upon them in the course of a robbery. Some of these people were dangerous. And yet this was Gaborone, on a Saturday afternoon, with the sun riding high in the sky, and people walking along Zebra Drive. This was not a time of shadows and inexplicable noises, a time of darkness. This was not a time to be afraid.

CHAPTER TWO

TROUSERS AND PUMPKINS

MMA RAMOTSWE did not consider herself to be a particularly courageous woman. There were some things of which she was frightened: curtainless windows at night, for example, because one could not see what was outside, in the darkness; and snakes, because there were snakes about which were truly dangerous—puff adders, for example, the lebolobolo, which was fat and lazy and had great curved fangs, or the mokopa, which was long and black and very poisonous and which was well-known to hate humans because of some distant wrong in snake memory. These were things about which one should be frightened; other things could be frightening if one allowed them to be so, but could be faced up to if one were only prepared to look them in the eye.

Yet there was something very strange about thinking that you were alone in the house and then discovering that you were not. Mma Ramotswe found this very frightening, and had to struggle with herself before she began her inspection, walking first through the door which led from the kitchen into the sitting room next door. She glanced about her, and quickly noticed that everything was in its normal place and that nothing seemed to have been disturbed. There was her ornamental plate with its picture of Sir Seretse Khama—a prize possession which she would have been mortified to have lost to a burglar. And there was her Queen Elizabeth II tea cup, with its picture of the Queen looking out in such a dignified way. That was another thing that she would have been very upset to have lost, because it reminded her of duty and of the traditional values in a world that seemed to have less and less time for such things. Not once had Seretse Khama faltered in his duty, nor had the Queen, who admired the Khama family and had always had a feeling for Africa. Mma Ramotswe had read that at the funeral of Sir

Garfield Todd, that good man who had stood up for decency and justice in Zimbabwe, a message had been read out from the Queen. And the Queen had insisted that her High Commissioner should go to the graveside in person, to the very graveside, to read out what she had to say about that brave man. And when Lady Khama had died, the Queen had sent a message too, because she understood, and that had made Mma Ramotswe feel proud of being a Motswana, and of all that Seretse and his wife had done.

She looked quickly at the wall to see whether the photograph of her father—her Daddy, as she called him—the late Obed Ramotswe was in place, and it was. And so was the velvet picture of mountains, which they had brought over from Mr J.L.B. Matekoni's house near the old Botswana Defence Force Club. There would have been many people who would have liked to steal that, so that they could run their fingers over it and feel the texture of the velvet, but it was safe too. Mma Ramotswe was not sure about that picture, and perhaps it would not be an altogether bad thing if somebody did steal it, but she corrected herself and suppressed the thought. Mr

J.L.B. Matekoni liked that picture, and she would not have wished him to be upset. So the picture would remain. And indeed, if they ever did have a real burglary, when everything was taken, she was sure that the picture would somehow be left, and she would have to look at it while she sat on cushions on the floor, all the chairs having gone.

She moved over to the door between the sitting room and the verandah and checked it. It was securely locked, just as they had left it. And the windows too, although open, had their wrought-iron bars intact. Nobody could have entered by any of those without bending or breaking the bars, and this had not been done. So the intruder, if he existed, could neither have come in nor gone out through that room.

She left the sitting room and walked slowly down the corridor to check the other rooms. There was a large walk-in cupboard a few paces along the corridor, and she stopped before this, peering gingerly past the edge of its door, which was slightly ajar. It was dark in the cupboard, but she could just make out the shapes of the items it contained: the two buckets, the sewing machine, the coats that Mr J.L.B.

Matekoni had brought with him and hung on the rail at the back. Nothing seemed out of place, and there was certainly no intruder hiding in the coats. So she closed the door and went on until she came to the first of the three rooms that gave off the corridor. This was Puso's room, which was very much a boy's room, with little in it. She opened the door cautiously, gritting her teeth as the door creaked loudly. She looked at the table, on which a home-made catapult was resting, and the floor, on which a discarded football and a pair of running shoes lay, and she realised that no intruder would come in here anyway. Motholeli's room also was empty, although here Mma Ramotswe thought it necessary to peer into the cupboard. Again there was nothing untoward.

Now she entered the bedroom she shared with Mr J.L.B. Matekoni. This was the largest of the three bedrooms, and it contained things that somebody might well wish to steal. There were her clothes, for instance, which were colourful and well-made. There would be a keen demand for these from larger ladies looking for dresses, but there was no sign that the hanging rail on which these garments were suspended had been tampered with. And nor was there any sign of disturbance on the dressing table on which Mma Ramotswe kept the few brooches and bangles that she liked to wear. None of these seemed to have gone.

Mma Ramotswe felt the tension leave her body. The house was obviously empty and the notion that somebody might be hiding in it was manifestly nonsense. There was probably some perfectly rational explanation for the open drawer and the ball of string on the dresser, and this explanation would no doubt emerge when Mr J.L.B. Matekoni and the children returned that evening. One possibility was that they had set off, forgotten something, and then come back to the house after Mma Ramotswe had herself left it. Perhaps they had bought a present for Mr J.L.B. Matekoni's relative and had come back to wrap it up, a task for which they would have needed the string. That was a perfectly rational explanation.

As Mma Ramotswe made her way back to the kitchen to make her tea, she thought of how things that appeared to be mysteries were usually no such thing. The unexplained was unexplained not because there was anything beyond explanation, but simply because the ordinary, day-to-day explanation had not made itself apparent. Once one began to enquire, so-called mysteries rapidly tended to become something much more prosaic. Not that people liked this, of course. They liked to think that there were things beyond explanation—supernatural things—things like tokoloshes, for example, who roamed at night and caused fear and mischief. Nobody ever saw a tokolosh for the simple reason that there was nothing to see. What one thought was a tokolosh was usually no more than a shadow of a branch in the moonlight, or the sound of the wind in the trees, or a tiny animal scurrying through the undergrowth. But people were not attracted by these perfectly straightforward explana-tions and spoke instead of all sorts of fanciful spirits. Well, she would not be like that when it came to intruders. There had been no in-truder in the house at all, and Mma Ramotswe was quite alone, as she had originally thought herself to be.

She made her tea and poured herself a large cup. Then, cup in hand, she returned to her bedroom. It would be a pleasant way of spend-ing what remained of the afternoon, resting on her bed, and falling asleep if she wished. She had a few magazines on her bedside table, and a copy of the **Botswana Daily News.** She would read these until her eyes began to shut and the magazine fell out of her hands. It was a very agreeable way of drifting off to sleep.

She opened wide the window to allow a cooling breeze to circulate. Then, having placed her tea cup on the bedside table, she lowered herself onto the bed, sinking down into the mattress that had served her so well for many years and which was holding up very well with the additional weight of Mr J.L.B. Matekoni. She had bought the bed and its mattress at the same time that she had moved into the house on Zebra Drive, and had resisted the temptation to buy cheaply. In her view a well-made bed was the one thing on which it was worthwhile spending as much money as one could possibly afford. A good bed produced happiness, she was sure of that; a bad, uncomfortable bed produced grumpiness and niggling pains.

She started to read the **Botswana Daily News.** There was a story of a politician who had made a speech urging people to take more care of their cattle. He said that it was a shocking thing to the conscience of a cattle-owning

country that there should be cases of mis-
treated cattle. People who allowed their cattle
to go thirsty while they were driving them to
the railway siding should be ashamed of themselves, he said. It was well-known, he went on,
that the quality of meat was affected by the
experience of the cattle in their last days. An
animal that had been stressed would always
produce beef that tasted less than perfect, and
perfection was what Botswana wanted for its
meat. After all, Botswana beef was fine, grass-
fed beef, and tasted so much better than the
meat of those poor cattle which were kept
cooped up or which were fed food that cattle
should not eat.

Mma Ramotswe found herself agreeing
with all of this. Her father had been a great
judge of cattle and had always told her that cattle should be treated as members of the family.
He knew the names of all his cattle, which was
a considerable feat for one who had built up so
large a herd, and he would never have tolerated
their suffering in any way. It was just as well,
she thought, that he was no longer able to hear
this news of thirsty cattle, nor to see the sort of
things that she had seen that very day while
having her tea at the shopping centre.

She finished the article on cattle and had embarked on another one when she heard a sound. It was a rather peculiar sound, rather like moaning. She lowered the newspaper and stared up at the ceiling. It was very strange. The sound was apparently coming from fairly nearby—from just outside her window, it seemed. She listened very hard and there it was again, once more emanating from somewhere not far away.

Mma Ramotswe sat up, and as she did so the sound occurred again—a soft, indistinct groaning, like the sound of a dog in pain. She got up off the bed and crossed to her window to look outside. If there was a dog in the garden, then she would have to go and chase it away. She did not like dogs to come into the garden, and in particular she did not like visits from the malodorous yellow dogs which her neighbour kept. These dogs were always moaning and whining, in a way which was very similar to the sound that she had heard while lying down.

She looked out into the garden. The sun was well down in the sky now, and the shadows from the trees were long. She saw the paw-paw trees and their yellowing leaves; she saw the spray of bougainvillaea and the mopipi tree which grew at the edge of Mr J.L.B. Matekoni's vegetable patch. And she saw the rough patch of grass in which a stray dog might like to hide. But there was no dog in sight, not under her window, nor in the grass, nor at the foot of the mopipi tree.

Mma Ramotswe turned round and went back to bed. Lying down again, her traditional frame sank deep into the mattress, which sagged down towards the floor. Immediately the moaning sound returned, louder this time, and it seemed rather closer. Mma Ramotswe frowned, and shifted her weight on the mattress. Immediately the moaning sound made itself heard again, this time even more loudly.

It was then that she realised that the sound was coming from within the room, and her heart skipped a beat. The sound was in the room, and it seemed as if it was directly under her, under the bed. And at that point, as this frightening realisation was reached, her mattress suddenly heaved beneath her, as if a great subterranean event had propelled it upwards. Then, with a scuffling sound, the figure of a man squirmed out from under the bed, seemed to struggle with some impediment as he emerged, and then shook himself free and dashed out of the room. It happened so quickly that Mma Ramotswe barely had time to see him before he disappeared through the bedroom door. She had no time to see his features, and she only barely took in the fact that although he was wearing a smart red shirt, he was not wearing any trousers.

She shouted out, but the man was already out of the room. And by the time that she struggled to her feet, she heard the kitchen door slamming as he made his exit from the house. She moved over to the window in the hope of seeing him as he ran across her yard, but he had taken another route, over to the side, and must have been heading towards the fence that ran along the side of her property.

Then she looked down at the floor and noticed, just at the side of the bed, where they were still snagged on the sharp end of a spring, a pair of khaki trousers. The man who had been hiding under her bed had become trapped and had been obliged to wriggle out of his trousers to make his getaway. Mma Ramotswe now picked up these trousers, releasing them from the spring, and examined them: an ordinary pair of khaki trousers, in quite good condition, and now separated from their owner. She felt gingerly in the pockets—one never knew what one would find in a man's pockets—but there was nothing other than a piece of string. There was certainly nothing that could identify this man.

Mma Ramotswe carried the trousers through to the kitchen. She had been shocked by what had happened, but the thought of the intruder having to run off without his trousers made her smile. How on earth would he be able to get home, wherever that might be, clad only in a shirt and socks, and without any trousers? The police would probably pick him up if they saw him, and then he would have some explaining to do. Would he say that he had simply forgotten to put on his trousers before he went out? That would be one way of explaining himself, but would anybody ever forget to put on his trousers before he ventured forth? Surely not. Or might he say that his trousers had been stolen? But how could one's trousers possibly be stolen while one was wearing them? It seemed rather difficult to see how this might happen, and she could not imagine the police being convinced by such an explanation.

She poured herself another cup of tea in the kitchen, the cup she had taken through to the bedroom having been knocked over while the man made his escape from under her bed. Then she took this cup of tea, and the trousers, out onto the verandah. She draped the trousers over the rail and sat down on her chair. This was really rather funny, she thought. It had been alarming to discover that there was a man under her bed, but it must have been much more alarming for him, especially when she lay down on the bed and he had been crushed underneath the sagging mattress. That explained the moaning; the poor man was having the breath crushed out of him. Well, that's what came of hiding where one had no business to hide. He would not hide under a bed again, she suspected, which meant that he had perhaps learned a bit of a lesson. However, there were obviously other lessons for that man to learn, and if she ever found out who he was, unlikely though that was, she would have something to say to him and would say it in no uncertain terms.

When Mr J.L.B. Matekoni and the children returned in the evening, Mma Ramotswe said nothing about the incident until both Puso and Motholeli had been settled in bed and were safely off to sleep. Puso had a tendency to nightmares, and she did not want him to start worrying about intruders, and so she would make sure that he did not hear about what had happened. Motholeli was less nervous, and seemed not to be scared of the dark, as her brother was. But if she were to be told, then she might tell him in an unguarded moment, and so it would be better for neither of them to know.

Mr J.L.B. Matekoni listened intently. When she described the man running out of the room without his trousers, he gasped, and put his hand to his mouth.

"That is very bad," he said. "I do not like the thought that there was this strange man in our bedroom without any trousers."

"Yes," said Mma Ramotswe. "But you must remember that he did not take them off himself. They came off when he was trying to escape. That is different."

Mr J.L.B. Matekoni looked doubtful. "I still don't like it. Why was he there? What mischief was he planning?"

"I suspect that he was just a thief who passed by and saw that nobody was in," suggested Mma Ramotswe. "Then he was disturbed when I came back and he had no way of getting out. I suspect that he was a very frightened man."

They did not discuss the matter further. The trousers were left out on the verandah, where Mma Ramotswe had hung them. Mr J.L.B. Matekoni had suggested that they might fit one of the apprentices and he could give them to him. If they did not, then he would pass them on to one of the second-hand clothes traders who would surely find a good pair of legs to fit into them; honest legs this time.

But the next morning, when Mma Ramotswe went out onto the verandah for her morning cup of bush tea, the trousers had gone. And directly below the place where they had been left, there was a large, yellow pumpkin, luscious and ready to eat.

CHAPTER THREE

FURTHER THOUGHTS
ON PUMPKINS

MMA RAMOTSWE inspected the pumpkin from all angles. There was nothing about pumpkins in Clovis Andersen's **Principles of Private Detection,** but Mma Ramotswe was perfectly capable of investigating a pumpkin herself without the need of guidance from others. She did not touch it at first, but peered at the pumpkin itself, and then at the ground around it. The pumpkin had been placed in what was nominally a flower bed, but which had not been cultivated very much since Mma Ramotswe had moved into the house. She devoted herself to vegetables and shrubs, holding the view that flowers required too much effort and gave too little reward. In the hot air of Botswana flowers tended to open briefly and then shut and wilt away, as if surprised, unless, of course, one protected them with shade netting and coaxed them daily with precious water. It was far better, thought Mma Ramotswe, to allow native plants to establish themselves. These plants knew the soil of Botswana and could cope with the sun. They knew when it was time to blossom and when it was time to hide away; they knew how to make the most of every little drop of moisture that came their way.

The bed in which the pumpkin sat ran along the low front wall of the verandah. It was mostly sand, but there were a few plants, small aloes and the like, which had taken root, and it was alongside one of these that the pumpkin had been deposited. Mma Ramotswe looked at the sand around the pumpkin: for the most part it was undisturbed, save for the tiny tracks made by ants, but there, clearly visible, a few feet away from the pumpkin was the print of a shoe—that was all; just the indentations of a shoe-sole, which told one nothing, other than that the person who put the pumpkin there was a man, judging from the size, and that he possessed a pair of shoes.

She stood above the pumpkin and contemplated its promising roundness. This would do for three meals, she thought, with perhaps a little left over to make some soup afterwards. It was exactly ready—with just that degree of ripeness which gives the flesh some sweetness without making it too soft. This was a fine pumpkin, and the person who had left it there must have been a good judge of pumpkins.

Mma Ramotswe bent forward and began to lift the pumpkin, gingerly at first but then more firmly. With the large yellow burden up against her chest, she smelled the sweet pumpkin smell, and she closed her eyes for a moment, imagining how it would be once it was cut up, cooked and gracing the plates on her table. Grasping the pumpkin, which was heavy, she made her way back to the kitchen and deposited it on the table.

"That is a very fine pumpkin," observed Mr J.L.B. Matekoni as he entered the kitchen a few minutes later.

Mma Ramotswe was about to tell him what had happened when she noticed that the children were directly behind him—Motholeli in her wheelchair and Puso neatly dressed in freshly ironed khaki shorts (Rose's ironing) and a short-sleeved white shirt.

"A pumpkin!" shouted Puso. "A very big pumpkin!"

Mr J.L.B. Matekoni raised an eyebrow. "You have been to the shops already, Mma Ramotswe?"

"No," said Mma Ramotswe. "Somebody left this pumpkin for us. I found it out at the front. It is a very fine present." That, at least, was true. Somebody had left the pumpkin outside the house, and it was quite reasonable to assume that it was a present.

"Who was the kind person?" asked Mr J.L.B. Matekoni. "Mrs Moffat said that she would give me a present for fixing the doctor's car. Do you think that she has left us a pumpkin?"

"It may be her," said Mma Ramotswe. "But I am not sure." She looked at Mr J.L.B. Matekoni, trying to signal to him that there was more to this pumpkin than met the eye, but that it was not something that should be discussed in front of the children. He caught her eye, and realised.

"Well, I shall put that pumpkin away in the cupboard," he said, "then we shall be able to take it out later today and cook it. Do you not think that a good idea?"

"I do," said Mma Ramotswe. "You put the pumpkin away and I can make some porridge for the children's breakfast. Then we can all go to church before it gets too hot."

THEY DROVE the short distance to the Anglican Cathedral, parking Mr J.L.B. Matekoni's van round the side, near the Dean's house. Mma Ramotswe helped Motholeli into her wheelchair and Puso pushed it round to the front, where a ramp allowed for entrance. Mma Ramotswe and Mr J.L.B. Matekoni made their way in through the side door, collected their hymn books from the table near the door, and walked to their favourite pew. A few minutes later the children arrived. Motholeli's wheelchair was parked at the end of the pew, and Puso sat between Mma Ramotswe and Mr J.L.B. Matekoni, where he could be watched. He had a tendency to fidget, and would usually be sent out, after fifteen minutes or so, to play on the Cathedral swing.

Mma Ramotswe read through the service sheet. She did not approve of the day's choice of hymns, none of which was known to her, and she quickly moved on to read the parish notes.

There was a list of the sick, and she ran her eye down this, noting, with sorrow, that many of those who had been on the list last week were still named. It was a time of sickness, and charity was sorely tested. There were mothers here, mothers who would leave children behind them if they were called. There were poor people and rich people too, all equal in their human vulnerability. **Remember these brothers and sisters** it said at the bottom of the list. Yes, she would. She would remember these brothers and sisters. How could one forget?

The choir entered and the service began. As she stood there, unenthusiastically mouthing the words of the unfamiliar hymns chosen for that day, Mma Ramotswe's thoughts kept returning to the extraordinary finding of the pumpkin. One possible explanation of the mystery, she thought, was that the intruder had come back for some reason—perhaps to break in again—and had discovered his trousers hung out on the verandah. He had been carrying a pumpkin, which he had probably stolen from somewhere else, and had put this down on the ground while he put the trousers back on. Then perhaps he had been disturbed—again—and had run away without picking up the pumpkin.

That was certainly possible, but was it at all likely? Mma Ramotswe looked up to the ceiling of the Cathedral, watching the blades of the great white fans as they cut slowly at the air. No, it was unlikely that the intruder would have returned, and even if he had, would he have had the time to steal a pumpkin from somewhere else? Surely his most pressing concern, without his trousers, would have been to get home or to find some other trousers.

What seemed much more likely was that the disappearance of the trousers and the appearance of the pumpkin were completely unconnected. The garment had been removed by a passer-by, who had spotted the opportunity to acquire a perfectly good pair of khaki trousers. Then, earlier that morning, a friend had dropped off a pumpkin as a present and had merely left it there, not wishing to wake people too early on a Sunday. That was much more probable, and indeed was the solution that Clovis Andersen himself would have identified. **Never go for the excessively complicated solution,** he had written. **Always assume that the simplest explanation is the most likely one. Nine times out of ten, you'll be right.**

Mma Ramotswe jolted herself back from

these realms of speculation. The service was proceeding, and now the Reverend Trevor Mwamba was ascending the pulpit. She put from her mind all thoughts of pumpkins and listened to what Trevor Mwamba had to say. He had married them, under that tree at the orphan farm, barely six months ago, on that day of which every minute was etched into her memory: the voices of the children, who sang; the canopy of leaves above their heads; the smiles of those present; and those echoing words which had marked the beginning of her married life to that kind man, Mr J.L.B. Matekoni, that great mechanic, who was now her husband.

The Reverend Trevor Mwamba now looked out over the congregation, and smiled. "We have visitors," he said, smiling. "Please stand up and tell us who you are."

They looked about them. Five people stood up, scattered amongst the regular congregation. One by one, to a turning of heads, they announced who they were.

"I am John Ngwenya, from Mbabane in Swaziland," said a stout man in a pearl-grey suit. He bowed slightly, and this was acknowledged by a burst of applause from the congregation, who then turned to look at the next visitor. In turn the others revealed who they were—a man from Francistown, a man from Brisbane, a woman from Concord, Massachusetts, and a woman from Johannesburg. Each was welcomed, solemnly but warmly. No distinction was made between those who were from Africa and those who were not. The American woman, Mma Ramotswe observed, was wearing a pumpkin-coloured dress. She noted that, but immediately corrected herself. This was a time of fellowship, and not a time to be thinking of pumpkins.

Trevor Mwamba adjusted his glasses. "My brothers and sisters," he began, "you are welcome here with us. Wherever you may come from, you are welcome."

He looked at his notes before him. "I am sometimes asked," he said, "why there is so much suffering in this world and how we can reconcile it with the faith which we have in a benevolent creator. This is not a new objection. Many people have made this point to those who hold to a faith, and they have often rejected the answers they have received. It is not good enough, they say. Your answers do not convince. Yet why should they imagine that we can explain every mystery? There are some mysteries that lie beyond our understanding. Such mysteries reveal themselves every day."

Yes, thought Mma Ramotswe. **There is one such mystery which has revealed itself in Zebra Drive this very morning. How does one explain a missing pair of trousers and a pumpkin that comes from nowhere?** She stopped herself. This was not the way to listen to Trevor Mwamba.

"There are many other mysteries in this world that we cannot explain and which we must accept. I think of the mystery of life, for instance. The scientists know a great deal about life, but they do not know how to make that spark that is the difference between life and no-life. That bit, that current, is a mystery to them, however much they know about how life works and perpetuates itself. And so we have to accept, do we not, that there are some mysteries in this world that we simply cannot understand? These things are simply there. They are beyond us."

The mystery of life! thought Mma Ramotswe. **The mystery of pumpkins. Why are pumpkins the shape they are? Why is the flesh of the pumpkin the colour it is? Can**

anybody explain that, or is it just something that is? Again she struggled to stop her train of thought and concentrated on what Trevor Mwamba was saying.

"And so it is with suffering. It may seem a mystery to us that there can be suffering in a world in which we claim to see a divine purpose. But the more we think about that mystery, the more an answer eludes us. We could, then, shrug our shoulders and fall into despair, or we could accept the mystery for what it is, as being something that we simply cannot understand. And that does not mean that we lapse into nihilism, into the philosophy that says that we can do nothing about the suffering and pain of the world. We can do something about it, and all of us in this place today have the chance to do something, even if only a small thing, to diminish the volume of suffering in the world. We can do that by acts of kindness to others; we can do that by relieving their pain.

"If we look about our world today, if we look about this dear home of ours, Africa, then what do we see but tears and sorrow? Yes, we see those. We see those even in Botswana, where we are so fortunate in many ways. We see those in the faces of those who are ill, in their fear and their sorrow at the thought that their lives will be so shortened. This is real suffering, but it is not suffering that we as Christians walk away from. Every day, every moment of every day, there are people who are working to alleviate this suffering. They are working at this task right now as I speak, right across the road in the Princess Marina Hospital. There are doctors and nurses working. There are our own people and generous-hearted people from far away, from America, for example, who are working there to bring relief to those who are very sick from this cruel illness that stalks Africa. Do those people talk about such suffering as proof that there can be no divine presence in this world? They do not. They do not ask that question. And many are sustained by that very faith at which some clever people like to sneer. And that, my friends, is the true mystery at which we should marvel. That is what we should think about in silence for a moment, as we remember the names of those who are ill, those members of this body, this Anglican church, our brothers and sisters. And I read them out now."

CHAPTER FOUR

TEA ISSUES

IN THE MORNINGS everybody arrived at Tlokweng Road Speedy Motors at different times, and there was no telling who would be in first. It used to be Mr J.L.B. Matekoni, in the days when the offices of the No. 1 Ladies' Detective Agency were housed separately, but since the two businesses began to share the same premises it was sometimes Mma Ramotswe or Mma Makutsi, or, very rarely, one of the apprentices. In general, the apprentices arrived late, as they liked to stay in bed until the last possible moment before they bolted down a quick breakfast and rushed to catch the overloaded minibus that would drop them off at the roundabout at the end of the Tlokweng Road.

After their marriage, of course, Mma Ramotswe and Mr J.L.B. Matekoni tended to arrive at exactly the same time, even if they drove in two vehicles, as in a convoy, with Mr J.L.B. Matekoni's truck leading the way and the tiny white van, at the wheel of which sat Mma Ramotswe, following valiantly behind.

On that particular morning it was Mma Makutsi, carrying a brown paper parcel, who was first to arrive. She unlocked the office of the No. 1 Ladies' Detective Agency, placed the parcel on her desk, and opened the window to let in some air. It was barely seven o'clock, and it would be half an hour or so before Mma Ramotswe and Mr J.L.B. Matekoni arrived. This would give her time to organise her desk, to telephone her cousin's sister-in-law about a family matter, and to write a quick letter to her father in Bobonong. Her father was seventy-one, and he had nothing very much to do, other than to walk to the small post office in the village and check for mail. Usually there was nothing, but at least once a week there would be a letter from Mma Makutsi, containing a few snippets of news from Gaborone and sometimes a fifty-pula note. Her father could not read English very well, and so Mma

Makutsi always wrote to him in Kalanga, which gave her pleasure, as she liked to keep her grasp of the language alive.

There was much to tell him that day. She had had a busy weekend, with an invitation to a meal at the house of one of her new neighbours, who was a Malawian lady teaching at one of the schools. This lady had lived in London for a year and knew all about places that Mma Makutsi had only seen in the pages of the **National Geographic** magazine. Yet she carried her experience lightly, and did not make Mma Makutsi feel at all provincial or untravelled. Quite the opposite, in fact. The neighbour had asked probing questions about Bobonong and had listened attentively while Mma Makutsi had told her of Francistown and Maun, and places like that.

"You are lucky to live in this country," said the neighbour. "You have everything. Lots of land, as far as the eye can see, and further. And all those diamonds. And the cattle. There is everything here."

"We are very fortunate," said Mma Makutsi. "We know that."

"And you now have that nice new house," the neighbour went on, "and that interesting job of yours. People must ask you all the time: What is it like to be a private detective?"

Mma Makutsi smiled modestly. "They think it is a very exciting job," she said. "But it is not really. Most of the time we are just helping people to find out things they already know."

"And this Mma Ramotswe people talk about?" asked the neighbour. "What is she like? I have seen her at the shops. She has a very kind face. You would not think she was a detective, just to look at her."

"She is a very kind lady," agreed Mma Makutsi. "But she is also very clever. She can tell when people are lying, just by looking at them. And she also knows how to deal with men."

The neighbour sighed. "That is a very great talent," she said. "I would like to be able to do that."

Mma Makutsi agreed with this. That would be very good; and indeed it would be good to have just one man to deal with. Mma Ramotswe now had Mr J.L.B. Matekoni, and this Malawian woman had a boyfriend, whom Mma Makutsi had seen coming to the house in the evenings. She herself had not yet found a man, apart from that one she had met at the Kalahari Typing School for Men and who had not lasted very long for some reason. After that she had made a rule: **Never become emotionally involved with one of your typing students**—a rule which was a variant on the advice which Mma Ramotswe had quoted from Clovis Andersen: **Always keep your distance from your client; hugs and kisses never solved any cases, and never paid any bills.**

Now the last part of that advice was very interesting, and Mma Makutsi had considered it at some length. She had no doubt that it was true that emotional involvement with a client would not help you to see a problem clearly, and would therefore not assist the solving of the case, but was it true to say that hugs and kisses never paid any bills? Surely one could argue the opposite of that. There were plenty of people who paid their way through life with hugs and kisses—the wives of rich men, for example, or at least some wives of some rich men. Mma Makutsi was in no doubt whatsoever that some of those glamorous girls who had been in her class at the Botswana Secretarial College, those girls who in some cases got scarcely fifty per cent in the College's final examinations (against her own ninety-seven per cent); some of these girls had made a very astute calculation that the way to get on financially was to make sure that their hugs and kisses went to the right sort of man. And that, in their view, was the sort of man who was earning many thousands of pula a month and who drove an expensive car, preferably a Mercedes-Benz.

Mma Makutsi now wrote to her father about the meeting with this neighbour, but said nothing of the discussion about men, or Mma Ramotswe, or being a private detective; rather, she told him what the woman had cooked for her. Then she told him about the trouble she was having with ants in the new house, and that there seemed to be nothing that could be done. He would sympathise with her on that. Everybody in Botswana had experienced trouble with ants, and everybody had a view on what to do. But nobody ever succeeded: the ants always returned. Perhaps it was because they had been there before people had arrived and regarded it as their place. Perhaps the country should be called Botshoswane, rather than Botswana; this meant the Place of the Ants. No doubt that's what the ants called it anyway.

The letter concluded, she attached a twenty-pula note to it with a pin, addressed the envelope and sealed it. That was her daughterly duty done for the week, and she smiled to herself as she imagined her father opening his small metal postal box (which she paid for) and his pleasure in receiving her letter. She had been told that he would read each letter again and again, extracting new significance each time from each phrase and each sentence. Then he would show it to his friends, the other old men, or read it to those who could not read, and they would talk about it for hours.

By the time the letter was finished, and the quick telephone call made, she heard Mr J.L.B. Matekoni's truck arriving outside. This truck always made more noise than any other vehicle, which was caused by its engine being different from the engines of other trucks. That was what Mr J.L.B. Matekoni had said, and he was undoubtedly right. He explained that the engine had been badly looked after by the previous owner and it had been impossible to undo the damage altogether. But it remained a good truck at heart; like a faithful beast of burden that has been maltreated by an owner but which has never lost its faith in man. And hard on the heels of the truck came the tiny white van, which drew to a halt in its parking place under the acacia tree at the side of the garage.

Mma Ramotswe and Mma Makutsi had already opened the morning mail by the time that the apprentices arrived. The older apprentice, Charlie, sauntered into their office, whistling a tune, and smiling cheekily at the two women.

"You look pleased with yourself," said Mma Ramotswe. "Have you won a big prize or something?"

The apprentice laughed. "Wouldn't you like to know, Mma? Just wouldn't you like to know?"

Mma Ramotswe exchanged glances with Mma Makutsi. "I hope you haven't come to borrow money," she said. "I am happy to help you, but you really should pay me back that fifty pula you borrowed at the beginning of the month."

The apprentice affected injured innocence. "Ow! Why do you think I should need to borrow money, Mma? Do I look like somebody who needs to borrow money? I do not, I think. In fact, I was just coming in to pay you back. Here. Look."

He reached into his pocket and took out a

small roll of notes, from which he peeled off fifty pula. "There," he said. "That is fifty pula, is it not? And that is what I owe you. I am giving it back right now."

Mma Ramotswe took the money and slipped it into her drawer. "You seem to have a lot of money there. Where did you get it? Have you robbed a bank?"

The apprentice laughed. "I would never rob a bank. That is just for fools. If you rob a bank, then the police will surely catch you. That is always true. So don't rob a bank, Mma!"

"I have no intention of robbing a bank," said Mma Ramotswe, laughing at the suggestion.

"Just warning you, Mma," he said casually, ostentatiously putting the roll of notes back into the pocket of his overalls. Then he sauntered out again, having resumed his whistling.

Mma Makutsi looked across the room at Mma Ramotswe. "Well!" she exclaimed. "What a performance!"

"He's up to something," said Mma Ramotswe. "Where would he have got hold of that money if he weren't up to something? Do you think he borrowed it from somebody, from some foolish person who doesn't know what those young men are like?"

"I have no idea," said Mma Makutsi. "But did you see the look on his face? Did you see how pleased he was with himself? And did you see that he was wearing one white shoe and one brown shoe? Did you notice that?"

"I'm afraid I didn't," said Mma Ramotswe. "What can that mean, do you think?"

"It means that he has two pairs like that," said Mma Makutsi, laughing. "Or it means that he thinks he looks smart. I think it is because he thinks it looks smart."

"He's a good enough boy at heart," said Mma Ramotswe. "He just needs to grow up a bit, don't you think?"

"No," said Mma Makutsi. She paused before continuing, "Do you know, Mma? I think that he is seeing a rich woman. I think that he has found some lady to give him money. That would explain the money itself, but it would also explain the fancy shoes, the grease on the hair, and the general air of being very pleased with himself. That is what is happening, if you ask me."

Mma Ramotswe laughed. "Poor woman!" she said. "I feel sorry for her."

Mma Makutsi agreed with this, but she felt concerned for the boy too. He was only a young man, and very immature, and if this woman was much older than he was, then she might be taking advantage of him in some way. It did not look good for a young man to be spoilt in this way by some bored, rich woman. He would be the one to be hurt when the whole thing came to an end, as it undoubtedly would. And in spite of everything, she liked the two apprentices, or at least felt some responsibility for them; the responsibility that an older sister feels for a younger brother, perhaps. The younger brother might be foolish and may get into all sorts of difficulties through his foolishness, but he remained the younger brother, and he had to be protected.

"I think we should watch this situation," she said to Mma Ramotswe. And Mma Ramotswe nodded her head in agreement.

"We'll think of something," she said. "But you are right, we do not want that young man to come to any harm. We must think of something."

THEY HAD A GREAT DEAL of work to do that day. A few days previously, they had received a letter from a firm of lawyers in Zambia, asking them to help in the tracing of a Lusaka financier who had disappeared. The circumstances of his disappearance were suspicious: there was a large hole in the company's finances and the natural conclusion was that he had taken the money. This was not the sort of matter with which Mma Ramotswe normally liked to concern herself; the No. 1 Ladies' Detective Agency preferred to deal with more domestic matters, but it was a matter of professional honour that no client would be turned away, unless, of course, they deserved to be. And there was also the question of money. This sort of work paid well, and there were overheads to be taken into account—Mma Makutsi's salary, the cost of running the tiny white van, and postage, to name just a few of the items that seemed to consume so much of the profits each month.

The financier was believed to be in Botswana, where he had relatives. Of course they were the first people who should be approached, but who were they? The lawyers had been unable to provide names, and this would mean that Mma Ramotswe and Mma Makutsi would have to make enquiries amongst

Zambians in Gaborone. That sounded simple enough, but it was not always easy to get foreigners to talk about their fellow citizens, especially if one of them was in trouble. They knew that it was wrong to close ranks, especially when it was a question of embezzled funds, but they did it nonetheless. So there were many telephone calls to be made to see if anybody was prepared to throw light on the case. There were also letters to hotels, asking them if they recognised the person in the photograph which they now sent them. All of this was time-consuming, and they worked solidly until ten o'clock, when Mma Ramotswe, having just finished an unsatisfactory telephone call to a rather rude Zambian woman, put down the receiver, stretched her arms wide, and announced that it was time for morning tea.

Mma Makutsi agreed. "I have written letters now to ten hotels," she said, taking a sheet out of her typewriter, "and my head is sore from thinking about missing Zambians. I am looking forward to a cup of tea."

"I will make it," offered Mma Ramotswe. "You have been working very hard, while I have just been talking on the telephone. You deserve a rest."

Mma Makutsi looked embarrassed. "That is very kind, Mma. But I was thinking of making tea in a different way this morning."

Mma Ramotswe looked at her assistant in astonishment. "In a different way? How can you make bush tea in a different way? Surely there is only one way to make tea—you put the tea leaves in the tea-pot and then you put in the water. What are you going to do? Put the water in first? Is that the different way you have in mind?"

Mma Makutsi rose to her feet, picking up the parcel which she had placed on her desk when she arrived. Mma Ramotswe had not noticed this, as it had been behind a pile of files. Now she looked at it with curiosity.

"What is that, Mma?" Mma Ramotswe asked. "Is it something to do with this new way of making tea?"

Mma Makutsi did not reply, but unwrapped the parcel and exposed a new china tea-pot, which she held up to Mma Ramotswe's gaze.

"Ah!" exclaimed Mma Ramotswe. "That is a very fine tea-pot, Mma! Look at it! Look at the flowers on the side. That is very fine. Our bush tea will taste very good if it is brewed in so handsome a tea-pot!"

Mma Makutsi looked down at her shoes, but there was no help from that quarter; there never was. In tight moments, she had noticed, her shoes tended to say: **You're on your own, Boss!** She had known all along that this would be awkward, but she had decided that sooner or later she would have to take this issue up with Mma Ramotswe and it could not be put off any longer.

"Well, Mma," she began. "Well . . ."

She paused. It was going to be more difficult than she had imagined. She looked at Mma Ramotswe, who stared back at her expectantly.

"I am looking forward to the tea," said Mma Ramotswe helpfully.

Mma Makutsi swallowed. "I will not be making bush tea," she blurted out. "I mean, I will make bush tea for you, as usual, but I want to make my own tea, ordinary tea, in this pot. Just for me. Ordinary tea. You can drink bush tea and I will drink ordinary tea."

After she had finished speaking, there was a complete silence. Mma Ramotswe sat quite still in her chair, her eyes fixed on the china tea-pot. Mma Makutsi, who had been holding the pot up as if it were a battle standard, a standard for the ranks of those who preferred ordinary tea to bush tea, now lowered it and put it down on her desk.

"I'm sorry, Mma," said Mma Makutsi. "I'm very sorry. I do not want you to think that I am a rude person. I am not. But I have tried and tried to like bush tea and now I must speak what is in my heart. And my heart says that I have preferred ordinary tea all along. That is why I bought this special tea-pot."

Mma Ramotswe listened carefully, and then she spoke. "I am the one who should say sorry, Mma. No, it is me. I am the one. I have been the rude person all along. I have never asked you whether you would prefer to drink ordinary tea. I never bothered to ask you, but I have bought bush tea and expected you to like it. I am very sorry, Mma."

"You have not been rude," protested Mma Makutsi. "I should have told you. I am the one who is at fault here."

It was all very complicated. Mma Makutsi had switched from bush tea to ordinary tea some time ago, and then she had gone back to bush tea again. Mma Ramotswe felt confused: What did Mma Makutsi really want when it came to tea?

"No," said Mma Ramotswe. "You have been very patient with me, drinking all that bush tea just for my sake. I should have seen it. I should have seen it in your face. I did not. I am very sorry, Mma."

"But I didn't dislike it **all** that much," said Mma Makutsi. "I did not make a face when I drank it. If I had made a face, then you might have noticed it. But I did not. I was happy enough drinking it—it's just that I shall be even happier when I am drinking ordinary tea."

Mma Ramotswe nodded. "Then we shall have different tea," she said. "Just as we did in the past. I have my tea, and you have yours. That is the solution to this difficult problem."

"Exactly," said Mma Makutsi. She thought for a moment. What about Mr J.L.B. Matekoni and the apprentices? They had all been drinking bush tea, but now that there was a choice, should they be offered ordinary tea? And if they were, then would they want to drink it out of her tea-pot? She would not mind sharing her new tea-pot with Mr J.L.B. Matekoni—nobody would mind that—but sharing with the apprentices was another matter altogether.

She decided to voice her concerns to Mma Ramotswe. "What about Mr J.L.B. Matekoni?" she asked. "Will he drink . . ."

"Bush tea," said Mma Ramotswe quickly. "That is the best tea for a man. It is well-known. He will drink bush tea."

"And the apprentices?"

Mma Ramotswe rolled her eyes towards the ceiling. "Perhaps they should have bush tea too," she said. "Although, heaven knows, it's not doing them much good."

With those decisions made, Mma Makutsi put on the kettle and, watched by Mma Ramotswe, she ladled into the new tea-pot a quantity of her tea, her ordinary tea. Then she fetched Mma Ramotswe's tea-pot, which looked distinctly battered beside the fine new china tea-pot, and into this she put the correct quantity of bush tea. They waited for the kettle to boil, each of them silent, each of them alone with her thoughts. Mma Makutsi was thinking with relief of the generous response that Mma Ramotswe had shown to her confession, which seemed so like an act of disloyalty, of treachery even. Her employer had made it so easy that she felt a flood of gratitude for her. Mma Ramotswe was undoubtedly one of the finest women in all Botswana. Mma Makutsi had always known this, but here was another instance which spoke to those qualities of understanding and sympathy. And for her part, Mma Ramotswe thought of what a loyal, fine woman was Mma Makutsi. Other employees would have complained, or moaned about drinking tea they did not like, but she had said nothing. And more than that, she had given the impression that she was enjoying what was given to her, as a polite guest will eat or drink what is laid upon the host's table. This was further evidence of those very qualities which obviously had been revealed at the Botswana Secretarial College and which had resulted in her astonishingly high marks. Mma Makutsi was surely a gem.

CHAPTER FIVE

AN ENCOUNTER WITH
A BICYCLE

FOR THE REST of that day, with the issue of
tea tactfully settled, Mma Ramotswe and Mma
Makutsi continued with their attempts to find
out about the missing Zambian. This was the
office stage of the project; they knew that in a
day or so they would have to go out and seek
people who might give them information, unless, of course, one of the letters which Mma
Makutsi wrote or the telephone conversations
which Mma Ramotswe conducted yielded results. At a quarter to five, when the afternoon
heat had abated and the sky was beginning to
redden over the Kalahari, Mma Ramotswe announced that although the working day still
technically had fifteen minutes to run, they

had achieved so much that they might in good conscience stop.

"I've made so many phone calls," she said. "I cannot speak any more."

"And are we any closer to finding him?" asked Mma Makutsi doubtfully.

Mma Ramotswe was not one to be defeatist. "Yes, we are," she said. "Even if we have not discovered anything concrete, every step along the path is one step closer to the solution. Mr Andersen says, doesn't he, that if there are one hundred questions to be asked in an investigation, you have to go through every one of them, and so you achieve something even if you get no answer. That is what he wrote."

"He must be right," said Mma Makutsi. "But I am not sure that we will ever find this man. He is too smart. He is not a man to be caught all that easily."

"But we are smart too," said Mma Ramotswe. "There are two smart ladies after him, and he is just one man. No man will escape in such circumstances."

Mma Makutsi still looked doubtful. "I hope that you're right, Mma," she said.

"I am," said Mma Ramotswe simply. And

with that conclusion she stood up and began to gather her things together. "I can take you home," she said. "I am going that way."

They locked the office behind them and made their way round to the place where the tiny white van awaited them under its acacia tree. Mma Makutsi got into the passenger seat, next to Mma Ramotswe, who strapped herself in and started the engine. As she did so, Mma Makutsi suddenly grabbed her arm and pointed to something that was happening outside the garage.

A large, silver-coloured car, a Mercedes-Benz, had drawn up at the road side. The windows of this vehicle were slightly tinted, but a woman could be made out at the driving wheel. No sooner had she stopped, than Charlie, the older apprentice, appeared from the front of the garage, sauntered across the ground between the garage and the road, and casually climbed into the passenger seat of the expensive car.

Mma Ramotswe looked at Mma Makutsi. They were both clearly thinking the same thing; Charlie had produced a roll of notes that morning, and Mma Makutsi had quite astutely suggested that he was seeing a rich woman.

Well, here was a rich woman in a rich woman's car, and there was Charlie setting off with her at the end of work. There was only one interpretation that anybody could put on that.

"Well," exclaimed Mma Makutsi. "That's that then."

Mma Ramotswe stared in fascination. "Who would have thought that that silly boy could take up with a woman like that? Who would have thought it?"

"There are some women like that," said Mma Makutsi, a strong note of disapproval in her voice. "They call them cradle snatchers. That is because they take young men away from girls of their own age. They steal these boys away."

"So that woman is a cradle-snatcher," said Mma Ramotswe. "That is very interesting." She paused, and then turned to Mma Makutsi. "I think that we shall have to come back on duty right now," she said. "I think that we should follow that car, just to see where they go."

"That's a very good idea," said Mma Makutsi. "I do not mind being back on duty."

The opulent silver car set off towards town, and as it did so the tiny white van swung out from the side of the garage and set off behind the other car, but at a respectable distance. For a powerful car, the Mercedes-Benz was being driven slowly; most Mercedes-Benz drivers, Mma Ramotswe had observed, seemed to be in a hurry to get somewhere, but this one, this woman of whom they had had only the briefest glimpse, seemed to be content to amble along.

"She's in no hurry," said Mma Ramotswe. "They must be talking."

"I can just imagine it," said Mma Makutsi grimly. "He'll be telling her some tale about us, Mma. She'll be laughing and urging him on."

When they reached the old Game Stores, the silver car suddenly turned into the Village and made its way down Odi Drive. The tiny white van, holding back in case the apprentice should turn and see them, proceeded at a safe distance, following the quarry past the school and the new flats until they reached the University gate. Now came a surprise: instead of turning left, which would have led them into town, the silver car went to the right, towards the prison and the old Gaborone Club.

"This is very odd," said Mma Makutsi. "I would have thought that they would be going somewhere like the Sun Hotel. What is there for them along here?"

"Maybe she lives along this way," said Mma Ramotswe. "But we shall see soon enough."

Mma Ramotswe turned to Mma Makutsi and smiled conspiratorially. The two women were enjoying themselves. There was no real reason for them to follow the apprentice and this woman. Indeed, had they stopped to consider what they were doing, they would have had to admit that it was surely no more than idle curiosity—nosiness, indeed, that motivated them. And it was interesting, in a gossipy sort of way. If Charlie was seeing an older woman, then it would be fascinating to see what sort of woman she would be. Not that there was much doubt about that, thought Mma Ramotswe.

"What would Mr J.L.B. Matekoni think of us?" ventured Mma Makutsi, giggling. "Would he approve?"

Mma Ramotswe shook her head. "He would say that we were two nosy women," she said. "And I think he would be more interested in the Mercedes-Benz than the people in it. That is what mechanics are like. They think . . ."

She did not complete her sentence. The silver car was now near the old Botswana Defence Force Club and was slowing down. Then an indicator light started to flash and the car turned into a driveway—into the driveway of Mr J.L.B. Matekoni's house.

When she saw the car turn, Mma Ramotswe swerved the tiny white van so violently that Mma Makutsi shouted out in alarm. A cyclist, who had been coming in the opposite direction, swerved too, wobbling off the road to avoid the van. Mma Ramotswe drew to a halt and climbed out.

"Rra, oh Rra," she shouted, as she ran towards the fallen man. "I'm so sorry, Rra."

The man picked himself up off the ground and then dusted his trousers. He used careful, deliberate gestures, as might be used by one who is dressed in expensive clothes; but his were worn, and crumpled. Then he looked up, and Mma Ramotswe saw that there were tears in his eyes.

"Oh, Rra," she said. "I've hurt you. I'm so sorry. I will take you straight to a doctor."

The man shook his head, and then wiped at his eyes with the back of a hand.

"I am not hurt," he said. "I am shaken, but I am not hurt."

"I was looking at something else," said Mma Ramotswe, reaching out to take the man's hand. "It was very silly of me. I took my eyes off the road, and then suddenly I saw you."

The man said nothing. Turning to his bicycle, he picked it up. The front wheel, which must have been caught in a rut in the ground, was now slightly twisted, and the handlebars were at a strange angle. He looked mutely at the bicycle, before trying, unsuccessfully, to straighten the handlebars.

Mma Ramotswe turned and beckoned to Mma Makutsi to come out of the van. She had been holding back, out of a mixture of tact and embarrassment, but now she appeared and made a sympathetic remark to the man.

"I will take you to where you are going," said Mma Ramotswe. "We can put the bike in the back of the van and then I shall take that to your place, wherever that is."

The man pointed back towards Tlokweng. "I live over that way," he said. "I would prefer to go home now. I do not want to go to the other place."

They lifted up the bicycle together and placed it in the back of the van. Then Mma Ramotswe and Mma Makutsi got into the tiny white van on one side and the man on the other. With the three of them in the cab, there was barely enough room for Mma Ramotswe to change gear, and each time she did it she dug Mma Makutsi in the ribs.

"This is not a big van," Mma Ramotswe said brightly to their passenger. "But it always goes. So it will get us to Tlokweng very easily."

She looked sideways at the man. He looked as if he was in his late forties. He had a good face, she thought; an intelligent face, the face of a teacher, perhaps, or of a senior clerk. And he spoke well too, enunciating each word clearly, as if he meant it. So many people spoke carelessly these days, she thought, running their words together so that it was sometimes quite difficult to make out what they were saying. And as for people on the radio, these so-called disc jockeys, they spoke as if they had hiccups. Presumably they thought that it was fashionable to talk like this; that it made them more alluring, which it probably did if one was star-struck, and with nothing much in one's head, but which only sounded ridiculous to her.

"I will have your bicycle fixed for you," she said to the man. "It will be made as good as new. I promise you that."

The man nodded. "I cannot pay myself," he said. "I have not got the money for that."

Mma Ramotswe nodded. She had thought as much. In spite of all the progress which Botswana had made, and in spite of the prosperity which the diamonds had brought to the country, there were still many, many poor people. They should not be forgotten. But why was this man, who seemed to be educated, not in a job? She knew that there were many people who could not find a job, but usually these were people who had no skills. This man did not seem to be like that.

It was Mma Makutsi who asked the question for her. She had been thinking the same thing as Mma Ramotswe. She had noticed the disparity between the signs of poverty—something that Mma Makutsi knew all about—and the educated voice. She had seen, too, that the man's hands were what she would describe as well-kept. These were not the hands of a manual labourer, nor those of a man who tended the land. She noticed such hands at her part-time typing classes at the Kalahari Typing School for Men. Many of her pupils there, who worked in offices, had hands like this man's.

"Do you work in an office, Rra?" she asked. "And may I ask you: What is your name?"

The man glanced at her, and then turned away.

"My name is Polopetsi," he said. "And no, I have no work. I am looking for work, but there is no place that will take me."

Mma Ramotswe frowned. "It is hard now," she said. "That must be very bad for you." She paused. "What did you do before?"

Mr Polopetsi did not answer directly, and the question seemed to hang in the air for a while. Then he spoke.

"I was in prison for two years. I have been out for six months."

The tiny white van swerved slightly, almost imperceptibly. "And nobody will give you a job?" asked Mma Ramotswe.

"They will not," he answered.

"And you always tell them that you have been in prison?" interjected Mma Makutsi.

"I do," said Mr Polopetsi. "I am an honest man. I cannot lie to them when they say what have you been doing this last year. I cannot tell them that I was in Johannesburg or something like that. I cannot tell them that I have been working."

"So, you are an honest man," said Mma Ramotswe. "But why were you in prison? Are there honest men in prison?" She asked the question before she thought about it and she immediately realised that it sounded very rude; as if she were questioning the man's story.

He did not seem to take objection. "I was not sent to prison for dishonesty," he said. "But there are honest men in prison, by the way. There are some very dishonest men there, and some very bad men. But there are also men who are there because of other things that they did."

They waited for him to continue, but he did not.

"So," said Mma Ramotswe. "What did you do, Rra? Why did they send you to prison?"

Mr Polopetsi looked at his hands. "I was sent to prison because of an accident."

Mma Makutsi turned to look at him. "An accident? They sent you instead of somebody else?"

"No," said the man. "I was sent to prison because there was an accident while I was in charge of something. It was my fault, and a person was killed. It was an accident, but they said that it would not have happened had I been more careful."

They were nearing Tlokweng now, and Mma Ramotswe had to ask for directions to the man's house. He pointed to a dusty side-road, not much more than a bumpy track, and she drove the tiny white van down that, trying to avoid the larger holes in the ground. If there was a grader in Tlokweng, then it must rarely have bothered to come this way.

"Our road is not very good," said Mr Polopetsi. "When it rains all these holes fill up with water and you can go fishing if you like."

Mma Makutsi laughed. "I have lived along a road like this in the past," she said. "I know what it is like."

"Yes," said Mr Polopetsi. "It is not easy." He stopped, and pointed at a house a short way down the road. "That is my place."

It was a simple, two-room house, and Mma Ramotswe could see that it was in need of painting; the lower part of the outside walls was specked with dried red mud, which had been splashed up at the last rains. The yard, which was small, was well-swept, which suggested that there was a conscientious woman in charge of it, and there was a small chicken coop to one side, again well-kept.

"This is a very tidy place," said Mma Ramotswe. "It is good to see a place that is well-kept, as this one is."

"It is my wife," said Mr Polopetsi. "She is the one who keeps this place so clean."

"You must be proud of her, Rra," said Mma Makutsi.

"And she must be proud of you," said Mma Ramotswe.

There was silence for a moment. Then Mr Polopetsi spoke. "Why do you say that, Mma?" he asked.

"Because you are a good man," said Mma Ramotswe quietly. "That is why I said that. You may have been in prison for two years, but I can tell that you are a good man."

THEY LEFT Mr Polopetsi in his house and drove back down the pothole-ridden road. The bicycle was still in the back of the tiny white van and Mma Ramotswe had agreed with Mr

Polopetsi that she would take it to be fixed the following day and bring it out to him when it was ready. As he had stepped out of the van, she had offered him money to compensate him for the accident, but he had shaken his head.

"I can tell when something is an accident," he said. "And people are not to blame for accidents. I know that."

She had not pressed the matter. This man had his pride, and it would have been rude for her to persist. So they agreed about the bicycle and left him outside his house. They were largely silent as they drove back. Mma Ramotswe was thinking of Mr Polopetsi, and his house, and the humiliation that he had suffered in his life. That must have been why he was in tears after the accident; it was just one more thing that he had to bear. Of course they had heard only his side of the story of the prison sentence. Surely people were not sent to prison in Botswana for nothing? She knew that they could be proud of their system of justice—of their judges who would not kow-tow to anybody, who were not afraid of criticising the Government. There were so many countries where this was not so, where the judges were browbeaten or chosen from amongst the ranks of the party faithful, but this had never been the case in Botswana. So surely these judges would never have sent a man to prison unless he deserved punishment?

Mma Makutsi was anxious about being late for the typing class she was due to give at seven o'clock, and so they did not linger on their way back, although they did go slightly out of their way in order to drive past Mr J.L.B. Matekoni's house—or, rather, the house which belonged to Mr J.L.B. Matekoni but which was now occupied by a tenant. The silver Mercedes-Benz was still there.

"Does she live in that house?" asked Mma Makutsi. "Did Mr J.L.B. Matekoni let the house to a woman?"

"No," said Mma Ramotswe. "He let it out—without first asking me, mind you—to a man whose car he used to fix. He does not know him very well, but he said that he always used to pay his bills."

"It is very strange," said Mma Makutsi. "We will have to find out more about this."

"We certainly shall," agreed Mma Ramotswe. "There are many mysteries developing in our lives, Mma Makutsi, what with these rich ladies in silver cars, bicycles, pumpkins, and all the rest, and we shall have to sort them all out."

Mma Makutsi looked puzzled. "Pumpkins?" she asked.

"Yes," said Mma Ramotswe. "There is a pumpkin mystery, but we do not have time to talk about it now. I shall tell you about it some other time."

THAT EVENING Mma Makutsi could not get pumpkins out of her mind, and it was one of the words which she got the typing class to type. She held these classes several times a week in a church hall that she rented for the purpose. The Kalahari Typing School for Men, which admitted only men, was based on the supposition that men usually cannot type very well but are afraid to admit this fact. And while it would be perfectly possible for them to register for any of the part-time courses provided by the Botswana Secretarial College, they tended not to do this for reasons of shame. Men would not wish to be outstripped by women in typing, which would be sure to happen. So Mma Makutsi's discreet classes had proved very popular.

She stood now before a class of fifteen men, all eager students of the art of typing, and all making good progress, although at different rates. This class had worked on finger position, had worked its way through the simple words which start every typing career (hat, cat, rat, and the like), and was now ready for more advanced tasks.

"Pumpkin," Mma Makutsi called out, and the keys immediately began to clatter. But she had something to add: "Do not leave out the p. That is very important."

A number of the keys stopped, and then started afresh, on a new line.

CHAPTER SIX

FURTHER DETAILS

Mma Ramotswe had intended to ask Mr J.L.B. Matekoni about his new tenant that evening, but it was busy at home, with the children making demands to be taken here and there and Rose staying late to talk to her about her sick child. So by the time that nine o'clock arrived, and the pots and pans had been washed in the kitchen, and sandwiches made and wrapped up for the children to take to school the next day, Mma Ramotswe was too tired to start a new conversation, particularly one which might prove awkward for Mr J.L.B. Matekoni. So they both retired to bed, where she read a magazine for a few minutes before drowsiness forced her to abandon her reading and she switched off the light.

So it was not until the next morning when Mr J.L.B. Matekoni came into the office for his mid-morning cup of tea, that she was able to raise the subject of what she and Mma Makutsi had seen the previous evening. She had told him about the accident, of course, and he had told the apprentices to fix the bicycle that morning.

Mma Ramotswe had expressed doubts about their abilities to fix it properly. "They are very rough with machinery," she said. "You've told me that yourself. And we've all seen it. I don't want them to make that poor man's bicycle worse."

"It is only a bicycle," said Mr J.L.B. Matekoni, reassuringly. "It's not a Mercedes-Benz."

Now the topic of Mercedes-Benzes came up again, as she passed Mr J.L.B. Matekoni his brimming mug of bush tea.

"Mma Makutsi and I saw a Mercedes-Benz yesterday," she began, glancing at Mma Makutsi for confirmation. "It stopped right outside this place."

"Oh yes," said Mr J.L.B. Matekoni, in a

tone which suggested that he was not very interested. "There are many Mercedes-Benzes these days. You see them all the time. What sort was it?"

"It was silver," offered Mma Makutsi.

Mr J.L.B. Matekoni smiled. "That is its colour. There are silver Toyotas too. Many cars are silver. I meant what model was it?"

"It was a Mercedes E class," said Mma Ramotswe.

This remark made Mma Makutsi look up in astonishment, and then look down in shame. Of course that was exactly the sort of detail which a detective should spot, and which Mma Ramotswe had indeed noted. Whereas she, Mma Makutsi, a mere assistant detective, had noticed nothing other than the colour.

"A good car," said Mr J.L.B. Matekoni. "Not that I would ever spend that much money—even if I had that much—on a car like that. There must be a lot of rich people around."

"I think that the driver was a rich lady," said Mma Ramotswe. "I think that she is a rich lady who is seeing Charlie out there. Yes. I believe that."

Mr J.L.B. Matekoni stared down into his

tea. He did not like to think of the private life of his apprentices, largely because he imagined that it would be distasteful in the extreme. It would all be girls, he thought, because that is all they had in their minds. Just girls. So he said nothing, and Mma Ramotswe continued.

"Yes. Mma Makutsi and I saw Charlie getting into this Mercedes-Benz with the rich lady who was driving it and then they drove off."

She waited for a reaction from Mr J.L.B. Matekoni, but he merely continued to drink his tea.

"So," she went on, "they drove off towards the old airfield and then they went to a house." She paused before adding, "Your house, in fact."

Mr J.L.B. Matekoni put down his mug of tea. "My house?"

"Yes," said Mma Ramotswe. "They went into your house, and that is what made me swerve and make that poor man fall off his bicycle. If it had not been your house, I would not have been so surprised and would not have swerved."

"And they stayed there for some time," said Mma Makutsi. "I think they were visiting the people who live there now, whoever they are."

"That could be true," said Mr J.L.B. Matekoni. "The people who live in my house will have friends, no doubt. Perhaps this lady with the Mercedes-Benz is a friend of those people."

Mma Ramotswe agreed that this was a possibility. But the apprentices were always happy to gossip, and if they were mixing socially with Mr J.L.B. Matekoni's tenants they might well have been expected to mention the fact, surely?

Mr J.L.B. Matekoni now shrugged. "It is Charlie's affair," he said. "If he is going round with this woman in his own time, then that is his business. I cannot stop those young men from having girlfriends. That is not my job. My job is to teach them to work on engines, and that is difficult enough. If I had to teach them about looking after themselves once they leave the garage, then . . ." He spread his hands in a gesture of hopelessness.

Mma Ramotswe glanced at Mma Makutsi, who asked, "Who is your tenant, Rra?"

"His name is Ofentse Makola," he said. "I do not know much about him, but he has been paying his rent very regularly every month. He has never been late with it—not once."

Mma Ramotswe caught Mma Makutsi's eye, signalling to her that they should bring this discussion to an end. Mr J.L.B. Matekoni looked a little bit awkward, she thought, and it would be best not to press him at this stage. Besides, she wanted to find out who owned the silver Mercedes, and this would require his co-operation. If he thought that the two of them were up to something, then he might decline to help. So there should be no more talk of Charlie's exploits for the time being.

After Mr J.L.B. Matekoni had returned to work, Mma Ramotswe busied herself with some telephone calls before she turned to Mma Makutsi and asked her directly what she thought they should do.

"Should we bother to find out anything about this woman?" she asked. "Is it really any of our business?"

Mma Makutsi looked thoughtful. "Charlie is a young man," she said. "He is responsible for himself. We cannot tell him what to do."

Mma Ramotswe agreed that this was true, but then, she asked, what should one do if, as an older person, one saw a younger person about to make a bad mistake, or do something wrong. Did one have the right to say anything? Or did one just have to stand by and let matters take their own course?

Mma Makutsi considered this for a moment. "If I was about to do something foolish—really foolish—would you tell me, Mma?"

"I would tell you," said Mma Ramotswe. "I would tell you and hope that you would not do it."

"So should we tell Charlie to be careful? Is that what we should do?"

Mma Ramotswe very much doubted whether Charlie would take advice when it came to the matter of a woman, but thought that perhaps they might try. "We could try talking to him about it," she said. "But we don't really have much to go on, do we? We don't know anything about this woman, other than that she has a Mercedes-Benz. That is not enough to go on. You can't warn somebody if you know only that. You can't say: Have nothing to do with ladies who drive Mercedes-Benzes! You can't say that, can you, Mma?"

"Some people would say that," suggested Mma Makutsi, mischievously.

"But I think we need to know a little bit more," said Mma Ramotswe.

"Then ask him. Isn't that the way we work in the No. 1 Ladies' Detective Agency? Don't we just ask people if we want to find out something?"

Mma Ramotswe had to agree that this was true. If she ever wrote a book like **The Principles of Private Detection,** she would add to what Clovis Andersen had to say. He suggested all sorts of clever ways of finding out facts—following people, looking at what they threw away in the bin, watching the sort of people they mixed with, and so on—but he did not say anything about asking them to their faces. That was often the best way of getting information, and in her book, if she ever wrote it (**Private Detection for Ladies** might be a good title), she would make much of this direct method. After all, this technique had served her well in many of her cases, and perhaps this was another occasion on which it might be used.

She rose from her desk and sauntered into the garage, followed by Mma Makutsi. Mr J.L.B. Matekoni was attending to a car which was parked outside, its owner standing anxiously by. Inside the garage, underneath the hydraulic ramp upon which a large red car was balanced, Charlie and the younger apprentice were peering up at the car's suspension.

"So," said Mma Ramotswe conversationally. "So you are going to fix the suspension of that car. The driver will be very grateful to you. He will not feel so many bumps once you have finished."

Charlie looked away from the car and smiled at Mma Ramotswe. "That is right, Mma. We are going to make this suspension so smooth that the driver will think he is riding along on a cloud."

"You are very clever," said Mma Ramotswe.

"That is right," said Charlie. "I am."

Mma Ramotswe glanced at Mma Makutsi, who bit her lip. It was sometimes very difficult to remain civil when dealing with these boys. It would have been so easy to be sarcastic, but the problem was that they did not understand sarcasm: it was wasted on them.

"We saw you yesterday afternoon," she said airily. "We saw you getting into a very smart car, Charlie. You must have some very smart friends these days."

The apprentice laughed. "Very smart," he said. "Yes. You're right, Mma. I have some very smart friends. Hah! You think I'm nothing, but I have friends who do not think that."

"I have never thought you were nothing," protested Mma Ramotswe. "You have no right to say that."

Charlie looked to the younger apprentice for support, but there was none forthcoming. "All right," he said. "Maybe you do not think that. But I'm telling you, Mma, my life is going to change. It's going to change very soon, and then . . ."

They waited for him to finish speaking, but he did not.

"You are going to get married?" suggested Mma Makutsi. "That is very good news! Marriage is always a big change for people."

"Hah!" said the apprentice. "Who said anything about marriage? No, I am not going to get married."

Mma Ramotswe drew in her breath. The time had come to be direct, and to see what response she could draw. "Is it because that girlfriend of yours, that rich lady, is already married? Is that it, Charlie?"

The moment her question had been posed, she knew that her instinct had been correct. There was no need for Charlie to tell them anything further. The way he had stood up and bumped his head on the bottom of the car made it abundantly clear that the question needed no answer. It was answered already.

THAT EVENING, Mma Ramotswe made sure that she and Mr J.L.B. Matekoni returned to the house on Zebra Drive well before five o'clock, something which seemed to be becoming more and more difficult. Both of them had busy working lives—she as a private detective whose services were increasingly in demand, and he as one of the finest mechanics in all Botswana. Both of these positions had been attained through hard work and a strict adherence to certain principles. For Mma Ramotswe the principle which governed her practice was honesty. Sometimes it was necessary to resort to minor deception—but never anything harmful—in order to get at the truth, but one should never do this with a client. One's duty to a client was never to mislead: if the truth was unpalatable or hurtful, then there were ways of presenting the truth in a gentle way. Often all that one had to do was to get clients to work out conclusions by themselves, merely assisting them by pointing out things that they might have found out for themselves had they been willing to confront them.

Of course there was more to Mma Ramotswe's success than that. Another reason why she was so popular was her sympathetic nature. People said that you could say anything to Mma Ramotswe, anything, and she would not scold you or shake her head in condemnation (as long you did not show an arrogant face; that she would not tolerate). So people could go to see her and tell her frankly of things that they had done wrong—things which had landed them in difficulty—and she would do her best to extricate them from the consequences of their selfishness or their folly. A man could go into Mma Ramotswe's office and confess to adultery, and she would not purse her lips or mutter under her breath, but would say, "I am sure that you are sorry, Rra. I know how difficult it is for you men, with all your weaknesses." This would reassure them, without giving them the impression that she was condoning what they had done. And once the confession was made, then Mma Ramotswe would often prove resourceful in finding a solution, and these solutions usually avoided too much pain. It seemed as if the forgiveness which she was capable of showing was infectious. Competitors and enemies, locked in pointless feuds, would find that Mma Ramotswe would hit upon a solution that preserved dignity and face. "We are all human," she would say. "Men particularly. You must not be ashamed."

And as for Mr J.L.B. Matekoni's reputation, again this was built on that most simple and immediately recognisable of human virtues: decency. Mr J.L.B. Matekoni would never overcharge nor allow shoddy work to go out of the garage (which brought him into frequent conflict with his feckless apprentices and their slipshod ways; "These boys will drive me to an early grave," he said, shaking his head. "Tlokweng Road Late Motors, that will be it: proprietor the late Mr J.L.B. Matekoni").

No less a person than the British High Commissioner, who was driven around in a handsome Range Rover, was amongst those who recognised the merits of Mr J.L.B. Matekoni. He, and his predecessor in office, had entrusted their cars to the care of Mr J.L.B. Matekoni when other diplomats took theirs to large garages with glittering forecourts. But the first British High Commissioner to use Tlokweng Road Speedy Motors had been a good judge of men and had immediately known that he had made a great discovery when Mr J.L.B. Matekoni, quite unasked, had adjusted something in the vehicle's engine when he had merely stopped to fill the tank. A change in the engine note had alerted Mr J.L.B. Matekoni to the fact that a problem was developing and he had dealt with it on the spot, and without charge. That was the beginning of a long relationship, in which the spotless diplomatic vehicle was routinely serviced by Tlokweng Road Speedy Motors.

And just as Mma Ramotswe was tactful in the breaking of difficult news, so too could Mr J.L.B. Matekoni convey bad news about a car in such a way as to soften the blow to the owner. He had seen some mechanics shake their heads when looking at an engine—even if the car's owner was standing right next to them. Indeed, when he had been an apprentice himself, he had served alongside a German-trained mechanic who would simply point at an engine and shout **Kaput!** This was no way of letting a customer know that all was not well, and Mr J.L.B. Matekoni wondered whether German doctors did the same with their patients and just shook their heads and said **Kaput!** Perhaps they did.

His ways were gentler. If a repair was going to be very expensive, he would sometimes offer the customer a chair before he told them what it would cost. And if there was nothing he could do, he would start off by telling them that there was a limit to the life of everything and this applied to shoes, cars, and even man himself. In this way the passing of a car might be seen by the customer as something inevitable. Mr J.L.B. Matekoni could understand, though, how people might be strongly attached to their cars, as he had found out in his dealings with both Mma Potokwane, the matron at the orphan farm, and with Mma Ramotswe herself. The orphan farm had an old minibus which Mma Potokwane had persuaded him to maintain (free of charge). This van should have been replaced some time ago, just as the water pump at the orphan farm should have been replaced well before it actually was. Mma Potokwane had no particular emotional attachment to the minibus, but was reluctant to spend money if she could possibly avoid it. He had pointed out to her that one day the suspension on the bus would have to be replaced, along with the braking system, the electric wiring, and several of the panels in the floor. He had pointed out the danger if those panels gave way through rust; an orphan could fall out onto the road, he said, and what would people say if that happened? It will not happen, she had replied. You will not let that happen.

In Mma Ramotswe's case, her attachment to the tiny white van was more emotional than financial in origin. She had bought the tiny white van when she first came to live in Gaborone, and it had served her loyally since that day. It was not a fast vehicle, nor a particularly comfortable one; the suspension had been in a bad way for some time, especially on the driver's side, in view of Mma Ramotswe's traditional build, which posed some degree of strain on the system. And the engine had a tendency to go out of tune very shortly after Mr J.L.B. Matekoni had attended to it, which meant that the tiny white van would splutter and jerk from time to time. In Mma Ramotswe's view, though, these were small matters: as long as the tiny white van was capable of getting her around, and as long as it did not break down too often, she proposed holding on to it. She thought of it as a friend, a staunch ally in this world, an ally to whom she owed a strong debt of loyalty.

These professional reputations meant that both Mma Ramotswe and Mr J.L.B. Matekoni were rather busier than they would have liked to be. So it was with some pleasure that Mma Ramotswe managed that evening to secure the hour between five and six as time when the two of them could sit on the verandah, and walk about their garden, and drink a cup of bush tea. She wanted to do this, not only to give Mr J.L.B. Matekoni a chance to unwind (he was, she thought, working far too hard), but also because she wanted to spend some time talking to him, alone, without Mma Makutsi or the apprentices, or even Motholeli and Puso listening in.

They sat together on the verandah, mugs of tea in hand. The sky was of that colour which it assumed at the end of the day—a late afternoon colour of tired blue—and was great and empty. On the leaves of the acacia trees that grew here and there in the garden, the gentle rays of the afternoon sun fell forgivingly, as if the battle between heat and life, between red and green, was temporarily over.

"I am very happy that we can just sit here," said Mma Ramotswe. "All the time these days it is work, work, work. We must be careful or we will work so much that we forget how to sit and talk about things."

"You are right, Mma," said Mr J.L.B. Matekoni. "But it is very hard, isn't it? You can't say to people: go away, we cannot help you. And I can't say to people: I can't fix your car. We cannot do that."

Mma Ramotswe nodded. He was right, of course. Neither of them would want to turn people away, no matter how busy they were. So where did the solution lie? Should they allow the businesses to expand? This was one of the matters that she wished to discuss with him—this, and the difficult issue of Charlie and the older woman.

"I suppose we could make the businesses bigger," she ventured. "You could get another mechanic to help you, and I could take on somebody else."

Mr J.L.B. Matekoni put down his mug and looked at her. "We could not do that," he said. "We are small businesses. If you allow your business to get too big, then you have many headaches. Headaches, headaches—all the time."

"But if you have too much work to do, you end up with a headache too," said Mma Ramotswe mildly. "And what is the point of working so much? We have enough money, I think. We do not need to be rich people. Other people can be rich if they want to. We are happy just as we are."

Mr J.L.B. Matekoni was sure that they were happy, but pointed out that he would not be happy if he had to turn people away, or cut corners in his work.

"I cannot do quick, shoddy work," he said. "That catches up with you sooner or later. The worst thing a mechanic can see is a car he looks after broken down at the edge of the road. Such a mechanic has to hide his face. I could not live like that."

"Well," said Mma Ramotswe. "Perhaps you could take another apprentice. A good one this time. Or you could employ an assistant mechanic—a qualified person."

"How would I know that he would be any good?" asked Mr J.L.B. Matekoni. "I cannot just employ the first person who walks into the garage."

Mma Ramotswe explained that there were ways of preventing this from happening. They could check up on references which the candidate provided, and they could even employ somebody on a temporary basis, on the understanding that they were on approval. Mr J.L.B. Matekoni listened to these suggestions but was noncommittal. Mma Ramotswe changed tack; she had an idea that had occurred to her during the day and which she wanted to put to him.

"Of course," she began, "it might be possible to employ somebody who could do a bit of work for you and a bit of work for me. There might be a person who could be taught some simple garage tasks—changing oil, for instance—and who would at the same time be able to do some enquiry work in the agency. I was not thinking of somebody who was a detective, but of somebody who could take some of the burden off Mma Makutsi and myself. We seem to have too much work these days and it would be useful."

Mr J.L.B. Matekoni said nothing for a moment. He did not appear to be rejecting the idea out of hand, and so Mma Ramotswe continued.

"There is somebody I met who is looking for a job," she said. "I would like to try him out. We could take him for a month maybe, and see how he does. If he is good, then he might be able to help us both."

"Who is this person?" asked Mr J.L.B. Matekoni. "Do you know anything about him?"

"He is a person I happened to bump into," said Mma Ramotswe, and then laughed. "Or I would have bumped into him if he had not swerved on his bicycle."

Mr J.L.B. Matekoni sighed. "You do not have to give him a job just because you almost knocked him over. You do not have to do that."

"I know that. And that is not the reason."

Mr J.L.B. Matekoni lifted up his mug and drained it of the last of his bush tea. "And do you know anything about him?" he asked. "What was his last job? How did he lose it?"

Mma Ramotswe thought carefully. She could not lie to her husband, but she realised that if she revealed that the man had been in prison, then it would be extremely unlikely that he would agree to employ him. They would then be no different from everybody else who was refusing to give him work because of his past. He would never get a job in these circumstances.

"I do not know exactly what happened," she said, truthfully. "But I shall ask him to speak to you himself. Then he could explain what happened."

It was some time before Mr J.L.B. Matekoni replied, but after a period, during which he seemed deep in reflection, he agreed to speak to the man when he came to collect his bicycle. This was all that Mma Ramotswe wanted. Now, with their tea finished, she thought that they might take a short stroll around the garden, in the last of the afternoon light, and discuss the other problem that needed to be resolved—the Charlie problem.

CHAPTER SEVEN

A TEA DISASTER . . .
AND WORSE

THERE WAS an unusually large pile of mail awaiting them the next morning at the No. 1 Ladies' Detective Agency. Letters for both businesses were opened in the same office, Mma Ramotswe normally dealing with those addressed to the agency and Mma Makutsi going through the garage mail. It was their policy to reply immediately to everything, and this often took up much of the morning. People wrote to the No. 1 Ladies' Detective Agency about all sorts of things, and with impossible requests. Some of them were under the impression that they were a branch of the police force and made allegations against others, usually anonymously. There was one such letter that morning.

"Dear Mma Ramotswe," it read, "I saw an

article about you in the **Botswana Daily News.**
It said that you are the only ladies' detective
agency in Botswana. Men will not deal with
this thing, and so that is why I am writing to
you. I want to bring to your notice something
that is happening in our village. I have not been
able to talk about this thing to anybody here,
because there are many people who would not
believe me and would only say that I am lying
and trying to make trouble. I wish to complain
about some teachers at the school. They are always drinking and taking girl pupils to bars
where they give them strong drink and make
them dance with them. I have seen this thing
myself many times, and I think that it is something which the police should deal with. But
the police here are also dancing in these bars.
So please will you do something about this. I
cannot give you my real name and address because I know that they will threaten me if they
hear about this. I am one such girl. That is how
I know about this. Please do something."

Mma Ramotswe read the letter aloud to
Mma Makutsi, who laid aside the spare-parts
bill she was dealing with and listened attentively.

"Well, Mma?" said Mma Ramotswe after
she had finished. "What do we do about that?"

"Which village is this?" asked Mma Makutsi. "We could pass it on to somebody. Maybe the district police superintendent, or somebody like that."

Mma Ramotswe studied the letter again, and sighed. "There is no address," she said. "This girl has not told us where she is writing from."

"And the postmark?" Mma Makutsi enquired.

"I cannot make it out," said Mma Ramotswe. "It is very indistinct. It could be anywhere. It could be out near Ghanzi for all we know. It could be somewhere very far away. There's nothing we can do. Nothing."

They both stared at the simple, ruled letter which Mma Ramotswe was holding. It was a piece of paper in which a great deal of anxiety had been invested.

"I am sure that this is true," said Mma Ramotswe, as she reluctantly let the letter fall into the wastepaper bin. "I am sure that this thing is really happening. I have heard about the bad behaviour of some teachers these days. They have forgotten what it is to be a teacher. They have forgotten that they should be worthy of respect."

Mma Makutsi agreed with this, but that, she

thought, was not the whole story. Teachers may have started behaving badly, like everybody else, but this was not altogether their fault. They now had to put up with children who had not been taught the basics of good behaviour, and it was difficult in such circumstances for the teachers to maintain discipline.

"It is not always the teachers' fault, Mma Ramotswe," she said. "The children are very bad too these days."

They sat in silence for a moment. There had been no alternative but to dispose of the letter, but that did not make it any easier to do. That girl, wherever and whoever she was, would be looking for justice, for the restoration of the balance between right and wrong, and her pleas would continue to go unheard.

Mma Ramotswe looked at the next letter on her desk and picked up her letter knife. "This is sometimes not a very easy job, is it?" she said.

Mma Makutsi spread her hands in a gesture of resignation. "No, it is not easy, Mma."

"But we get by, don't we?" Mma Ramotswe went on, more cheerfully. "Sometimes we are able to do something that helps somebody else. That's the important thing. That makes our job a good one."

"Yes," said Mma Makutsi. "That is it. And you have helped me, Mma. I shall always remember that."

Mma Ramotswe looked surprised. "I don't think I have, Mma. You have helped yourself."

Mma Makutsi shook her head. "No, you are the one who has helped me. You gave me this job and you kept me on even when we were not making any money. Remember that time? Remember how we had very few cases and you said that it didn't matter and I could stay on? I thought that I was going to be out of a job then, but you were kind to me and promoted me. That's what you did."

"You deserved it," said Mma Ramotswe modestly.

"I shall never forget," said Mma Makutsi. "And I shall never forget how kind you were to me when my brother was called."

"You were good to your brother," said Mma Ramotswe gently. "I saw what you did for him. He could not have wished for a better sister. And he is at peace now."

Mma Makutsi said nothing. She looked down at her desk, and then took off her large round spectacles and polished them with the threadbare lace handkerchief that she liked to carry. Mma Ramotswe glanced at her quickly, and then picked up the next letter and began to slit it open.

"This looks like a bill," she said, in a businesslike manner.

WHEN THE TIME CAME for morning tea, they had replied to just about all the letters and sorted out all the bills, both outgoing and incoming.

"This morning's going very quickly," said Mma Ramotswe, as she looked at her watch. "I am ready for tea."

Mma Makutsi agreed. She had a slight tendency to stiffness if she sat at her desk too long, and so she rose to her feet and rocked from side to side for a few moments, stretching her arms up and down as she did so. Then she turned round to get her tea-pot off the shelf behind her desk.

Mma Ramotswe looked up sharply when she heard the exclamation.

"My new tea-pot!" said Mma Makutsi. "Have you seen my tea-pot?"

"It was on that shelf," said Mma Ramotswe. "Next to the files."

"It is not there any longer," said Mma Makutsi. "Somebody has stolen it."

"But who would steal it?" asked Mma Ramotswe. "Nobody has been in here since we locked up last."

"Well, where is it, then?" retorted her assistant. "Tea-pots don't just walk. If it's not here, then somebody has taken it."

Mma Ramotswe scratched her head. "Maybe Mr J.L.B. Matekoni took it to make himself some tea. He came in very early this morning—before I did. That must be what happened."

Mma Makutsi thought about this. It was just possible that Mr J.L.B. Matekoni had moved the tea-pot, but it seemed unlikely. If he had wanted to make himself tea, then surely he would have used the normal tea-pot which Mma Ramotswe used. And what was more, she could not remember ever seeing him make tea himself, which again made the explanation somewhat unlikely.

Mma Ramotswe had now got up from her chair and was making her way to the door.

"Let's go and ask," she said. "I'm sure that it will turn up. Tea-pots don't just vanish."

Mma Makutsi followed her out into the

garage workshop. Mr J.L.B. Matekoni, together with the two apprentices, was standing at the far side. He had in his hand a piece of an engine, and was pointing out something to the two young men, who were peering at the part with interest. As the two women came into the garage, he looked over in their direction.

"Have you seen . . ." Mma Ramotswe began to call out, but then stopped. At the very same instant, she and Mma Makutsi had seen the tea-pot, sitting on top of an upturned oil drum.

Mma Makutsi was smiling with relief. "There it is," she said. "Mr J.L.B. Matekoni must have made tea, as you said."

She walked over to the oil drum and picked up the tea-pot, only immediately to replace it on the surface of the drum. Watching her, Mma Ramotswe instantly knew that something was very wrong. She hurried over to join Mma Makutsi, who was standing in mute dismay, peering into the open top of the tea-pot.

"Diesel oil," Mma Makutsi muttered. "Somebody has filled it with diesel oil."

Mma Ramotswe bent down and sniffed at the tea-pot. The unmistakable smell of diesel was strong in her nostrils.

"Oh!" she exclaimed. "Who has done this? Who has done this?"

She turned and looked at the three men. They stood there, two of them looking puzzled and a third looking sheepishly down at his overalls.

"Charlie!" shouted Mma Ramotswe. "You come over here right now! Right now!"

Charlie sauntered over, accompanied by Mr J.L.B. Matekoni.

"What is all this?" asked Mr J.L.B. Matekoni, wiping his hands on a piece of cotton lint. "What is all this fuss?"

"He's put diesel oil in my new tea-pot," wailed Mma Makutsi. "Why did he do that?"

There was a defensive note in Charlie's voice. "I was draining a tank," he explained. "I had nothing to catch the diesel. So I found that thing in the office and it was empty. I thought I'd use it. Don't worry, I'll wash it."

"Can't you see it's a tea-pot?" snapped Mma Ramotswe. "Can't you see even that?"

"It is not the usual tea-pot," said Charlie defiantly. "The tea-pot we use does not look like that."

"That's because it's my new tea-pot," interjected Mma Makutsi. "You stupid, stupid boy. You are more stupid than a cow."

Charlie bristled at the insult. "Don't you call me stupid, Mma. Just because you got ninety per cent."

"Ninety-**seven** per cent," shouted Mma Makutsi. "You can't even get that right. You are as stupid as a warthog."

"She must not call me a warthog," Charlie protested to Mr J.L.B. Matekoni. "Boss, you cannot let this foolish woman call me a warthog. She is the warthog. A warthog with big round glasses."

Mr J.L.B. Matekoni wagged a finger. "You must not say that, Charlie. You are the one who is in the wrong here. You put diesel oil in Mma Makutsi's new tea-pot. That is not a clever thing to do."

Charlie took a deep breath. His eyes had widened now, and his nostrils were flaring slightly. It was clear that he was very angry.

"I may be stupid," he said. "But I am not stupid enough to stay in this useless garage. That's it, Boss. I quit now. Right now."

Mr J.L.B. Matekoni grasped the apprentice's arm in an attempt to reassure him, but was brushed off. "But what about the apprenticeship?" he said quietly. "You cannot give that up."

"Oh, can't I?" said Charlie. "You'll see. I am not a slave, Boss. I am a free Motswana. I can go when I want. Now I am looked after by a friend. I have a rich friend. I have a Mercedes-Benz—have you not seen me? I do not have to work any more."

He turned away and started to unbutton his overalls. He then ripped these off, and threw them into a puddle of oil on the floor.

"You cannot go," said Mr J.L.B. Matekoni. "We can talk about this."

"No, I am not talking," said Charlie. "I have had enough of being treated like a dog. I am going to have a better life now."

It had all been so sudden and so dramatic that it was difficult to take it all in. But after a few minutes, as they watched Charlie walking quickly away in the direction of the town, they realised that something serious and potentially irremediable had happened. They saw before them the ruins of a career; the wrecking of a life.

MR J.L.B. MATEKONI sat astride the client's chair in the office of the No. 1 Ladies' Detective

Agency, his head sunk in his hands, his expression glum.

"I have always tried very hard with that young man," he said to Mma Ramotswe and Mma Makutsi. "I really have. He has been with me now for two years, and I have worked and worked to make him into a good mechanic. And now this has happened."

"It is not your fault, Mr J.L.B. Matekoni," said Mma Ramotswe reassuringly. "We know what you have done. We have seen it, haven't we, Mma Makutsi?"

Mma Makutsi nodded vigorously. She was particularly shocked by the apprentice's outburst and wondered whether in the eyes of Mr J.L.B. Matekoni and Mma Ramotswe she was responsible for his abrupt resignation and departure. It had been wrong of her, perhaps, to lose her temper with Charlie, and she regretted that, but at the same time there was the question of her new tea-pot and its ignominious fate as a receptacle for diesel oil. She doubted whether she would be able to get the smell of fuel out of it now, and tea was such a sensitive substance—the slightest contamination could make it taste peculiar. She had once been served tea out of a flask that had been regularly used for coffee, and she remembered how long the acrid, confusing taste had lingered in her mouth. But she would not have shouted at him like that if she had imagined that it would lead to this—the garage could ill afford the loss of one set of hands, particularly a trained set, if one could call Charlie's hands that.

"I'm very sorry," she said quietly. "I should not have been so cross with him. I'm sorry. I did not think that he would run away like that."

Mma Ramotswe raised a hand to stop her. "You do not need to apologise, Mma," she said firmly. "It was Charlie who called you a warthog. He had no right to say that. I shall not have the Assistant Detective at the No. 1 Ladies' Detective Agency called a warthog."

She looked at Mr J.L.B. Matekoni, as if to challenge him to defend the indefensible. It was true that Mma Makutsi had initiated the trade of insults, but that was only under the gravest provocation. Had Charlie apologised for ruining the tea-pot, then Mma Makutsi would surely not have spoken in the intemperate way in which she did speak.

Mr J.L.B. Matekoni, it transpired, was of much the same view.

"It is not Mma Makutsi's fault at all," he said simply. "It is just not her fault. That young man has been heading this way for some time. You told me only a little time ago about this woman of his. I was foolish and did not speak to him firmly. Now he has decided that he can give everything up just because his rich lady is running after him in her Mercedes-Benz. Oh dear! Those cars have a lot to answer for."

Mma Ramotswe nodded her head in vigorous agreement. "They do, Rra. They certainly do. They turn people's heads, I think. That is what they do."

"And women turn heads too," continued Mr J.L.B. Matekoni. "Women turn the heads of young men and make them do silly things."

There was a short silence. Mma Makutsi was about to say something, but decided against it. It was arguable, she thought, whether women turned the heads of men any more than men turned the heads of women. She would have thought that responsibility was shared in that respect. But this was not the time to engage in debate on this issue.

"So what do we do now?" asked Mr J.L.B. Matekoni. "Should I go and try to talk to him tonight? Should I see if I can persuade him to come back?"

Mma Ramotswe thought about this suggestion. If Mr J.L.B. Matekoni were to try to persuade the apprentice to return, it might work, but at the same time it could have dire consequences for his future behaviour. It was not right that an employer should run after a subordinate like that; that would mean that the young man could throw his weight around in the future because he would know that ultimately he could get away with anything. It would also give him the impression that he was in the right and Mma Makutsi was in the wrong, and that was simply unfair. No, she thought, if Charlie were to come back, it would have to be at his own request, and preferably accompanied by a proper apology to Mma Makutsi, not only for calling her a warthog but also for spoiling her tea-pot. In fact, he should probably be obliged to buy her a new tea-pot, but they would not press that aspect of the matter in these delicate circumstances. An apology, then, would suffice.

She looked directly at Mr J.L.B. Matekoni. "I don't think that is a good idea," she said.

"You are the boss. He is a young man who has run away from work after being rude to a superior. It would not look good, would it, if the boss were to run after the young man and beg him to come back? No, he should be allowed to come back, but only when he has said sorry."

Mr J.L.B. Matekoni looked resigned. "Yes," he said. "You are right. But what are we to do here? What if he does not come back? There is work for three people here at the garage, even if his work has many faults. It will be hard without him."

"I know that, Rra," said Mma Ramotswe. "And that is why we need a plan with two parts. It is always a good idea to have a plan with two parts."

Mma Makutsi and Mr J.L.B. Matekoni looked at her expectantly. This was the Mma Ramotswe they appreciated: the woman with a clear idea of what to do. They had no doubt at all that she would solve this problem, and now all that they wanted was to hear how she was going to do it. A plan with two parts sounded very impressive.

Now it was as if Mma Ramotswe had herself become imbued with the confidence that they had in her. She sat back in her chair and smiled as she laid out the contours of her plan.

"The first part," she said, "is to go immediately to Tlokweng and get the man whose bicycle has been broken. We can offer him work here, as I have discussed with you, Mr J.L.B. Matekoni. This man can then do all the unskilled work in the garage, as if he were an apprentice on the first day of his apprenticeship. I think that he will be a good worker. He will not be a proper apprentice, of course, but Charlie's young friend will imagine that this is just what he is. That means that the news will get back to Charlie straightaway that we have found somebody to replace him. That will give him a big shock, I am sure of it."

On hearing this, Mma Makutsi let out an exclamation of delight. "That will teach him to take off his overalls and throw them in a puddle of oil," she said gleefully.

Mma Ramotswe looked at her disapprovingly and she lowered her eyes.

"The second part of the plan," Mma Ramotswe continued, "is to find out more about this woman of Charlie's and then to see if there is anything we can do to help him come to his senses. I am sure that she is a married lady. Now, if that is so, then there will be a husband somewhere, and it may be that he is paying for that expensive silver Mercedes-Benz. Do you think that men like to pay for cars like that to be driven around in by young men who are seeing their wives? I do not think they do. So all we have to do is to find out where this man is and see to it that he finds out what is going on. Then we let things sort themselves out, and I think that we shall soon have Charlie back, knocking on the door, asking for us to forget what he said about the garage."

"And about me," added Mma Makutsi.

"Yes," said Mma Ramotswe. "About you too."

Mma Makutsi was emboldened. "And would it not help if Mr J.L.B. Matekoni beat him?" she asked. "Just a bit. Would that not help him to behave better in the future?"

They both looked at her, Mma Ramotswe in astonishment, Mr J.L.B. Matekoni in alarm.

"Those days are past," said Mma Ramotswe. "That is no longer possible, Mma."

"Pity," said Mma Makutsi.

CHAPTER EIGHT

AT THE ACADEMY OF DANCE AND MOVEMENT

EVERYBODY'S SPIRITS were considerably lifted by the way in which a credible plan of action had emerged from a shocking and disagreeable row. Mma Makutsi was particularly pleased that she could go home that evening without a burden of worry and guilt over what had happened. For that evening she was due to embark on a new and exciting project—the most important thing that she had done since the founding of the Kalahari Typing School for Men. Unlike the typing school, however, this did not involve work for her, which would be a pleasant change. For as long as she could remember, her life had been a matter of work: as a girl she had worked at home in all the usual tasks of the household, unremittingly; she had

walked six miles to school each morning and
six miles back to acquire an education; and
then, when her great opportunity had presented itself and she had taken up that place at
the Botswana Secretarial College, paid for by
the scrimping and saving of her entire family,
she had worked harder than ever before. Of
course she had been rewarded—with that glorious result of ninety-seven per cent—but it
had all been such hard work. Now it was time
to dance.

She had seen the advertisement in the newspaper and had been immediately intrigued by
the name of the person who had placed the advertisement. Who was this Mr Fano Fanope? It
was an unusual name, but its musical qualities
seemed very suitable for one who offered
classes in "dance and movement, and the social
skills that go with those things." As to the
name, Fano Fanope was a bit like Spokes
Spokesi, the famous radio disc jockey. These
names had a forward lilt to them; they were the
names of people who were **going somewhere.**
She reflected on her own name: Grace
Makutsi. There was nothing wrong with a
name like that—she had certainly encountered
stranger names in Botswana, where people

seemed to like naming their children in an individual and sometimes rather strange way—but it was not a name which suggested much movement or ambition. Indeed, one might even describe it as a safe name, a rather stodgy name, the sort of name that might well be held by the leader of a knitting circle or a Sunday School teacher. Of course, it could have been much worse, and she could have been burdened with one of those names which children then spend the rest of their days in living down. At least she was not called, as one of the teachers at the Botswana Secretarial College had been called, a name which, when translated from Setswana, meant: **This one makes a lot of noise.** That was not a good name to give a child, but her parents still did it.

Now this well-named Fano Fanope was proposing to offer dancing classes (with other skills included) every Friday night. These would take place in a room at the President Hotel, and there would be a small band provided. The advertisement also revealed that instruction would be given in a wide range of ballroom dances, and that Fano Fanope, who had achieved recognition in dancing circles in four countries, would personally instruct all those who registered for the class. It would be wise not to wait, the advertisement went on, as there were many people who were keen to improve their social skills in this way and demand would be high.

Mma Makutsi read the advertisement with close interest. There was no doubt in her mind that it would be good to be able to do some of those obscure dances that she had read about—the tango, for one, looked interesting— and there was also no doubt that dancing classes were a good place to meet people. She met people at work, of course, and there were her new neighbours, who were perfectly friendly, but she was looking forward to a rather different sort of meeting. She wanted to meet people who had been places, people who could talk about fascinating things, people whose lives encompassed rather more than the daily round of work and home and children.

And there was no reason why she should not enter into such a world, thought Mma Makutsi. After all, she was an independent woman with a position. She was an assistant detective at the No. 1 Ladies' Detective Agency; she had her own small business in the shape of the part-time Kalahari Typing School for Men; and she had a new house, or part of a house, in a good area of town. She had something behind her now, and it did not matter if she wore very large round glasses and had a difficult complexion; it was her turn to enjoy life a bit more.

She prepared for the evening with care. Mma Makutsi did not have many dresses, but there was one, at least, a red dress with a line of small bows along the hem, that would be ideal for a dancing class. She took this dress out of the cupboard and ironed it carefully. Then she showered, under cold water, as there was no hot water in the house, and spent some time in the other tasks of making herself ready to go out. There was nail varnish to be applied, a very fine pink one that she had bought at ridiculous expense the previous week; there was lipstick; there was powder; there was something to put on her hair. All this took the best part of an hour, and then she had to walk off to the end of the road to catch the minibus into town.

"You're looking smart, Mma," said an older woman in the crowded vehicle. "You must be meeting a man tonight. Be careful! Men are dangerous."

Mma Makutsi smiled. "I am going to a

dancing class. It is the first time that I have gone to it."

The woman laughed. "Oh, there will be plenty of men at a dancing class," she said, offering Mma Makutsi a peppermint from a small bag she had extracted from a pocket. "That's why men go to dancing classes. They go to meet pretty girls like you."

Mma Makutsi said nothing, but as she sucked on the peppermint she thought about the prospect of meeting a man. She had not been strictly honest with herself, and she was prepared to admit it, even if only to herself. She would like to learn to dance, and she would like to meet interesting people in general, but what she really wanted to do was to meet an interesting man, and she hoped that this would be her chance. So if what her neighbour in the minibus said was true, then perhaps this was the night that it would happen.

She alighted from the bus at the top of the mall. There were no lights on in the Government buildings behind her, as it was Friday evening and no civil servant would ever work late on a Friday evening, but the mall itself was lit and there were people strolling about, enjoying the cool night air and chatting with friends.

There was always so much to talk about, even if nothing much had happened, and now people were going over the events, or non-events perhaps, of the day, catching up on gossip, hearing about things that were happening, or might just happen if one waited long enough.

Outside the President Hotel there was a small knot of young people, mostly in their teens. They were standing about the open staircase that went up to the verandah where Mma Ramotswe liked to have lunch on special occasions. They fell silent as Mma Makutsi approached the stairs.

"Going to learn to dance, Mma?" muttered one of the young men. "I'll teach you how to dance!"

There were titters of laughter.

"I don't dance with little boys," said Mma Makutsi as she went past.

There was silence for a moment, and she added, "When you're big, come and ask me then."

This brought laughter from the rest of the young people, and she turned and smiled at them as she went up the stairs. Her success in this good-natured repartee gave her confidence as she entered the hotel and asked for directions to the room in which the class was to be held. She had felt some trepidation about the outing—what if she failed to remember the steps of the tango, or whatever it was they were going to learn? Would she look stupid? Would she possibly even trip and fall over? And who would be there? Would the people who went to classes like this be much more sophisticated than she was, much richer? It was all very well being the most distinguished graduate of her year from the Botswana Secretarial College, but would that count for much here, in the world of music and elegant dancing and mirrors?

The dancing class was to be held in a room at the back of the hotel, a room which was used for business lunches and cheaper private parties. As Mma Makutsi made her way along the corridor, she heard the sound of an amplified guitar and drums. This was the band which had been promised in the advertisement, and it was a sound which filled her with a feeling of anticipation. And there were voices too, the sound of people talking amongst themselves; there were going to be a lot of people there, it seemed.

At the entrance to the room there was a small table at which a comfortable-looking woman in a red sequinned dress was seated. She smiled at Mma Makutsi and pointed to a small printed notice which gave the cost of the class. It was forty pula, which was not cheap, but then this was a proper dancing class, thought Mma Makutsi, with a real two-piece band and a room in the President Hotel. She reached into her purse, took out the money, and paid.

"Are you experienced, or are you a beginner?" asked the woman.

Mma Makutsi thought about this. She had danced before, of course, but then so had just about everybody. From the point of view of this woman, with her sequinned dress, though, Mma Makutsi must be very much a novice.

"I have done some dancing," said Mma Makutsi. "Like everybody else. But not very much."

"Beginner," said the woman.

"I suppose so," said Mma Makutsi.

"Yes," said the woman. "If you have not been to a dance academy before, then you are a beginner. But you need not be ashamed. Everybody has to begin somewhere."

The woman smiled at her encouragingly and pointed at the doorway. "Go in. We shall be starting very soon," she said. "Mr Fanope is in the bar, but will come very soon. He is a very famous dancer, you know. Johannesburg. Nairobi. He has danced in all these places."

Mma Makutsi went in. It was a large room, the centre of which had been cleared and the carpet taken up. Chairs had been placed around the sides, and at the far end, on a small platform, the two musicians, the drummer and the guitarist, were perched on stools. The guitarist was fiddling with a lead to his instrument, while the drummer, a thin man wearing a silver-coloured waistcoat, was staring up at the ceiling, tapping his drumsticks against his knee.

Most of the chairs were occupied, and for a moment Mma Makutsi felt awkward as the eyes of those already there fell upon her. She felt that she was being appraised, and she searched quickly for any face that she knew, for any person whom she could approach and greet. But there was nobody, and under the gaze of the sixty or so people present, she crossed the floor to take a seat on one of the few chairs which were still free. Glancing around, she saw, to her relief, that she was dressed in much the same way as the other women, but none, she saw, was wearing glasses. For a moment she thought about taking hers off and putting them away, but the difficulty with doing that was that she really needed them and without them she would not be able to make out what was happening.

A few minutes later Mr Fanope entered the room, followed by the woman in the red sequinned dress. He was a rather small, dapper man, wearing a white evening jacket and a bow tie. Mma Makutsi noticed that he was wearing black patent leather shoes. She had not seen a man in patent leather footwear before and she thought them most becoming. Would Mr J.L.B. Matekoni wear such shoes, she wondered? It was difficult to see him in shoes like that at the garage—the oil would spoil them so quickly—but she could hardly imagine him in shoes like that even in other circumstances. This was definitely not his world, nor the world of Mma Ramotswe, when one came to think about it. Would Mma Ramotswe be a good dancer? Traditionally built women could be rather good at dancing, thought Mma Makutsi, as they have the right bearing, at least for some dances. The tango would hardly suit somebody of Mma Ramotswe's build, but she could certainly imagine her doing a waltz, perhaps, or a sedate jive. Traditional dancing presented no problems, of course, because the whole point about traditional dancing was that everybody could join in. A few weeks previously they had been at the orphan farm for Mma Potokwane's birthday party, and the children's traditional dancing group had performed in the matron's honour, with all the housemothers joining in. Some of them were of a very traditional build—from all that sampling of the good food they cooked for the children—and they had looked very dignified as they had joined in the line of shuffling, singing dancers. But all of that was a long way away from the world of Mr Fanope and his President Hotel dance academy.

"Now then, **bomma** and **borra,**" said Mr Fanope into the microphone. "Welcome to the first class of the Academy of Dance and Movement. You have made a very good choice coming here tonight because this is the number-one place to learn ballroom dancing in Botswana. And I am the best teacher for you people. I will make dancers out of all of you, even if you have never danced before. Everybody here has a dancer inside, and I will let that dancer out. That is what I will do."

Somebody clapped at this point, and a number of others followed suit. Mr Fanope acknowledged the applause with a small bow.

"We are going to start this evening with a simple dance. This is a dance that anybody can do, and it is called the quickstep. It goes slow, slow, quick; slow, slow, quick, quick. It is very simple, and Mma Betty and I are going to show you how to do it."

He nodded to the musicians. As they began to play, he moved away from the microphone and turned to the woman in the red sequinned dress. Mma Makutsi watched in fascination as they danced across the floor. They were both extraordinarily light on their feet, and they both moved in such perfect harmony, as if they were one body, moving on strings pulled by a single hand.

"Watch what we do," shouted Mr Fanope, above the music. "Watch us now. Slow, slow, quick, quick."

After a few minutes, he disengaged from Mma Betty and the band stopped playing.

"Choose your partners," he shouted. "Men,

you get up and ask the ladies. If anybody is left over, Mma Betty and I will take it in turns to be your partner. Mma Betty will dance with men, and I shall dance with the ladies. Men, get up and choose a lady."

At this signal, the men rose to their feet and crossed the floor or turned to a lady sitting nearby. There was a sudden flurry of activity, and Mma Makutsi caught her breath in the excitement of it all. A man was coming towards her, a tall man with a moustache and a blue shirt. She looked down at her shoes. He would be a good man to dance with, a man who would lead his partner confidently.

But he did not ask her; he approached the woman sitting next to her, who rose up smiling and took his hand. Mma Makutsi waited. Everybody seemed to be finding a partner and moving onto the floor—everybody except her. She lowered her eyes. This was the humiliation she had feared; she should not have come. She would end up being danced with by Mr Fanope, out of charity, and everybody would know that nobody had asked her. It's my glasses, she told herself. It's my glasses, and the fact that I am a plain girl. I am just a plain girl from Bobonong.

She looked up. A man was standing in front of her, bending down to speak to her. In the general hubbub of noise she could not make out exactly what he was saying, but he was clearly a man, and he was clearly asking her to dance.

Mma Makutsi smiled and stood up. "Thank you, Rra," she said. "I am called Grace Makutsi."

He nodded, and pointed back to the dance floor, and they made their way together into the thick of the crowd. Mma Makutsi took a surreptitious glance at her partner. He was slightly older than she was, she thought; not very good-looking, but with a kind face. And he walked in a slightly strange way, as if his shoes did not quite fit him.

"What is your name, Rra?" she asked, as they stood together amongst the other couples, waiting for the music to start.

The man stared at her. It seemed that it was an effort for him to speak.

"I am called Phuti Radiphuti," he said. That is what he said, but it did not come out as directly as that. Called was c...c...c... called and Phuti was ph...ph...phuti.

It was a bad speech impediment, and Mma Makutsi's heart sank. She was a kind woman, like Mma Ramotswe, but it was typical of her luck, she thought, that she should be the last to be picked and then to be chosen by a man who moved in an odd way and had a very pronounced stutter. But he was still a man, wasn't he, and at least she was dancing with somebody and not sitting unhappily, unwanted. So she smiled encouragingly and asked him whether he had ever danced before.

Phuti Radiphuti opened his mouth to speak, and Mma Makutsi waited for his answer, but no words were formed. He bit his lip, and looked apologetic.

"Don't worry, Rra," said Mma Makutsi lightly. "We don't have to talk now. We can talk a bit later, after we have danced. Don't worry. It is my first time at a dance class too."

Mr Fanope was now organising the couples and was signalling the band to start.

"Take your partners," he called out. "No, do not crush them, gentlemen. A good dancer holds his partner lightly. Like this. See?"

They began to dance, and it became straightaway apparent to Mma Makutsi that

her partner had very little sense of rhythm.
While she counted slow, slow, quick, quick, as
they had been instructed to do by Mr Fanope,
he seemed to be counting slow, slow, slow,
quick, or even slow, slow, slow, slow. Whatever
he was doing, it bore no relation to what Mma
Makutsi herself was doing.

After a few minutes of uncoordinated shuffling, Mr Fanope came up to them and tapped
Phuti Radiphuti on the shoulder.

"No, Rra," he said, shaking a finger at him.
"You are all over the place. This is not football.
This is a quickstep. You go slow, slow, quick,
quick, like this."

Phuti Radiphuti looked ashamed.

"I am very so . . . so . . . sor . . . sorry," he
stuttered. "I am not a good dancer. I am sorry."

"Let me do the counting," said Mma
Makutsi. "You just listen to me this time."

They resumed the dance, with Mma
Makutsi counting loudly and guiding Phuti
Radiphuti in an attempt to bring their movements into unison. It was not easy; Phuti
Radiphuti seemed inordinately clumsy, and no
matter how clearly she counted he appeared to
be following a quite different rhythm.

"It is important to move quickly after I count two," shouted Mma Makutsi above a particularly loud passage of drumming. "That is why the dance is called the quickstep."

Phuti Radiphuti nodded. He looked rather miserable now, as if he was regretting the decision to attend the lesson. Mma Makutsi, for her part, was sure that people were looking at them as they stumbled along. She had changed her mind about whether it would have been better to remain firmly seated, unapproached by any man, than to be subjected to this awkward, bumbling performance. And there, only a few couples away, was somebody she recognised. She stole a glance and then looked away. Yes, it was her, one of the women from her year at the Botswana Secretarial College, one of those fun-loving glamorous girls who ended up getting barely fifty per cent, and there she was, dancing with a confident and attractive man. Mma Makutsi hardly dared look again, but was forced to do so when they found themselves getting closer and closer together.

"So!" shouted the glamorous girl. "So there you are! Grace Makutsi!"

Mma Makutsi affected surprise, smiling at

the other girl. She noticed the eyes of the other move quickly to Phuti Radiphuti and then come back to rest on her, amused.

"Who is that?" stuttered Phuti Radiphuti. "Who . . ."

"She is just somebody I know," said Mma Makutsi carelessly. "I have forgotten her name."

"She is a very good dancer," said Phuti Radiphuti, stumbling over each word.

"Dancing is not the only thing," said Mma Makutsi quickly. "There are other things, you know."

THE DANCE CLASS lasted for almost two hours. There were further exhibitions of the quickstep, performed with shimmering fluidity by Mr Fanope and Mma Betty, and then demonstrations of the waltz, which they were then all invited to attempt. Mma Makutsi, who had detached herself from Phuti Radiphuti while the demonstration was being performed, was hoping that somebody else would come and ask her to dance, but was quickly sought out by Phuti Radiphuti, who guided her clumsily back onto the floor.

At the end of the evening, he thanked her and offered to drive her home.

"I have a car outside," he said. "I can take you."

She hesitated. She felt sorry for this man, who seemed harmless enough, but this was not what she had hoped for, nor anticipated, for the evening. She had seen at least four men who looked attractive and interesting, but they had not looked at her, not for so much as an instant. Instead it had been her luck to have the attention of this poor man, decent though he was, with his terrible stutter and his awful clumsiness. So she should say no to his offer, so as not to encourage him, and wait for a minibus, or even walk home. It would take her no more than thirty minutes, and it was perfectly safe at this hour of night.

She looked at him, and noticed that there were dark patches in the armpits of his shirt. We are all human, all creatures of water and salt, all human. And she thought for a moment of her brother, her poor brother Richard, whom she had loved and looked after, and who had suffered from those dreadful fevers that bathed him in sweat at night. She could not hurt this man; she could not say to him, no, I cannot accept your kindness.

She agreed, and they left the room together. At the doorway, Mr Fanope smiled at them and said that he looked forward to seeing them the following Friday.

"You make a very good couple," he said. "You are coming on nicely. You are a good dancer, Mma, and you, Rra, I think you will be good in the future."

Mma Makutsi's heart sank. If she had feared that she might be landed with this man at every class, then this fear had just been confirmed.

"I'm not sure that I shall be able to come here again," she blurted out. "I am very busy."

Mr Fanope shook his head. "You must come, Mma. Your friend here needs you to help him with his dancing, don't you, Rra?"

Phuti Radiphuti beamed with pleasure, wiping his brow with a red handkerchief. "I am very happy dancing with . . ." The words came painfully slowly, and he was interrupted by Mr Fanope before he could finish.

"Good," said the instructor. "We shall see you both then, next Friday. That is very good." He gestured at the other dancers. "Some of these people over there don't really need lessons. But you do."

Outside, they walked in silence to the car park behind the hardware store. Phuti Radiphuti's car was at the far end, a modest white car with a twisted aerial. Yet it was a car, which told Mma Makutsi something about him. As Mma Ramotswe would have pointed out to her, the mere fact that he has a car tells us something, Mma. It means that he has a good job. Now look at his hands, Mma, and his shoes, and see what they say about him. As he started the car, Mma Makutsi looked at his hands, but they told her nothing. Or at least they told her one thing, she thought, with an inward smile. He has all his fingers. He is not a butcher.

She directed him back to her house, where he dropped her, keeping the engine running. She was relieved that he had no expectations beyond that, and she thanked him politely as she alighted.

"I will see you next week," she said, although she had not planned to say this. She had not planned to give any commitment, but she had done it, more out of pity for him than anything else. And she noticed that he appeared to appreciate the gesture, as he smiled and started to say something. But he did not finish. The words were stuck, and he became mute. So she closed the door, and waved to him, and he drew away in his white car, and she watched the red lights of the car disappear down the road, into the darkness.

CHAPTER NINE

MR POLOPETSI STARTS
AT THE GARAGE

THE REPAIR of the bicycle had been effected by the younger apprentice. He had managed to straighten the handlebars and attend to a buckle in the wheel, with the result that even if the bicycle was not as good as new, it was possible to ride it safely. Mma Ramotswe had her misgivings about this; she would have liked to be able to say to its owner that it was perfect, indeed that it had been improved upon, but she felt that she could not claim this. Instead she would have to say that they had done their best, and that she hoped that he might be satisfied with the repair. Of course, in view of the offer she was about to make him, he would be unlikely to protest very much.

She had asked him to come to the garage to

fetch the bicycle and now he was here, knocking at the door of her office, his hat in his hand. She had bade him enter and he had done so, not boldly as men usually entered, but almost apologetically. Mma Ramotswe noticed this, and thought how this must be the effect of prison, at least its effect on an honest man who had been sent there unjustly. What greater wrong can there be than that, what greater hurt? To know that you were reviled for something that you had not done, or for something for which you did not deserve to be punished; that must be very painful, she thought.

She rose to her feet to greet him.

"You are very welcome, Rra," she said. "You must come in and sit down, and we can talk. Then . . ."

"It is not ready? It is not fixed?"

She smiled to put him at his ease. "Of course it's ready, Rra. We have done our best, or rather the apprentice through there—you might have seen him—has done his best. I hope that it is all right."

His relief was visible. "I am glad of that, Mma. I need that bicycle to look for work."

Mma Ramotswe looked across the room to

where Mma Makutsi was sitting at her desk and they exchanged glances.

"Well, Rra," she began. "On that thing I have something to say to you. I can tell you . . ."

As she spoke, Mr Polopetsi suddenly raised a hand to stop her. "No, Mma," he said, his tone becoming firmer. "Please do not tell me. I have had so many people telling me how I can find work. They all tell me that I must look in this place and look in that place. And I do that, and it is no good. It is always the same thing—I tell them about what happened to me and they say thank you, but we cannot help you. That is what they tell me. Every time. So please do not tell me again. I know you are being kind, but I have heard these things so many times."

He stopped, and again there was an apologetic look, as if the courage that his declaration had required had now run out.

Mma Ramotswe stared at him. "I was not going to say that, Rra," she said quietly. "I was not going to give you advice. No, I was going to offer you a job. That is all."

For a few moments Mr Polopetsi said nothing, but looked at her, and then looked over his shoulder at Mma Makutsi, as if for confirmation. Mma Makutsi smiled encouragingly.

"Yes, Rra," she said. "Mma Ramotswe does not say things that she does not mean. She is going to offer you a job."

Mma Ramotswe leaned forward and tapped her desk. "This job is right here in the garage," she said. "And maybe you will do a bit of work for us too. You can help us. It is not a big job."

Mr Polopetsi appeared to be having difficulty in taking in what was being said to him. He opened his mouth to speak, and closed it again. Then he asked a question.

"Is this job for a long time?" he asked. "Or just for a few days?"

Mma Ramotswe looked down at her desk. She had not discussed this matter with Mr J.L.B. Matekoni and now, faced with the hopes of Mr Polopetsi, she had to make a decision.

"It will be for at least a year," she said confidently. "We cannot see what will happen beyond that. But you will be safe for a year."

After she had spoken, she glanced at Mma Makutsi, who raised an eyebrow. Mma Makutsi understood that there was an impulsive side to her employer, just as there sometimes was to Mr J.L.B. Matekoni. Both of them could act in that way when they were being kind, and then find that there were reproaches from the other. There were two fine examples of this that Mma Makutsi knew about. Mma Ramotswe had acted in exactly that way when she had promoted her to Assistant Detective. Mma Makutsi knew that this had been done in times of financial difficulty when sound economic sense should have dictated precisely the opposite course of action. But Mma Ramotswe had been unable to disappoint her and had gone ahead and done what her heart dictated. And then Mr J.L.B. Matekoni had done just the same thing, had he not, when he had adopted the two children from the orphan farm? Everybody knew that Mma Potokwane pushed Mr J.L.B. Matekoni around and must have browbeaten or tricked him into that decision, but the wily matron knew exactly how to play on his good nature. So this decision was nothing unusual, although Mma Ramotswe would at some point have to own up to Mr J.L.B. Matekoni that she had given this assurance.

"Well, Rra?" asked Mma Ramotswe. "Would you like this job?"

Mr Polopetsi nodded his head. "My heart is

too full to speak," he said. "My heart is too full, Mma. You are a very kind lady. God was watching when he made you knock me over. That was God's act."

"That is kind of you," said Mma Ramotswe in a businesslike tone. "But I think it was something altogether different. Now I think that we should go through there to speak to Mr J.L.B. Matekoni so that he can start you off."

Mr Polopetsi stood up. "I am very happy," he said. "But I know nothing about cars. I hope that I can do this job."

"For years we have had two young men working here who know nothing about cars," interjected Mma Makutsi. "That did not stop them. So it should not stop you, Rra."

"That is true," said Mma Ramotswe. "But let us talk about that later." She paused before adding, "There is one thing, Rra."

Mr Polopetsi hesitated. "Yes?"

"You have this job now," said Mma Ramotswe, "so you can tell us about what happened to you. Tell us at lunchtime today, right from the beginning, so that we know all about it and will not have to wonder what happened.

Tell us so that we no longer have to think about it."

"I can do that," said Mr Polopetsi. "I can tell you everything."

"Good," said Mma Ramotswe. "Now you can start work. There is a lot to do. We are very busy these days and we are very pleased to have another man . . ."

"To order about," interjected Mma Makutsi, and then laughed. "No, Rra, do not worry. I am only joking about that."

Mr J.L.B. Matekoni was busy at lunchtime, taking the remaining apprentice off with him to deal with a breakdown out on the Molepolole Road. So it was only Mma Ramotswe and Mma Makutsi who sat in the office listening to Mr Polopetsi while he told his story. Mma Makutsi had made sandwiches for them with the bread they kept in the office cupboard—thick slices with generous helpings of jam—and Mma Ramotswe noticed how eagerly Mr Polopetsi tackled the food. He is hungry, she thought, and realised that he had probably been giving what little food there was to his family. She signalled to Mma Makutsi to make more sandwiches, which Mr Polopetsi wolfed down as he spoke.

"I was born in Lobatse," he began. "My father was one of the attendants at the mental hospital there. You will know the place. His job was to help the doctors control the very sick people who struggled when the doctors tried to treat them. There were some very strong patients and they would shout and strike out at everybody. My father was a strong man too, and he had a special jacket that he could put on these people and tie their arms behind them. That would make it easier for the doctors.

"I worked hard at school. I wanted to be a doctor when I grew up, but when the examinations came along I did not do well enough. I knew the answers to the questions, because I had worked so hard, but I became very frightened when the examinations started and I could not write properly. My hand would shake and shake and the examiners must have wondered who was this stupid boy who could not even write neatly. So I never did as well as I should have. If I hadn't shaken like that, then maybe I would have been given a scholarship and gone off to South Africa to study medicine. That happened to one boy at my school, but it did not happen to me.

"But I did not sit and complain about this because I knew that God would find me some other work. And He did. When I was sixteen I was given a job in the hospital where my father worked. There is a pharmacy in the hospital and they needed somebody to wash the bottles and to help carry and lift things. I also had to write notes in the drugs stock book, and I had to count the bottles and the pills. I was very good at that and they made me a pharmacy assistant when I was twenty. That was a very good job. I even took some examinations to do with that work and I found that I was not so frightened this time. I wrote neatly and I passed.

"I worked down there for twelve years before they sent me up to Gaborone. I was very pleased to get this new job because it was more senior and I was given more money. I became a pharmacy assistant at the Princess Marina, which is a very fine hospital. There is a very big pharmacy there and they have many, many shelves of bottles. I worked very hard and did well. Now I could marry a lady whom I had met at my church. She is a very good lady and she has given me two children, two girls, this big and this big, and they are very good children.

"I was a very happy man and a very proud one too. Then one day a very bad thing happened to me, a thing which changed my life forever and which I can never forget. And it was just an ordinary day, the same as any day. When I left my house that morning I did not know what was going to happen to me. I did not know that this was the last day that I would be happy."

Mr Polopetsi paused to bite into the fresh sandwich which Mma Makutsi had passed him. He took a large mouthful, and the two ladies watched him in silence as he chewed on the food. Mma Ramotswe wondered what it was that could have suddenly brought his world to an end. He had said when they had first met them that there had been an accident, but what accident could have resulted in his spending two years in prison? A road accident? Had he driven while drunk and killed somebody? He seemed an unlikely candidate for that.

"We were very busy that morning," continued Mr Polopetsi, wiping crumbs from his mouth with the back of his hand. "Sometimes it was like that. All the wards would run out of medicines at the same time and there would be a whole line of out-patients waiting for their prescriptions. So we would be running this way and that, trying to get things sorted out. There were two pharmacists who were ill that day because there was a lot of flu in the town. So we were very busy.

"We were not allowed to do many things. We were just pharmacy assistants, and so we were not allowed to measure out drugs and things like that. But when it was busy like that they sometimes told us that we could do simple things, like counting out pills and putting them in bottles. So we did that.

"I was doing that sort of thing on that morning. And that is when I made a mistake. I took pills from the wrong place and put them into the bottle which the pharmacist had given me. I put these pills in because I thought that he had pointed to one place and not to another. I misunderstood him.

"The drugs that I put in that bottle were very strong. They killed a lady who took them. It was because of what I did.

"They were very cross when this lady died. They found the bottle with the wrong drugs in it and they asked who had put them in there. The pharmacist said that he had passed the right drugs to me to put in and that I must have disobeyed him. He was very frightened because he thought that they would blame him. He was just a junior person, a foreigner who used to work there, and who has gone now. So he lied. I heard him lying and I shouted out that what he said was not true. So they asked him again and he said that he remembered that morning very well and he remembered giving me the right drugs, and that there were no other pills around at the time. That was not true. There were many containers of pills and he should have realised that I might misunderstand his instructions.

"That evening when I went home I sat at my place and said nothing. I could not speak. My wife tried to comfort me. She said that it was not my fault that somebody had died and that what had happened was a true accident, like a dog running across the road or a plate falling off the table. But I could not even hear her words very well because my heart was cold, cold within me, and I knew that I would lose my job. How would we get anything to eat if I had no job? My father was late now and I could not go back to his place. We would be finished.

"I had no idea then how much worse things would be. It was only a few weeks later, after the police had spoken to me three or four times, that they told me that they were going to charge me with culpable homicide. That's what they called it. They said that it was culpable homicide to do something so careless that another person died. I could not believe that they would blame me so much, but the family of the lady who died were making a very big fuss about this and they kept asking the police when the man who had killed their mother would be punished for what he had done.

"I went to see them. They lived over there in Old Naledi, and I went to their house and begged them to forgive me. I said that I had never intended to harm the mother. Why should I want to harm her? I said that I felt as bad as if I had killed my own mother. I asked them if they would stop asking the police to send me to prison and tell them that I had explained to them what had happened. I went down on my knees to them. But they did not even look at me. They said I was to get out of their house or they would run and fetch the police.

"So I left their place and went home and waited for the day to come when I would have to go to court. I had a lawyer who said that he would work for me if I could pay him. I went to the Post Office and took out almost all the money I had saved and I gave this to the lawyer. He said that he would do his best for me, and I am sure that he did. But the prosecutor said that what I had done was very careless. He said that nobody who was being careful would have done what I did. And the magistrate was looking at me all the time, and I could tell that he thought I was a very careless man who had gone and killed somebody with his carelessness.

"When he said that I would have to go to prison for two years, at first I could not look behind me. My wife was there, and I could hear her cry out, and so I turned round and saw her there with my two little girls, and the girls were looking at their daddy and wondering whether I was coming home with them now, and I did not know what to do, whether I should wave goodbye to them, and so I just stood there until the policemen who were standing on either side of me said that I would have to go. These policemen were kind to me. They did not push me; they did not speak unkindly. One of them said, 'I am sorry, Rra. I am sorry about this thing. You must come now.' And I left, and I did not look behind me again, and I went away."

He stopped, and there was silence. Mma Ramotswe reached forward to pick up a pencil from the table top. Then she put it down again. Mma Makutsi was quite still. Neither of them spoke, because there was nothing that either of them felt that she could say.

CHAPTER TEN

THERE IS ALWAYS TIME FOR TEA AND CAKE (IF AVAILABLE)

It was time for Mma Ramotswe to visit Mma Silvia Potokwane, the redoubtable matron of the orphan farm. There was no particular reason for Mma Ramotswe to pay a visit; she had received no summons from the matron, and there was no request to borrow Mr J.L.B. Matekoni for some maintenance task that needed doing. This was purely a social visit, of the sort that Mma Ramotswe liked to make when she felt that it was time to sit and talk. People did not spend enough time sitting and talking, she thought, and it was important that sitting and talking time be preserved.

The two women had known one another for many years, and had moved into that most comfortable of territories, that of an old friendship that could be picked up and put down at will without damage. Sometimes several months would go by without the two seeing one another, and this would make no difference. A conversation left unfinished at the beginning of the hot season could be resumed after the rains; a question asked in January might be answered in June, or even later, or indeed not at all. There was no need for formality or caution, and the faults of each were known to the other.

What were the faults of Mma Potokwane? Well, Mma Ramotswe might list those quite readily, were she to put her mind to it. Everybody knew that Mma Potokwane was pushy; she had pushed Mr J.L.B. Matekoni around for years, and he had meekly submitted to such treatment. There had been innumerable requests for help in keeping that water pump alive, well beyond the limits of its natural life, and then there had been the unreliable minibus, which should have been scrapped years before but which was still on the road thanks to the unsurpassed mechanical skills of Mr J.L.B. Matekoni. At least the pump had been disposed of when he had eventually stood up to her and told her that its time had come, but he had yet to make a similar stand over the minibus.

But the worst instance of all had been that business with the sponsored parachute jump, when Mma Potokwane had cajoled Mr J.L.B. Matekoni into agreeing to jump from an aeroplane to raise money for the orphan farm. That had been a dreadful thing to do, and Mma Ramotswe had found herself quite cross over the whole episode. Although she had managed to arrange for Charlie to jump in his employer's stead—and she would never forget how Charlie had landed on a large acacia thorn—the whole matter had caused great anxiety to Mr J.L.B. Matekoni. One had to watch Mma Potokwane, then, so that she did not manoeuvre people into positions in which they felt uncomfortable. This was always the case with pushy people; their pushy schemes were sometimes put into effect without one's being aware of what was going on. And then suddenly one would discover that one had agreed to do something one had no wish to do.

Of course, let she who is without pushiness cast the first stone. Mma Ramotswe would have to admit that she herself was not above the occasional attempt to get people to do

things. She would not have called that pushiness; she would rather have described it as . . .
Well, it was difficult for her to think of an exact word to express the mixture of psychology
and determination which one had to be able to
invoke if one was to get anything done. And it
should always be borne in mind that even if
Mma Potokwane was pushy, she never pushed
for things for herself. She used her undoubted
talents in this direction for the benefit of the
orphans, and there were many of them who
had a great deal to thank her for.

There was that small boy with the club foot,
for example. Mma Ramotswe remembered
when she had first seen him at the orphan farm
four or five years ago. He had been taken in at
the age of six, having been sent down from
Selibi Pickwe, or somewhere in those parts.
Mma Potokwane had explained the background to her, and had told her how the boy
had been deserted by his mother, who had
gone off with a man and had left him with an
aunt who was an alcoholic. This aunt had let a
fire get out of control, and the small traditional
house in which they lived, with its walls of
brushwood, had gone up in flames while the
boy was inside it. The aunt had staggered off,

and nobody had been aware of the fact that the boy was inside until the fire had died down. He had spent months in hospital and had then been given a home at the orphan farm.

Mma Ramotswe had seen him playing with the other boys, running after a ball with them in one of those strange spontaneous games which boys will make up for themselves. And she had seen his efforts to keep up, in vain because he had to drag his misshapen left foot behind him.

"That is a brave boy, that one," Mma Potokwane had said. "He is always trying to do things. He tries to climb trees, but he cannot because of that foot. And he would like to play football, but he cannot kick the ball. He is a brave boy."

Mma Ramotswe had noticed that look in Mma Potokwane's eyes as she spoke, that look of determination; and it was no surprise to her to hear some months ago that the matron had packed the boy onto a bus with her and had made the long journey to Johannesburg. There she had taken him to the surgery of a doctor she had heard about and had insisted that he see the boy. It was an act of breathtaking bravery. She had later heard, from Mma Potokwane herself, who related the story with frequent chuckles, how she had taken the boy into the waiting room of this doctor, a waiting room in a glittering tall building, and had ignored the protestations of the receptionist that the doctor would never be able to see her.

"The doctor can decide that," Mma Potokwane had announced. "You cannot speak for the doctor. He can look at this boy and then he can tell me, himself, whether he will see him or not."

She had waited and waited, and at last the doctor had poked his head round the door and this had been the signal for Mma Potokwane to leap to her feet and take from her bag a large fruit cake that she had prepared. This was thrust into the astonished man's hands, while the boy, hanging on to Mma Potokwane's skirts, had followed her into the doctor's office.

"He could not say no after that," said Mma Potokwane. "I cut a piece of the cake straightaway and told him that he could eat it while the boy took his shoes and socks off. So he did. He ate the cake and then he could not say that he would not look at the boy. And once he had done that, I asked him when he could do the operation, and while he was trying to think of something to say I cut another piece of fruit cake for him. So that boy had his foot repaired and now it is not too bad at all. He still limps, but not nearly so badly. He can play football. He can even run. That was a very good doctor. And he did not charge anything either. He said that the fruit cake was payment enough."

Achievements like that, Mma Ramotswe thought, were more than enough to make up for the occasional irritation that one might feel over Mma Potokwane's pushiness, and anyway, on this occasion, Mma Ramotswe was not minded to think of her friend's faults. She wanted, rather, to hear her views on several difficult issues with which she was confronted. At least one of these issues was serious—the question of what to do about Charlie—and others merely needed to be aired, to see what insights Mma Potokwane might bring to them.

She spotted the matron on the verandah outside her office, engaged in conversation with one of the groundsmen. These men were important members of the orphan farm staff; they attended to all the minor tasks which cropped up on an orphan farm, problems with blocked drains, or the broken boughs of trees, or the chasing away of a snake or a stray dog.

She waited in the tiny white van until the business between the two appeared to be finished, and then she got out and walked over the dusty car park towards the matron's verandah.

"So, Mma," Mma Potokwane called out. "You have arrived at exactly the time I was thinking that it would be a good time to make some tea. You are very good at that."

Mma Ramotswe laughed, and raised a hand in greeting. "And you always arrive at my office at exactly the same time," she responded. "We are both good at that."

Mma Potokwane called out to a young woman who was standing in the doorway of a neighbouring office, asking her to make tea for both of them, and then she gestured for Mma Ramotswe to follow her inside. Once seated, they looked at one another to see who would begin the conversation.

It was Mma Ramotswe who broke the silence. "I have been very busy, Mma," she began, shaking her head. "We have had a lot of work in the agency, and the garage is always busy, as you know. Mr J.L.B. Matekoni takes on too much."

She had not intended this to be a reference

to the fact that some people—principally Mma Makutsi—thought that Mma Potokwane shamelessly added to Mr J.L.B. Matekoni's burdens in this life. Fortunately Mma Potokwane did not appear to interpret her remark in this way.

"He is a good, kind man," said Mma Potokwane. "And such men are often too busy. I have noticed that round here too. That man I was talking to just then—one of our groundsmen—he is like that. He is so kind that everybody asks him to do everything. We had a bad-tempered man working here once and he had nothing to do because nobody, apart from myself, of course, had the courage to ask him to do anything."

Mma Ramotswe agreed that this was the way that people sometimes behaved, and further agreed with Mma Potokwane when she went on to say that people never really changed. It was almost impossible to get a busy man to do less; that was not the way they were made.

"Are you worried about him?" asked Mma Potokwane bluntly. "After that illness he had, maybe you should watch him. Didn't Dr Moffat say that he should not work too hard?"

"He did," said Mma Ramotswe. "But then when Mr J.L.B. Matekoni was told this, he said: 'And what about Dr Moffat himself? He is the hardest worker of them all. I have seen him. He is always rushing off to the hospital and looking after people. If he thinks that I should not work so hard, why is he working so hard himself?' That is what he said, Mma, and I found it difficult to answer that."

Mma Potokwane snorted. "That is no answer," she said. "Doctors are allowed to tell us things which they might not do themselves. They know what the right thing is, but they may not be able to do it themselves. That does not mean that their advice is bad advice."

This was an interesting observation, and Mma Ramotswe thought carefully about it before she replied.

"I must think about what you have said, Mma," she said. "Should we really go around telling other people what not to do?"

The question was asked and hung heavily in the air while the tea tray was brought in and laid on Mma Potokwane's desk. Mma Ramotswe looked discreetly at its contents; yes, there was cake—two large slices of fruit cake of the sort that she always hoped for when she visited the orphan farm. The absence of cake from the tray could have meant that she was for some reason in disfavour or disgrace; but fortunately that was not the case today.

Mma Potokwane reached forward and placed the larger slice of cake on her friend's plate. Then she placed the other piece on her own plate and began to pour the tea.

"The question you have asked is a very important one, Mma," she pronounced, picking up her slice of cake and taking a bite. "I must think about it. Maybe there are people who would say that I eat too much cake."

"But you do not eat too much, do you?" observed Mma Ramotswe.

Mma Potokwane's response came quickly. "No, I do not. I do not eat too much cake." She paused, and looked wistfully at her now emptying plate. "Sometimes I would like to eat too much cake. That is certainly true. Sometimes I am tempted."

Mma Ramotswe sighed. "We are all tempted, Mma. We are all tempted when it comes to cake."

"That is true," said Mma Potokwane sadly. "There are many temptations in this life, but cake is probably one of the biggest of them."

For a few moments neither of them said anything. Mma Ramotswe looked out of the window, at the tree outside, and beyond that at the sky, which was an empty light blue, endless, endless. A large bird, a buzzard perhaps, was circling on high on a current of air, a tiny, soaring point of black, looking for food, of course, as all of us did, in one way or another.

She looked away from the sky and back towards Mma Potokwane, who was watching her, the faintest of smiles playing about her lips.

"Temptation is very difficult," said Mma Ramotswe quietly. "I do not always resist it. I am not a strong woman in that respect."

"I am glad you said that," said Mma Potokwane. "I am not strong either. For example, right at the moment, I am thinking of cake."

"And so am I," confessed Mma Ramotswe.

Mma Potokwane stood up and shouted to the girl outside. "Two more pieces of cake, please. Two big slices."

THE CAKE FINISHED and the tray tidied away, they settled down with their mugs of tea to continue the conversation. Mma Ramotswe thought that she would begin with the puzzle of the pumpkin, which had been rather forgotten about in all the recent excitement, but which was still something of a mystery. So she told Mma Potokwane about the disturbing experience of finding herself in the house with an intruder, and then the even more alarming discovery that the intruder was under her bed.

Mma Potokwane shrieked with laughter when Mma Ramotswe described how the intruder's trousers had been caught on a bedspring.

"You might have crushed him, Mma," she said. "You could have broken his ribs."

Mma Ramotswe thought that the same might be said of any intruder who was unwise enough to hide under Mma Potokwane's bed, but she did not point this out.

"But then the next morning," she went on, "I found a beautiful pumpkin in front of the house. Somebody had taken the trousers and left a pumpkin in the place of the trousers. What do you make of that, Mma?"

Mma Potokwane frowned. "You have decided that the pumpkin was put there by the person who took the trousers, but are they connected? Might the pumpkin and the trousers be two quite separate matters? You have a pumpkin person, who brings the pumpkin— while the trousers are still there—and then you have a trousers person who takes the trousers and does not touch the pumpkin. That might be what happened."

"But who would bring a pumpkin and leave it there without any explanation?" asked Mma Ramotswe. "Would you do such a thing?"

Mma Potokwane scratched her head. "I do not think that I would leave a pumpkin at somebody's house unless I told them why. You would leave a message with the pumpkin, or you would tell the person later: that was me who left that pumpkin there."

"That is right," said Mma Ramotswe. "That is what most people would do."

"Mind you," said Mma Potokwane, "we have had people leave gifts out here at the gate. Once I found a box of food just sitting there, with no note. Some kind person had left it for the children."

"That is good," said Mma Ramotswe. "But then it is a bit different, isn't it? I am not a charity. Nobody would leave a pumpkin because they felt that I was in need of pumpkins."

Mma Potokwane saw the reason in this and was about to make an observation to this effect when she stopped herself short. Another possibility had occurred to her. Mma Ramotswe was assuming that the pumpkin had been intended for her, but what if somebody had placed it there by mistake? It was possible that somebody had intended the pumpkin for somebody else who lived on Zebra Drive but had delivered it to the wrong house. She was about to suggest this when she was stopped by Mma Ramotswe.

"Does it matter?" mused Mma Ramotswe. "Here we are talking about a pumpkin. There are plenty of pumpkins in this country. Is it sensible to spend one's time talking about pumpkins when there are more important things to talk about?"

Mma Potokwane agreed with this. "You are quite right," she said. "We have talked about this pumpkin for long enough. So let us talk about something more important."

Mma Ramotswe did not waste time. "Well," she said. "We have a very big problem with

Charlie. I think that this problem is even bigger than the thorn that he got in the back of his trousers when he did that parachute jump."

"It is to do with a woman?" prompted Mma Potokwane.

"Yes," said Mma Ramotswe. "Now listen to this."

Mma Potokwane settled back in her chair. She had had a soft spot for Charlie since he had done the parachute jump for the benefit of the orphan farm. She considered him something of a character, and the prospect of hearing some juicy bit of information about his amorous entanglements was an interesting one. But then she remembered that there was something that she had meant to mention to Mma Ramotswe. It would be important to bring this up before Mma Ramotswe got into full flow, otherwise she might forget. So she raised a hand to interrupt.

"Before you begin, Mma," she said, "there's something I thought I should tell you about."

Mma Ramotswe looked at her friend expectantly. She wondered whether Mma Potokwane perhaps already knew about Charlie's affair and might even be able to tell her about the woman involved. Mma Potokwane knew so much about what was going on that it would not be at all surprising if she knew exactly who it was who had been at the wheel of that sleek silver Mercedes-Benz.

"You'll never guess who I saw in town the other day," said Mma Potokwane. "I could hardly believe it."

"I cannot guess," said Mma Ramotswe. "Was it somebody well-known?"

"A bit," said Mma Potokwane enigmatically. "Well-known in the jazz world, perhaps."

Mma Ramotswe said nothing, waiting for Mma Potokwane to continue.

"Note," she said simply. "Note Mokoti, your first husband. Remember him?"

CHAPTER ELEVEN

MMA MAKUTSI FINDS OUT MORE ABOUT MR PHUTI RADIPHUTI

WHILE MMA RAMOTSWE was embarking on her second slice of cake with Mma Potokwane, Mma Makutsi was still at the No. 1 Ladies' Detective Agency, tidying up. Mma Ramotswe had given her permission to close early that day since she herself was effectively taking the entire afternoon off. They were still busy with the affairs of a number of clients, but there was nothing that could not wait, and Mma Ramotswe knew that Mma Makutsi would like to have adequate time to get ready for her dancing class, the second one, which would be held that evening.

Mma Makutsi had finished the day's filing—a task which, as had been drummed into her at the Botswana Secretarial College, should never be left to lie over for the following day. This message had come from no less a person than the Principal herself, a tall, imposing woman who had brought the highest standards to the secretarial profession in Botswana.

"Don't let paper lie about, girls," she had admonished them. "Let each paper cross your desk once, and once only. That is a very good rule. Put everything away. Imagine that at night there are big paper rats that will come out and eat all the paper on your desk!"

That had been a very clever way of putting it, thought Mma Makutsi. The idea of the paper rat coming out at night to eat unfiled letters was a vivid one, and she had thought that it was not helpful of those silly, glamorous girls in the back row to laugh like that at what the Principal had said. The trouble with those girls had been that they were not committed secretaries. Everybody knew that most of them came to the Botswana Secretarial College simply because they had worked out that the best way of marrying a man with a good job and a lot of money was to become a secretary to such a man. So they went through the College course looking bored and making very little effort. It would have been different, it occurred to Mma Makutsi, had there been a part of the curriculum entitled: **How to Marry Your Boss.** That would have been very popular with those girls, and they would have paid very close attention to such a course.

In an idle moment, Mma Makutsi had speculated as to the possible contents of a course of this name. Some of the time would be devoted to psychology and this part would include lessons on how men think. That was very important if one was the sort of girl who planned to trap a man. You had to know what attracted men and what frightened them. Mma Makutsi thought about this. What attracted men? Good looks? Certainly if a girl was pretty then she tended to get the attention of men; that was beyond any doubt at all. But it was not just prettiness that mattered, because there were many girls who did not look anything special but who seemed to find no difficulty in making men notice them. These girls dressed in a very careful way; they knew which colours appealed to men (red, and other bright colours; men were like cattle in that respect), and they knew how to walk and sit down in a way which would make men sit up and take notice. The walk was important: it should not be a simple walk, with one leg going forward, to be followed by the other; no, the legs had to bend and twist a bit, almost as if one was thinking of walking in a circle. And then there was the delicate issue of what to do with one's bottom while one was walking. Some people thought that one could just leave one's bottom to follow one when one was walking. Not so. A mere glance at any glamorous girl would show that the bottom had to be more **involved.**

Mma Makutsi thought about all this as she tidied the office that afternoon. It was all very dispiriting. She had been dismayed to see that woman at the dance class—the woman whose name she had forgotten but who had been one of the worst, the very worst, of the glamorous girls at the Botswana Secretarial College. The sight of that woman dancing with such a handsome man, while she, Mma Makutsi, stumbled about the floor with poor Phuti Radiphuti, struggling to make out what he was trying to say; that sight had been immensely depressing. And then there was the question of her glasses, so large that people saw themselves reflected and did not even bother to see the person behind the lenses. What could she do about those? Glasses were very expensive, and although she was better off now, she had so many other costs to meet—higher rent for her new house, new clothes to be bought, and more money needed by those at home in Bobonong.

Her thoughts were interrupted by the arrival at the door of Mr Polopetsi. He had been working at the garage for several days now and had made a very good impression on all of them. Mr J.L.B. Matekoni had been particularly pleased with the way in which he had tidied the store cupboards. Cans of oil had been placed on shelves according to size, and parts had been organised according to make.

"You need a system," Mr Polopetsi had announced. "Then you will know when it is time to order more spark plugs and the like. This is called stock control."

He had also scrubbed the garage floor, removing several large patches of oil which the apprentices had never bothered to do anything about.

"Somebody might slip," said Mr Polopetsi. "You have to be very careful."

Mr J.L.B. Matekoni was delighted with this pronouncement, and drew it to the attention of the remaining apprentice.

"Did you hear that, young man?" he said. "Did you hear what Polopetsi said? Carefulness. Have you heard that word before? Do you know what it means?"

The younger apprentice said nothing, but stared at Mr Polopetsi in a surly way. He had been suspicious of this new employee ever since he had arrived, although Mr Polopetsi had been polite to him and had made every effort to win him over. Observing this, it had been clear to Mr J.L.B. Matekoni that their assumption that Charlie would soon hear that his place had been usurped was perfectly correct. But he was not sure that Charlie would respond in quite the way Mma Ramotswe had anticipated. However, they would see in due course, and for the time being the important thing was that the work in the garage was getting done.

Mr Polopetsi, in fact, had shown considerable talent for the simpler mechanical tasks which Mr J.L.B. Matekoni had given him. Watching the way he changed an air filter, or examined the oil on an engine's dip stick, made Mr J.L.B. Matekoni realise that this man had a feeling for cars, something which some mechanics never developed but which was a necessity if one was to become really good at the job.

"You like engines, don't you?" he said to Mr Polopetsi at the end of his first day. "I can tell that you understand them. Have you worked with them before?"

"Never," admitted Mr Polopetsi. "I do not know the names of all the parts or what they do. This bit here, for example, what does it do?"

Mr J.L.B. Matekoni peered at the engine. "That," he said, "is a very interesting bit. That is the distributor. It is the bit which sends the electric current in the right direction."

"So you would not want any dirt or water to get in there," said Mr Polopetsi.

Mr J.L.B. Matekoni nodded appreciatively. This showed that Mr Polopetsi intuitively understood how engines **felt.** Charlie would never have said anything so perceptive.

Now Mma Makutsi asked Mr Polopetsi whether everything was all right.

"Oh yes," he replied enthusiastically. "Everything is all right. I just thought that I would tell you that I have finished all my work in the garage this afternoon and I wondered if you had anything for me to do."

Mma Makutsi was most impressed. Most people would not ask for more work, but if they had nothing to do would merely pretend to work until five o'clock came and they could go home. In asking for something to do, Mr Polopetsi was proving that Mma Ramotswe had been right in her positive judgement of him.

She looked about the office. It was difficult to see what there was for him to do. She could hardly ask him to do any filing, which had been done anyway, and it would be too much to expect him to be able to type, even if he had been a pharmacy assistant and was therefore an indoor sort of man. So she could not ask him to do any letters; or could she?

Mma Makutsi looked sideways at Mr Polopetsi. "You can't type, can you, Rra?" she asked hesitantly.

Mr Polopetsi was matter-of-fact in his reply; there was no hint of boasting. "I can type very quickly, Mma. My sister went to the Botswana Secretarial College and she taught me."

Mma Makutsi stared at him. Not only was he a hard and resourceful worker, but he had a sister who was a graduate of the Botswana

Secretarial College! She thought of the name—Polopetsi. Had she known anybody of that name at the College?

"She has a different name," Mr Polopetsi explained. "She is my sister by a different father. Her name is Difele. Agnes Difele."

Mma Makutsi clapped her hands together. "She was my friend," she exclaimed. "She was just before me at the College. She did very well . . . too."

"Yes," said Mr Polopetsi. "She got eighty per cent in the final examinations."

Mma Makutsi nodded gravely. That was a good mark, well above the average. Of course it was not ninety-seven per cent, but it was perfectly creditable.

"Where is she now?" asked Mma Makutsi.

"She is a secretary in the Standard Bank," said Mr Polopetsi. "But I do not see her much these days. She was very ashamed when I was sent to prison and she has not spoken to me since then. She said that I disgraced her."

Mma Makutsi was silent. It was difficult to imagine somebody disowning her own brother like that. She herself would never have done that; one's family was one's family whatever happened; surely that was the point of having a family in the first place. One's family gave one unconditional support, whatever happened.

"I am sorry to hear that, Rra," she said.

Mr Polopetsi looked away for a moment. "I am not cross with her. I hope that she will change her mind some day. Then we will talk again."

Mma Makutsi looked at her desk. There were several letters which had to be typed, and she had intended to type them the following day. But here was Mr Polopetsi, with his ability to type, and it occurred to her that she had never once been in a position to dictate a letter and have somebody else type it. Now here she was with letters to be typed and a good typist at her disposal.

"I have some letters to dictate," she said. "You could type them as I dictate. That will save time."

Mr Polopetsi lost no time in setting himself up behind the typewriter at Mma Makutsi's desk, while she installed herself in Mma Ramotswe's chair, several sheets of paper in her hand. This is delicious, she thought. After all these years, I am now sitting in an office chair and dictating **to a man.** This was a very long way from those early days in Bobonong.

MMA MAKUTSI was late in arriving at the dancing class that evening, and as she walked along the corridor at the President Hotel she could hear the band in full flow and the sound of numerous feet on the wooden floor. She appeared at the entrance and made her way to a seat at the side, only to be intercepted by Phuti Radiphuti, who had been waiting for her. Her heart sank. She did not wish to be unkind, but she had hoped that perhaps he would not be there and that she might have the chance to dance with somebody else. Now she was trapped, and there would be more stumbling and tripping while everybody else made progress and moved with greater and greater ease.

Phuti Radiphuti beamed with pleasure as he led her onto the floor. The band, which had been augmented by another guitarist, was playing more loudly than the last time, with the result that it was difficult for her to hear what anybody was saying, let alone to understand those with a speech impediment. So Mma

Makutsi had to strain to make out her partner's words, and even when she thought she could do so, she was puzzled by their apparent lack of sense.

"This is a waltz," he tried to say, as they started to dance. But Mma Makutsi heard: **This is all false.** She wondered why he would say such a thing. Did he sense that she was only dancing with him out of pity, or a sense of duty? Or did he mean something quite different?

So she decided to seek clarification. "Why?" she asked.

Phuti Radiphuti looked puzzled. Waltzes were waltzes, of course; that was just what they were. He could not answer her question, and instead concentrated on doing the steps correctly, which was difficult for him. One, two, together is what Mr Fanope had said; or had he said that they should count three before they did the side-step?

Sensing her partner's confusion, Mma Makutsi took control. Drawing him to the side of the floor, she showed him how the steps were to be executed and made him repeat them himself while she watched. From the corner of her eye she noticed that the woman she had seen at the first lesson, the one whose name she had forgotten, was watching her in a bemused fashion from the other side of the room. That woman was dancing with the same elegant man who had partnered her before, and she waved at Mma Makutsi over her shoulder as she spun round in his expert arms.

Mma Makutsi pursed her lips. She was determined not to feel put down by this woman with her showy dress and her condescending manner. She knew what she would think of her, that she would be thinking: there's poor Grace Makutsi, who never managed to get any man to pay attention to her, and look what she's landed herself with now! Life has passed her by, of course, in spite of the fact that she graduated top of our class. It's no good getting ninety-whatever per cent if you end up like that.

It did not help to imagine what that woman would be thinking; it would be far better to ignore her, or, better still, to remind herself that it was the other woman who deserved the pity. After all, what did she have in life? She would have no career, that woman, only a life of running around with men. And the problem with that is that as you get older it becomes harder and harder to interest men. There would be a new generation of young women then, women with young faces and flashing teeth, while all the time one's own face sagged with age and one's teeth seemed to get a little less white.

Over the next half hour, they danced in almost complete silence. Mma Makutsi had to acknowledge that Phuti Radiphuti was making an effort and seemed to be improving slightly. He trod on her toes less frequently now, and he seemed to be making some progress with keeping in time. She complimented him on this, and he smiled appreciatively.

"I think I'm getting better," he stuttered.

"We must take a break," said Mma Makutsi. "I'm very thirsty after all this dancing."

They left the dance room and made their way down the corridor and onto the hotel verandah. A waiter appeared and took their orders: a cold beer for Phuti Radiphuti and a large glass of orange juice for Mma Makutsi.

The conversation was slow to begin with, but Mma Makutsi noticed that as he began to relax in her company, Phuti Radiphuti's speech became more confident and clearer. She was now able to understand most of what he had to say, although every now and then he seemed to stumble over a word, and when this happened it could be some time before something intelligible emerged.

There seemed to be a lot to talk about. He explained where he was from (the South) and what he was doing in Gaborone (he had a job in a furniture store in Broadhurst, where he sold chairs and tables). He asked about her; about the school she had gone to in Bobonong, about the Botswana Secretarial College, and about her job at the No. 1 Ladies' Detective Agency. He confessed that he had no idea of what a private detective agency would do and he was interested to find out.

"It's very straightforward," said Mma Makutsi. "Most people think that it is very exciting. But it isn't, it really isn't."

"There are very few exciting jobs," observed Phuti Radiphuti. "Most of us have very dull work to do. I just sell tables and chairs. There is nothing exciting in that."

"But it is important work," Mma Makutsi countered. "Where would we be if we had no chairs and tables?"

"We would be on the floor," said Phuti Radiphuti solemnly.

They thought about this for a moment, and

then Mma Makutsi laughed. He had answered her with such gravity, as if the question had been an important one, rather than a mere reflection. She looked at him, and saw him smile in response. Yes, he understood that what he had said was funny. That was important in itself. It was good to be able to share such things with somebody else; the little jokes of life, the little absurdities.

They sat together for a few more minutes, finishing their drinks. Then Mma Makutsi rose to her feet and announced that she was going to the ladies' room and would meet him back in the dance hall for the rest of the class.

She found a door labelled **Powder Room** which bore an outline picture of a woman in a long, flowing skirt. She went in, and immediately regretted it.

"So! There you are, Grace Makutsi!" said the woman standing at the basin.

Mma Makutsi stopped, but the door had closed behind her, and she could hardly pretend that she had come into the wrong room.

She looked at the woman at the basin, and the name came back to her. This was the woman she had seen in the dance class, and her name was Violet Sephotho. She was one of the worst of the glamorous, empty-headed set at the Botswana Secretarial College, and here she was applying powder to her face in the aptly named Powder Room of the President Hotel.

"Violet," said Mma Makutsi. "It is good to see you again."

Violet smiled, closed her powder compact, and leant back against the edge of the basin. She had the air of one who was settling in for a long chat.

"Yes, sure," she said. "I haven't seen you for ages. Ages. Not since we finished the course." She paused, looking Mma Makutsi up and down, as if appraising her dress. "You did well, didn't you? At that college, I mean."

The thrust of the comment was unambiguous. One might do well at college, but this was very different from the real world. And then there was the disdainful reference to **that** college, as if there were better secretarial colleges to be attended.

Mma Makutsi ignored the barb. "And you, Violet? What have you been doing? Did you manage to find a job?"

The implication in this remark was that those who got barely fifty per cent in the final examinations might be expected to experience some difficulty in finding a job. This was not lost on Violet, whose eyes narrowed.

"Find a job?" she retorted. "Mma, I had them lining up to give me a job! I had so many offers that I could think of no way of choosing between them. So you know what I did? You want to know?"

Mma Makutsi nodded. She wanted to be out of this room, and away from this person, but she realised that she had to remain. She would have to stand up for herself if she were not to feel completely belittled by the encounter.

"I looked at the men who were offering the jobs and I chose the best-looking one," she announced. "I knew that that was how they would choose their secretary, so I applied the same rule to them! Hah!"

Mma Makutsi said nothing. She could comment on the stupidity of this, but then that would enable Violet to say something like, "Well that may be stupid in your eyes, but look at the jobs I got." So she said nothing, and held the other woman's challenging glance.

Violet lowered her eyes and inspected her brightly polished nails. "Nice shoes," she said.

"Those green shoes of yours. I've never seen anybody wear green shoes before. It's brave of you. I would be frightened that people would laugh at me if I wore shoes like that."

Mma Makutsi bit her lip. What was wrong with green shoes? And how dare this woman, this empty-headed woman, pass comment on her taste in shoes? She looked at Violet's shoes, sleek black shoes with pointed toes and quite unsuitable for dancing. They looked expensive—much more expensive than these shoes which Mma Makutsi had treated herself to and of which she felt so proud.

"But let's not talk about funny shoes," Violet went on breezily. "Let's talk about men. Don't you love talking about men? That man through there. Is that your uncle or something?"

Mma Makutsi closed her eyes and imagined for a moment that Mma Ramotswe was by her side. What would Mma Ramotswe advise in such circumstances? Could Mma Ramotswe provide the words to deal with this woman, or would she say, "No, do not allow yourself to be belittled by her. Do not stoop to her level. You are worth more than that silly girl." And Mma

Makutsi saw Mma Ramotswe in her mind's eye, and heard her too, and that is exactly what she said.

"The man you are dancing with is very handsome," said Mma Makutsi. "You are lucky to have such a handsome man to dance with. But then you are a very pretty lady, Mma, and you deserve these handsome men. It is quite right that way."

Violet stared at her for a moment, and then looked away. Nothing more was said, and Mma Makutsi went about her business.

"Well done, Mma," said Mma Ramotswe's voice. "You did just the right thing there. Just the right thing!"

"It was very hard," replied Mma Makutsi.

"It often is," said Mma Ramotswe.

CHAPTER TWELVE

MMA RAMOTSWE REVEALS
A PROBLEM WITHOUT
A SOLUTION

Mma Potokwane had mentioned it so casually, as if it had been no more than a piece of unimportant gossip. But the news that Note Mokoti had been seen in Gaborone was much more than that, at least to Mma Ramotswe. She had put Note out of her mind and very rarely thought of him, although there were times when he came to her in dreams, taunting her, threatening her, and she would wake up in fright and have to remind herself that he was no longer there. He had gone to South Africa, she understood, and had pursued his musical career in Johannesburg, apparently with some success, as she had seen the occasional magazine photograph featuring him.

I'm a forgiving lady, Mma Ramotswe told

herself. I see no point in keeping old arguments alive when it is so simple to lay them to rest. She had made a deliberate attempt to forgive Note, and she thought that it had worked. She remembered the day on which she had done this, when she had gone for a walk in the bush and had looked up at the sky and emptied her heart of its hatred. She had forgiven him on that day: she had forgiven him the physical cruelty, the beatings which she had endured when he had taken drink; she had forgiven him the mental torment which he had inflicted on her when he had promised her something or other and had immediately torn up the promise. And when it came to the money which he had taken from her, she forgave him that too, saying to herself that she did not want it back.

When Mma Potokwane had made her disclosure about having seen Note Mokoti, Mma Ramotswe had not shown much of a reaction. Indeed, Mma Potokwane felt the news was of little importance to her friend, so uninterested did she appear, and so she said nothing more about it. They continued their conversation about Charlie and his worrying behaviour; Mma Potokwane had a great deal to say about this, and made some valuable suggestions, but later, when Mma Ramotswe tried to remember what she had said, she could recall very little. Her mind had been almost completely occupied by the sheer awfulness of the news that had been broken to her so casually. Note was back.

As she drove back from Tlokweng that day, Charlie was far from her mind. If Note Mokoti had been seen in Gaborone, then this could mean that he had returned to live there—and that raised certain very obvious difficulties—or it could mean no more than that he had come back for a visit. If he was on a visit, then he might already have gone back to Johannesburg, and she need worry no more. If, however, he had moved back to Gaborone, then it would be inevitable that she herself would see him sooner or later. The town was bigger these days, and it was possible that two people might live in it without ever seeing one another, but there was a very good chance that their paths would cross. After all, there were not all that many supermarkets and she was always bumping into people at such places. And then there was the mall, the centre of the town, where everybody went sooner or later; what if she were to be walking down the mall and she saw Note walking towards her? Would she turn round and walk in the opposite direction, or would she just walk past him as if he were any other stranger?

She thought about this, as she drove the tiny white van back along the Tlokweng Road. Presumably there were many who felt that they had to avoid somebody or other. People were always having arguments with one another, feuds about land and cattle, family scraps over inheritance—which were rich sources of dispute wherever one went in this world. Some of these people made it up with one another and talked again; others never did this, and kept their anger and resentment alive. Then there were people who split up from a lover or a spouse. If you left your wife for another woman, and your wife failed to see this as a good thing, then what if you were walking down the road with your new woman, holding hands, as those who are newly in love might do, and you saw your old wife coming towards you? This must happen a great deal, thought Mma Ramotswe, and presumably people faced it and coped, as they usually end up doing.

People got by in life in spite of all these social pitfalls.

She tried to imagine what she might say to Note if she were to find herself with no alternative but to talk to him. Perhaps it would be best to speak in a very ordinary way and ask him how he was and how life had been treating him. Then she could say something about how she hoped that his music was going well and how she imagined what an exciting life he was leading in Johannesburg. Yes, that would be all. With that she would have shown that she wished him no evil, and even Note, even that unkind man who had treated her so badly, might leave her alone after that.

She turned the tiny white van into Odi Drive to cut through the Village. As she did so, she saw Mrs Moffat walking back along the side of the road, a heavy bag of shopping in her hand. It was not far to the Moffat house, and it would not have taken Mrs Moffat long to walk, but nobody drove past a friend in Botswana, and she drew up alongside and reached over to open the passenger door.

"Your bag looks very heavy," she said. "I will take you back."

Mrs Moffat smiled. "You are very kind, Mma Ramotswe," she said. "And sometimes I feel very lazy. I'm feeling very lazy now."

She climbed into the van and they resumed the short journey back up the road to the Moffat house. Samuel, who worked in the Moffat garden once a week, was standing near the gate, and he opened it for the tiny white van to sweep through.

"Thank you," said Mrs Moffat, turning to her friend. "This bag was getting rather heavy, I'm . . ." She did not finish her sentence, for she had seen the expression on Mma Ramotswe's face.

"Is something wrong, Mma Ramotswe?"

Mma Ramotswe looked away before she gave her reply. "Yes. There is something wrong. I did not want you to know, but there is something wrong."

Mrs Moffat's first thought was of the obvious. Mma Ramotswe and Mr J.L.B. Matekoni had recently married. Their wedding, which she and the doctor had attended, had been a surprise to everybody as they had all decided that Mr J.L.B. Matekoni, fine man though he was, would never make up his mind to get to the altar. Perhaps he had not been ready after all; perhaps the seemingly interminable engagement had been his way of saying that his heart was not really in marriage, and perhaps she was now discovering this. The thought of this appalled her. She knew that Mma Ramotswe had been married before, a long time ago; she had heard a little about this marriage—that it had been one of those awful violent marriages which so many women had to put up with—and it seemed so unfair that things should be going wrong again, if that is what was happening. It would be impossible, though, that they would be going wrong in the same way: Mr J.L.B. Matekoni was incapable of being violent—at least that was certain.

Mrs Moffat reached across and touched Mma Ramotswe lightly on the forearm. "Come," she said. "You can talk to me. We can sit in the garden, or on the verandah if you prefer."

Mma Ramotswe nodded, and turned off the engine. "I do not want to burden you," she said. "It is not a big thing."

"Tell me about it," said Mrs Moffat. "Sometimes it's good just to talk."

They decided to sit on the verandah, where it was cool, and where they could look out over the garden that Mrs Moffat had spent so much time in creating. There was a towering jacaranda tree directly adjacent, and its great canopy of leaves gave shade to the house. It was a good place to sit and reflect.

Mma Ramotswe came straight to the point and told Mrs Moffat about the news which Mma Potokwane had given her. As she spoke, she saw her friend's expression change from one of concern to one of what appeared to be relief.

"So that's all," said Mrs Moffat. "That's all it is."

Mma Ramotswe managed a smile. "I said it was not a big thing."

Mrs Moffat laughed. "It certainly isn't a big thing," she said. "I imagined that there was something wrong with your marriage. I was busy thinking that Mr J.L.B. Matekoni had run away, or something like that. I was wondering what I would be able to say."

"Mr J.L.B. Matekoni would never run away," said Mma Ramotswe. "He is enjoying all the good food that I am putting on the table for him. He would never run away."

"That is a good way to keep a man," said Mrs Moffat. "But, going back to this other man, to Note Mokoti, so what if he's back? You needn't worry about that. Just be polite to him if you see him. You don't have to engage further than that. Tell him you're married . . ."

Mma Ramotswe had been looking at Mrs Moffat as she spoke, but when her friend said **Tell him you're married,** she looked away sharply and Mrs Moffat hesitated. Her words appeared to have upset Mma Ramotswe for some reason and she wondered what it was. Could it be that Mma Ramotswe did not want Note to know this, that for some reason she retained feeling for this man and that she would not want him to know about her marriage to Mr J.L.B. Matekoni?

"You will tell him," she said, "if he shows up, that is. You will tell him that you're married?"

Mma Ramotswe was holding the hem of her dress between her fingers, worrying at it. She looked up and met Mrs Moffat's gaze.

"I am still married to him," she said quietly, her voice barely above a whisper. "I am still married to that man. We did not get a divorce."

In the ensuing moments of silence, a grey African dove moved delicately along a branch of the jacaranda tree, looking down, with quick movements, at the two women below. On a rock just outside the penumbra of shade cast by the tree, a small lizard, tinted blue along its flanks, lifted its head towards the late afternoon sun.

Mrs Moffat said nothing. She was not waiting for Mma Ramotswe to continue; it was just that she had nothing to say.

"So you see, Mma," said Mma Ramotswe. "I am very unhappy. Very unhappy."

Mrs Moffat nodded. "But why did you not get a divorce? He left you, didn't he? You could have got a divorce."

"I was very young," said Mma Ramotswe. "That man frightened me. When he left I just put him out of my mind and tried to forget that we were ever married. I made myself not think about it."

"But surely you remembered later?"

"No," said Mma Ramotswe. "I should have done something about it, but I could not bring myself to face it. I just couldn't. I'm sorry, Mma . . ."

"You don't have to apologise to me!" exclaimed Mrs Moffat. "It's just that this is a bit complicated, isn't it? You're not meant to get married again until you're divorced."

"I know that," said Mma Ramotswe. "I have done a very silly thing, Mma."

They sat together for a short time longer. Mrs Moffat tried to think of something to say, of some advice to give, but she simply could not think of any way out of the situation in which Mma Ramotswe found herself. Friends sometimes behaved in a foolish way—she knew that very well—and this was a good example of that happening. It was not as if Mma Ramotswe had done anything morally reprehensible—it was more a case of being careless about a legal formality. But this was a legal formality which was really rather important, and she simply could not think of any way out of it.

After a few minutes, Mma Ramotswe sighed and stood up. She straightened her blouse and brushed some dust off the side of her skirt, dust more imaginary than real.

"This is my problem, Mma," she said to Mrs Moffat. "I cannot expect you to help me with this. I shall have to do something myself to sort it all out." She paused, before continuing, "Although I cannot think of anything that I can do, Mma. I cannot think of anything at all!"

CHAPTER THIRTEEN

MMA MAKUTSI AND MR J.L.B. MATEKONI VISIT MR J.L.B. MATEKONI'S HOUSE

MMA MAKUTSI realised the next day that Mma Ramotswe's mind was on other things. Her employer was rarely moody, but there were occasions when it seemed as if some problem was preventing her from giving her full attention to the affairs of the agency. It was usually something domestic—one of the children might be experiencing difficulty at school or Rose, her maid, might have told her of the hardship being endured by a relative or friend. There was so much need, even in a fortunate country such as Botswana; it seemed as if the reservoirs of suffering were never empty, and no matter what progress was made there would always be people for whom there was no job, or no place to live, or not enough food. And when you became aware of these needs, especially if they were being felt by those who had a claim on you, then it was hard to put them out of your mind.

Everybody knew somebody in need. Mma Makutsi herself had just heard of a young girl whose parents had both died. This girl, who lived with an aunt, was clever. She had done well in her examinations, but now there was no money to pay her school fees and she would have to give up her education if this money were not found. What could one do? Mma Makutsi could not help her; although she had a bit of spare money now from the Kalahari Typing School for Men, she had her own people to look after up in Bobonong. So there was nobody to help this child, and she would lose her chance to make something of her life.

Of course you could not allow yourself to think too much about these issues. One had to get on and to attend to the day-to-day business of living. The No. 1 Ladies' Detective Agency was there to solve the problems in people's lives—that's what they did, as Mma Ramotswe often pointed out—but they could not solve all the world's problems. And so you had to turn away from so much that you would like to do something about, and hope that things would work out somehow for those who were in need. That was all you could do.

Mma Makutsi looked at Mma Ramoswe, seated at her desk on the other side of the room, and wondered. She asked herself whether she should say something to her employer, or whether she should remain silent. After a moment's thought, she decided to speak.

"You are looking very worried, Mma Ramotswe," she ventured. "Are you feeling all right?"

For a while Mma Ramotswe said nothing, and Mma Makutsi's question hung awkwardly in the air.

Then Mma Ramotswe spoke. "I am worried about something, Mma," she said. "But I do not wish to burden you with my worries. This is a private thing."

Mma Makutsi looked at her. To describe something as a private thing was a big step. There were very few matters in Botswana which people would treat as a private thing; this was a society in which people knew one another's business. "I do not wish to pry into private things," she said. "But if you are worried about that thing, then you should let me take up your worries about other things. That way I can help you."

Mma Ramotswe sighed. "I do not know which worries I can pass on to you. There are so many . . ."

Mma Makutsi's interjection was brisk. "Well, there's Charlie, for a start. He is a big worry. Let me deal with Charlie. Then you can stop worrying about him."

For a moment Mma Ramotswe thought of ways to decline this offer. Charlie was a garage matter, and his welfare was thus the concern of Mr J.L.B. Matekoni, and of herself, indirectly, as the wife of Mr J.L.B. Matekoni. She and Mr J.L.B. Matekoni had always worried about the apprentices, and it seemed perfectly natural that they should continue to do so. And yet, it was undoubtedly an attractive offer that Mma Makutsi was making. She had no idea what she could do about Charlie—if, indeed she could do anything at all. Mma Makutsi was a resourceful and intelligent lady who was quite capable of sorting out young men. She had taken the apprentices in hand before, with conspicuous success, and so perhaps it was appropriate that she should try to do so again.

"What would you do about Charlie?" she asked. "What can any of us possibly do?"

Mma Makutsi smiled. "I can go and find out just what's going on," she said. "Then I can look at ways of dealing with it."

"But we know perfectly well what's going on," said Mma Ramotswe. "The goings-on are between him and that rich lady with the Mercedes-Benz. Anybody can tell what that's all about. That's what's going on."

Mma Makutsi agreed that this was so. But in her view there was always more beneath the surface, and they had of course seen the lady and the apprentice drive into Mr J.L.B. Matekoni's yard. That remained something of a mystery.

"There are still some things to be looked at," she said to Mma Ramotswe. "I have been thinking that Mr J.L.B. Matekoni and I should have a closer look. That's what I've been thinking."

"You must be careful of Mr J.L.B. Matekoni," cautioned Mma Ramotswe. "He is a very good mechanic, but I do not think that he will be a very good detective. In fact, I am sure he will not be."

"I shall be in charge," said Mma Makutsi. "I shall make sure that Mr J.L.B. Matekoni comes to no harm."

"Good," said Mma Ramotswe. "He is the only husband I . . ." She stopped. She had been about to say that he was the only husband she had, but then she realised, with a feeling of dark foreboding, that this was not strictly true.

WHEN MMA MAKUTSI suggested to Mr J.L.B. Matekoni that they pay a visit to his new tenant, he looked at his watch and scratched his head.

"I have so much to do, Mma," he said. "There is that car over there which has no brake pads left. Then there is that van which is making a noise like a donkey. There are many sick vehicles here, and I cannot leave them."

"They are not dying," said Mma Makutsi firmly. "They will still be here when we come back."

Mr J.L.B. Matekoni sighed. "I do not see why we need to go to the house. They are paying their rent. The house has not been burned down."

"But there is Charlie," pointed out Mma Makutsi. "We should find out why he is going to your house. What if he is being sucked into some sort of criminal activity, with that fancy lady of his and that Mercedes-Benz?"

At the mention of criminal activity, Mr J.L.B. Matekoni grimaced. He had taken those boys on several years ago, and he had imagined their involvement in all sorts of affairs with girls. He did not like to enquire about that, and it was their own business after all. But criminal activity was another matter. What if there were to be an article in the newspapers reporting that an apprentice from Tlokweng Road Speedy Motors had been arrested by the police in connection with some racket? The shame that this would bring on him would be too much to bear. His was a business dedicated to looking after customers and their cars, and doing so honestly. Mr J.L.B. Matekoni had never used cheap, unsuitable spare parts and then charged the customer for expensive, proprietary parts; he had never paid or accepted a bribe. He had done his best to instill this sense of morality—this commercial, or even mechanical, morality—in the boys, but he was not at all sure whether he had succeeded. He sighed again. These women were always pushing him into things against his will. He did not want to interfere with his tenant. He did not want to go back to his old house, now that he was so safely settled in the house at Zebra Drive. But it seemed that he was being given very little alternative, and so he agreed. They could go that evening, he conceded, shortly after five o'clock. Until then he wanted to work on these poor vehicles without interruption.

"I will not disturb you," promised Mma Makutsi. "But at five o'clock I shall be standing here, ready to go."

And at exactly five o'clock she waved goodbye to Mma Ramotswe as her employer drove off homewards in the tiny white van and she went to remind Mr J.L.B. Matekoni that it was time for them to go. He had just finished working on a car, and was in a cheerful mood, as the job had worked out well.

"I hope that we shall not have to be long," he said as he wiped his hands on a piece of lint. "I do not have very much to say to that man who has rented my house. In fact, I have nothing to say to him at all."

"We can say that we have come to see that everything is all right," said Mma Makutsi. "And then we can say something about Charlie. We can ask him if he has seen Charlie."

"I don't see any point in that," said Mr J.L.B. Matekoni. "If he has seen Charlie he will say yes, and if he has not seen him, then he will say no. What is the point of asking him this?"

Mma Makutsi smiled. "You are not a detective, Rra. I can tell that."

"I am certainly not a detective," said Mr J.L.B. Matekoni. "And I do not want to be a detective. I am a mechanic."

"You have married a detective," said Mma Makutsi gently. "People who marry people sometimes pick up a bit about the job. Look at the President's wife. She must know all about opening schools and signing things now."

"But I do not expect Mma Ramotswe to fix cars," objected Mr J.L.B. Matekoni. "So she should not expect me to be a detective."

Mma Makutsi decided not to respond to this remark. Glancing at her watch, she pointed out that they should leave, or they would arrive at a time when the tenant and his family were sitting down to their evening meal, and this would be rude. Reluctantly, Mr J.L.B. Matekoni peeled off his overalls and reached for his hat off its accustomed peg. Then the two of them set off in his truck, to make the short journey along the road that led to his house near the old Botswana Defence Force Club.

As they neared the house, Mr J.L.B. Matekoni began to slow down. Peering over the steering wheel, he remarked to Mma Makutsi, "This feels very strange, Mma. It is always strange coming back to a place where you used to live."

Mma Makutsi nodded. It was true: she had only been back to Bobonong a few times since she had moved to Gaborone, and it had always been an unsettling experience. Everything was so familiar—that was true—but in a curious way it did not seem the same. To begin with, there was the smallness, and the shabbiness. When she had lived in Bobonong the houses seemed perfectly normal to her and the house in which her family lived had seemed quite comfortable. But looking at it with eyes that had seen Gaborone, and the large buildings there, their house had seemed mean and cramped. And as for the shabbiness, she had never noticed when she lived there how Bobonong could have done with a lick of paint, but having been in Gaborone, where things were kept so smart, it was impossible not to notice all the flaking paint and the dirt-scarred walls.

The people too seemed diminished. Her favourite aunt was still her favourite, of course, but whereas she had always been impressed by the wisdom of what her aunt said, now her words seemed no more than trite. And what was worse, she had actually felt embarrassed at some of her pronouncements, thinking that such observations would seem quaint in Gaborone. That had made her feel guilty, and she had tried to smile appreciatively at her aunt's remarks, but somehow the effort seemed too great. She knew this was wrong; she knew that you should never forget what you owed to home, and to family, and to the place that nurtured you, but sometimes it was difficult to put this into practice.

Mma Makutsi had always been impressed by the way in which Mma Ramotswe seemed to be completely at ease with who she was and where she came from. She was clearly very attached to Mochudi, and when she spoke of her childhood there it was always with fondness. This was great good fortune: to love the place in which you were brought up; not everybody could do that. And even greater good fortune would be to have a father like Obed Ramotswe, about whom Mma Makutsi had heard so much from Mma Ramotswe. Mma Makutsi almost felt as if she knew him now, and that at any moment she herself would start quoting things he had said, although of course she had never met him. She could just imagine that happening. She would say to Mma Ramotswe, "As your father used to say, Mma . . ." and Mma Ramotswe would smile and say, "Yes, he always said that, didn't he?"

Of course she would not be the only one to do that sort of thing. Mma Ramotswe was always talking about Seretse Khama and quoting the things that he had said, but Mma Makutsi was a bit suspicious of this. It was not that Seretse Khama had not said a great number of wise things—he had—it was just that she felt that Mma Ramotswe had a slight tendency to express a view—her own view—and then attribute it to Seretse Khama, even if Sir Seretse had never expressed an opinion on the matter in question. There had been an example of this recently when Mma Ramotswe had told her that you should never drive a goat across water and that Seretse Khama himself had said something to that effect. Mma Makutsi was very doubtful about this; Seretse Khama had never said anything about goats, as far as she could remember—and she had studied his speeches when she was at school—and in her view this was merely Mma Ramotswe giving authority to a peculiar view of her own.

"When did he say that?" she had challenged.

Mma Ramotswe had looked vague. "A long time ago, I think," she said. "I read it somewhere or other."

This answer had failed to satisfy Mma Makutsi, and she had been tempted to say to her employer, "Mma Ramotswe, you must remember that you are not Seretse Khama!" But she had not done so, fortunately, because it would have sounded rude, and Mma Ramotswe meant well when she talked about Seretse Khama, even if she did not always get her facts right. The real problem, thought Mma Makutsi, is that Mma Ramotswe did not go to the Botswana Secretarial College. Had she done that, then she would have perhaps been a little bit more careful about some of the things she said. There was no substitute for formal training, Mma Makutsi thought; intuition and experience would get one so far, but you really needed a little bit more than that to round things off. And had Mma Ramotswe been fortunate enough to attend the Botswana Secretarial College, then what mark, Mma Makutsi wondered, would she have achieved in the final examinations? That was a fascinating question. She would have surely done very well, and might even have finished up with . . . well, with about seventy-five per cent. That was a distinguished result, even if it was some twenty-two per cent below what she herself had achieved. The problem with having got ninety-seven per cent is that it set the bar artificially high for others.

Mma Makutsi's thoughts were interrupted by Mr J.L.B. Matekoni, who tapped her lightly on the shoulder.

"Do you want me to drive up the drive, Mma?"

Mma Makutsi thought for a moment. "It would be best, Rra. Remember that you have nothing to hide here. You are just calling on this man to see that everything is all right."

"And you?" asked Mr J.L.B. Matekoni, as he guided the truck through his familiar gates. "What will they think about you?"

"I could be your niece," said Mma Makutsi. "Many men of your age have nieces who ride with them in their trucks. Have you not seen that, Mr J.L.B. Matekoni?"

Mr J.L.B. Matekoni gave her a strange look. He had never known quite how to take Mma

Makutsi, and this sort of ambiguous remark was typical of the sort of thing she said. But he made no reply, and concentrated on positioning the truck next to one of the two cars which had been parked beside the house.

Together they walked round to the front door, where Mr J.L.B. Matekoni knocked loudly, calling out as he did so.

"The yard is not very tidy," Mma Makutsi muttered, discreetly pointing to several up-turned paraffin tins that had been used for some purpose or other and had then just been left where they lay.

"They are busy people, I think," said Mr J.L.B. Matekoni. "Maybe they do not have much time to look after the yard. You cannot blame them for that."

"You can," retorted Mma Makutsi, her voice rather louder now.

"Hush," said Mr J.L.B. Matekoni. "There is somebody coming."

The door was opened by a woman somewhere in her mid-forties, who was wearing a colourful red blouse and a full length green skirt. She looked them up and down, and then gestured for them to come in.

"There aren't many people here," she said

before they had the chance to utter a greeting. "But I'll get you something if you go and sit in the back. I've got some rum, or you can just have a beer. What will it be?"

Mr J.L.B. Matekoni half-turned to Mma Makutsi in surprise. He had not expected such a businesslike welcome, and it was rather strange, was it not, to offer somebody a drink like that before anything else had been said? How did this woman, whoever she was, know who he was? Perhaps she was the tenant's wife: he had dealt only with the tenant himself and had not seen anybody else.

If Mr J.L.B. Matekoni was at a loss to speak, then the same was not true of Mma Makutsi. She smiled at the woman and immediately accepted the offer of a beer for Mr J.L.B. Matekoni. She would have something soft, she said—as long as it was cold. The woman nodded and disappeared into the kitchen, leaving Mr J.L.B. Matekoni and Mma Makutsi to make their way into the room which used to be Mr J.L.B. Matekoni's dining room.

It had been his favourite room when he had lived in the house, as it had a good view of the back yard with its pawpaw trees, and beyond that of a small hill in the distance. Now, as they entered, there was no view, as curtains had been drawn across the window and the only light was provided by two red-shaded lamps that had been placed on a low table in front of the curtains. Mr J.L.B. Matekoni looked about him in astonishment. He knew that people had different tastes, but it seemed extraordinary that somebody would wish to plunge a room into darkness—and waste electricity—when there was perfectly good natural light available outside for nothing.

He turned to Mma Makutsi. Perhaps she had seen this sort of thing before and would be unsurprised. He looked at her for an explanation, but she was just smiling at him in a curious way.

"What have they done to my dining room?" he whispered. "This is very strange."

Mma Makutsi continued to smile. "It is very interesting," she said, her voice lowered. "Of course you know that . . ."

She did not finish what she was saying; the woman in the red blouse had returned with a tray bearing a beer and a glass of cola. She placed the tray on the table and pointed to a large leather-covered sofa at one side of the room.

"You can sit down," she said. "I will put on some music if you would like that."

Mma Makutsi picked up her glass of cola. "You join us, Mma. It has been a hot day and I think that you might like a beer. You can charge it to us. We will buy you a beer."

The woman accepted readily. "That is kind of you, Mma. I will fetch it and come back."

Once she had left the room, Mr J.L.B. Matekoni turned to Mma Makutsi. "Is this . . ." he began.

"Yes," Mma Makutsi interrupted. "This is a shebeen. Your house, Mr J.L.B. Matekoni, has been turned into an illegal bar!"

Mr J.L.B. Matekoni sat down heavily on the sofa. "This is very bad," he said. "Everybody will think that I am involved in it. They will say that man is running a shebeen while he pretends to be a respectable person. And what will Mma Ramotswe think?"

"She'll understand that it has nothing to do with you," said Mma Makutsi. "And I'm sure that other people will think the same."

"I do not like such places," said Mr J.L.B. Matekoni, shaking his head. "They let people run up big bills and spend all their money on drink."

Mma Makutsi agreed. She was amused by the discovery, which she had not expected to make, but she knew that there was nothing very funny about shebeens. Although people could easily go to legitimate bars, there were those who needed to drink on credit, and shebeens exploited such people. They encouraged people to spend too much and then, every month, they would end up taking a larger and larger portion of the drinker's salary. And there were other things too: shebeens were associated with gambling and again in this respect they preyed on human weakness.

The woman returned, an opened bottle of beer in her hand. She raised the bottle in a toast, and Mr J.L.B. Matekoni half-heartedly reciprocated, although Mma Makutsi's response was more convincing.

"So, Mma," said Mma Makutsi brightly, "this is a nice place you have. Very nice!"

The woman laughed. "No, Mma. It is not my place. I am just somebody who works here. There is another woman who runs this place."

Mma Makutsi thought for a moment. Of course: a woman like that, a woman who drove a large Mercedes-Benz, would not go to a shebeen as a mere customer—she was the shebeen queen herself.

"Oh yes," Mma Makutsi said. "I know that

woman. She is the one who drives that big Mercedes-Benz and has that young boyfriend, the new one. I think he's called Charlie."

"That is her," said the woman. "Charlie is her boyfriend. He comes here with her sometimes. But there's a husband too. He is in Johannesburg. He's a big man there. He has some bars, I think."

"Yes," said Mma Makutsi. "I know him well." She paused. "Do you think that he knows about Charlie?"

The woman took a swig from her bottle of beer and then wiped her mouth with the back of her hand. "Hah! I think that he will not know about Charlie. And if I were Charlie I'd be very careful. That man comes back to Botswana to see her every few months and then Charlie had better be away for the weekend! Hah! If I were Charlie I'd go right up to Francistown or Maun when that happens. The further away the better."

Mma Makutsi glanced at Mr J.L.B. Matekoni, who was following the conversation closely. Then she looked back at the woman and asked her question. "Does that man, the husband, help to run this place? Does he come here ever?"

"Sometimes," said the woman. "He phones us sometimes to leave messages for her."

Mma Makutsi took a deep breath. Mma Ramotswe had told her that when one asked the important question—the question upon which an entire investigation might turn—one should be careful to sound calm, as if the answer to the question really did not matter all that much. This was the moment for such a question, but Mma Makutsi found that her heart was beating loud within her and she was sure that this woman would hear it.

"So he phones? Well, you wouldn't have his telephone number over there, would you? I'd like to speak to him about a friend we have in Johannesburg who wants to see him about something. I had his number, but . . ."

"It is here," said the woman. "It is through in the kitchen on a piece of paper. I can fetch it for you."

"You are very kind," said Mma Makutsi. "And when you go through to the kitchen, you can get yourself another beer, Mma. Mr J.L.B. Matekoni will pay."

CHAPTER FOURTEEN

REMEMBER ME?

Mma Ramotswe had tried very hard to contain the feeling of dread which stalked her now, like a dark shadow. She had tried to put Note Mokoti out of her mind; she had told herself that just because Mma Potokwane had seen him this did not mean that she would do so. But none of this had worked, and she found herself unable to take her mind off her first husband and the meeting that she knew he would seek with her.

Her immediate inclination had been to tell Mr J.L.B. Matekoni what Mma Potokwane had said, but then she found that she simply could not do this. Note Mokoti belonged to her past—to a painful part of that past—and she had never brought herself to speak to Mr

J.L.B. Matekoni about this. She had told him, of course, that she had been married before, and that her husband had been a cruel man. But that was all that she had said, and he had sensed that this was something that she did not wish to discuss, and he had respected that. Nor had she discussed it to any great extent with Mma Makutsi, although they had touched upon it once or twice when the subject of men, or husbands in particular, had come up.

But no matter how firmly she had relegated Note to this wished-for oblivion, in real life he was a flesh and blood man who was now back in Gaborone and who would cross her path sooner or later. It happened in the mid-morning, just two days after her meeting with Mma Potokwane, when Mma Ramotswe and Mma Makutsi were working in the office of the No. 1 Ladies' Detective Agency. Mr J.L.B. Matekoni was off fetching spare parts from the motor trades distributor with whom he dealt, and Mr Polopetsi was helping the younger apprentice to fix the suspension on a hearse. It was a very ordinary morning.

Mr Polopetsi made the announcement. Knocking on the door that led from the garage into the agency office, he looked cautiously in and said that there was somebody to see Mma Ramotswe.

"Who is it?" asked Mma Makutsi. They were busy and did not want to be disturbed, but one always had to be ready to receive a client.

"It is a man," said Mr Polopetsi, and with this answer Mma Ramotswe knew that it was Note.

"Who is this man?" asked Mma Makutsi. "Has he given his name?"

Mr Polopetsi shook his head. "He would not give me his name," he said. "He is a man wearing dark glasses, and a brown leather jacket. I did not like him."

Mma Ramotswe rose to her feet. "I will come and see him," she said quietly. "I think I know who this is."

Mma Makutsi looked at her employer quizzically. "Could you not get him to come in here?"

"I will see him outside," said Mma Ramotswe. "I think that he has private business with me."

She made her way out of the office, avoiding Mma Makutsi's gaze. It was bright outside—a day on which the sun cast hard, short shadows; a day on which there was no shelter from the growing heat; a day on which the air seemed heavy and sluggish. As she went out through the wide door of the garage, leaving Mr Polopetsi to return to his labour, she saw the petrol pumps and the acacias and a car driving down the Tlokweng Road, and then, just to the left of the garage, standing under the shade of an acacia tree, looking in her direction, Note Mokoti, thumbs tucked into his belt, standing in that pose that she remembered so well.

She took the few steps that would bring her up to him. She raised her eyes and saw that his face was fleshier, but still cruel, and bore a small scar to the side of his chin. She saw that he had developed a slight paunch, but that this was almost hidden by the leather jacket which he wore in spite of the heat. And she thought, suddenly, how strange it was that one would notice these things when one was frightened of another; that the prisoner facing execution might notice, in those last terrible moments, that the man who was about to take his life had a barber's rash round his throat or that he had hair on the back of his hands.

"Note," she said. "It is you."

The muscles around the mouth slackened, and he smiled. She saw the teeth, so important, he had always said, for a trumpeter, good teeth. And then she heard the voice.

"It is me, yes. Yes, you are right there, Precious. It is me after all these years."

She looked into the lenses of the dark glasses, but could see only the tiny reflection of the acacia tree and the sky.

"Are you well, Note? Have you travelled from Johannesburg?"

"Joeies," he said, laughing as he spoke. "Egoli. Joburg. The place of many names."

She waited for him to say something more. For a few moments there was nothing, then he spoke.

"I've heard all about you," he said. "I've heard that you are the big detective around these parts." He laughed again, as if the suggestion that this should be so was ridiculous. Of course he had thought that about all women: that no woman, in his view, could do a job as well as a man. **How many woman trumpeters do you see?** he had asked her all those years ago, mockingly. She had been too young then to stand up to him, and now, when she could do so, when she had the facts of her success with which to confront him, she felt only the same ancient fear, the fear which had made women through the ages cower before such men.

"I have a good business," she said.

He looked over her shoulder into the garage and then he glanced up at their business sign, the sign which she had proudly displayed over her first office under Kgale Hill and which they had brought with them when they made the move.

"And your father?" he said casually, looking at her now. "How is the old man? Still going on about cattle?"

She felt her heart lurch, and then a rush of emotion that seemed to stifle the very breath within her.

"Well?" he said. "What about him?"

She steadied herself. "My father is late," she said. "It is many years ago now. He is late."

Note shrugged. "There are many people who are dying. You may have noticed."

For a moment Mma Ramotswe could think of nothing, but then she thought of her father, the late Daddy, Obed Ramotswe, who had never said anything unkind or dismissive to this man, although he had known full well what sort of person he was; of Obed Ramotswe who represented all that was fine in Botswana and in the world, whom she still loved, and who was as fresh in her memory as if he had been alive only yesterday.

She turned away and took a few faltering steps back towards the garage.

"Where are you going?" called Note, his voice harsh. "Where are you going, fat lady?"

She paused, still looking away from him. She heard him come towards her, and now he was standing directly behind her, his acrid body odour in her nostrils.

He leaned forward so that his mouth was close to her ear. "Listen," he said. "You have married that man, haven't you? But what about me? Am I not still your husband?"

She looked down at the ground, and at her toes sticking out of the sandals she was wearing.

"Now," said Note. "Now you listen to me. I haven't come back for you—don't worry about that. I never really liked you, you know? I wanted a woman who could have a child, a strong child. You know that? Not a child who wasn't going to last very long. So I haven't come back for you. So you just listen to me. I'm planning a concert here—a big event at the

One Hundred Bar. But I need a bit of help with the cost of that, you know? Ten thousand pula. I'll come and collect it in two or three days, from your place. That'll give you time to get the money together. Understand?"

She remained quite immobile, and he moved away suddenly.

"Goodbye," he said. "I'll come for that loan. And if you don't pay, then maybe I can tell somebody—maybe the police, I don't know—that you've married a man before you got rid of the first husband. That's a careless thing to do, Mma. Very careless!"

SHE WENT BACK into the office, where Mma Makutsi was sitting at her desk, immersed in the task of addressing an envelope. The search for the delinquent Zambian financier had brought forth nothing so far. Most of the letters they had written had been ignored by their recipients, although one, which had been sent to a Zambian doctor who was thought to know just about everybody in the local Zambian community, had drawn a hostile reply. "You people are always saying that Zambians are dishonest and that if there is any money missing then you should look in Zambian pockets. This is defamation and we are fed up with such stereotypes. Everybody knows that you should be looking in Nigerian pockets . . ."

Mma Ramotswe made her way to her desk and sat down. She reached for a sheet of paper, folded it, and picked up her pen. Then she put down the pen and opened a drawer, not knowing why she was doing this, but filled with dread and fear. The picking up of a pen, the opening of a drawer, the lifting of the telephone handset—all of these were actions that might be performed in distress by one who did not know what to do, but who hoped that by such movements the fear might be defeated, which of course it never would.

Mma Makutsi watched, and knew that whoever it was who had arrived that morning had upset and frightened her employer.

"You saw that person?" she asked gently. "Was it somebody you knew?"

Mma Ramotswe looked up at her and Mma Makutsi saw the pain in her eyes.

"It was somebody I knew," she said quietly. "It was somebody I knew very well."

Mma Makutsi opened her mouth to ask a

question, but stopped herself as Mma Ramotswe raised a hand.

"I do not want to talk about that, Mma," she said. "Please do not ask me about this thing. Please do not ask."

"I will not," said Mma Makutsi. "I will not ask."

Mma Ramotswe looked at her watch and muttered something about being late for a meeting. Again Mma Makutsi was about to ask what meeting this was, as nothing had been said about a meeting, but then she thought better of it and simply watched as Mma Ramotswe gathered her things together and left the office. Mma Makutsi waited for a few minutes, until she heard the engine of the tiny white van start, and then she stood up and looked out of the window to see Mma Ramotswe drive out onto the Tlokweng Road and disappear in the direction of town.

Leaving the office, Mma Makutsi found Mr Polopetsi with the apprentice.

"I need to ask you something, Rra," she said. "That man who came to see Mma Ramotswe—who was he?"

Mr Polopetsi stood up and stretched. It was

difficult working on cars in confined spaces, although he was beginning to get used to it. It amused him to think that throughout his education he had worked and worked to get himself a job which would involve no manual labour, and here he was enjoying the rediscovery of his hands. Of course they had said that this job was only temporary, but he had begun to settle in to being a mechanic and perhaps he would ask about becoming a real apprentice. And why not? Botswana needed mechanics—everyone knew that—and there was no reason why older people should be prevented from acquiring such skills.

Mr Polopetsi scratched his head. "I have not seen him before," he said. "He was a Motswana, judging from the way he spoke. But there was something about him that seemed foreign. You know how it is when people are away for a long time. They carry themselves in a different way."

"Johannesburg?" asked Mma Makutsi.

Mr Polopetsi nodded. It was sometimes difficult to put it into words, but there was an unmistakable air about people who came from Johannesburg or who had lived a long time there. There was a way of walking in Johannesburg, a way of holding oneself, that was different from the way in which people did these things in Botswana. Johannesburg was a city of swagger, and that was something which people in Botswana would never do. There were some people who swaggered these days, particularly those who had more money, but it was not really the Botswana way of doing things.

"And what do you think this man wanted from Mma Ramotswe?" asked Mma Makutsi. "Did he bring her bad news, do you think? Did he tell her that somebody is late?"

Mr Polopetsi shook his head. "I have very good hearing, Mma," he said. "I can hear a car when it is far, far away. I can hear an animal before you can see it in the bush. I am like one of those people out in the bush who can tell you everything just by listening to the wind. So I can tell you that he did not tell her that somebody is late."

Mma Makutsi was surprised by this sudden disclosure on the part of Mr Polopetsi. He had seemed such a quiet and inoffensive man, and now he was admitting to the talents of a bush tracker. Such a person could be useful in a detective agency. You were not allowed to tape a person's telephone line, but then there would be no need to do so if you had a Mr Polopetsi. You could just position him on the other side of the street, with his ears pointed in the right direction, and he could report what was said behind closed doors. It would be one of those low technology solutions that people sometimes talked about.

"It must be useful to have hearing like that," said Mma Makutsi. "We must talk about it more some day. But in the meantime, you might wish to tell me what this man said to Mma Ramotswe."

Mr Polopetsi looked Mma Makutsi straight in the eye. "I would not normally tell somebody about Mma Ramotswe's business," he pronounced. "But this is different. I was going to tell you anyway—later on."

"Well?" said Mma Makutsi.

Mr Polopetsi lowered his voice. The apprentice was standing beside the car on which they had been working and was looking at them intently.

"He asked her for money," he whispered. "He asked her for ten thousand pula. Yes, ten thousand!"

"And?"

"And he said that if she didn't pay, then he was going to go to the police and tell them that she is still married to him and that she should not have married Mr J.L.B. Matekoni." He stopped, watching the effect of his words.

For a few moments Mma Makutsi did nothing. Then she reached forward and placed a finger across her lips.

"You must never mention this to anybody," she said. "You must promise me that."

He nodded gravely. "Of course I shall not."

Mma Makutsi turned away and went back into her office, her heart cold within her. You are my mother and my sister, she thought. You gave me my job. You helped me. You held my hand and wept with me when my brother became late. You are the one who made me feel that it was possible for a person from Bobonong to do well and to hold her head up in anybody's company. And now this man is threatening to bring shame upon you. I cannot allow that. I cannot.

She stopped. Mr Polopetsi had been watching her silently, but now he called out. "Mma! Do not worry. I will do something to stop that man. Mma Ramotswe is the woman who gave me a job. She is the one who knocked me down—but then she picked me up again. I will deal with that man."

Mma Makutsi turned round and looked at Mr Polopetsi. It was kind of him to say that, and she was touched by his loyalty. But what could a man like that do? Not very much, she feared.

CHAPTER FIFTEEN

MMA RAMOTSWE AND MR J.L.B. MATEKONI HAVE DINNER IN THEIR HOUSE ON ZEBRA DRIVE

Mr J.L.B. Matekoni was late coming home for dinner that evening. Normally he came back to the house at about six o'clock, which was almost an hour later than Mma Ramotswe. She would leave the office at five, or thereabouts, although she sometimes came back even earlier. If there was nothing particular happening at the agency, she would look at Mma Makutsi and ask her if there was any reason why they should stay in the office. Sometimes she did not even have to say anything, but would give a look that said, "I've had enough; it's a hot afternoon and it would be so much better being at home." And Mma Makutsi would return the look with a look of her own which said, "You're right, as usual,

Mma Ramotswe." And with that unspoken exchange, Mma Ramotswe would pick up her bag and close the window that looked out to the side of the garage. Then she would give Mma Makutsi a ride into town, or back to her house in Extension Two, before she went home to Zebra Drive.

One advantage of getting home early was that she would be there for the children when they returned from school. Motholeli always came back a little later than Puso, as her wheelchair had to be pushed all the way from the school. The girls in her class had arranged a rota for this, and took it in turns, week and week about, to wheel their classmate home. The boys had been involved in this too, and had vied with one another for the privilege, but they had, on the whole, been found to be unsatisfactory. Several of the boys—indeed most of them—had been unable to resist the temptation of pushing the wheelchair too fast and there had been an unfortunate incident when one of them had lost control of the chair and Motholeli had careered into a ditch and tumbled out. She had been unharmed by this fall, but the boy had run away in fright and a passer-by, a cook at one of the large houses on

Nyerere Drive, had come to her rescue and had helped her back into the chair and pushed her back, at reasonable speed, to the house.

"That boy is very stupid," said the cook.

"He is usually a nice boy," Motholeli replied. "He became frightened. Maybe he thought that he had killed me or something."

"He should not have run away," said the cook. "That is what they call a hit and run. It is very bad."

Puso was too young to be involved in getting his sister home. He could manage the wheelchair, but he had a tendency to be unreliable. He could not be counted upon to come to Motholeli's classroom at the right time, and it was also quite possible that he would lose interest halfway through and run after a lizard or something else that attracted his attention. He was a dreamy boy, moody even, and it was sometimes rather difficult to make out what he was thinking about.

"He thinks differently," observed Mma Ramotswe, not saying, out of delicacy, that the obvious reason for this—in her mind, and in the mind of most, no doubt—was that Puso had in his veins a fair measure of bushman blood. People were funny about that. Some were unkind to such people, but in Mma Ramotswe's opinion there was no need for this. There should be room in our hearts for all the people of this country, she said, and those people are our brothers and sisters too. This is their place as much as it is ours. That seemed clear to her, and she had no time for those who had raised an eyebrow when she and Mr J.L.B. Matekoni had taken on these children from the orphan farm. There were some households where this would not have happened, on the grounds that they were not of pure Tswana blood, but not that house on Zebra Drive.

Yet Mma Ramotswe had to admit that there were aspects about Puso's behaviour that people could well point to and say, "Well, there you are! That is because he is thinking of the Kalahari all the time and wants to be out in the bush. It is just the way his heart works." Well, thought Mma Ramotswe, that might be so; perhaps there stirred within this strange little boy some ancient yearnings which came to him from his people. But even if this were so, then what difference did it make? The important thing was that he should be happy, and in his way he was. He would never be a mechanic, he would never take over the business from Mr J.L.B. Matekoni, but then did that matter all that much? His sister, to the surprise of all, had shown great interest in machinery and had declared her intention of training as a mechanic. So that left it open for him to pursue some quite different career, even if it was difficult to think at the moment what such a career might be. He liked to chase lizards and to sit under trees and look up at the birds. He also liked to make small piles of rocks—they were all over the yard—on which Mma Ramotswe's maid, Rose, sometimes stubbed her toes when she went to hang out the washing. What might such a boy expect to do when he grew up? What clues did such pursuits give to the turn his life would take?

"There are jobs with the game department," Mr J.L.B. Matekoni had pointed out. "They need people who can track animals. Maybe he will be happy out there in the bush, tracking giraffe or whatever it is they do. For some people that is the best job there is."

On that evening, after the awful encounter with Note Mokoti, the children had noticed that there was something wrong with Mma Ramotswe. Puso had asked a question to which she had begun to respond before she had trailed off into silence, as if her thoughts had drifted off elsewhere. He had repeated his question, but this time she had said nothing, and he had gone off in puzzlement. Motholeli, finding her standing in the kitchen staring blankly out of the window, had offered to help her with the preparation of the evening meal, and had received a similar, rather distracted response. She had waited for Mma Ramotswe to say something else, and when nothing further came she had asked her whether there was anything wrong.

"I am thinking of something," said Mma Ramotswe. "I'm sorry if I am not listening to you. I am thinking of something that happened today."

"Was it a bad thing?" asked Motholeli.

"It was," said Mma Ramotswe. "But I cannot talk about it now. I'm sorry. I am feeling sad and I do not want to talk."

The children had left her to herself. Adults were sometimes strange in their behaviour—all children knew that—and the best thing to do in such circumstances was to leave the adult alone. Matters preyed on their mind, matters to which children could never be party; a tactful child understood that very well.

But when Mr J.L.B. Matekoni came home that evening and he too seemed to be preoccupied and distant, they knew that something was very wrong.

"There is something bad happening at the garage," whispered Motholeli to her brother. "They are very unhappy."

He had looked at her anxiously. "Will we have to go back to the orphan farm?" he asked.

"I hope not," she said. "I am happy living here in Zebra Drive. Perhaps they will get over it."

She tried to sound confident, but it was difficult, and her spirits sank even further when they sat down at the table for supper and Mma Ramotswe forgot even to say grace and remained silent for almost the whole meal. Afterwards, wheeling herself into her brother's room, where she found him lying disconsolately on his bed, she told him that whatever happened, he was not to worry about being by himself.

"Even if we go back to Mma Potokwane," she said, "she will make sure that we are kept together. She has always done that."

Puso stared at her miserably. "I do not want to leave. I am very happy here in this house.

This is the best food I have ever eaten in my life."

"And they are the best people we have ever met," she said. "There is nobody in Botswana, nobody, as good and kind as Mma Ramotswe and Mr J.L.B. Matekoni. Nobody."

The little boy nodded vigorously. "I know that," he said. "Will they come and see us at the orphan farm?"

"Of course they will come—if we have to go back," she reassured him. But her reassurance could not prevent the tears that he now began to shed, tears for everything that had happened to him, for the loss of the mother whom he could not remember, for the thought that in this large and frightening world there was nobody, other than his sister, to whom he could turn, who might not be taken away from him.

AFTER THE CHILDREN had gone off to their rooms for the night, Mma Ramotswe made herself a cup of bush tea and walked out onto the verandah. She had thought that Mr J.L.B. Matekoni was in the living room, as she had heard the radio on in there and had assumed that he was sitting in his favourite chair brooding over whatever mechanical problem it was that had made him so quiet that night. She imagined that it was a mechanical problem, because that was all that seemed to upset Mr J.L.B. Matekoni; and such problems inevitably solved themselves.

"You are very quiet tonight," she observed.

He looked up at her. "And so are you," he replied.

"Yes," she said. "We are both quiet."

She sat down beside him, balancing her tea cup on her knee. As she did so, she glanced at Mr J.L.B. Matekoni; the thought had occurred to her that he might be feeling depressed—and that was an alarming prospect—but she quickly discounted this. He had behaved very differently when he had been depressed, acting in a listless, vague way. Now, by contrast, he was very obviously thinking of one particular thing.

She looked out into the garden, and the night. It was warm and the moon was almost full, throwing shadows of the acacia, of the mopipi tree, of shrubs that had no name. Mma Ramotswe liked to walk in her garden in the evening, taking care to move slowly and with firm tread; those who crept about at night risked stepping on a snake if they were not careful, as snakes move out of our way only if they feel vibrations in the ground. A light person—a person of non-traditional build, for example—was at far greater risk of being bitten by a snake for that very reason. That was another argument, of course, for maintaining traditional build—consideration for snakes, and safety too.

Mma Ramotswe was well aware of the difficulties now faced by traditionally built people, particularly by traditionally built ladies. There was a time in Botswana when nobody paid much attention to thin people—indeed thin people might sometimes simply not be seen at all, as they could so easily be looked past. If a thin person stood against a background of acacia trees and grass, then might he not either merge into the background or be thought to be a stick or even a shadow? This was never a danger with a traditionally built person; such a person would stand in the landscape with the same prominence and authority as a baobab tree.

There was no doubt in Mma Ramotswe's mind that Botswana had to get back to the values which had always sustained the country and which had made it by far the best country in Africa. There were many of these values, including respect for age—for the grandmothers who knew so much and had seen so much hardship—and respect for those who were traditionally built. It was all very well being a modern society, but the advent of prosperity and the growth of the towns was a poisoned cup from which one should drink with the greatest caution. One might have all the things which the modern world offered, but what was the use of these if they destroyed all that which gave you strength and courage and pride in yourself and your country? Mma Ramotswe was horrified when she read of people being described in the newspapers as consumers. That was a horrible, horrible word, which sounded rather too like cucumber, a vegetable for which she had little time. People were not just greedy consumers, grabbing everything that came their way, nor were they cucumbers for that matter; they were **Batswana,** they were **people**!

But it was not on these matters, grave as they were, that Mma Ramotswe's mind was dwelling; she was thinking, rather, of the meeting with Note and of the threat he had made. He had said that he would come for the money in a few days, and it was the prospect of this visit, rather than the paying over of the money itself, which was unsettling her. She could afford the money—just—but she was dreading the idea that Note would come to the house. It seemed to her that this would be a form of defiling; the house on Zebra Drive was a place of sun and of happiness, and she did not want it to be associated in any way with him. In fact, she had already made her decision, and was now mulling over how to put it into operation. She had written a cheque that afternoon and would take it to him, and the sooner that she did that the better.

Mr J.L.B. Matekoni took a sip of his tea. "You are very worried about something," he said quietly. "Do you want to tell me what it is?"

Mma Ramotswe did not reply. How could she tell him about what Note had said? How could she tell him that they were not married; that the ceremony which the Reverend Trevor Mwamba had conducted was legally meaningless, and that, moreover, it involved the commission of a criminal offence on her part? If there were words for all this, then they were words which she could not bring herself to utter.

The silence that hung so heavy between them was broken by Mr J.L.B. Matekoni.

"That man came to see you, didn't he?" he said.

Mma Ramotswe gripped her tea cup. Mma Makutsi must have told him, or perhaps it was Mr Polopetsi. This should not surprise her: there were few secrets in a business that small.

"He did," she said, sighing. "He came and asked me for some money. I am going to give it to him—just to get him to go away."

Mr J.L.B. Matekoni nodded. "It is often like that with such people," he said. "They come back. But you have to be careful. If you give them money, then they might just ask for more and more."

Mma Ramotswe knew that what he said was true. She would tell Note that there would be no more money, and next time, if he came to see her again, she would refuse him. Or would she? What if he were to threaten her again with the police? Surely she would do anything rather than face the shame which that would involve?

"I will give him this money and tell him not to come back," she said. "I do not want to see him again."

"All right," he said. "But you must be careful."

She looked at him. They had not spoken at any length, and she had kept the real truth from him, but even so she felt better after this brief airing of her worry. Now she could ask about him.

"What about you?" she said.

Mr J.L.B. Matekoni groaned. "Oh dear," he said. "I am in a bad mess. I have discovered something about my house."

Mma Ramotswe frowned. She knew that tenants were always a risk. They treated furniture with disrespect; they burned holes in the floor and on the edge of tables with their cigarettes. She had even heard of a farmhouse not far from town which had been rented by python smugglers. Some of the pythons had escaped and taken up residence in the roof even after the tenants had been evicted. One of these had almost succeeded in taking the owners' baby when they returned. The father had gone into the bedroom and had found the python lying on the baby, its jaws opened wide around its feet. He had saved the child, but both of them had been badly bitten by the python's needle-like teeth.

Mr J.L.B. Matekoni was unlikely to have pythons in his house, of course, but it was obviously something troublesome, nonetheless. She looked at him expectantly.

"It's being used as a shebeen," he blurted out. "I did not know this. I would not have allowed it to be a shebeen. But that is what it is."

Mma Ramotswe let out a hoot of laughter. "Your house? A shebeen?"

Mr J.L.B. Matekoni looked at her slightly reproachfully. "I do not think it is funny," he said.

She corrected herself quickly. "Of course not." Her tone became concerned. "You are going to have to do something about that." She paused. Poor Mr J.L.B. Matekoni: he was far too gentle and kind. He would never be able to take on a shebeen queen. She herself would have to sort this out; shebeen queens held no dread for her.

"Would you like me to sort all that out?" she asked. "I can get rid of those people. It's the sort of thing that a detective agency can do quite easily."

Mr J.L.B. Matekoni's gratitude was palpable. "You are very kind," he said. "It is really my problem, but I am not very good at these things. I am happy sorting out cars, but people . . ."

"You are a great mechanic," said Mma Ramotswe, reaching across to pat him on the forearm. "That is enough for one person."

"And you are a very great detective," said Mr J.L.B. Matekoni. This was true, of course, and he meant every word of the compliment, but it was also inadequate. He knew that not only was Mma Ramotswe a great detective, but she was also a great cook, and a great wife, and a great foster-mother for the children. There was nothing that Mma Ramotswe could not do—in his view, at least. She could run Botswana if only they would give her the chance.

Mma Ramotswe drained the last of the tea from her cup and rose to her feet. She looked at her watch. It was only eight o'clock. She would go and seek out Note, hand him the cheque, and have put the whole matter to rest before she turned in that night. Her conversation with Mr J.L.B. Matekoni had filled her with a new resolve. There was no point in waiting. She had a pretty fair idea where Note would be staying—his people lived in a small village about ten miles to the south. It would only take her half an hour at the most to get out there, to pay him off, and to put him out of her life again. Then she could return to Zebra Drive and go to sleep without any dread. He would not be coming there.

CHAPTER SIXTEEN

THE TINY WHITE VAN

MMA RAMOTSWE did not like driving at night. She was not a timid driver, but she knew that there was one danger on the roads at night against which no amount of care could protect one—wandering cattle. Cattle liked to stand on the roadside at night and would suddenly step out into the paths of oncoming cars, almost as if they were curious to find out what lay behind the headlights. Perhaps they thought that the headlights were torches, held by their owners, and came out to see if they brought food; perhaps they were looking for warmth and thought the lights were the sun. Perhaps they thought nothing in particular, which was always possible with cattle, and with some people too, for that matter.

Mma Ramotswe's friend Barbara Mooketsi was just one of the many people Mma Ramotswe knew who had collided with a cow at night. She had been driving down from Francistown late one evening and had hit a cow north of Mahalapye. The unfortunate animal, which was black, and therefore almost completely invisible at night, had been scooped up by the collision and had entered the car through the windscreen. One of its horns had scraped Mma Mooketsi's shoulder and would have killed her had she been sitting in a slightly different position. Mma Ramotswe had visited her in her hospital bed and had seen the myriad of cuts on her face and arms from the shattered glass. This was the danger of driving at night, and it had been enough to put her off. Of course, in the town it was different. There were no cattle wandering about, although sometimes they drifted into the outlying parts of Gaborone and caused accidents there.

Now, leaving the edge of the town and peering into the darkness ahead of her, she searched the road for obstacles. It was not much of a road—a track ploughed out of the red earth and eroded into tiny canyons by the rains. Note's people lived in the village at the end of this track, along with some twenty other families. It was the sort of place that was halfway between town and country. The young people here would work in Gaborone and walk out along this track to the main road each morning to catch a minibus into town. Others would live in town and come out for weekends, when they would slip back into the role of village people, looking after cattle and ploughing a few meagre fields.

Mma Ramotswe hoped that she would remember the house where Note's people lived. It was late now for village people, and there was a chance that there would be no light on in the house and she would have to turn round and go back home. It was also possible that Note would not be there—that he would be staying somewhere in the town. As she thought of these possibilities it occurred to her that the whole idea of coming out here was ridiculous. Here she was coming in search of a man who had ruined years of her life, planning to give him hard-earned money so that he could pursue some absurd plan, and all of this being done out of fear. She was a strong woman, a resourceful woman who had built up a business from scratch, and who had shown on numerous occasions in her professional life that she was prepared to take men on head to head. But not this man. This man was different; he made her feel inadequate, and had always done so. It was a curious experience, to feel so young again, and as uncertain and in awe as she had been so long ago.

She reached the first of the houses, a brown block caught in the tiny white van's wavering headlights. If her memory served her correctly, the Mokoti place was three houses down; and there it was, just as she remembered it—a whitewashed building of four rooms joined together, with a lean-to shed to one side and an old granary at the edge of the front yard. And there was a light on in the front room.

She stopped the van. There was time to go back if she wished, to turn round and drive home. There was time to tear up the cheque which she had written out—the cash cheque, payable to bearer, for ten thousand pula. There was time to stand up to Note and to dare him to go to the police, after which she could go and make a clean breast of things to Mr J.L.B. Matekoni, who would surely understand. He was a kind man and he knew that people sometimes forgot to do important things, such as getting a divorce before they remarried.

She closed her eyes and took a deep breath. She knew what she should do now, but something deep within her, that part of her which had survived from all those years ago, that part which just could not stand up to Note, which drew her to him like a light draws in a moth— that part propelled her to the gate and to the door beyond the gate.

They were slow to open the door to her knocking, and when it was opened it was done in such a way that it could be quickly slammed shut. She saw a figure within which at first she could not make out, and then she recognised her mother-in-law, and she caught her breath. She was aged now, and stooped, but it was the same woman whom she had not seen for many years, and who recognised her too, after a moment's hesitation.

For a while neither woman spoke. There was so much that could be said, and Mma Ramotswe might have wept in the saying of it, but that was not what she had come for, and this woman did not deserve that. She had always sided with Note, of course, and had turned a blind eye to what was going on, but then what mother would admit to others, or to herself, that her own son was capable of such cruelty?

After a minute or so, the older woman moved slowly to one side and nodded. "You should come inside, Mma," she said.

Mma Ramotswe stepped into the house, noticing the smell as she did so. This was the odour of poverty, of life on the edge of making do; the smell of carefully husbanded cooking fuel, of clothes that were not washed frequently enough—for lack of soap. She glanced around. They were in a room which served as a living room and kitchen. A naked bulb burned weakly above a table on which a half-empty jar of jam stood flanked by a couple of knives and a folded cloth. On a shelf at the other end of the room was stacked a small number of tin plates and several steel cooking pots. A picture, cut out of a magazine, had been pinned to the wall beside the shelves.

She had been in this house many times before. That had been a long time ago, and she was now feeling the usual effect of memory, which was to diminish places, to make them more cramped and shabbier than they had once appeared. It was as though one was looking at the world from a long way away, and it was smaller. She tried to remember exactly when it was that she had last been here, but it was too many years ago, and the painful memories had been obliterated.

"I am sorry that I have come to your house so late at night," said Mma Ramotswe. She spoke respectfully, because this was an old woman she was addressing, and it did not matter that she was the mother of Note Mokoti—she was an old Motswana lady and that was enough.

The woman looked down at her hands. "He is not here," she said. "Note is not here."

Mma Ramotswe did not say anything. On the other side of the room two doors led off into the rest of the house, the bedrooms. These were both closed.

Mma Mokoti saw her look at the doors. "No," she said. "There is only my husband in one room and in the other there is a lodger, a young woman who works in a Government office. She pays us to stay here. That is all."

Mma Ramotswe felt embarrassed that Note's mother had sensed her doubts. "I believe you, Mma," she said. "Can you tell me where I can find him?"

The old woman pointed vaguely in the direction of the town, and then dropped her hand. "Somewhere in town. He is staying somewhere in town."

"But you don't know where?"

Mma Mokoti sighed. "I do not know. He has come to see us, and he will come again. But I do not know when." She muttered something else that Mma Ramotswe did not catch, and then looked up at her visitor, and Mma Ramotswe saw the clouded eyes, with their brown irises and their muddy, milky whites. They were not the eyes of a malevolent person, but the eyes of one who had seen a great deal and had done her best to make something of a hard life. They were the eyes of the sort that one could see anywhere, at any time, of people who had a life of difficulty and who still managed to keep their human dignity in the face of suffering and want.

She had no idea why she should say it—certainly she had not planned it—but Mma Ramotswe suddenly spoke. "I want you to know, Mma," she began. "I want you to know that I do not think ill of you, or of Note. What happened was a long time ago. It was not your fault. And there are things about your son of which you can be proud. Yes. His music. That is a great gift and it makes people happy. You can be proud."

There was a silence. Mma Mokoti was staring at her hands again. Then she turned away and looked at the shelf with the pots. "I did not want him to marry you, you know," she said quietly. "I argued with him. I told him that you were a young girl and that you were not ready for the life that he was leading. And there was another girl he was seeing. You didn't know about that, did you? There was another girl, who had a baby. She was already there when he met you. He had already married that girl."

Mma Ramotswe stood quite still. From within one of the rooms a man coughed. She had suspected, all those years ago, that Note was seeing other women, but she had never thought that he had been married. Did this change anything, she wondered? What should I feel about this? It was another of his lies, of his concealments, but she should not feel any surprise about that. Everything he had said to her was a lie, it seemed; there was simply no truth in him.

"Do you know who this other girl was?" she

asked. She did not think about the question, nor whether she really wanted to know the answer. But she felt that she had to say something.

Mma Mokoti turned back to face her. "I think that she is late, now," she said. "And I never saw that baby. He is my grandchild, but I have never seen him. I feel very sad about that."

Mma Ramotswe took a step forward and put her arm gently about the old woman. The shoulder was hard and bony. "You must not feel too sad, Mma," she said. "You have worked hard. You have made this home for your husband. You must not feel sad about any of that. The other things are not so important, are they?"

The old woman said nothing for a moment, and Mma Ramotswe kept her arm about her shoulder. It was a strange feeling, she had always thought; feeling the breathing of another, a reminder of how we all share the same air, and of how fragile we are. At least there was enough air in the world for everybody to breathe; at least people did not fight with one another over that. And it would be difficult, would it not, for the rich people to take all the air away from the poor people, even if they could take so many other things? Black people, white people: same air.

The old woman looked up at her quite suddenly. "Your father," she said. "I remember him from the wedding. He was a good man, wasn't he?"

Mma Ramotswe smiled. "He was a very good man. He is late now, as perhaps you know. But I still go to his grave, out there at Mochudi. And I think of him every day."

The old woman nodded. "That is good."

Mma Ramotswe took her arm away, gently. "I must go now," she said. "I must get back to my place."

She said goodbye to Mma Mokoti, who saw her to the door, and then she went out into the night to where the tiny white van was parked. The engine started first time, as it always did, now that it was being regularly looked after by Mr J.L.B. Matekoni, and she was soon negotiating her way back up the rough dirt track, the undelivered cheque still firmly in her pocket. It will remain undelivered, she thought, because of the conversation which she had had with Mma Mokoti. So Note had been married before he met her. Well, if that were the case, then one might well ask the question: **Did he get divorced?**

SHE HAD ALMOST REACHED the end of the track when the tiny white van died. The end came suddenly, just as the end may come to those who suffer a stroke or a heart attack, without notice, when they are least expecting it. Certainly Mma Ramotswe was not thinking of the possibility of mechanical failure; her thoughts, rather, were on the conversation she had had with Mma Mokoti. It had been a painful visit for her, at least at the beginning. It had been hard to go back to that house, which had actually been the scene of one of Note's assaults on her, one weekend all those years ago when they had been the only people there and he had been drunk and had turned on her with vicious suddenness. But she was glad that she had gone now, and had been able to talk to Note's mother. Even if she had not revealed that information about her son, it had done both of them good, she thought, to talk. For the mother, it would perhaps be easier for her to know that she, Precious Ramotswe, did not hold anything against her, and had forgiven her son. That would be one less thing in a life which she suspected had been full of things to worry about. And for her part, saying to the mother what she had said had cost her very little, and had made her feel much better anyway. And then there had been the massive relief of realising that perhaps she had not committed bigamy after all. If Note had still been married when he had married her, then there was no marriage in the first place. That meant that her marriage to Mr J.L.B. Matekoni was perfectly legal.

It was while she was thinking of this that the tiny white van suddenly lost all power. She was not going at all fast when it happened, barely ten miles an hour on that pitted surface, but the drawing to a halt happened very quickly and the engine stopped.

Mma Ramotswe's first thought was that she had run out of fuel. She had filled the tank only a few days ago, and when she looked down, it showed that it was still half full. So that possibility was excluded. Nor had there been electrical failure, as the lights were still illuminating the track ahead. So the problem, she felt, was in the engine itself.

With sinking heart, she switched off the ignition and then tried to turn it on again. There was the sound of the starter turning over, but nothing else happened. She tried again, with the same result.

Mma Ramotswe switched off the headlights and opened the door of the van. There was some moonlight, if not very much, and for a moment she stood there, looking up at the sky, humbled by its sheer immensity and by the quiet of the bush. The tiny white van had been a cocoon of safety in the darkness; now it was just her, an African lady, under this great sky and with a long walk ahead of her. She would be able to reach the main road, she thought, in twenty minutes or so, and then they were about ten miles from the town. She could walk that far, of course, if she had to, but how long would that take? She knew that an average person could cover four miles in an hour, as long as there were no hills. She was not an average person, she feared; the rate for traditionally built people was probably three miles an hour. So that would mean a walk of about three hours, just to reach the outskirts of town. From there it would be at least half an hour—probably rather more—to Zebra Drive.

Of course there was the chance that she

would be able to flag down a minibus, if there was one on the prowl. The driver would probably take advantage of her need and charge much more than was normal, but she would readily pay whatever it cost to get home before midnight. Or she might be able to persuade a passing driver to stop and pick her up as an act of charity. There had been a time when people would do that, and indeed Mma Ramotswe would still let people ride in the back of the van when she went up to Mochudi. But she doubted whether people would stop at night out here to pick up a woman who for no apparent reason was standing by the roadside.

She locked the door of the tiny white van and was about to start her walk when she heard a sound. There were many sounds in the bush at night—the screeching of insects, the scurrying of small creatures. This sound, though, was not one of those; it was the sound of liquid dripping. She stood where she was and strained her ears. For a few moments there was only silence, but then it came again and this time it was clear that it emanated from under the van itself.

Unlike Mma Makutsi, and indeed unlike Motholeli, Mma Ramotswe was no mechanic.

But it was difficult to be married to a mechanic and not to pick up some knowledge of engines, and one thing that she did know was that if an engine lost its oil it would seize up. The dripping sound which she heard from under the van must be oil, and then she remembered. Coming down the track she had certainly felt a bad bump when she hit one of the rocks which protruded from the dirt surface. She had not thought much about it, but now she realised just what it could have done. The rock could have damaged the sump and the oil simply drained out of the van. If the crack in the sump were not too large it would have taken some time, but once it had occurred, then the engine would simply stop, just as hers had done that night. And Mma Ramotswe further knew that when an engine seized, awful damage was done. She and Mma Makutsi could survive for long periods without tea, but engines, alas, were different.

She turned away with a heavy heart and began to trudge up the track. She was closer to the main road than she had thought and in less than fifteen minutes she was at the junction. The road to Lobatse was relatively busy, and it was not long before a set of headlights swung into view over the brow of the hill. She watched as a truck sped by, the wind from its passing brushing against her face. That had been going in the wrong direction, down towards Lobatse, but there would be vehicles going the other way. She began to walk.

It was easy walking along the road, along the well-used tar. This was a properly maintained road, with a smooth surface, and walking along it one might make good progress. But it still felt strange to her to be so utterly isolated in the night, with darkness stretching out on either side of the road. How far away, she wondered, was the nearest creature that might wish to eat her? There were no lions this close to Gaborone, but if one went forty miles to the east, then that might be different. And what would happen if a lion decided to wander? Forty miles for a lion was nothing, and after having covered forty miles a lion might be hungry and in just the right mood to find a traditionally built meal . . .

It did not help to think about lions, and so Mma Ramotswe moved on to something different. She began to think, for some reason, of Mr Polopetsi, and of how well he had fitted into his new job at the garage. She had not discussed the situation with Mr J.L.B. Matekoni, but she was going to propose to him that their new employee be taken on permanently and be trained for the job. There was simply too much work to be handled at the garage, and she was beginning to get concerned over how much Mr J.L.B. Matekoni had to do. The apprentices had always been a worry for him, and when they finished their apprenticeship—if they ever did—then he should encourage them to go elsewhere. That would leave him without an assistant, unless Mr Polopetsi stayed. And there was another reason why he was so suitable. Mma Makutsi had already used him for some secretarial work and had spoken highly of his abilities. He could be attached to the detective agency in some vague, unspecified capacity. Yes, he was certainly the best choice, and it had been a happy accident when she had made him fall off his bicycle. Life was full of these happy accidents, if one came to think of it. Had she not taken her tiny white van to Tlokweng Road Speedy Motors—and she could quite easily have gone to another garage—then she would not have met Mr J.L.B. Matekoni and she would never then have found herself marrying him. And had

Mma Makutsi not been looking for a job just at the time that she was setting up the No.1 Ladies' Detective Agency, then she would never have got to know her and Mma Makutsi would never have become an assistant private detective. That was a fortunate coincidence, and for a few minutes she thought of what might have happened had she employed one of those useless secretaries about whom Mma Makutsi had told her, one of those girls who got barely fifty per cent in the final examinations of the Botswana Secretarial College. That hardly bore thinking about.

This train of thought, speculative though it was, might have sustained her for a good part of her walk, but it was interrupted by the sound of a vehicle approaching from behind her and by the sudden appearance of lights. Mma Ramotswe stopped where she was and stood in such a position that the driver of the vehicle would see her face-on.

The car came up quickly, and Mma Ramotswe took a step backwards as the lights came towards her. But she still waved her arm up and down, in the recognised way of one pleading for a lift. The car shot past, which was just what she had feared it would do. But then, once it had gone past her, and she had turned round in disappointment, its rear lights glowed red and it drew to a halt. Mma Ramotswe, hardly believing her good fortune, ran up to the side of the vehicle.

A man looked out at her from the driver's window, a face in the darkness that she could not see.

"Where are you going, Mma?"

"I am going into town, Rra," she said. "My van has broken down back there."

"You can get in the back. We are going that way."

She opened the door gratefully and slipped into the back seat. She saw now that there was another person in the car, a woman, who turned to her and greeted her. Mma Ramotswe could just make out the face, which seemed vaguely familiar even if she could not say who it was.

"It is very bad when your car breaks down," said the woman. "That would have been a long walk back into town."

"It would," said Mma Ramotswe. "I used to be able to walk for long distances, years ago, before I had a van. But now . . ."

"It is easy to forget how to walk," the

woman agreed. "Children used to walk ten miles to school. Remember that?"

"Some children still do," said Mma Ramotswe.

They continued the conversation for a while, agreeing with one another on a variety of subjects. Now the lights of Gaborone were visible in the distance, a glow that lit up the sky, even at that late hour. Soon they would be home.

CHAPTER SEVENTEEN

MMA RAMOTSWE, MR J.L.B. MATEKONI, AND MR POLOPETSI GET AN UNPLEASANT SURPRISE

MR J.L.B. MATEKONI was sound asleep by the time that Mma Ramotswe arrived home from her visit to the Mokoti house. When he awoke the next morning, Mma Ramotswe was already out of bed and walking in the garden, nursing a cup of bush tea in her hands. Mr J.L.B. Matekoni got up, washed and dressed, and went out to find her standing sunk in thought in front of the mopipi tree.

"It is a fine morning again," he said, as he walked up to her.

She turned to him and smiled. "I am always happiest in the early morning," she said. "Standing here in the garden watching the plants wake up. It is very good."

Mr J.L.B. Matekoni agreed. He found it difficult to get out of bed quite as early as she did, but he knew that the first few hours of light was the best part of the day, a time of freshness and optimism. He particularly liked it when he was in at the garage early enough to feel the first rays of the sun on the back of his neck as he worked on an engine. That was perfection itself—a state of bliss for a mechanic—to be warm (but not too warm) and comfortable while he worked on a challenging engine. Of course it depended to a great extent on the engine. There were some engines that made one despair—engines with inaccessible corners and parts that were difficult to reorder—but an engine that was **cooperative** was a delight to work on.

Mma Ramotswe's tiny white van was a case in point. He had spent a great deal of time on that van and felt that he knew it quite well now. Its engine was not a difficult one to deal with, as all the essential parts could be got at without too much trouble, but it could not be kept going forever and he was not sure whether Mma Ramotswe understood that. He had the same problem with Mma Potokwane and the old minibus that she used to transport the orphans. It was a miracle that that vehicle was still going—or rather it was down to the constant nursing by Mr J.L.B. Matekoni. Sooner or later, though, one had to face reality with an old vehicle and accept that it had come to the end of its life. Mr J.L.B. Matekoni understood the attachment that people developed to a car or a truck, but sentiment had got to be kept in its place. If we are prepared to throw away old clothes, then why not throw away old vehicles once they had had their day? He had noted that Mma Ramotswe had been ready to throw out his clothes, and it was only after a spirited defence on his part that he had succeeded in keeping some of the jackets and trousers which had served him well and which—in his opinion at least—still had a great deal to offer. But his opposition had not prevented her from getting rid of several pairs of trousers (which still had a lot of wear in them and which had only one or two patches), a favourite pair of old brown veldschoens, and a jacket which he had bought at OK Bazaars over the border in Mafikeng with his first pay cheque as a qualified mechanic. He had wanted to ask her how she would feel if he had gone through her wardrobe and thrown out some of her dresses, but he had refrained from doing so. It was an entirely hypothetical question anyway; it would never have occurred to him to do such a thing. And he readily admitted that he knew nothing about women's clothing, as most men would have to admit; and yet women always claimed to know what clothes were right for a man. There was some injustice here, thought Mr J.L.B. Matekoni, although he was not quite sure how one might pursue the point.

Standing beside Mma Ramotswe, Mr J.L.B. Matekoni took a lungful of the early morning air.

"And how did it go?" he asked, as he breathed out. "Did you find him?"

"He was not there," said Mma Ramotswe. "But I spoke to his mother and that was useful. I learned something important."

"And what was this important thing?" asked Mr J.L.B. Matekoni, closing his eyes and breathing in deeply again.

Mma Ramotswe did not answer his question. She should not have said anything about it, she realised, even if she wanted to share the overwhelming sense of relief that the visit had brought her.

"Well?" said Mr J.L.B. Matekoni, opening his eyes and looking around the yard. "The important thing. Why is it . . ." He stopped. Then, frowning, asked, "Where is the white van?"

Mma Ramotswe sighed. "It broke down on the way back. It is sitting out over there." She waved a hand in the general direction of the south, the direction of Lobatse, the Cape, and the oceans to the south of the Cape. "It is down there."

"Broke down?" asked Mr J.L.B. Matekoni sharply. "What happened?"

Mma Ramotswe told him of how the engine had suddenly lost power and then stopped. She told him that there had been no warning, but that it had all happened rather quickly, just before she reached the main road. Then she mentioned the oil and her suspicions that it had something to do with the cracking of the sump on a rock.

Mr J.L.B. Matekoni grimaced. "You are probably right," he said reproachfully. "Those rocks can do a lot of damage. You really shouldn't take a small van like that on those roads. They're not built for that sort of work."

Mma Ramotswe took the rebuke quietly. "And if the engine has seized? What then?"

Mr J.L.B. Matekoni shook his head. "It is very bad news. You'll need a new engine block. I don't think it would be worth it."

"So I would need a new van?"

"Yes, you would."

Mma Ramotswe thought for a moment. "I have had that van for a long time," she said. "I am very fond of it. They do not make vans like that any more."

Mr J.L.B. Matekoni looked at her and was suddenly filled with a great sense of pride. There were some women who would be only too eager to get hold of a new van or car and who would willingly scrap a faithful vehicle for the sake of something flashier and smarter. It made him feel proud to know that Mma Ramotswe was not like that. Such a woman would never want to trade in an old and useless husband for a newer, smarter man. That was very reassuring.

"We'll take a look at it," he said. "You must never say that a van is finished until you've had a good look. We can go out in my truck and collect it. I'll tow you back."

THERE WAS NOTHING very much happening at the No. 1 Ladies' Detective Agency that morning. Mma Makutsi was planning to go out, with a view to pursuing, without any real hope of success, the elusive Zambian financier, and with her correspondence up to date, there was little for Mma Ramotswe to do. Mr J.L.B. Matekoni had a car to service, but it was an uncomplicated job and could safely be left to the remaining apprentice. As for Mr Polopetsi, he never liked to be idle, and would fill any spare minutes tidying the garage, sweeping the floor, or even polishing the cars of customers. On several occasions a client of the agency had come out of a meeting with Mma Ramotswe to discover that his car had been washed and waxed while he was consulting the agency. This was often very much appreciated, and was another point in favour of Mr Polopetsi.

"Just imagine if everybody in Botswana was like that," Mma Ramotswe had remarked to Mma Makutsi. "Imagine how successful this country would be. We would be so rich we wouldn't know what to do."

"Can you ever be that rich?" asked Mma Makutsi. "Surely there is always something to spend your money on. More shoes, for example."

Mma Ramotswe had laughed. "You can only wear one pair of shoes at a time," she said. "Rich people are like the rest of us—two feet, ten toes. We are all the same that way."

Mma Makutsi was not sure about this. One might not be able to wear more than one pair of shoes at a time, but that did not mean that one could not wear a different pair each day, or even one pair in the morning and another in the afternoon. Did rich people do that sort of thing, she wondered. She only had two pairs of shoes at the moment, although she was planning to acquire another pair before too long. She had her ordinary working shoes, which were brown and had been resoled and repaired rather more times than she would care to remember; and then there was her special pair of shoes, green on the outside and with sky-blue linings—the pair of shoes which she had bought with the first profits of the Kalahari Typing School for Men and of which she was so inordinately proud. She wore these shoes to work from time to time, but it seemed a pity to waste them on such mundane use and so she usually reserved them now for occasions such as the dancing class. What she needed now was to buy a smarter pair of shoes for use in the office, and she had in fact identified just such a pair in one of the stores. The shoes were red, and although they had no special coloured lining, they had two large gold ornamental buckles which gave them an air of authority which her other shoes did not have. These were bold shoes, and she would wear them when confronting difficult men, as she occasionally had to do. Men would be mesmerised by the buckles, and this would give her just the advantage that one needed when dealing with men like that.

Although she was reluctant to raise the issue, Mma Makutsi had long been wanting to say something to Mma Ramotswe about the sort of shoes which the older woman wore. Mma Ramotswe was not a flashy dresser, preferring good, reliable skirts and loose blouses, but she nonetheless had a good eye for colour and always looked smart. But when it came to shoes, then it seemed that her dress sense let her down, as she was usually to be seen in a pair of rather shapeless brown shoes with bulges on both sides reflecting the shape of her toes. These shoes were in no sense elegant, and it seemed to Mma Makutsi that they should be replaced by something rather more in keeping with Mma Ramotswe's position as Botswana's senior lady private detective.

Mma Ramotswe's shoes had been touched upon in conversation once before, and the outcome had not been satisfactory. Mma Makutsi had mentioned that there was a shoe sale at one of the shops at the Game Centre, and that in her view there were bargains to be had.

"Perhaps people who have been wearing the same shoes for a long time would be able to find something suitable there," she remarked casually.

Mma Ramotswe had looked at her. "You mean somebody like me?" she said.

Mma Makutsi had laughed to cover her embarrassment. "No, I was not just thinking of you. But maybe you would like to get yourself some new shoes. You can afford them."

"But what's wrong with the shoes I have?" asked Mma Ramotswe. "I have very wide feet. These are very wide shoes and they suit my feet. What would my feet say if I bought a thin pair of fashionable shoes? Surely they would think that something was wrong."

Mma Makutsi decided to stand her ground. "But you can get wide shoes which look very good," she said. "They have something for everybody."

"I am very happy in these shoes," said Mma Ramotswe. "They never give me any trouble."

"You might buy some for Mr J.L.B. Matekoni, then," suggested Mma Makutsi.

"And what is wrong with Mr J.L.B. Matekoni's shoes?"

Mma Makutsi was beginning to regret raising the subject. There was a great deal wrong with Mr J.L.B. Matekoni's shoes in her opinion. To begin with, they were covered in oil stains and she had seen the beginnings of a hole in the toe cap of one of them. Like Mma Ramotswe, he had a position in society as the proprietor of Tlokweng Road Speedy Motors, and shoes in good order were expected of such a person.

When Mma Makutsi did not provide an answer to her question, Mma Ramotswe went on to explain that new shoes would be wasted on Mr J.L.B. Matekoni. "There is no point in buying men new shoes," she said. "They are wasted on them. Men are not interested in shoes. That is very well known. If a man is always thinking about shoes, then there is something wrong with that man."

"And what do men think about?" asked Mma Makutsi. "If they cannot think about shoes, what can they think about?"

Mma Ramotswe raised an eyebrow. "Men

think about ladies a great deal of the time," she said. "They think about ladies in a disrespectful way. That is because men are made that way, and there is nothing that can be done to change them. Then if they are not thinking about ladies, they are thinking about cattle and cars. And some men think a lot about football too. These are all things that men like to think about."

On that morning, though, the main topic of conversation was not shoes, nor the foibles of men, but the drama of the tiny white van. Mr Polopetsi had been dismayed to hear about the break-down of the van, to which he felt he owed a debt of gratitude as it was the van that had brought him into contact with Mma Ramotswe and given him his new job. When Mma Ramotswe said that she and Mr J.L.B. Matekoni would shortly be going to retrieve the van and tow it back into Gaborone, he asked whether he could accompany them. Mma Ramotswe agreed, and once Mr J.L.B. Matekoni had explained to the apprentice what needed to be done to the car which had been brought in for servicing, the three of them set off in the truck, leaving Mma Makutsi alone in the office.

The morning had remained fine, and as

they drove down past Kgale Hill the sun seemed to paint with gold the trees and rocks on the hillside. Above them the sky was quite empty, apart from a few soaring birds of prey, circling high in the currents of rising warm air; ahead of them the road was clear and straight, a ribbon of black making its way through the grey-green acacia scrub. It was a morning which made one happy to be alive, and to be in that place.

Mr Polopetsi was in a talkative mood, and gave them his views on a speech which Chief Linchwe had recently given in Gaborone and which had given rise to a lot of discussion in the papers. Was Chief Linchwe right in what he had said? Mr Polopetsi thought he was. He had a lot of respect for Chief Linchwe, he said, and he thought that more attention should be paid to his views. Then he moved on to the issue of what should be done about people who dropped litter. There had been some talk about this out at Tlokweng, where he lived, and some people had suggested that those who abandoned litter should be made to go on litter picking-up squads. Either that, or they should be obliged to wear large signs on their backs saying DIRTY PERSON. That would soon stop littering, in Mr Polopetsi's view.

Mma Ramotswe was not sure about that. "Shame can be a very strong way of encouraging people to behave well," she said. "Yes, I can see that. But you couldn't put signs on people saying DIRTY PERSON because that would make others think that those people did not wash. But they might wash quite a lot."

"I think that signs are a good idea," said Mr J.L.B. Matekoni. "You could put signs on cars too. DANGEROUS DRIVER, for example, or SPEEDER. That would make people drive more safely, I think."

"But it would look a bit silly, wouldn't it?" said Mma Ramotswe. "Everybody would eventually have some sort of sign. I would have a sign saying MMA RAMOTSWE on my back, or DETECTIVE perhaps. That would be silly." And then she thought, but did not say it: **And Mma Makutsi would have a sign on her back which said 97 per cent**.

"I did not suggest that," said Mr Polopetsi, rather peevishly. "All I said was that people who drop litter could have a sign. That is all."

It was Mr J.L.B. Matekoni who brought the

discussion to an end. "We are almost there," he said. "Is this not the turning that you said you took?"

They slowed down, and Mr J.L.B. Matekoni cautiously headed the truck down the track. By daylight the potholes and rifts in the ground looked far worse than they had at night. It was no surprise to Mma Ramotswe that the tiny white van had been damaged in these conditions; stones, exposed by the movement of soil, reared up in jagged points and at places there jutted onto the track the fallen limbs of trees, plastered now in dried red mud by energetic white ants. Beside the track, watching the truck with mournful eyes, was a small herd of cattle, standing listlessly under the shade of a tree.

"Those cattle are not in good condition," said Mr J.L.B. Matekoni. "Look at the ribs on that one."

Mma Ramotswe cast an expert eye over the light grey beast and agreed. "It is ill," she said. "My father would have known what to do about that."

"Yes, he knew about cattle," said Mr J.L.B. Matekoni. He had never met Obed Ramotswe, of course, but he knew of his reputation as a fine judge of cattle. Mr J.L.B. Matekoni was always prepared to listen to stories about Obed Ramotswe, although he had heard them all from Mma Ramotswe many times over. He had heard the story of how Obed Ramotswe had met Seretse Khama once when he had come to Mochudi, and had shaken the great man's hand. He had heard the story of his hat, and how it had once been left near the kgotla and carefully placed on a wall where he might find it again. He had also heard about how the hat had been blown off his head once in a dust storm and had ended up in a tree. There were many such stories, and he understood just how important they were, and listened with patience and with respect. A life without stories would be no life at all. And stories bound us, did they not, one to another, the living to the dead, people to animals, people to the land?

They drove slowly down the track. After a while, Mr J.L.B. Matekoni turned to Mma Ramotswe. "You said that it happened very close to the turn-off," he said. "But it must have been further than you thought."

Mma Ramotswe cast an anxious glance over her shoulder. She was sure that it was about there, at that bend, where the track went off in a different direction. Yes, it must have been that spot, but there was no sign of the van.

She looked at Mr J.L.B. Matekoni. "We must stop here," she said. "I am very sure that it was here."

Mr Polopetsi, who was sitting between Mr J.L.B. Matekoni and Mma Ramotswe, now leaned forward in his seat. "It has been stolen!" he exclaimed. "Your van has been stolen!"

"We'll see," said Mma Ramotswe. She feared that he was right, even though she felt cross with him for saying it. If her van had been stolen, then it was for her to make the announcement, not Mr Polopetsi.

They alighted from the truck and Mma Ramotswe walked over the edge of the track, a few yards behind the place where they had stopped. Looking down at the ground, she saw what she had been looking for, a patch of oil in the sand. The patch measured only six inches or so across, but it was dark and obvious, and there was now no doubt in her mind. She was looking at the place where she had had her last sight of the tiny white van, and it was undoubtedly no longer there.

Mr J.L.B. Matekoni joined her and followed her gaze, down towards the sand. "Ah!"

he said, and then, turning to face her, "Ah!" again.

"It has been taken," she said, her voice cracking. "My van. It is gone now."

Mr Polopetsi now came to stand beside them. "Somebody must have fixed it and driven it away."

"Very strange," said Mr J.L.B. Matekoni. "But that means that your engine can't have seized. It must have been something else. They would not have been able to drive it away if it had seized."

Mma Ramotswe shook her head. "We will have to go to the police and report it. That is all we can do. They will have driven it far away by now."

"I'm afraid that you're right," said Mr J.L.B. Matekoni gently. "When a vehicle is stolen, it disappears very quickly. Just like that. It's gone."

Mma Ramotswe turned away and began to walk back to the truck, followed by Mr J.L.B. Matekoni. Mr Polopetsi, though, stood where he was.

"We must get back," called Mr J.L.B. Matekoni over his shoulder.

Mr Polopetsi looked down at the place

where the van had been, and then out into the bush beside the track, through the trees and the shrubs and the termite mounds, as if he might see something other than the brown of the grass and the red, red earth and the thorn trees; as if he might hear something other than the screech of the cicadas and the call of birds.

"Leave me here," he said. "I want to look for clues. You go back to town. I'll get a minibus from the main road later on. You leave me here."

Mma Ramotswe turned and stared at him. "There will be no clues," she said. "They have come and gone. That is all."

"Just let me try," said Mr Polopetsi.

"If he wants to," said Mr J.L.B. Matekoni. "There is no harm. There is not much for him to do at the garage this morning."

They climbed into the truck and Mr J.L.B. Matekoni manoeuvred it back to face up the track. As they drove slowly past him, Mr Polopetsi raised a hand in farewell. Mma Ramotswe noticed that he looked excited, and remarked on this a little later to Mr J.L.B. Matekoni.

"He is playing the detective," she said. "But there is no harm in that. He is very keen to do some detective work."

Mr J.L.B. Matekoni laughed. "He is a good man," he said. "And you did the right thing when you asked him to join us."

The compliment pleased Mma Ramotswe, and she touched him gently on the forearm. "You have been good to him too," she said.

They travelled on in silence. A few minutes later, Mr J.L.B. Matekoni glanced at Mma Ramotswe, and he saw that she was crying, silently, but there were tears on her cheeks.

"I am sorry," she said. "I am sorry. My white van. I loved it very much. It had been my friend for many years."

Mr J.L.B. Matekoni shifted in his seat. He found it difficult when women became emotional; he was a mechanic, after all, and these things were awkward for mechanics.

"I will find a new one for you," he said gently. "I will find you a good van."

Mma Ramotswe said nothing. It was kind of him, she knew, but the finding of a new van was not the point. She wanted only that tiny white van that had driven her all over Botswana. That was all she wanted.

CHAPTER EIGHTEEN

THE DOUBLE COMFORT
FURNITURE STORE

IT WAS THAT MORNING, while Mma Ramotswe was finding out about the loss of the tiny white van, that Mma Makutsi made a discovery of her own. The matter of the missing Zambian financier was proving frustrating. Letters had been sent out to no avail, and telephone calls had taken them no further. Mma Ramotswe had suggested a few personal calls on prominent members of the Zambian community in Gaborone, and that was what she was proposing to do. They had three names— a dentist with a long list of patients, many of them Zambians, a minister of religion, and a businessman who ran a thriving import-export agency. Looking at the list that morning, she had decided not to try to speak to the dentist, as she knew that dentists were usually very busy and she would be unlikely to get past the receptionist. Of course she could make an appointment to see him—she had not had her teeth checked for some time and it might be a good idea to have that done—but it would be difficult to ask questions while one's mouth was full of dental equipment. It was for this reason, perhaps, that conversations with dentists were often somewhat one-sided.

She had telephoned the minister of religion but had been spoken to by his answering machine. **I am not in, but you may leave a message,** a careful voice had announced, **and in the meantime, my prayers are with you.** Mma Makutsi had been momentarily taken by surprise when she heard this message, and she put down the receiver without saying anything. How could his prayers be with her if he did not even know who it was who had called? It would be different, she thought, if he had said that his prayers would be with her in the future, once he had heard that she had called. That, at least, would have been honest. Of course, he was only trying to be kind—she understood that—but it was important, she felt, that one should always speak the truth, and ministers of religion, more than others, should understand that.

Mma Makutsi thought about this for a few minutes, and the more she pondered it, the crosser she became. Eventually, picking up the telephone she dialled the number again and listened, with irritation, to the insincere message. Then, after hearing the tone which indicated that she could leave a message, she spoke. "This is Grace Makutsi of the No. 1 Ladies' Detective Agency here. I am calling you about some important matters. But how can your prayers be with me until you have heard who I am? Should you not say that you will pray for people after you find out who they are? Shouldn't you do that? Thank you very much, Reverend, and goodbye."

She felt better for having struck a blow for truth-telling and accuracy. She would tell Mma Ramotswe about that when she came back with the van; she would approve of it, she imagined, as she was a very truthful woman and did not like people who made false claims. She would certainly approve of this . . . or would she? Suddenly Mma Makutsi was visited by doubts. It occurred to her now that Mma Ramotswe might think it rather unkind to give a lecture of this sort—and a recorded lecture to boot—to a minister of religion who was only trying to be helpful to the people who telephoned him. Might not Mma Ramotswe say something like, "Well, Mma, many of the people who call that man will be troubled in some way. Maybe they will have somebody who is late and they will be phoning him about that. Maybe that is why he is trying to make them feel better."

Mma Makutsi thought a little longer and then picked up the telephone and dialled the number again. She had decided to leave another message saying that she had not quite meant what she had said, but this time the telephone was answered by the minister.

For a few moments, Mma Makutsi was unsure what to say, and even considered putting down the receiver, like a child who is caught playing with the telephone.

But better judgement prevailed. "It is Mma Makutsi," she said. "I left a message a few minutes ago and . . ."

"I have listened to your message, Mma," the minister interrupted her. "And you are right. I was not thinking when I said 'in the meantime.' I shall re-record the message and say,

'When I hear your message, I shall put you in my prayers.' That is what I shall say."

Mma Makutsi felt a flush of shame. "I did not mean to be rude," she said hurriedly.

"I know that," said the minister. "And you did not sound at all rude. You were very polite about it."

A short silence ensued before the minister continued. "But you said that you had something to say to me. May I ask what that was?"

Mma Makutsi told him of her business with him, and when she had finished, he said, "What exactly are you asking of me, Mma? Are you asking me to tell you whether any such person, any businessman from Zambia, has spoken to me? Is that what you are asking?"

"Yes," said Mma Makutsi. "You will know many of your countrymen down here. They come to ask you for help. I thought that perhaps this man had done that too."

The minister was silent. At the other end of the line, sitting at her desk in the No. 1 Ladies' Detective Agency, Mma Makutsi watched a small white gecko climb expertly and effortlessly up a wall. The creature's head moved from side to side as it made its journey, watchful for predators and prey.

Then the minister cleared his throat. "I cannot speak about these things, Mma," he said, his tone now reproachful. "When people come to me in their sorrow and their difficulties, they do not expect me to talk to other people about that. They do not think that I shall discuss their affairs with the first private detective who telephones."

Mma Makutsi felt her embarrassment increase at the rebuke. What would he think of her? Not only had she left an unsolicited lecture on his answering machine, but now she had quite improperly asked him to disclose a confidence. She would have to apologise and bring the conversation to an end before the reputation, in his eyes, of the No. 1 Ladies' Detective Agency suffered even further.

"I am very sorry, Reverend," she began. "I did not mean . . ."

"People think," interrupted the minister, "people think that ministers sit in judgement on them. They think that we sit here and think, now that's a very bad thing to do, or that's a very wicked person. But we do not do that, you know. We recognise that all of us are weak and that we all do things that we should not. There is not one of us who is not a sinner, you know. Not one. And so when this poor man came to see me with his troubled soul, I did not sit here and think you should not have taken that money. I did not think that. Nor did I tell him that he should not go running off to Johannesburg, to his cousin, who works in a big hotel there, as he was intending to do. I did not do that. But I did tell him that he could speak to me in complete confidence and that I would not go to the police. And I have not gone to the police, because that would be to break the secrecy of the conversation that a minister has with one of his flock, whoever he might be. So, you see, Mma, I cannot talk to you about this man. I just cannot do that."

Mma Makutsi sat bolt upright at her desk. In front of her, on a small piece of paper, she had written the words: **Gone to Johannesburg. Cousin. Hotel.**

She smiled to herself. "You have been very kind," she said to the minister. "I am sorry for asking about these private matters."

"And I am sorry that I cannot help you," said the minister.

"But you have been most helpful," said Mma Makutsi. And with that, the conversation came to an end, as did the case of the missing Zambian financier. The problem could now be passed on to somebody else, but passed on in a useful way, and with some positive information attached to it. Their quarry was now in Johannesburg, which was a very large place, of course, but there were not all that many big hotels there, and now those who were after this man would know precisely where to start looking.

They had enough information now to report back to the attorneys, and to do so with their heads held high. Their report would be well worth their fee, she thought; and from her point of view, she was eagerly awaiting the chance to tell Mma Ramotswe about what she had discovered. It was always satisfying to be able to make a positive report.

When she heard the truck come back, she got up from her desk and went outside. She had expected, of course, to see Mma Ramotswe's van ignominiously tied to the truck with a tow-rope, and was dismayed when she saw only the truck and a disconsolate looking Mma Ramotswe getting out of the passenger seat.

Mma Ramotswe told her what had happened, and Mma Makutsi let out a wail of sorrow, for a moment quite forgetting the good news which she had intended to welcome her back.

"Ow, Mma!" she cried. "Your van! They have stolen your van! Ow!"

Mr J.L.B. Matekoni stood back from the two women, looking miserable. He tried to calm them, saying, "We will find another van. There are many vans . . . ," only to be hushed by Mma Makutsi, who felt that this was not the moment for sensible male advice.

Later, when she and Mma Ramotswe were sitting down together in their office for a quickly brewed cup of bush tea—which Mma Makutsi had now decided that she liked—it was Mma Ramotswe who set out to calm her assistant.

"I suppose that it had to go sometime," she said. "Mr J.L.B. Matekoni has often said that cars and vans do not last forever. We have to face that. And he's right, isn't he?"

Mma Makutsi had to admit that this was so. But that did not make this monstrous misfortune any easier to bear. "You are being very calm about it. I would be very angry if this had happened to me."

"Well," said Mma Ramotswe, "I have felt

that anger. I felt it when I saw that the van had gone. I felt it a bit in the truck on the way back. But what is the point of anger now, Mma? I don't think that anger will help us."

Mma Makutsi sighed. "You are right about anger," she said. "There is no point in it."

"So tell me what has been happening here," said Mma Ramotswe.

At this invitation, Mma Makutsi sat up in her chair and grinned. At least here was something to make up, even in small part, for the news of the van. "I have solved a case," she said modestly. "That Zambian . . ."

Mma Ramotswe let out a cry of delight. "You've found him? Where is he?"

Mma Makutsi held up a hand. "Not exactly found him," she said. "But I've found out that he's no longer here. He's in Johannesburg."

She explained to Mma Ramotswe about the telephone call to the minister and about his in-advertent disclosure of the whereabouts of their quarry.

"You assume that it was inadvertent," corrected Mma Ramotswe. "But I rather think that the minister may have known exactly what he was saying. He did know that you were looking for somebody who had probably stolen a very large amount of other people's money? He did know that?"

"He did," said Mma Makutsi. "He knew all about that."

"Well," said Mma Ramotswe, "I think that this minister is not as stupid as you think he is. It sounds to me as if he was looking for a way of telling you something without running up problems with his own conscience. He knew that he should not break any confidences, but if he could do it indirectly, as he obviously has done, then perhaps he would not feel so bad about it."

"But is that the way that ministers think?" asked Mma Makutsi.

"It certainly is," said Mma Ramotswe. "One thing I have learned in this job is that everybody, even ministers, find ways of telling you things that they feel they should not tell you directly. And in the case of this minister, he probably thinks that it would be a very good thing for somebody to catch up with this man. So he has told you all that he knew, but he has done it in a special, roundabout way."

Mma Makutsi was thoughtful. "So, what should we do now, Mma? Is that enough?"

"What would Clovis Andersen suggest?" asked Mma Ramotswe.

Mma Makutsi looked at the well-thumbed copy of **The Principles of Private Detection**. She had never actually read the book from cover to cover, although she knew that one day she should do this.

"He would say that you should always remember when to stop asking questions," she ventured. "I think he says that, doesn't he?"

"Exactly!" exclaimed Mma Ramotswe, adding, "I don't think we even need that book any more. I think we know enough to start writing our own book, Mma. Do you agree?"

"I do," said Mma Makutsi. "**Private Detection for Ladies** by Precious Ramotswe and Grace Makutsi. I can see that book already."

"So can I," said Mma Ramotswe, taking a further sip of her tea. "It will be a very good book, Mma. I am sure of that."

To reward Mma Makutsi for her success, Mma Ramotswe gave her the rest of the day off.

"You have worked very hard," she said to

her assistant. "Now you can go and spend the bonus I am going to give you."

Mma Makutsi could not hide her surprise. No mention had ever been made of bonuses, but she had heard people who worked for large companies talk about them.

"Yes," said Mma Ramotswe, smiling, and reaching for the cash box which she kept in the top drawer of her desk. "We shall get a very good fee for this Zambian work. I think that it will be about ten thousand pula altogether." She paused, watching the effect of her words on Mma Makutsi. "So your bonus will be twenty-five per cent of that, which is . . ."

"Two thousand five hundred pula," said Mma Makutsi quickly.

"That much?" said Mma Ramotswe absent-mindedly. "Well, yes, I suppose it will be two thousand five hundred pula. Of course you'll have to wait until we're paid before you get all of that, but here is five hundred pula to be going on with."

Mma Makutsi accepted the notes gratefully and tucked them into the top of her blouse. She had already decided what she would do with her bonus, or this portion of it, and it seemed to her that this was exactly the time to do it. She looked down at her shoes, her work shoes, and shook a finger at them.

"More new shoes?" asked Mma Ramotswe, smiling.

"Yes," said Mma Makutsi. "New shoes and some new handkerchiefs."

Mma Ramotswe nodded her approval. The tiny white van had crossed her mind again, and the thought threatened to darken the mood of joy. But she said nothing to Mma Makutsi, who was now preparing to leave the office and catch a minibus to the shops. She deserves this happiness, thought Mma Ramotswe. She has had so many years in which there has been little for her. Now with her typing school and her new house, and this bonus of course, her life must be taking a marked turn for the better. Perhaps she would find a man too, although that might be too much to ask for at the moment. Still, it would be good for her to find a nice man, if there were any left, which was a matter about which Mma Ramotswe was beginning to feel some doubt. The tiny white van would not have been stolen by a woman, would it? That would have been a man. And this dishonest Zambian financier—he was a man too, was he not? Men had a lot to answer for, she thought; except for Mr J.L.B. Matekoni, of course, and Mr Polopetsi, and her late father. So there were good men around, if one looked hard enough. But where, she wondered, were these good men when one was looking for a husband? Where could Mma Makutsi find a good man at her age, with her large spectacles and her difficult complexion? It would not be easy, thought Mma Ramotswe, and there really was very little that she, or anybody else, could do to help.

THE BUYING OF THE NEW SHOES took remarkably little time. She had already seen the pair that she wanted—the red shoes with the gold buckles—and to her delight they were still prominently displayed in the shop window when she reached it. There was a moment of anxiety while the assistant searched for her size, but the shoes were soon produced and they fitted perfectly.

"You look very good in those," said the assistant admiringly. "Those buckles, Mma! They will dazzle the men all right!"

Mma Makutsi looked at her anxiously. "I am not always trying to dazzle men, you know."

"Oh, I can tell that," the assistant corrected herself. "Those shoes would be good for work too. They are very good shoes for all sorts of things."

Mma Makutsi decided to wear the shoes immediately, and as she walked along the pavement she felt that extraordinary pleasure that comes from having fresh leather soles beneath your feet. It was a feeling of satisfaction, of security, and in this case it was compounded by the flashing of the buckles in the sunlight. This is what it must feel like to be a rich person, she thought. And rich people would feel like this all the time, as they walked about in their fine clothes and their new shoes. Well, at least she had a bit of that feeling, as long as the shoes were new and the leather unscuffed.

She decided to walk a bit further down the line of shops. Not only would this give her the chance to wear in her new shoes, but she had a bit of money left over from the purchase of the shoes and she might find something else which would take her fancy. So she set off, walking past a small radio shop of no interest, and a shop that sold garden equipment. None of this seemed at all promising, and she wondered whether she should catch a minibus that would take her to the shopping centre where Mma Ramotswe liked to sit and have tea. There were shops there that might have something tempting.

Mma Makutsi stopped. She was in front of a shop which sold furniture, the Double Comfort Furniture Shop, and standing inside the shop, looking out at her through the plateglass window, was Phuti Radiphuti.

Mma Makutsi smiled and waved. Yes, of course: he worked in a furniture store, and here he was, selling furniture. Well, it would be interesting to see his shop, even if she had not been planning to buy any furniture.

Phuti Radiphuti waved back and moved towards the door to open it for her. As she went in, he greeted her warmly, stumbling over the words, but making his pleasure at seeing her clear enough.

"And look at your sh . . . sh . . . sh . . . shoes," he said. "They are very pr . . . pr . . ."

"Thank you," said Mma Makutsi. "Yes, they are very pretty. I have just bought them with my bonus."

Phuti Radiphuti smiled and wrung his hands together.

"This is my shop," he said. "This is where I work."

Mma Makutsi looked around. It was a large furniture shop, with all sorts of inviting-looking sofas and chairs. There were also tables and desks, set out in serried ranks.

"It is a very big place," she said. "Are there many people who work here?"

"I have about ten people working here," he said, the words now coming more easily. She had noticed that his stammer was most pronounced when he started a conversation and that it became less marked when he got into his stride.

She thought for a moment. He had said that he had ten people working here; this sounded rather as if he was the manager, which seemed a little bit unlikely.

"Are you the manager then?" she asked jokingly.

"Yes," he said. "My father owns the store and I am the manager. He is mostly retired these days. He likes to spend his time with his cattle, you know, but he still comes here. He is in the office back there now."

For a few moments Mma Makutsi said nothing. The knowledge that Phuti Radiphuti effectively owned a store should have made no difference to how she viewed him, but it did.

He was no longer the inept dancer, the likeable, but rather vulnerable man with whom she danced at the dance academy. Here he was an important man, a man of wealth. The money did not matter. It did not matter.

The silence was broken by Phuti Radiphuti. "You must meet my father," he said. "Come to the office and meet him."

They walked to the back of the showroom, past the tables and chairs and into a large room with a blue carpet and a couple of cluttered desks. As they entered, an elderly man who had been sitting behind one of the desks looked up from behind a pile of invoices. Mma Makutsi moved forward to greet him, using the traditional and respectful greeting appropriate for an older man.

"This is my friend from the dancing class," said Phuti Radiphuti. There was pride in his voice, and Mma Makutsi noticed it.

The old man looked up at Mma Makutsi and rose slowly to his feet. He grimaced as he did so, as if he was in pain.

"It is very good to see you, Mma," said Mr Radiphuti. Then, turning to his son, he told him that he could see a customer in the showroom waiting for attention. He should not be kept waiting, he said.

With Phuti Radiphuti out of the room, the old man gestured for Mma Makutsi to sit down on a chair beside his desk.

"You have been very kind to dance with my son," he said quietly. "He is a shy boy. He does not have many friends."

"He is a good person," said Mma Makutsi. "And his dancing is getting better. It was not so good to begin with, but now it is getting better."

The old man nodded. "He speaks more clearly too, when he is with people he knows," he said. "I am sure that you have helped him in that way too."

Mma Makutsi smiled. "Yes, he is less shy now." She looked down at her new shoes, wondering what this old man would make of them. Would he think her flashy to be wearing shoes with such large buckles?

Mr Radiphuti did not seem to notice her shoes. "What do you do, Mma? Do you have a job? My son has spoken about you many times, but he has not told me what you do."

"I work at the No. 1 Ladies' Detective

Agency," said Mma Makutsi. "I am an assistant there. There is a lady . . ."

"Called Mma Ramotswe," said Mr Radiphuti.

"You know her?"

"Of course I do," said the old man. "And I knew her father too. He was called Obed Ramotswe and he was a very good man. I bought cattle from him, you know, and I still have some of the descendants of those cattle down on my farm near Lobatse. They are fine beasts." He paused. "So you work with Precious Ramotswe. Well, that is very interesting. Do you solve many cases?"

"I solved one today," said Mma Makutsi lightly. "I almost found a man who had taken a lot of money."

"Almost? Did he get away?"

Mma Makutsi laughed, and explained about the information that she had obtained which would enable people in Johannesburg to track him down. The old man listened carefully and smiled with pleasure.

"I can tell that you are very clever," he said. "That is good."

Mma Makutsi did not know how to take this remark. Why was it good that she was clever? Why would it make any difference to this old man? For a brief moment she wondered whether she should tell him about her ninety-seven per cent at the Botswana Secretarial College, but eventually decided against it: one should not speak too often about these things.

They talked for a few minutes more, mostly about the shop and the furniture which it sold. Then Phuti Radiphuti returned with a tray on which three cups of tea were balanced, and they drank this before he offered to run her back to her house in his car, and she accepted. It would be good, she thought, not to have to walk too far in these new red shoes, which were beginning to pinch a little bit on the right foot—not a great deal, but noticeable nonetheless.

When they arrived at her house, Phuti Radiphuti stopped the engine of his car. Then he reached into the back and took out a large parcel, which he gave to Mma Makutsi.

"This is a present for you, Mma," he said. "I hope that you like it."

Mma Makutsi looked at the carefully wrapped gift. "May I open it now?" she asked.

Phuti Radiphuti nodded proudly. "It is from the shop," he said.

Mma Makutsi tore open the paper. Inside was a cushion, an ornate gold velvet cushion. It was the most beautiful thing she had seen for a good while, and she struggled with her tears. He was a fine man this, a good man, who liked her enough to give her this beautiful cushion.

She looked at him and smiled. "You are very kind to me," she said. "You are very kind."

Phuti Radiphuti looked at the steering wheel. He could not speak.

CHAPTER NINETEEN

DOING THE DONKEY WORK

M R POLOPETSI stood under the empty sky, beside the track and a half-dead acacia tree. His excitement was making itself felt physically: a pulse that was becoming more rapid and a prickling in his skin at the back of his neck. He had watched Mr J.L.B. Matekoni's truck make its bumpy way up the track in the direction of the main road, a small cloud of dust being thrown up behind it as the heavily treaded tyres engaged with the surface dirt. Now it had disappeared and he was alone in the middle of the bush, looking down at the stain on the ground where Mma Ramotswe's van had bled its final drops of oil. He smiled. If his father could see him now, how proud he would be. He would never have dreamed, of course, that the skills which he had taught his son would be put to this use, nor would he have dreamed that his son would end up in prison, nor work as a mechanic at Tlokweng Road Speedy Motors, nor be, if he dared to think of it, an assistant private detective at the No. 1 Ladies' Detective Agency. He could not really claim that last title, of course, but if only they gave him the chance to prove himself then there was surely no reason why he should not be every bit as good as Mma Makutsi. He would not aspire to become another Mma Ramotswe—nobody could do that—but at least he might be able to do the things that Mma Makutsi did, ninety-seven per cent or no ninety-seven per cent.

Mr Polopetsi's father, Ernest Polopetsi, had been a small-scale farmer who had enjoyed hunting in his spare time. He had rarely shot any game, as he had no rifle and relied on others for that, but he had been adept at following animal spoor and had taught his son how to do it too. He had shown him the prints made by the different animals—by civet cats, by duiker, by rock rabbits—and he had shown him how to tell how long ago an animal had passed by. There was the wind, which blew small grains of sand into the indentations made by the animal hoof or pads; there was rain, which washed everything away; there was the sun which dried out freshly turned soil. Then there was the bending of the grass, which could spring back, but slowly and in a time that could be read as a person might read the hands of a clock. This knowledge had been passed on to Mr Polopetsi as a boy and now, so unexpectedly, he was presented with the chance to use it.

He looked down at the ground and began his examination. There were prints which he could rule out at the outset: his own, to begin with; the marks of Mr J.L.B. Matekoni's veldschoens—a flat footprint reflecting soft rubber soles; then there were Mma Ramotswe's footprints, one set more recent than the other, because she had walked around the van the night before, immediately after it had broken down. Then there were other prints—a pair of boots that had walked along a path that joined the track from the right. The boots had been accompanied by a set of bare feet, small in size and therefore the feet of a child, perhaps, or of a small woman. That pair of boots had walked round and round in a circle and had then stopped and done something near the oil stain.

After that, the boots had gone off and, yes, they had come back with another set of prints. Mr Polopetsi bent down and looked at the confusion of spoor: boots, tyres (small tyre prints—the prints of the tiny white van itself), and then, quite unmistakably, the prints of donkey hoofs. Yes! thought Mr Polopetsi. And then, yes! again.

He stood up and stretched. It was uncomfortable bending down like that, but it was the only thing to do when one was tracking. One had to get down to that level, to see the world from the point of view of the grains of sand and the blades of grass. It was another world down there, a world of ants and tiny crusts of earth, like miniature mountain ridges, but it was a world that could tell you a great deal about the world of a few feet up; all you had to do was ask it.

He stooped down again and began to move off, following the donkey spoor. This went up the road a short way and then turned off to the right, in the same direction as the path down which the pair of boots had walked. Now, in the ground between the shrubs, the picture was becoming much clearer. There had been much activity on the track itself; now the donkeys, inspanned to the tiny white van, had pulled their burden across undisturbed ground and the tracks were tell-tale. The donkeys—and there had been four of them, concluded Mr Polopetsi—had been led, whipped no doubt, by the man in boots and behind them, moving over at least some of the donkey tracks and obliterating them—had come the tiny white van itself. There must have been somebody else sitting at the wheel and steering the van as it was pulled along. Of course that was the pair of bare feet—a boy no doubt. Yes, the boy had steered while his father drove the donkeys. That is what had happened.

It was easy from there. Mr Polopetsi followed the tracks across the virgin ground for about half a mile before he saw the small cluster of single-room traditional houses and the stock pen made from brushwood. He paused. He was sure that the tiny white van would be there, concealed, perhaps, under a covering of sticks and leaves, but there nonetheless. What should he do? One possibility would be to run back to the track and make his way up the main road. He could be back in Gaborone within a couple of hours and he could tell the police about it, but by that time the van might well have vanished altogether. He stood and thought, and as he stood there he noticed a boy looking at him from the doorway of one of the houses. That decided it for him. He could not leave now as his presence would be reported and action would be taken to get rid of the van.

Mr Polopetsi walked towards the nearest of the four buildings and, as he did so, he saw the tiny white van. It was parked behind the house he was approaching, half covered with an old tarpaulin. The sight filled him with indignation. He had never been able to understand dishonesty, and here was a blatant example of the most bare-faced thievery. Did these people—these useless people—know what sort of person's van they had stolen? The worst in Botswana had stolen from the finest in Botswana; it was as straightforward as that.

As he came closer to the house, a man came out. This man, clad in khaki shirt and trousers, now walked towards Mr Polopetsi and greeted him.

"Are you lost, Rra?" the man asked. His tone was neutral.

Mr Polopetsi felt his heart thumping within him. "I am not lost," he said. "I have come to fetch my employer's van." He gestured towards the half-concealed van, and the man's eye followed him.

"You are the owner of that van?" asked the man.

"No," said Mr Polopetsi. "As I told you, it is owned by my boss. I have come to get it back."

The man looked away. Mr Polopetsi watched him, and realised that the man was thinking. It would be difficult for him to explain its presence, half hidden, behind his house.

Mr Polopetsi decided to be direct. "You have stolen that van," he challenged. "You had no right to take it."

The man looked at him, his eyes narrowed. "I did not steal it, Rra. Watch what you say. I merely brought it here for safe-keeping. You cannot leave vans out in the bush, you know."

Mr Polopetsi drew in his breath. The sheer effrontery of this man's explanation astonished him. Did this man think that he was quite that gullible?

"But how would we have found out that you were looking after this van for us?" he asked sarcastically. "Perhaps you left a note that we missed?"

The man shrugged. "I do not want to discuss this with you," he said. "Please take that van away. It is cluttering up our yard."

Mr Polopetsi stared at the other man, struggling with his indignation. "Now listen to me, Rra," he said. "You listen very carefully. You have made a very bad mistake in taking that van. A very bad mistake."

The man laughed. "Oh yes?" he said. "Let me think now. Does it belong to the President? Or maybe it belongs to Ian Khama or the Chief Justice or somebody just as important! What a bad mistake I have made!"

Mr Polopetsi shook his head. "That van belongs to nobody like that," he said quietly. "That van belongs to Mma Ramotswe, who is a senior detective in Gaborone. You have heard of the CID, Rra? You know about detectives? Detectives are plain-clothes senior policemen. You do know that, Rra?"

Mr Polopetsi saw that his words were having the desired effect. The attitude of the other man now changed, and he was no longer off-hand.

"I'm telling the truth, Rra," he whined. "I was just trying to look after that van. I am not a thief. Believe me, Rra. It is true."

Mr Polopetsi knew that it was not in the slightest bit true, but now he changed tack.

"I am prepared to forget all about this," he said. "You just return this van to the main road up there—you get your donkeys out—and then we shall arrange for a tow truck to come out."

The man frowned. "All the way up to the main road? That will take a long time."

"I'm sure that you have plenty of time," said Mr Polopetsi. "That is, unless you want to spend some of that time in prison."

The man said nothing. Then he turned round and called out to the boy who had been watching from afar. "Get the donkeys," he shouted. "The van is going up to the main road."

Mr Polopetsi smiled. "And there's another thing," he said. "The detective—the chief detective, I should call her—has had her time wasted by having to come out to look for her van and then finding it gone. I see that you have grown some very good pumpkins down here. I suggest that you put four of your best pumpkins into the back of the van. That will make up for her wasted time."

The man opened his mouth to protest, but

thought better of it, and sulkily went off to fetch the pumpkins. Then, with its fine cargo of yellow vegetables stacked in the back, the tiny white van was connected to the team of donkeys, and the journey began. Mr Polopetsi began to walk alongside, but thought better of it and decided to make the rest of the journey in the van, with the pumpkins. It was comfortable there, resting on some old sacking, watching the sky above and thinking with some satisfaction of the pleasure which Mma Ramotswe would experience when he told her that the tiny white van was safe, rescued from captivity vile, ready to resume duties—after some necessary repairs, of course.

CHAPTER TWENTY

NOTE

THE DAY AFTER the return of the tiny white van—which had been fetched by Mr J.L.B. Matekoni from the side of the main Lobatse road and towed back with the apprentice at the wheel—was a day of taking stock. Mr J.L.B. Matekoni had to decide what to do about the van, the engine of which had seized up, just as he had feared. His instinct was to scrap it, and to explain to Mma Ramotswe that it was hardly worth pouring money into such an old vehicle, but he knew what reaction such an opinion would bring, and so he devoted some time to looking at just what needed to be done and how long it would take to do it. Mr Polopetsi felt justly proud of himself. He had explained to an attentive audience of Mma

Ramotswe and Mma Makutsi how he had followed the tracks through the bush and how he had intimidated the thief with references to senior detectives. Mma Ramotswe had smiled at that. "I suppose I am a senior detective," she said. "In one sense at least. I suppose that strictly speaking you told no lies."

For Mma Ramotswe, it seemed that things were improving rapidly. Only recently, her situation had seemed rather bleak, with the loss of the van, the absence of any progress on the Zambian case, and Note's demands hanging over her. Now the van was back, and in the expert hands of Mr J.L.B. Matekoni; they could claim something of a victory in the Zambian case; and she was positively looking forward to seeing Note and confronting him with the information she had received from his mother.

She now no longer cared whether Note came to the house or to the office. She had nothing to hide from Mr J.L.B. Matekoni—she had not been married before, and the marriage which Trevor Mwamba had performed for them under the tree at the orphan farm was perfectly valid. She also realised that if Note had already been married at the time of her marriage to him, then her marriage to him was null and void, and this meant that Note had never been her husband at any point. That was a liberating thought for her, and it had a curious effect on her feelings for him. She was not afraid now. He had never been her husband. She felt free of him, quite free.

Note chose that afternoon to come to the garage, and she was ready for him. It was Mr J.L.B. Matekoni who spoke to him first, and he came through to the office to let her know that he had arrived.

"Do you want me to get rid of him?" he whispered. "I can tell him to go away. Do you want me to do that?"

Mma Makutsi watched from her desk, pretending not to be too interested, but excited nonetheless. She would be happy to tell Note to go away too; they had only to ask her and she would deal with him in a most decisive manner.

Mma Ramotswe rose from her chair. "No," she said. "I want to speak to him. I want to say something to him."

"Do you want me to be there?" asked Mr J.L.B. Matekoni.

Mma Ramotswe shook her head. "This is something that I wish to do for myself," she said. And Mr J.L.B. Matekoni knew, from her tone, that she was resolved. Note would have to be a strong man to stand up to Mma Ramotswe in this mood. He glanced at Mma Makutsi, who raised an eyebrow, and made a slow cutting movement across her throat. She too realised what a risk Note was running.

Mma Ramotswe walked out of the office and saw Note standing next to a customer's car, running a hand across the highly polished bodywork.

"Nice car," he said. "There are some rich people in this town these days. Lots of cars like this."

"Don't put your finger-marks on it, please," said Mma Ramotswe. "The apprentice has spent hours polishing that car."

Note looked at her in astonishment. He opened his mouth to speak, but before he could say anything Mma Ramotswe launched into her attack.

"I went to see your mother," she said. "I went to your place the other night. Did she tell you?"

Note shook his head. "I have not been down there over the last few days."

"Poor woman," said Mma Ramotswe. "She must be very ashamed of you."

Note's eyes widened. "You mind your own business," he spat out. "You keep away from her."

"Oh, I have no plans to go there again," retorted Mma Ramotswe. "And I don't want to see you again, either."

Note sneered. "You're getting a bit cheeky, aren't you? You know what I do to cheeky women?"

Mma Ramotswe closed her eyes, but only briefly. She remembered the violence, yes, but now it seemed less frightening.

"You listen to me," she said. "If you've come for money from me, the answer is that I do not have to give you a single thebe, not one. Because I was never your wife in the first place, and I owe you nothing. Nothing."

Note moved slowly towards her. "You say you were not my wife? Why do you say that?"

"Because you were still married when you married me," she said. "That makes you the bigamist, not me. I am not the one who could be reported to the police. You are. You were married to another girl and you had a child by her, didn't you? I know that now."

Note stopped in his advance. She saw his lip quiver, and she saw his fingers move in that strange way, as if he were practising the trumpet. She wondered for a moment whether he would strike her, as he had struck her before those many years ago, but decided that he would not. Behind her she could hear Mr J.L.B. Matekoni cough, and drop a spanner loudly—his way of signalling that he was at hand, that he would intervene should it be necessary. And there was Mr Polopetsi too, standing at the entrance to the garage, pretending to sweep the floor, but watching closely. Her two friends, those two good men who were so different from Note: her husband—her real husband—and that kind and helpful Mr Polopetsi were there at hand, ready to come to her aid. Note was no threat while they stood there; cruelty was a thing of shadows and hidden places, not a thing that flourished under the eyes of such men as those.

Note looked at her, a look of pure hate, and for a moment Mma Ramotswe was afraid again, but then she stopped herself and taking a deep breath, she stepped towards him. Now they were face to face, and when she spoke she did not have to speak loudly.

"I loved you," she said, making sure that he should hear each word. "You were not good to me. Now that is all over. I do not hate you, Note Mokoti, and I am . . ."—she paused. It was hard to say this, but she knew that she had to. "I want you to go in peace. That is all." And she spoke in Setswana those two simple words that mean Go in Peace, Go Slowly.

Then she reached into the pocket of her skirt and took out a small envelope. Inside there was some money—not ten thousand pula by any means, but some money to help him.

"I do not hate you, Note Mokoti," she repeated. "This is a gift from me. It is to help you. Please go now."

Note looked at the envelope which was being held out to him. For a moment he hesitated, but then he reached forward and took it. He looked at her.

"Thank you," he said, and then he turned and began to walk away. But he stopped after a few paces, and turned round to face her again. She thought that he was going to say something, and there were things that she wished he might have said; but he did not speak, but left her standing there outside the garage, with the afternoon sun on her face. She turned back, to see Mr J.L.B. Matekoni coming towards her slowly, wiping his hands on a piece of greasy rag; and Mr Polopetsi with his broom, quite still, all pretence of work abandoned. And she wanted to cry, but somehow there were no tears, for they had been shed many years ago, and now she was beyond tears for that part of her life and for that particular suffering. She might weep for her tiny white van, yes, and for its travails, but she could no longer weep for the man to whom she had now said a final farewell.

"THERE," said Mma Ramotswe as she raised a cup of bush tea to her lips. "That has settled that. No more Note Mokoti. No more searching for our friend from Zambia. Everything is settled. Except for one thing."

"And what is that thing, Mma?" asked Mma Makutsi.

"Charlie," said Mma Ramotswe. "What are we going to do about Charlie?"

Mma Makutsi picked up her cup and looked at Mma Ramotswe over the rim. "What makes you think that has not yet been settled?" she asked.

"Well, he's not here," said Mma Ramotswe. "He hasn't come back to work. Presumably he is still with that woman."

Mma Makutsi put her cup down and examined her nails.

"Charlie will be back very soon," she said. "Either tomorrow, or early next week. I dealt with that matter myself, as I thought you had enough on your plate at the moment."

Mma Ramotswe frowned. Mma Makutsi's methods were sometimes rather unconventional, and she wondered what measures she had resorted to in order to deal with Charlie.

"Don't worry," said Mma Makutsi, sensing her employer's concern. "I handled it very tactfully. And I think he will be coming back just as soon as he leaves that flashy lady, which I think will be very soon."

Mma Ramotswe laughed. "And how do you know that he's going to leave her? Are you sure that you are not just hoping that he will come to his senses?"

"That boy has very few senses," said Mma Makutsi. "No, I think that he will very soon be persuaded by that lady's husband to come back. I telephoned him, you see. I managed to get his number from the shebeen queen who is living in Mr J.L.B. Matekoni's house. Then I telephoned the husband in Johannesburg and said that I thought that he should know that his wife was carrying on with a young man. He said that he would come over to Gaborone and sort out that young man. I said that he should not harm Charlie, but should just warn him off and tell him to get back to his job. He was unwilling to agree to this, of course, but then I said that if he did not, then he would have to look for another wife. I said that if he would promise not to harm Charlie, then I would see to it that Charlie stopped carrying on with his wife."

Mma Ramotswe looked puzzled.

"Yes," Mma Makutsi went on. "I told him that this wife of his was ready to run away with this young man. The only way of stopping that would be to get the young man to leave her of his own accord."

"And how could that be done?" asked Mma Ramotswe. She had seen how headstrong Charlie could be, and she could not imagine him yielding to advice from Mma Makutsi, or anybody else for that matter.

"I then got hold of Charlie and told him that I had heard that the woman's husband was coming to deal with him," she said. "He looked very frightened and asked me how I knew this thing. That's the point at which I had to tell a small lie, although it was a lie for Charlie's benefit. I told him that I had a cousin in the police who had told me that this man was suspected of disposing of another of his wife's boyfriends. They had not been able to prove it, but they said that he had done it."

"That was not a very big lie," observed Mma Ramotswe. "It may even be true."

"It could be," said Mma Makutsi. "That man certainly talked about Charlie in a very threatening way."

"So Charlie is now scared off?" asked Mma Ramotswe.

"Yes," said Mma Makutsi. "And he asked me whether Mr J.L.B. Matekoni would take him back. I said that I thought that he might, provided that he promised to work very hard and not to spend all his time looking at girls."

"And what did he say to that?"

"He said that he had always been hard-working and, anyway, he was getting a bit tired of women. Apparently this lady with the Mercedes-Benz is a bit demanding. She wants him to pay a lot of attention to her."

"I have always thought that about people who drive around in expensive cars," said Mma Ramotswe. "But I have never thought that about ladies who drive vans."

They laughed at this, and each of them poured another cup of tea.

CHAPTER TWENTY-ONE

A VISIT FROM MR PHUTI RADIPHUTI'S FATHER, THE ELDER MR RADIPHUTI

IN THE DAYS and weeks that followed, life returned to normal at the No. 1 Ladies' Detective Agency and at Tlokweng Road Speedy Motors.

"I have had quite enough excitement," observed Mma Ramotswe to Mma Makutsi. "There was that bad business with Note. There was the terrible thing that happened to the tiny white van. And then there was the row over Charlie. I do not think that I could have taken much more."

"You are right, Mma," said Mma Makutsi. "We have never had so much happen all at the same time. It is better for things to happen separately. I have always said that." She paused to think for a moment before continuing. "At the

Botswana Secretarial College they taught us to do one thing at a time. That is what they said we should do. One thing at a time."

Mma Ramotswe nodded. "That is very true," she said. She was not sure that everything that Mma Makutsi attributed to the Botswana Secretarial College could really have been taught there; after all, surely they had much more to teach than aphorisms. And for her part, of course, Mma Makutsi had those doubts about Mma Ramotswe's attribution of sayings and views to Seretse Khama. But neither expressed their doubts very much, which was what civility required.

It was true that rather too much had happened. Now both Mma Ramotswe and Mma Makutsi were looking forward to a period of stability and peace. That is not to say that they were averse to the appearance of an interesting client with a challenging problem; such clients were always welcome—indeed they were necessary—but it would be helpful if such a person did not cross their threshold for a week or two.

Mma Ramotswe was sure that Mr J.L.B. Matekoni would share her views on this. He had busied himself with the repair of the tiny white van—a task that had taken him several days—but now that was finished and she was once again at the wheel of the vehicle she loved so much.

"That van will not last forever," Mr J.L.B. Matekoni had warned her. "You know that, don't you?"

Mma Ramotswe had admitted this, as she had done on many occasions, "A few more years will be enough," she said. "Five, six years maybe. Then I shall say goodbye to it."

"Five or six years?" Mr J.L.B. Matekoni had repeated. "Oh, no. No. That is too long. You cannot hope for that. A machine is like a person. It gets tired."

"We shall see," said Mma Ramotswe. "You never know. There are some very old cars that are still working. I have seen some that are older than my van."

They had left the subject there, as there were other things for Mr J.L.B. Matekoni to do. Charlie had returned, as had been anticipated by Mr Polopetsi, and had asked for his job back. Mma Makutsi had witnessed the scene from the office doorway, standing just far back enough not to be seen by the chastened apprentice, but in a good position to listen to what was said. Later she told Mma Ramotswe with considerable satisfaction about the exchange.

"You should have seen his face, Mma," she said, smiling at the memory. "He looked like this." She turned down the corners of her mouth and gazed glumly at the floor.

Mma Ramotswe smiled. She took no pleasure in the young man's humiliation, but there were lessons he had to learn and there was a certain justice in what had happened.

"He shifted his weight from foot to foot," went on Mma Makutsi. "Like this. And Mr J.L.B. Matekoni stood like this, with his hands on his hips, like a teacher speaking to a naughty boy."

"What did he say?" asked Mma Ramotswe.

"I heard it all," said Mma Makutsi. "Charlie said, 'I am back here now, Boss. I have been away for a few days. I have taken a little holiday. Now I am back.'

"Mr J.L.B. Matekoni said, 'A holiday? I thought you said that you were quitting the job. I thought you said that you didn't need to work any more? Did you not say that?'

"And then Charlie said that this was a mistake. He said that he had not been serious when he said that he was not going to work any more. He said that he had meant to say that he was going on a holiday."

Mma Ramotswe sighed. "That young man has not learned anything yet," she said. "Did he really expect Mr J.L.B. Matekoni to believe that nonsense?"

"I think he did," said Mma Makutsi. "But then, you know what Charlie is like. He is not a boy with first-class brains. He is a forty-two per cent boy, at the most. That is the sort of result he would get in an exam. Forty-two per cent. I am pretty sure of that, Mma."

Mma Ramotswe's eyes wandered up for a moment to the certificate on the wall behind Mma Makutsi's head. It was the certificate from the Botswana Secretarial College, proudly framed, with the motto of the College in bold letters under the College title: **Be Accurate.** And under that, the remarkable result, inscribed in a hand that must have marvelled at the figures it was obliged to pen: 97 **per cent.**

"Anyway," went on Mma Makutsi, "Mr J.L.B. Matekoni listened to all this, and then he leaned forward and he shook a finger at Charlie, just as he did when Charlie shouted at me that day and called me the rude name."

A warthog, thought Mma Ramotswe. Yes, he called you a warthog, and I think you called him one too, if I remember correctly. She thought this and tried not to smile as for a brief moment an image of a warthog in big round glasses crossed her mind. Big round glasses and green shoes with blue linings.

"Mr J.L.B. Matekoni told him that he was a very silly young man," continued Mma Makutsi. "He said that young men should not run off with ladies who were much older than they were. He said that it was asking for trouble. He also told him that he should act more responsibly and find a nice girl of his own age whom he could marry. He said that this was what the Government was saying men should do, and that Charlie should listen to what the Government had to say on this subject.

"And all the time Charlie was looking down at the ground and wringing his hands, like this. I almost felt sorry for him. In fact, maybe I did feel a little bit sorry for him, although he had asked for all of it and only had himself to blame.

"And then I heard him promise Mr J.L.B. Matekoni to behave better in the future and I heard him say that he knew that he had been very stupid and that he would not be stupid again. Those were his very words, Mma, and I wrote them down on a piece of paper which we can keep in the office here and take out and wave at him some time in the future if we need to do so."

Mma Ramotswe looked at the piece of paper which Mma Makutsi had produced. Yes, it might be useful, but they should remember, she said, that Charlie was still a young man and that young men were apt to do foolish things, and that they probably all had to learn by their mistakes. Mma Makutsi was more grudging about it, but eventually agreed that he had probably suffered enough and should be given another chance. Perhaps he would meet a nice girl now, and all would change, although she had to admit to some reservations about that.

"But Charlie said something else," added Mma Makutsi. "He said something about a pumpkin."

Mma Ramotswe looked up sharply. "A pumpkin?"

"Yes," said Mma Makutsi. "He said that Mr J.L.B. Matekoni should not think that he was all bad. He said that he should remember that he had given you a pumpkin."

"I see," said Mma Ramotswe, and then, again, "I see."

She gazed out of the window. So it was Charlie who had brought that pumpkin, which meant that the man under the bed was not the person who had brought it, and this in turn meant that she still did not know the identity of the intruder. It was certainly not Charlie, because she would have recognised him, so . . . She stopped. An idea came to her, and it was an icy one. Perhaps it had been Note Mokoti under her bed. But she put that out of her mind, as there was no point in scaring herself after the event.

"Well, just think of that," said Mma Ramotswe to Mma Makutsi. "Charlie brought me a pumpkin! Don't young men do strange things, Mma Makutsi?" And everybody might be kind, she thought to herself—even a young man like Charlie, with his thoughts of women and his vanity and all the rest.

"They do," agreed Mma Makutsi. "Especially that young man." She would not mention her tea-pot again, but she had not forgotten.

Of course, Charlie's return had raised issues about Mr Polopetsi's future. Mr Polopetsi himself had been silent when Charlie had been re-engaged. He had continued to work conscientiously, but he had noticed Charlie's hostile glances and seen the two apprentices whispering to one another and looking in his direction. He had assumed that the return of the apprentice would mean the end of his job, and there was a resignation about his manner that day and the next. At last, waiting for a quiet moment, he had slipped into the office and spoken to Mma Ramotswe.

"I have come to thank you, Mma," he blurted out. "Now that my job is over, I am coming to thank you for what you did for me. I have been happy here. You have been kind to me."

Mma Ramotswe looked up from her desk. "I do not know what you are talking about, Rra," she said. "What is over? What are you talking about?"

"My job," he said. "The apprentice has come back. Now there will be no more work for me."

Mma Ramotswe, who had been adding up garage receipts, put down her pen and looked at Mr Polopetsi.

"I do not think your job is finished," she said. "Has Mr J.L.B. Matekoni said anything to you?"

Mr Polopetsi shook his head. "He is a very kind man," he said. "I do not think that he wants to tell me. But I think that this thing has happened anyway. I think that I shall have to go soon. Maybe tomorrow. I do not know."

Mma Ramotswe rose to her feet. "We will go and speak to him," she said. "You come with me, Rra."

Mr Polopetsi raised a hand. "No, Mma. Please, no. I do not want to make a fuss."

But Mma Ramotswe had brushed aside his objections and had ushered him out of the office and into the garage, where Mr J.L.B. Matekoni was standing over a handsome red car, deep in thought, contemplating its exposed engine.

"These people who make these cars are trying to make our lives difficult," he said. "They put in all these computers and what are we to do when they go wrong? They are trying to make cars into space ships, that is what they are doing. But we do not need space ships here in Botswana. We need good cars with engines that do not mind the dust. That is what we need."

"You should write to the people who make these cars," said Mma Ramotswe. "You could tell them."

"They would not listen to me," said Mr J.L.B. Matekoni. "I am just one man. I am just Mr J.L.B. Matekoni of Tlokweng Road Speedy Motors. They would look at my letter in Japan or America and say, 'Who is this Mr J.L.B. Matekoni? Do we know him? What is he writing to us about?' And then they will throw my letter in the bin. That is what would happen. I am not important."

"You are," said Mma Ramotswe. "You are very important. You are the best mechanic in Botswana."

"Yes," said Mr Polopetsi. "That is true, Rra. You are the very best mechanic. I have been proud to work with you."

Mr J.L.B. Matekoni turned and looked at them, first at Mma Ramotswe, and then at Mr Polopetsi.

"You are a good mechanic too, Rra," he said to Mr Polopetsi. "I have seen the way you handle an engine. You respect machinery. That comes from having worked in the hospital. You are like a doctor dealing with a patient."

Mma Ramotswe glanced at Mr Polopetsi, and then she addressed Mr J.L.B. Matekoni. "And he is a good detective too," she said. "He is the one who followed the tracks of the van. That was a fine piece of detective work. We could use him from time to time, as a sort of assistant. Maybe he could be an assistant-assistant detective to Mma Makutsi. She would like that."

Mr J.L.B. Matekoni looked thoughtful. "Yes," he said. "That would be a good idea." He paused, and frowned. "You did not think that your job was over, did you, Rra? Just because Charlie has come back?"

Mr Polopetsi nodded. "I did think that, Rra. And it is all right with me. I cannot expect you to give a job to everyone."

Mr J.L.B. Matekoni laughed. "But I never thought that you should go, Rra. I should have told you. I never thought that you should go. What is going to happen to this place once those boys finish their apprenticeship—if they ever finish it? Where would I be then if I did not have somebody like you to help me? And now you have heard what Mma Ramotswe says about your doing some work for her from time to time. You are going to be a very busy man, Rra."

THAT AFTERNOON, just as Mma Ramotswe was on the point of suggesting that they close the agency an hour earlier than normal, as she needed to go to the butcher to collect some meat for that evening's meal, Mr Polopetsi came into the office to announce that there was a man who was asking to see her. He was an elderly man, he said, who had arrived in a car driven by a driver, and he did not wish to come inside. Could Mma Ramotswe speak to him outside, under the tree?

Mma Ramotswe smiled. This was what an elderly person, a traditional person, might feel comfortable doing: talking under a tree, as people had always done. She went outside, and saw that her visitor was already standing under the tree, his hat in his hand. He looked so like her father, she thought, with a pang of regret; he had enjoyed talking to people while standing or sitting under a tree, watching the cattle grazing, or simply looking at the sky and the hills of the country that he had loved so much.

"Dumela, Mma Ramotswe, you remember me, do you not?"

She reached forward and they shook hands.

"I remember you well, Rra. You were a friend of my father. I have not seen you for a long time, but of course I remember you. You are well, Rra?"

He tapped his head lightly with a forefinger. "My head is getting very old now," he said, smiling as he spoke. "And that means that I forget many things. But I have not forgotten Obed Ramotswe. We were boys together. You do not forget that."

She nodded. "You were his good friend," she said.

"And he was a good man, your father."

There was a silence. She wondered whether she should invite him into the office for tea, but decided that this was not what he wanted. But what then did he want? Sometimes old people just liked to talk about the past, that was all, and perhaps that was why he had come to see her.

But no, there was something else. "I have a

son," he said. "I have a son who is called Phuti. He is a very good man, but he has not found a wife. That is because he is a very shy man, and has always been like that. He cannot speak properly, and his words come out very slowly. That makes him very shy with women. I think that maybe the girls used to laugh at him when he was younger."

"People can be very cruel," said Mma Ramotswe.

"Yes," said Mr Radiphuti. "But now he has met a very nice lady."

Ah, thought Mma Ramotswe. This is why he has come to see me. He has come to ask me to find out something about this lady. She had been asked many times to do that sort of thing—to investigate a prospective marriage partner. It was a common thing for detectives to do, and indeed there was a whole section in Clovis Andersen's book about how to approach such a task.

"Who is this lady?" asked Mma Ramotswe. "If you give me her name, then I shall see if I can find out anything about her for you. I can find out whether she would make a good wife for your son."

Mr Radiphuti fingered his hat awkwardly.

"Oh, I am sure that she would make a very good wife for him," he said. "And I think that you would know that thing already."

Mma Ramotswe looked at him in incomprehension, and he broke into a smile. "You see, Mma," Mr Radiphuti went on, "the lady works in that office over there, just behind you. So you will know her very well."

For a few moments Mma Ramotswe did not say anything. Then, very quietly, she said, "I see." Then she paused, and said again, "I see."

"Yes," said Mr Radiphuti. "My son has been seeing your assistant. She has been very kind to him and has made his dancing much better. She has also helped his speaking, because she has given him confidence. I am very happy about that. But there is a problem."

Mma Ramotswe's heart sank. She had allowed herself to hope, on Mma Makutsi's behalf, but now it seemed that there was some difficulty. It would be a familiar story of disappointment for Mma Makutsi. That seemed inevitable now.

Mr Radiphuti slowly drew breath before proceeding—a thick, wheezy sound. "I know that my son would like to marry this lady, I am sure of that. But I am also sure that he will never get round to asking her. He is too shy. In fact, he has told me that he cannot ask her because he would just stutter and stutter and no words would come. So he does not feel that he can ask her this important question."

He stopped, and looked imploringly at Mma Ramotswe.

"So what can we do, Mma?" he went on. "You are a clever lady. Maybe you can do something."

Mma Ramotswe looked up at the sky through the branches of the acacia tree. The sun was lower now, which always seemed to make the sky seem emptier. It was a time of day that made her feel a bit sad; a time of thinness and soft light.

"It is a very strange thing," she said. "But it seems to me that there is no reason that I know of why one person should not act as the messenger for another person in a matter like this. Have you seen those love messages that Zulu women used to make in beads and send to others? Those messages might contain a proposal of marriage. So why should we not use a messenger in a case like this? I see no reason."

Mr Radiphuti's gnarled fingers worked more anxiously on the brim of his hat. "Do you mean that I should ask her, Mma? Is that what you want me to do? Do you think . . ."

She raised a hand to stop him. "No, Rra. Do not worry. A woman is the best messenger in a case like this. But I must first ask you: Are you sure that your son wishes to marry this lady? Are you one hundred per cent sure?"

"I am," he said. "He told me that. And, what is more, he knows that I was coming to talk to you about it."

Mma Ramotswe listened carefully to his reply. Then, telling him to wait where he was, she made her way back into the office, where her assistant was sorting a pile of papers on her desk. Mma Makutsi looked up as Mma Ramotswe entered the room.

"What did he want?" she asked casually. "Is it a client?"

Mma Ramotswe said nothing, but stood there, smiling.

"Is it something funny?" asked Mma Makutsi. "You look as if you have heard something amusing."

"No," said Mma Ramotswe. "It is not funny. It is very important."

Mma Makutsi put down a piece of paper and looked quizzically at her employer. There were times when Mma Ramotswe was opaque in her manner, when she seemed to want Mma Makutsi to work something out for herself, and this seemed to be one of those occasions.

"I cannot guess, Mma," she said. "I just cannot guess. You are going to have to tell me what it is."

Mma Ramotswe took a deep breath. "Would you like to get married some day, Mma?" she asked.

Mma Makutsi looked down at her shoes. "Yes," she said. "I would like to get married one day. But I do not know if that will happen."

"There is a man who wishes to marry you," said Mma Ramotswe. "I understand that he is a good man. But he is too shy to ask you himself because he is very worried about his stammer . . ."

She tailed off. Mma Makutsi was staring at her now, and her eyes were wide with astonishment.

"He has sent his father to ask you whether you will marry him," Mma Ramotswe continued. "And I have come as the messenger from the father. All you have to do is think very carefully. Do you like this man? Do you love him enough to marry him? Is that what you want? Do not say yes unless you are sure. Be very careful, Mma. This is a very important decision."

As she finished her sentence, it seemed to her as if Mma Makutsi was unable to speak. She opened her mouth, but then she closed it again. Mma Ramotswe waited. A fly had landed on her shoulder and was tickling her, but she did not brush it off.

Mma Makutsi suddenly stood up, and looked at Mma Ramotswe. Then she sat down again, heavily, almost missing her chair. She took off her glasses, those large round glasses, and polished them quickly with her threadbare lace handkerchief, the handkerchief that she had treasured for so long and which, like the tiny white van, was near to the end of its life.

When she spoke, her voice was distant, almost a whisper. But Mma Ramotswe heard what she said, which was, "I will marry him, Mma. You can tell the father that. I will marry Phuti Radiphuti. My answer is yes."

Mma Ramotswe clapped her hands in delight. "Oh, I am happy, Mma Makutsi," she shrieked. "I am happy, happy, happy. His father said that Phuti was one hundred per cent certain that he wanted to marry you. One hundred per cent, Mma. Not ninety-seven per cent—one hundred per cent!"

They went outside together, to the place where Mr Radiphuti was standing. He looked at them anxiously, but could tell from their expressions what answer they were bringing him. Then the three of them spoke together for a short time, but only a short time, as Mr Radiphuti was keen to get back to his son to tell him what Mma Makutsi's response was.

Back in the office, Mma Ramotswe tactfully said nothing. Mma Makutsi gathered her thoughts, standing before the window, looking out to the trees in the distance and the evening sun on the grey-green hills beyond the trees. She had so much to think about: her past, and the place from where she had come; her family, who would be so pleased with this news, up there in Bobonong; and her late brother, Richard, who would never know about this, unless, of course, he was watching from somewhere, which he might be, for all she knew. She loved this country, which was a good place, and she loved those with whom she lived and worked. She had so much love to give—she had always felt that—and now there was somebody to whom she could give this love, and that, she knew, was good; for that is what redeems us, that is what makes our pain and sorrow bearable—this giving of love to others, this sharing of the heart.

africa
africa africa
africa africa africa
africa africa
africa

ABOUT THE AUTHOR

Alexander McCall Smith is the author of the acclaimed No. 1 Ladies' Detective Agency series. He was born in what is now known as Zimbabwe and taught law at the University of Botswana. He is the author of more than fifty books: novels, stories, children's books, and specialized titles such as **Forensic Aspects of Sleep.** A professor of medical law at Edinburgh University, he lives in Scotland.